Queen of Babble

MEG CABOT

Queen of Babble

AVON

An Imprint of HarperCollinsPublishers

ISBN: 978-0-06-085199-6
ISBN-10: 0-06-085199-6

The William Morrow hardcover edition contains the following Cataloging-in-Publication Data:

Cabot, Meg.
   Queen of babble / Meg Cabot.—1st ed.
     p. cm.
1. Young women—Fiction. 2. Americans—Europe—Fiction. I. Title.

PS3553.A278Q44 2006
813'.6—dc22   2005058369

07 08 09 10 11   ❖/RRD   10 9 8 7 6 5 4 3

For Benjamin

Many thanks to all the extremely generous people who helped with the writing of this book, including Beth Ader, Jennifer Brown, Megan Farr, Carrie Feron, Michele Jaffe, Laura Langlie, Laura McKay, Sophia Travis, and especially Benjamin Egnatz.

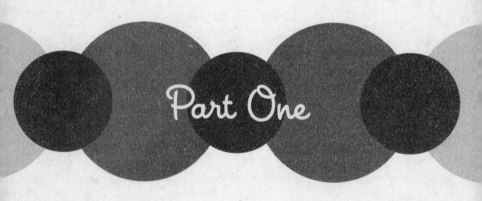

Part One

Clothing. Why do we wear it? Many people believe that we wear clothing out of modesty. In ancient civilizations, however, clothing was developed not to cover our private parts from view, but merely to keep the body warm. In other cultures, clothing was thought to protect its wearers from magic, while in still others clothing served merely ornamental or display purposes.

In this thesis, I hope to explore the history of clothing—or fashion—starting with ancient man, who wore animal hides for warmth, to modern man, or woman, some of whom wear small strips of material between their buttocks (see: thong) for reasons no one has yet been able to adequately explain to this author.

History of Fashion
SENIOR THESIS BY ELIZABETH NICHOLS

Our indiscretion sometime serves us well
When our deep plots do pall
—*William Shakespeare (1564–1616), British poet and playwright*

I can't believe this. I can't believe I don't remember what he looks like! How can I not remember what he *looks* like? I mean, *his tongue has been in my mouth*. How could I forget what someone whose tongue has been in my mouth *looks* like? It's not like there've been that many guys who've had their tongues in my mouth. Only, like, three.

And one of those was in high school. And the other one turned out to be gay.

God, that is so depressing. Okay, I'm not going to think about that right now.

It isn't like it's been THAT long since I last saw him. It was just three months ago! You would think I'd remember what someone I've been dating for THREE MONTHS looks like.

Even if, you know, for most of those three months we've been in separate countries.

Still. I have his photo. Well, okay, you can't really see his face in it. Actually, you can't see his face at all, since it's a photo of his—oh God—naked ass.

Why would anyone send someone something like that? I didn't

ask for a photo of his naked ass. Was it supposed to be erotic? Because it so wasn't.

Maybe that's just me, though. Shari's right, I've got to stop being so inhibited.

It was just so shocking to find it in my in-box, a big photo of my boyfriend's naked ass.

And okay, I know they were just goofing around, he and his friends. And I know Shari says it's a cultural thing, and that the British are much less sensitive about nudity than most Americans, and that we should strive as a culture to be more open and carefree, like they are.

Also that he probably thought, like most men do, that his ass is his best feature.

But still.

Okay, I'm not going to think about that right now. Stop thinking about my boyfriend's ass. Instead, I'm going to look for him. He has to be here somewhere, he swore he'd be here to pick me up—

Oh my God, that can't be him, can it? No, of course it's not. Why would he be wearing a jacket like that? Why would ANYONE be wearing a jacket like that? Unless they're being ironic. Or Michael Jackson, of course. He is the only man I could think of who would wear red leather with epaulets. Who isn't a professional break-dancer.

That CAN'T be him. Oh, please God, don't let that be him . . .

Oh no, he's looking this way . . . he's looking this way! Look down, look down, don't make eye contact with the guy in the red leather jacket with the epaulets. I'm sure he's a very nice man; it's a shame about his having to shop for coats from the 1980s at the Salvation Army.

But I don't want him to know I was looking at him, he might think I like him or something.

And it's not that I'm prejudiced against homeless people, I'm not, I know all about how many of us are really only a few paychecks away from being homeless ourselves. Some of us, in fact, are less than a paycheck away from being homeless. Some of us, in fact, are so broke that we still live with our parents.

But I'm not going to think about all that right now.

The thing is, I just don't want Andrew to get here and find me talking to some homeless guy in a red leather break-dancing jacket. I mean, that is so not the first impression I want to give. Not that, you know, it will be his FIRST impression of me, since we've been dating for three months and all. But it will be the first impression he'll have of the New Me, the me he hasn't met yet . . .

Okay. Okay, it's safe, he's not looking anymore.

Oh God, this is awful, I can't believe this is how they welcome people to their country. Herding us down this walkway with all these people LOOKING at us . . . I feel like I'm personally disappointing each and every one of them by not being the person they're waiting for. This is a very unkind thing to do to people who just sat on a plane for six hours, eight in my case if you count the flight from Ann Arbor to New York. Ten if you count the two-hour layover at JFK—

Wait. Was Red Break-dancing Jacket just checking me out?

Oh my God, he WAS! Red leather jacket with the epaulets totally checked me out!

Oh God, this is so embarrassing. It's my underwear, I KNOW it. How could he tell? That I'm not wearing any, I mean? It's true I don't have any visible panty lines, but for all he knows, I could be wearing a thong. I SHOULD have worn a thong. Shari was right.

But it's so uncomfortable when they go up your—

I KNEW I shouldn't have picked a dress this tight to get off the plane in—even if I did personally modify it by hemming the skirt to above the knee so I'm not hobbled by it.

But for one thing, I'm freezing—how can it be this cold in AUGUST?

And for another, this silk is particularly clingy, so there's the whole panty line thing.

Still, everyone back at the shop said I look great in it . . . though I wouldn't have thought a mandarin dress—even a vintage one—would actually work on me, seeing as how I'm Caucasian and all.

But I *want* to look good, since he hasn't seen me in so long, and I did lose those thirty pounds, and you wouldn't be able to tell I'd lost all that weight if I got off the plane in sweats. Isn't that always what celebrities are wearing when they show up on *Us Weekly*'s "What Were They Thinking?" page? You know, when they get off a plane in sweats and last year's Uggs, with their hair all crazy? If you are going to be a celebrity, you need to LOOK like a celebrity, even when you're getting off a plane.

Not that I'm a celebrity, but I still want to look good. I went to all this trouble, I haven't had so much as a crumb of bread for three months, and—

Wait. What if he doesn't recognize me? Seriously. I mean, I did lose thirty pounds, and with my new haircut and all—

Oh God, could he be here and not recognize me? Did I already walk right by him? Should I turn around and go back down that walkway thingie and look for him? But I'll seem like such an idiot. What do I do? Oh my God, this is so not fair, I just wanted to look good for him, not be stranded in a foreign country because I look so different my own boyfriend doesn't recognize me! What if he thinks I haven't shown up and just goes home? I don't have any money—well, twelve hundred bucks, but that has to last me until my flight home at the end of the month—

RED LEATHER JACKET IS STILL LOOKING THIS WAY!!! Oh God, what can he want from me?

What if he's part of some kind of airport white slavery ring? What if he hangs out here all the time looking for naive young tourists from Ann Arbor, Michigan, to kidnap and send to Saudi Arabia to be some sheikh's seventeenth bride? I read a book where that happened once . . . although I have to say the girl seemed to really enjoy it. But only because at the end the sheikh divorced all his other wives and just kept her because she was so pure and yet so good in the sack.

Or what if he just holds girls for ransom instead of selling them? Except that I am so not rich! I know this dress looks expensive, but I got it at Vintage to Vavoom for twelve dollars (with my employee discount)!

And my dad doesn't have any money. He works at a cyclotron, for crying out loud!

Don't kidnap me, don't kidnap me, don't kidnap me—

Wait, what is this booth? Meet Your Party. Oh, great! Customer service! That's what I'll do! I'll have Andrew paged. And that way, if he's here, he can come find me. And I'll be safe from Red Leather Break-dancing Jacket; he won't dare kidnap me and send me to Saudi Arabia in front of the pager guy—

"Hullo, love, you look lost. What can I do for you, then?"

Oh, the booth guy is so nice! And such a cute accent! Although that tie was an unfortunate choice.

"Hi, I'm Lizzie Nichols," I say. "I'm supposed to be picked up by my boyfriend, Andrew Marshall. Only he doesn't seem to be here, and—"

"Want me to page him for you, then?"

"Oh! Yes, please, would you? Because there's a guy following me, see him over there? I think he might be a kidnapper or the operator of a white slavery ring—"

"Which one?"

I don't want to point, but I do feel I have a duty, you know, to report Red Leather Break-dancing Jacket to the authorities, or at least to the Meet Your Party booth attendant, because he DOES look very odd in that jacket, and he IS still staring at me, really rudely, or at least suggestively, like he still wants to kidnap me.

"Over there," I say, nodding my head toward Red Leather Break-dancing Jacket. "That one in the hideous jacket with the epaulets. See him? The one staring at us."

"Oh, right." The Meet Your Party booth attendant nods. "Right. Very menacing. Hold on, then, I'll have your boyfriend over here, giving that git the thrashing he so richly deserves, in a second. AN-DREW MARSHALL. ANDREW MARSHALL, MISS NICHOLS IS WAITING FOR YOU AT THE MEET YOUR PARTY BOOTH. ANDREW MARSHALL, PLEASE FIND MISS NICHOLS AT THE MEET YOUR PARTY BOOTH. There? How was that?"

"Oh, that was great," I say encouragingly, because I feel a little sorry for him. I mean, it must be hard to sit in a booth all day, yelling over a loudspeaker. "That was really—"

"Liz?"

Andrew! At last!

Only when I turn around, it's Red Leather Break-dancing Jacket. Except.

Except that it WAS Andrew, all along.

And I just didn't recognize him, because I was distracted by the jacket—the most hideous jacket I've ever seen. Plus he seems to have had his hair cut. Not very flatteringly.

Sort of menacingly, in fact.

"Oh," I say. It is extremely difficult to hide my confusion. And dismay. "Andrew. Hi."

Behind the glass of the Meet Your Party booth, the attendant bursts into very, very loud laughter.

And I realize, with a pang, that I've done it.

Again.

The first woven material was made of vegetable fibers such as bark, cotton, and hemp. Animal fibers were not employed until the Neolithic period, by cultures that—unlike their nomadic ancestors—were able to establish stable communities near which sheep could graze, and in which looms could be constructed.

Nevertheless, the ancient Egyptian refused to wear wool until after the Alexandrian conquest, obviously citing its itchiness in warm climates.

History of Fashion
SENIOR THESIS BY ELIZABETH NICHOLS

Gossip isn't scandal and it's not merely malicious.
It's chatter about the human race by lovers of the same.
—*Phyllis McGinley (1905–1978), U.S. poet and author*

Two Days Earlier Back in Ann Arbor
(or maybe three days—wait, what time is it in America?)

You're compromising your feminist principles." That's what Shari keeps saying.

"Stop it," I say.

"Seriously. It's not like you. Ever since you met this guy—"

"Shari, I love him. Why is it wrong that I want to be with the person I love?"

"It's not wrong to want to be with him," Shari says. "It's wrong to put your own career on hold while you wait for him to finish his degree."

"And what career would that be, Shar?" I can't believe I'm even having this conversation. Again.

Also that she would station herself next to the chips and dip like this when she knows perfectly well I'm still trying to lose five more pounds.

Oh well. At least she's wearing the fifties black-and-white Mexican swing skirt I picked out for her at the shop, even though she claimed it made her butt look too big. It so doesn't. Except maybe in a good way.

"You know," Shari says. "The career you could have, if you would just move to New York with me when you get back from England, instead of—"

"I told you, I'm not arguing with you about this today," I say. "It's my graduation party, Shar. Can't you let me enjoy it?"

"No," Shari says. "Because you're being an ass, and you know it."

Shari's boyfriend, Chaz, comes over to us and scoops up some onion dip with a barbecue-flavored potato chip.

Mmm. Barbecue-flavored potato chips. Maybe if I just had one . . .

"What's Lizzie being an ass about now?" he asks, chewing.

But you can never have just one barbecue-flavored potato chip. Never.

Chaz is tall and lanky. I bet he's never had to lose five more pounds before in his entire life. He even has to wear a belt to hold up his Levi's. It's a mesh leather weave. But on him, mesh leather works.

What doesn't work, of course, is the University of Michigan baseball cap. But I have never successfully managed to convince him that baseball caps, as an accessory, are wrong on everyone. Except children and actual baseball players.

"She still plans to stay here after she gets back from England," Shari explains, plunging a chip of her own into the dip, "instead of moving to New York with us to start her real life."

Shari doesn't have to watch what she eats, either. She's always had a naturally fast metabolism. When we were kids, her school sack lunches consisted of three peanut butter and jelly sandwiches and a pack of Oreo cookies, and she never gained an ounce. My lunches? A hard-boiled egg, a single orange, and a chicken leg. And I was the blimp. Oh yes.

"Shari," I say, "I have a real life here. I've got a place to stay—"

"With your parents!"

"—and a job I love—"

"As an assistant manager of a vintage clothing store. That's not a *career*!"

"I told you," I say for what has to be the nine hundredth time, "I'm going to live here and save my money. Then Andrew and I are moving to New York after he gets his master's. It's just one more semester."

"Who's Andrew again?" Chaz wants to know. And Shari hits him in the shoulder.

"Ow," Chaz says.

"You remember," Shari says. "The R.A. at McCracken Hall. The grad student. The one Lizzie hasn't stopped talking about all summer."

"Oh, right, Andy. The British guy. The one who was running the illegal poker ring on the seventh floor."

I burst out laughing. "That's not Andrew! He doesn't *gamble*. He's studying to be an educator of youth so that he can preserve our most precious resource . . . the next generation."

"The guy who sent you the photo of his naked ass?"

I gasp. "Shari, you *told* him about that?"

"I wanted a guy's perspective," Shari says with a shrug. "You know, to see if he had any insights into what kind of individual would do something like that."

Coming from Shari, who'd been a psych major, this is actually a fairly reasonable explanation. I look at Chaz questioningly. He has lots of insights into lots of things—how many times around Palmer Field make a mile (four—which I needed to know back when I was walking it every day to lose weight); what the number 33 on the inside of the Rolling Rock bottle means; why so many guys seem to think man-pris are actually flattering . . .

But Chaz shrugs, too. "I was unable to be of any aid," he says, "not ever having taken a photo of my bare ass before."

"Andrew didn't take a photo of his own ass," I say. "His friends took it."

"How homoerotic," Chaz comments. "Why do you call him Andrew when everybody else calls him Andy?"

"Because Andy is a jock name," I say, "and Andrew isn't a jock. He's getting a master's in education. Someday he'll be teaching children to read. Could there be a more important job in the whole entire world than that? And he's *not* gay. I checked this time."

Chaz's eyebrows go up. "You *checked*? How? Wait . . . I don't want to know."

"She just likes pretending he's *Prince* Andrew," Shari says. "Um, so where was I?"

"Lizzie's being an ass," Chaz helpfully supplies. "So wait. How long's it been since you saw this guy? Three months?"

"About that," I say.

"Man," Chaz says, shaking his head, "there is going to be some major bone-jumping when you step off that plane."

"Andrew isn't like that," I say warmly. "He's a romantic. He'll probably want to let me get acclimated and recover from my jet lag in his king-size bed and thousand-thread-count sheets. He'll bring me breakfast in bed—a cute English breakfast with . . . Englishy stuff on it."

"Like stewed tomatoes?" Chaz asks with feigned innocence.

"Nice try," I say, "but Andrew knows I don't like tomatoes. He asked in his last e-mail if there are any foods I dislike, and I filled him in on the tomato thing."

"You better hope breakfast isn't all he brings you in bed," Shari says darkly. "Otherwise what is the point of traveling halfway around the world to see him?"

That's the problem with Shari. She's so unromantic. I'm really surprised she and Chaz have gone out as long as they have. I mean, two years is really a record for her.

Then again, as she likes to assure me, their attraction is almost purely physical, Chaz having just gotten his master's in philosophy and thus, in Shari's opinion, being virtually unemployable.

"So what would even be the point of hoping for a future with him?" she often asks me. "I mean, eventually he'll start to feel inadequate—even though he's got his trust fund, of course—and consequently suffer from performance anxiety in the bedroom. So I'll just keep him around as a boy toy for now, while he can still get it up."

Shari is very practical in this way.

"I still don't get why you're going all the way to England to see him," Chaz says. "I mean, a guy you haven't even slept with yet, who obviously doesn't know you very well if he isn't aware of your aversion to tomatoes and thinks you'd enjoy seeing a photograph of anyone's naked ass."

"You know perfectly well why," Shari says. "It's his accent."

"Shari!" I cry.

"Oh, right," Shari says, rolling her eyes. "He saved her life."

"Who saved whose life?" Angelo, my brother-in-law, moseys over, having discovered the dip.

"Lizzie's new boyfriend," Shari says.

"Lizzie's got a new boyfriend?" Angelo, I can tell, is trying to cut back on his carbs. He's only dipping celery sticks. Maybe he's on South Beach to control his belly fat, which is not enhanced by the white polyester shirt he is wearing. Why won't he listen to me and stick to natural fibers? "How did I not hear about this? The LBS must be on the fritz."

"LBS?" Chaz echoes, his dark eyebrows raised.

"Lizzie Broadcasting System," Shari explains to him. "Where have you been?"

"Oh, right," Chaz says, and swigs his beer.

"I told Rose all about it," I say, glaring at all three of them. Someday I'm going to get my sister Rose back for that Lizzie Broadcasting

System thing. It was funny when we were kids, but I'm twenty-two now! "Didn't she tell you, Ange?"

Angelo looks confused. "Tell me what?"

I sigh. "This freshman on the second floor let her potpourri boil over on her illegal hot plate and the hall filled with smoke and they had to evacuate," I explain. I am always eager to relate the story of how Andrew and I met. Because it's superromantic. Someday, when Andrew and I are married and live in a ramshackle and tomato-free Victorian in Westport, Connecticut, with our golden retriever, Rolly, and our four kids, Andrew Jr., Henry, Stella, and Beatrice, and I'm a famous—well, whatever I'm going to be—and Andrew's the headmaster at a nearby boys' school, teaching children to read, and I get interviewed in *Vogue,* I'll be able to tell this story—looking funky yet fabulous in vintage Chanel from head to toe—while laughingly serving a perfect cup of French roast to the reporter on my back porch, which will be decorated entirely in tasteful white wicker and chintz.

"Well, I was taking a shower," I go on, "so I didn't smell the smoke or hear the alarm going off or anything. Until Andrew came into the girls' bathroom and yelled *'Fire!'* and—"

"Is it true the girls' bathrooms in McCracken Hall have gang showers?" Angelo wants to know.

"It's true," Chaz informs him conversationally. "They all have to shower together. Sometimes they soap each other's backs while gossiping about their girlish hijinks from the night before."

Angelo stares at Chaz, bug-eyed. "Are you shitting me?"

"Don't pay any attention to him, Angelo," Shari says, going for another chip. "He's making it up."

"That kind of thing happens all the time on *Beverly Hills Bordello,*" Angelo says.

"We didn't shower all together," I say. "I mean, Shari and I did sometimes—"

"Tell us more about that, please," Chaz says, opening a new beer with the church key my mom had provided near the cooler.

"Don't," Shari says. "You'll just encourage him."

"Which bits were you washing when he came in?" Chaz wants to know. "And was there another girl with you at the time? Which bits was *she* washing? Or was she helping to wash *your* bits?"

"No," I say, "it was just me. And naturally, when I saw a guy in the girls' shower, I screamed."

"Oh, naturally," Chaz said.

"So I grabbed a towel and this guy—I couldn't really see him all that well through the steam and the smoke and all—goes, in the cutest British accent you ever heard, 'Miss, the building's on fire. I'm afraid you'll have to evacuate.'"

"So wait," Angelo says. "This dude saw you in the raw?"

"In her nudie-pants," Chaz confirms.

"So by then the halls were all smoky and I couldn't see, so he took my hand and guided me down the stairs and outside to safety, where we struck up a conversation—me in my towel and everything. And that's when I realized he was the love of my life."

"Based on one conversation," Chaz says, sounding skeptical. But then, having a philosophy master's degree, he is skeptical about everything. They train them to be that way.

"Well," I say, "we made out the rest of the night, too. That's how I know he's not gay. I mean, he got a full stiffy."

Chaz choked a little on his beer.

"So, anyway," I say, trying to steer the conversation back on track, "we made out all night. But then he had to leave the next day for England, because the semester was over—"

"—and now, since Lizzie's finally done with school, she's flying to London to spend the rest of the summer with him," Shari finishes for me. "Then coming back here to rot, just like her—"

"Come on, Shar," I interrupt quickly. "You promised."

She just grimaces at me.

"Listen, Liz," Chaz says, and reaches for another beer, "I know this guy's the love of your life and all. But you have all next semester to be with him. Are you sure you don't want to come to France with us for the rest of the summer?"

"Don't bother, Chaz," Shari says. "I already asked her eighty million times."

"Did you mention we're staying in a seventeenth-century French château with its own vineyard, perched on a hilltop overlooking a lush green valley through which snakes a long and lazy river?" Chaz wants to know.

"Shari told me," I say, "and it's sweet of you to ask. Even if you're not exactly in a position to be inviting people, because doesn't the château belong to one of your friends from that prep school you went to, and not you?"

"A trifling detail," Chaz says. "Luke would love to have you."

"Ha," Shari says, "I'll say. More slave labor for his amateur wedding franchise."

"What're they talking about?" Angelo asks me, looking confused.

"Chaz's childhood friend from prep school, Luke," I explain to him, "has an ancestral home in France that his father rents out during the summer sometimes as a destination wedding spot. Shari and Chaz are leaving tomorrow to spend a month at the château for free, in exchange for helping out at the weddings."

"Destination wedding spot," Angelo echoes. "You mean like Vegas?"

"Right," Shari says. "Only tasteful. And it costs more than one ninety-nine to get there. And there's no free breakfast buffet."

Angelo looks shocked. "Then what's the *point*?"

Someone tugs on the skirt of my dress and I look down. My sister Rose's firstborn, Maggie, holds up a necklace made of macaroni.

"Aunt Lizzie," she says. "For you. I made it. For your gradutation."

"Why, thank you, Maggie," I say, kneeling down so that Maggie can drop the necklace over my head.

"The paint's not dry," Maggie says, pointing to the red and blue splotches of paint that have now been transferred from the maca-roni to the front of my 1954 Suzy Perette rose silk party dress (which wasn't cheap, even with my employee discount).

"That's okay, Mags," I say. Because, after all, she's only four. "It's beautiful."

"There you are!" Grandma Nichols teeters toward us. "I've been looking for you everywhere, Anne-Marie. It's time for *Dr. Quinn.*"

"Grandma," I say, straightening up to grasp her spool-thin arm before she can topple over. I see that she has already managed to spill something all down the green crepe de chine 1960s tunic top I got her at the shop. Fortunately the paint stains from the macaroni necklace Maggie made for her are somewhat hiding the stain. "It's Lizzie. Not Anne-Marie. Mom's over by the dessert table. And what have you been drinking?"

I seize the Heineken bottle in Grandma's hand and smell its con-tents. It should, by prior agreement with the rest of my family, have been filled with nonalcoholic beer, then resealed, due to Grandma Nichols's inability to hold her liquor, which has resulted in what my mom likes to call "incidents." Mom was hoping to head off any "in-cidents" at my graduation party by letting Grandma have only non-alcoholic beer—but not telling her it was nonalcoholic, of course. Because then she would have raised a fuss, telling us we were trying to ruin an old lady's good time and all.

But I can't tell if the beer in the bottle is of the nonalcoholic va-riety. We had stashed the faux Heinekens in a special section of the cooler for Grandma. But she may have managed to find the real thing somewhere. She's crafty that way.

Or she could just THINK she's had the real thing, and conse-quently thinks she's drunk.

"Lizzie?" Grandma looks suspicious. "What are you doing here? Shouldn't you be away at college?"

"I graduated from college in May, Grandma," I say. Well, sort of, anyway. Not counting the two months I just spent in summer school getting my language requirement out of the way. "This is my graduation party. Well, my graduation-slash-bon voyage party."

"Bon voyage?" Grandma's suspicion turns to indignation. "Where do you think you're going?"

"To England, Grandma, the day after tomorrow," I say. "To visit my boyfriend. Remember? We talked about this."

"Boyfriend?" Grandma glares at Chaz. "Isn't that him right there?"

"No, Grandma," I say. "That's Chaz, Shari's boyfriend. You remember Shari Dennis, right, Grandma? She grew up down the street?"

"Oh, the Dennis girl," Grandma says, narrowing her eyes in Shari's direction. "I remember you now. I thought I saw your parents over by the barbecue. You and Lizzie going to do that song you always do when you get together?"

Shari and I exchange horror-filled glances. Angelo hoots.

"Hey, yeah!" he cries. "Rosie told me about this. What song was it you two used to do? Like at the school talent show and shit?"

I give Angelo a warning look, since Maggie is still hanging around, and say, "Little pitchers." It's clear from his expression that he has no idea what I'm talking about. I sigh and begin steering Grandma toward the house.

"Better come on, Grandma," I say, "or you'll miss your show."

"What about the song?" Grandma wants to know.

"We'll do the song later, Mrs. Nichols," Shari assures her.

"I'm going to hold you to that," Chaz says with a wink. Shari mouths *In your dreams* at him. Chaz blows a kiss at her over the top of his beer bottle.

They're so cute together. I can't wait until I'm in London and Andrew and I can be that cute together, too.

"Come on, Grandma," I say. "*Dr. Quinn*'s starting now."

"Oh, good," Grandma says. To Shari, she confides, "I don't care about that dumb Dr. Quinn. It's that hunk who hangs out with her—him I can't get enough of!"

"Okay, Grandma," I say quickly as Shari spurts out the mouthful of Amstel Light she's just taken. "Let's get you inside before you miss your show—"

We hardly get a few yards down the deck, however, before we're waylaid by Dr. Rajghatta, my dad's boss at the cyclotron, and his pretty wife, Nishi, beaming in a pink sari at his side.

"Many congratulations on your graduation," Dr. Rajghatta says.

"Yes," his wife agrees. "And may we say, you are also looking so slim and lovely?"

"Oh, thank you," I say. "Thank you so much!"

"And what will you be doing now that you have your bachelor's degree in . . . what is it again?" Dr. R wants to know. It's unfortunate about the pocket protector he's wearing, but then I haven't been able to wean my own father from the habit, so it's unlikely I'll ever make any headway with his boss.

"History of fashion," I reply.

"History of fashion? I was not aware this school offered a major in that field of study," Dr. R says.

"Oh, it doesn't. I'm in the individualized major program. You know, where you make your own major?"

"But fashion history?" Dr. Rajghatta looks concerned. "There are many opportunities available in this field?"

"Oh, tons," I say, trying not to remember how just last weekend I picked up a copy of the Sunday *New York Times* and saw that every fashion-related job in the want ads—besides merchandising—either didn't exactly require a bachelor's degree, or did require years of experience in the field, which I don't have. "I could get a job in the Costume Institute of the Metropolitan Museum of Art." Sure. As a janitor. "Or as a costume designer on Broadway." You know, if all the other costume designers in the world suddenly died at the same time. "Or even as a buyer for a major high-end fashion retailer like Saks Fifth Avenue." If I had listened to my dad, who'd begged me to minor in business.

"What do you mean, a buyer?" Grandma looks scandalized. "You're going to be a designer, not a buyer! Why, she's been ripping her clothes apart and sewing them back together all weird since she was old enough to pick up a needle," she tells Dr. and Mrs. R, who look at me as if Grandma has just announced I like to salsa naked in my spare time.

"Huh," I say with a nervous laugh. "It was just a hobby." I don't mention, of course, that I only did this—reinvented my clothing— because I was so chubby I couldn't fit into the fun, flirty clothes in the junior department, and so I had to somehow make the stuff Mom got me from the women's department look younger.

Which is, of course, why I love vintage clothes so much. They're so much better made—and more flattering, no matter what your size.

"Hobby my ass," Grandma says. "See this shirt here?" Grandma points at her stained tunic. "She dyed it herself! It was orange, and now look at it! And she hemmed the sleeves to make them sexier, just like I asked!"

"It's a very beautiful top," Mrs. Rajghatta says kindly. "I'm sure Lizzie will go very far with such talents."

"Oh," I say, feeling myself blush beet red. "I mean, I could never . . . you know. For a living. It's just a hobby."

"Well, that's good," her husband says, looking relieved. "No one should spend four years at a top college just so that she can sew for a living!"

"That would be such a waste!" I agree, deciding not to mention to him that I'd be spending my first semester out of college continuing in my assistant shop manager position while waiting for my boyfriend to graduate.

Grandma looks annoyed. "What do you care?" she asks, giving me a poke in the side. "You went for those four years for free anyway. What does it matter what you do with what you learned there?"

Dr. and Mrs. Rajghatta and I smile at one another, all equally embarrassed by Grandma's outburst.

"Your parents must be so proud of you," Mrs. Rajghatta says, still smiling pleasantly. "I mean, having the confidence to study something so . . . arcane when so many qualified young people can't even find jobs in today's market. That is very brave of you."

"Oh," I say, swallowing down the little bit of vomit that always seems to rise into my throat when I think about my future. Better not to think about it right now. Better to think about the fun I'm going to have with Andrew. "Well, I'm brave all right."

"I'll say she's brave," Grandma chimes in. "She's going to England day after tomorrow to hump some guy she barely knows."

"Well, we have to be going inside now," I say, grabbing Grandma's hand and tugging her along. "Thanks so much for coming, Dr. and Mrs. Rajghatta!"

"Oh, wait. This is for you, Lizzie," Mrs. Rajghatta says, slipping a small gift-wrapped box into my hand.

"Oh, thank you so much," I cry. "You didn't have to!"

"It's nothing, really," Mrs. Rajghatta says with a laugh. "Just a book light. Your parents said you were going to Europe, so I thought, if you are reading on a train or something—"

"Well, thank you very much," I say. "That will come in handy all right. Bye now."

"Book light," Grandma grumbles as I hurry her away from Dad's boss and his wife. "Who the hell wants a book light?"

"Lots of people," I say. "They are very handy things to have."

Grandma says a very bad word. I'll be happy when I get her safely tucked in front of the rerun of *Dr. Quinn*.

But before I can do that, there are several more obstacles we have to hurdle, including Rose.

"My baby sister!" Rose cries, looking up from the infant she's got in a high chair by the picnic table, into whose mouth she's shoveling mashed peas. "I can't believe you're graduating from college! It just makes me feel so old!"

"You *are* old," Grandma observes.

But Rose just ignores her, as is her custom where Grandma is concerned.

"Angelo and I are just so proud of you," Rose says, her eyes filling with tears. It's a shame she didn't listen to me about the length of her jeans. The cropped look just doesn't work unless you've got legs as long as Cindy Crawford's. Which none of us Nichols girls do. "Not just for the graduating thing, but for—well, you know. The weight loss. Really. You just look terrific. And . . . well, we got you a little something." She slips a small gift-wrapped package in my hand. "It isn't anything much . . . you know, with Angelo out of work, and the baby in day care and all . . . But I thought you might be able to use a book light. I know how much you love to read."

"Wow," I say. "Thank you so much, Rose. That was really thoughtful of you."

Grandma starts to say something, but I squeeze her hand, hard.

"Ow," Grandma says. "Stab me next time, why don't you?"

"Well, I have to get Grandma inside," I say. "Time for *Dr. Quinn*."

Rose looks down her nose at Grandma. "Oh God," she says. "She didn't talk about her lust for Byron Sully in front of everyone, did she?"

"At least *he's* got a job," Grandma begins, "which is more than I can say for that husband of—"

"Okay," I say, grabbing Grandma and heading for the sliding doors. "Let's go, Grandma. Don't want to keep Sully waiting."

"That is no way," I hear Rose wail behind us, "to talk about your grandson-in-law, Gram! Wait till I tell Daddy!"

"Aw, go ahead," Grandma retorts. Then, as I drag her away, she complains, "That sister of yours. How could you stand her all these years?"

Before I can form a reply—that it wasn't easy—I hear my other sister, Sarah, call my name. I turn around and see her staggering toward us, a casserole dish in her hands. Sadly, she is in a pair of white stretch capris that are far too tight on her.

Will my sisters never learn? Some things *need* to be left a mystery.

But I guess since that's the look that won Sarah her husband, Chuck, she's sticking with it.

"Oh, hey," Sarah says, not very distinctly. She's clearly been hitting the Heineken herself. "I made your favorite for you, in honor of your big day." She whisks the plastic wrap off the casserole dish and waves it under my nose. A wave of nausea grips me.

"Tomato ratatouille!" Sarah shrieks, laughing uproariously. "Remember that time Aunt Karen made that ratatouille and Mom told you you had to eat it to be polite and you threw up over the side of the deck?"

"Yes," I said, feeling like I was about to throw up over the side of the deck all over again.

"Wasn't that funny? So I made it for old times' sake. Hey, what's the matter?" She seems to notice my expression for the first time. "Oh, come on. Don't tell me you still hate tomatoes! I thought you grew out of that!"

"Why should she?" Grandma demands. "I never did. Why don't you take that stuff and put it up—"

"Okay, Gram," I say quickly. "Let's go. *Dr. Quinn*'s waiting . . ."

I hustle Grandma away before punches are thrown. Inside the sliding doors stand my parents.

"There she is," Dad says, brightening when he sees me. "The first of the Nichols girls actually to finish college!"

I hope Rose and Sarah don't overhear him. Even though it is, technically, true.

"Hi, Dad," I say. "Hi, Mom. Great par—" Then I notice the woman standing next to them. "Dr. Sprague!" I cry. "You came!"

"Of course I came." Dr. Sprague, my college adviser, gives me a hug and a kiss. "I wouldn't have missed it for the world. Look at you, so skinny now! That low-carb thing really worked."

"Aw," I say, "thanks."

"Oh, and here, I even brought you a little going-away present . . . sorry I didn't have time to wrap it," Dr. Sprague says, stuffing something into my hands.

"Oh," my father says. "A book light! Look at that, Lizzie! Bet you'll find a use for that."

"Absolutely," Mom says. "On those trains you'll be taking across Europe. A book light always comes in handy."

"Jesus H. Christ," Grandma says. "Was there a sale on 'em somewhere?"

"Thank you so much, Dr. Sprague," I hurry to say. "That was so thoughtful of you. But you really didn't have to."

"I know," Dr. Sprague says. She looks, as always, coolly professional in a red linen suit. Although I'm not sure that particular red is the right color for her. "I was wondering if we could talk privately for a moment, Elizabeth?"

"Of course," I say. "Mom, Dad, if you'll excuse us. Maybe one of you can help Grandma find the Hallmark Channel? Her show is on."

"Oh God," my mother says with a groan. "Not—"

"You know," Grandma says, "you could learn a lot from Dr.

Quinn, Anne-Marie. She knows how to make soap from a sheep's guts. And she had twins when she was fifty. Fifty!" I hear Grandma cry as Mom leads her toward the den. "I'd like to see you having twins at fifty."

"Is something wrong?" I ask Dr. Sprague, guiding her into my parents' living room, which has changed very little in the four years since I've been living in a dormitory more or less down the street. The pair of armchairs in which my mom and dad read every night—him, spy novels, her, romance—are still slipcovered against Molly the sheepdog's fur. Our childhood photos—me looking fatter in each consecutive one, Rose and Sarah slimmer and more glamorous—still line every inch of available wall space. It's homey and threadbare and plain and I wouldn't trade it for any living room in the world.

With the possible exception of the one in Pam Anderson's Malibu beach house, which I saw last week on *MTV Cribs*. It was surprisingly cute. Considering.

"Didn't you get my messages?" Dr. Sprague wants to know. "I've been calling your cell all morning."

"No," I say. "I mean, I've been busy running around helping Mom set up the party. Why? What's the matter?"

"There's no easy way to say this," Dr. Sprague says with a sigh, "so I'll just say it. When you signed up for the individualized major, Lizzie, you did realize one of the graduation requirements was a written thesis, didn't you?"

I stare at her blankly. "A what?"

"A written thesis." Dr. Sprague, apparently seeing by my expression that I have no idea what she's talking about, sinks with a groan into my dad's armchair. "Oh God. I knew it. Lizzie, didn't you read *any* of the materials from the department?"

"Of course I did," I say defensively. "I mean . . . most of it, anyway." It was all so *boring*.

"Didn't you wonder why, at commencement yesterday, your diploma tube was empty?"

"Well, sure," I say. "But I thought it was because I hadn't finished my language requirement. Which is why I took both summer sessions—"

"But you had to write a thesis, too," Dr. Sprague says, "summarizing, basically, what you learned about your field of concentration. Liz, you haven't officially graduated until you turn in a thesis."

"But"—my lips feel numb—"I'm leaving for England day after tomorrow for a month. To visit my boyfriend."

"Well," Dr. Sprague says with a sigh, "you'll have to write it when you get back, then."

It's my turn to sink into the armchair she's just vacated.

"I can't believe this," I murmur, letting all of my book lights fall into my lap. "My parents put on this huge party—there must be sixty people out there. Some of my teachers from high school are coming. And you're saying I'm not even really a college graduate?"

"Not until you write that thesis," Dr. Sprague says. "I'm sorry, Lizzie. But they're going to want at least fifty pages."

"Fifty pages?" She might as well have said fifteen hundred. How am I going to enjoy having English breakfast in Andrew's king-size bed knowing I have fifty pages hanging over my head? "Oh God." Then a worse thought hits me. I'm no longer the first of the Nichols girls actually to finish college. "*Please* don't mention this to my parents, Dr. Sprague. *Please*."

"I won't. And I'm really sorry about this," Dr. Sprague says. "I can't imagine how it happened."

"I can," I say miserably. "I should have gone to a small private college. In a huge state university, it's so easy to get lost in the shuffle and turn out not to have actually graduated after all."

"But an education at a small private college would have cost you thousands of dollars, which you'd have to be worrying about paying back now," Dr. Sprague says. "By attending the huge state university in which your father works, you got a superior education for absolutely nothing, and so now, instead of having to get a job right away, you can flit off to England to spend time with—what's his name again?"

"Andrew," I say dejectedly.

"Right. Andrew. Well." Dr. Sprague shoulders her expensive leather purse. "I guess I'd better be going now. I just wanted to drop by to give you the news. If it's any comfort to you, Lizzie, I'm sure your thesis is going to be just *great*."

"I don't even know what to write it *on*," I wail.

"A brief history of fashion will suffice," Dr. Sprague says. "To show you learned something while you were here. And," she adds brightly, "you can even do some research while you're in England."

"I could, couldn't I?" I'm starting to feel a little better. The history of fashion? I *love* fashion. And Dr. Sprague is right—England would be the perfect place to research this. They have all sorts of museums there. And I could go to Jane Austen's house! They might even have some of her clothes there! Clothes like they wore in *Pride and Prejudice* on A&E! I *loved* those clothes!

God. This might even turn out to be fun.

I have no idea whether Andrew is going to want to go to Jane Austen's house. But why wouldn't he? He's British. And so is she. Naturally he's going to be interested in his own country's history.

Yeah. Yeah, this is going to be great!

"Thanks for coming by personally to deliver the news, Dr. Sprague," I say, getting up and showing her to the door. "And thanks so much for the book light, too."

"Oh," Dr. Sprague says, "don't mention it. I shouldn't say this, of course, but we're going to miss you around the office. You always made such a splash whenever you'd show up there, in one of your, um"—I notice her gaze drop to the macaroni necklace and my paint-splashed dress—"*unusual* outfits."

"Oh," I say with a smile. "Well, thank you, Dr. Sprague. Any time you want me to find you an unusual outfit of your own, just stop by Vintage to Vavoom, you know, over in Kerrytown—"

Just then my sister Sarah bursts into the living room, her anger over the tomato ratatouille incident apparently forgotten, since she's laughing a little hysterically. She's followed by her husband, Chuck, my other sister, Rose, her husband, Angelo, Maggie, our parents, the Rajghattas, various other party guests, Shari, and Chaz.

"Here she is, here she is," Sarah yells. She, I can tell right away, is drunker than ever. Sarah grabs my arm and starts dragging me toward the landing—the one we used to use as a stage, when we were little, for putting on little plays for our parents. Well, the one Rose and Sarah used to push ME onto, to put on little plays for our parents. And for them.

"Come on, graduate," Sarah says, having a little trouble with the word. "Sing! We all want you and Shari to sing your little song!"

Only it comes out sounding like, *Shing! We all want you and Shari to shing your liddle shong!*

"Uh," I say, noticing that Rose has Shari in a grip about as tight as Sarah's on me. "No."

"Oh, come *on*," Rose cries. "We want to see our baby sister and her little fwiend do their song!" And she throws Shari hard against me, so that the two of us stumble and almost fall across the landing.

"Your sisters," Shari grumbles in my ear, "have the worst cases of sibling envy I have ever seen in my life. I can't believe how much they resent you because you, unlike them, did not become impregnated by a bohunk your sophomore year and have to drop out and stay home all day with drooling sprog."

"Shari!" I am shocked by this assessment of my sisters' lives. Even if it is, technically, accurate.

"All college gwaduates," Rose continues, apparently unaware that she's using baby talk while speaking to adults, "have to shing!"

"Rose," I say. "No. Really. Maybe later. I'm not in the mood."

"All college graduates," Rose repeats, this time with dangerously narrowed eyes, "have to *sing*!"

"In that case," I say, "you're going to have to count me out."

And then I turn to face thirty dumbfounded expressions.

And realize what I've just let slip.

"Kidding," I say quickly.

And everyone laughs. Except for Grandma, who's just come in from the den.

"Sully's not even in this episode," she announces. "Goddammit. Who's going to get an old lady a drink?"

Then she topples over onto the carpet and lets out a gentle snore.

"I love that woman," Shari says to me as everyone rushes forward to attempt to revive my grandmother, completely forgetting about Shari and me.

"So do I," I say. "You have no idea how much."

The ancient Egyptians, who invented both toilet paper and the first known form of birth control (lemon rind as cervical cap, plus alligator dung, which made an effective, if pungent, spermicide), were extremely hygienic, preferring fine linen to any other material, as it was easily washable—a not entirely surprising attitude, considering the alligator dung.

History of Fashion
SENIOR THESIS BY ELIZABETH NICHOLS

Anyone who has obeyed nature by transmitting a piece of gossip experiences the explosive relief that accompanies the satisfying of a primary need.
—*Primo Levi (1919–1987), Italian chemist and author*

thought that was you!" Andrew gushes in that cute accent that had all the girls in McCracken Hall swooning—even if his *th*'s do sound like *f*'s. "What's the matter? You walked right past me!"

"She thought you were a kidnapper," the guy from the Meet Your Party booth explains between guffaws.

"Kidnapper?" Andrew looks from the guy in the booth to me. "What's he talking about?"

"Nothing," I say, grabbing Andrew's arm and rushing him away from the booth. "Nothing, really. Oh my gosh! It's good to see you!"

"Good to see you, too," Andrew says, putting an arm around my waist and giving me a hug—so tight that the epaulets from his jacket dig into my cheek. "You look fucking fantastic! Did you lose weight or something?"

"Just a little," I say modestly. No need for Andrew to know that no starch whatsoever—not so much as a French fry or even a lousy crumb of bread—has touched my lips since he waved good-bye to me last May.

Then Andrew notices me looking at an older bald man who has

come up to us and is smiling politely at me. He is wearing a navy-blue windbreaker and a pair of brown corduroy pants. In August.

This is not a good sign. I'm just saying.

"Oh, right!" Andrew cries. "Liz, this is my dad. Dad, this is Liz!"

Oh, how sweet! He brought his dad to meet me at the airport! Andrew really MUST be taking our relationship seriously if he would go to so much trouble. I've already forgiven him for the jacket.

Well, almost.

"How do you do, Mr. Marshall?" I say, putting out my hand to shake his. "It's so nice to meet you."

"Nice to meet you, too," Andrew's father says with a nice smile. "And please, call me Arthur. Don't mind me, I'm just the chauffeur."

Andrew laughs. So do I. Except—Andrew doesn't have his own car?

Oh, but wait, that's right. Shari said things are different in Europe, that lots of people don't own cars because they're so expensive. And Andrew *is* trying to get by on a teacher's salary . . .

I've got to stop being so judgmental about other cultures. I think it's just cute as can be that Andrew doesn't have a car. So environmentally conscious! Besides, he lives in London. I imagine lots of people in London don't have cars. They take public transportation, or they walk, like New Yorkers. Which is why there are so few fat people in New York. You know, because they're all such healthy walkers. Probably there aren't many fat people in London, either. I mean, look at Andrew. He's thin as a toothpick, practically.

And yet he's got those marvelous grapefruit-size biceps . . .

Although now that I look at them, they seem sort of more orange-size.

But how could anybody really tell beneath a leather jacket, anyway?

It's sweet he has such a close relationship with his dad, too. I mean, that he could ask him to come with him to pick up his girl-friend at Heathrow. My dad is always too busy working to take time out for things like that. But then, his job at the cyclotron is very im-portant, since they're always smashing atoms up there and things. Andrew's dad is a teacher, like Andrew wants to be. Teachers get summers off.

Dr. Rajghatta would laugh his head off if my dad ever asked for a summer off.

Andrew takes my bag, which has wheels, so it's actually the light-est thing I'm carrying. My carry-on is way heavier, since it has all my makeup and beauty supplies in it. I wouldn't mind so much if the airline lost my clothes, but I would totally die if they lost my makeup. I look like a total beast without it. I have eyes that are so small and squinty without liner and mascara I actually resemble a pig . . . even if Shari, who's lived with me for the past four years, swears this isn't true. Shari says I could get away without makeup if I wanted to.

But why would I want to when makeup is such a brilliant and helpful invention for those of us cursed with piggy eyes?

Still, makeup does weigh an awful lot, at least when you have as much of it as I do. Not to mention all of my hairstyling equipment and products. Having long hair is no joke. You have to bring about nine tons of stuff with you in order to keep it properly shampooed, conditioned, tangle-and-frizz-free, dry, shiny, and full of body. Not to mention all the different adapters I had to bring for my hair dryer and curling iron, since Andrew was remarkably unhelpful in describing what British electrical outlets look like ("They look like *outlets,*" he kept saying on the phone. Isn't this just like a guy?), so I had to bring every different kind I could find at CVS.

But maybe it's just as well Andrew is pulling the wheelie bag and not carrying my carry-on. Because then if he asks what's inside and why it's so heavy, I'll have to tell him the truth, as I have resolved this relationship will not be founded on artifice, like the one with that guy T.J. I met at the McCracken Hall Movie Night, who turned out to be a practicing warlock—which would have been all right, I totally respect other people's religions . . .

Except that he also turned out to be a chubby-chaser, as I learned when I caught him making out in the quad with Amy De Soto. He tried to tell me his familiar *made* him sleep with her.

Which is why I plan to always tell the truth to Andrew, because T.J. did not give me even that much respect.

But that doesn't mean I'm not going to go out of my way to avoid having to tell him the truth, if I can. Like, there is absolutely no reason he needs to know that the reason my carry-on bag is so heavy is because it's filled with approximately seventy-five billion Clinique cosmetic samples; a container of astringent pads (because I shine so much, thanks to Mom's side of the family); a family-size container of Tums (because I've heard English food isn't necessarily the best); a family-size container of chewable fiber tablets (because ditto); the aforementioned curling iron and hair dryer; the clothes I wore on the plane before I changed into my mandarin dress; a Game Boy loaded with Tetris; the latest Dan Brown (because you can't go on a transatlantic flight with nothing to read); my mini iPod; three book lights; Sun-In for my highlights; all of my pharmaceuticals, such as aspirin, Band-Aids for the blisters I am undoubtedly going to get (from strolling hand in hand with Andrew through the British Museum, soaking in all the art), and prescriptions, including my birth control pills and antibiotic acne medication; and of course the notebook in which I've begun my senior thesis. I had to repack my sewing kit—for emergency clothing repairs—into my suitcase because of the stitch scissors and seam ripper.

There is no reason at this point in our relationship for Andrew to find out I wasn't actually born this good-looking—that a great deal of artifice goes into it. What if he turns out to be one of those guys who like naturally pink-cheeked beauties like Liv Tyler? What kind of chance do I stand against an English rose like that? A girl has to have *some* secrets.

Oh, wait, Andrew is talking to me. He's asking how my flight went. Why is he wearing that jacket? He can't seriously think it looks good, can he?

"The flight was great," I say. I don't tell Andrew about the little girl in the seat next to mine who ignored me throughout the flight when I was just wearing my jeans and T-shirt, with my hair in a ponytail. It wasn't until after I came back from doing my hair and makeup and changing into my silk dress a half hour before we landed that the kid did a double take, and the next thing I knew she was asking shyly, "Excuse me. But are you the actress Jennifer Garner?"

Jennifer Garner! Me! This kid thought *I* was Jennifer Garner!

And okay, she was only like ten or whatever, and wearing a shirt with Kermit the Frog on it (surely she meant this ironically and is not actually a current viewer of *Sesame Street,* as she seemed a bit old for it).

But still! No one has ever mistaken me for a movie star in my life! Let alone a skinny one like Jennifer Garner.

And the thing is, with my makeup on and my hair done, I guess I *do* look a bit like Jennifer Garner . . . you know, if she hadn't quite lost all the baby fat. And had bangs. And was only five feet six.

I guess it never occurred to the kid that Jennifer Garner would hardly be flying coach, by herself, to England. But whatever.

And before I could stop myself, I was going, "Why, yes. I AM Jennifer Garner," because, whatever, I'm never going to see this kid again in my life. Why not give her a thrill?

The kid's eyes practically bugged out, she was so excited.

"Hi," she said, bouncing a little in her seat. "I'm Marnie! I'm your biggest fan!"

"Well, hi, Marnie," I said. "It's nice to meet you."

"Mom!" Marnie turned to whisper to her dozing mother. "It IS Jennifer Garner! I TOLD you!"

And the little girl's drowsy mother looked over at me, her eyes still bleary with sleep, and went, "Oh. Hello."

"Hi," I said, wondering if I sounded Jennifer Garnery enough.

But I guess I did, since the next words out of the kid's mouth were, "I just loved you in *13 Going on 30.*"

"Why, thank you," I said. "I do consider that some of my best work. Besides *Alias,* of course."

"I'm not allowed to stay up late enough to watch that," Marnie said mournfully.

"Oh," I said. "Well, maybe you can see it on DVD."

"Can I have your autograph?" the little girl wanted to know.

"Of course you can," I said, and took the pen and the British Airways cocktail napkin she offered me and scrawled *Best wishes to Marnie, my biggest fan! Love, Jennifer Garner* on it.

The little girl took the napkin reverently, as if she couldn't believe her good fortune. "Thanks!" she said.

I just knew she was going to take that napkin back to America when she got home from her fun European vacation and show it to all of her friends.

I didn't really start feeling bad until then. Because what if one of Marnie's friends has an autograph from the REAL Jennifer Garner and they compare the handwriting? Then Marnie is going to be all suspicious! And she might even ask herself why Jen wasn't with her publicist or even why she was flying commercial. And then she'll realize I wasn't the REAL Jennifer Garner, and that I was lying the whole time. And that could shake her faith in the goodness of humankind. Marnie could develop serious trust issues, like the kind I myself developed when my prom date, Adam Berger, told me he had to go home and paint the ceiling instead of taking me to the after-party, when really he went ahead and attended the after-party with skinny-as-a-stick Melissa Kemplebaum after dropping me off.

But then I told myself that it didn't matter, since I'd never see Marnie again. So who even cared?

Still, I don't mention the incident to Andrew because, seeing as how he's getting a master's in education, I highly doubt he approves of lying to young children.

Also, the truth is, I am feeling kind of sleepy, even though it is eight o'clock in the morning in England, and I am wondering how far it is to Andrew's apartment, and if there's any chance at all he might have some diet Coke there. Because I could totally use one.

"Oh, not too far at all," is what Andrew's dad, Mr. Marshall, says when I ask Andrew how far he lives from the airport.

It's kind of strange that Andrew's dad answered, and not Andrew. But then again, Mr. Marshall's a teacher and answering questions is basically his job. He probably can't help it, even when he's off duty.

It's such a good thing there are men like Andrew and his dad who are willing to undertake the education of our youth. The Marshalls are truly a dying breed. I'm so glad I'm with Andrew and not, say, Chaz, who chose to pursue a philosophy degree solely so that he could argue more effectively with his parents. How is *that* supposed to help future generations?

Whereas Andrew has purposefully chosen a career that will never make him much money, but that will ensure that young minds don't go unmolded.

And isn't that the noblest thing you've ever heard of?

It's a long, long way to Mr. Marshall's car. We have to go through all of these hallways, where, along the walls, there are advertisements for products I've never heard of. Chaz had been complaining, last time he'd gone to visit his friend Luke—the one with the château—about the Americanization of Europe and how you couldn't go anywhere without seeing a Coca-Cola ad.

But I don't see any Americanization here in England. So far. I don't see anything even vaguely American. Not even a Coke machine.

Not that this is a bad thing. I'm just saying. Although a diet Coke wouldn't be so bad right about now.

Andrew and his dad are talking about the weather, and how lucky I am to have come at a time when it's so nice out. But when we step out of the building and into the parking garage, I realize it's maybe sixty degrees, at most, and that the sky—what I can see of it at the end of the garage level—is gray and overcast.

If this is good weather, what do the British consider bad? And, granted, it's certainly cold enough for a leather jacket. But that doesn't excuse the fact that Andrew is wearing one. Surely there's some rule somewhere—like the one about no white pants before Memorial Day—about no leather in August.

We're almost to the car—a small red compact, exactly what I'd expect a middle-aged teacher to drive—when I hear a shriek, and look around to see the little girl from the plane standing next to an SUV with her mother and an older couple I can only assume are her grandparents.

"There she is!" Marnie is screaming, pointing at me. "Jennifer Garner! Jennifer Garner!"

I keep walking, my head down, trying to ignore her. But both Andrew and his father are looking over at her, bemused smiles on their faces. Andrew does look a bit like his dad. Will he, too, be totally bald when he's fifty? Is baldness a trait passed on by the mother's side of the family or the father's? Why didn't I take a single bio course while I was designing my own major? I could have squeezed in at least one . . .

"Is that child speaking to you?" Mr. Marshall asks me.

"Me?" I glance over my shoulder, pretending to notice for the first time that a small child is shrieking at me from across the garage.

"Jennifer Garner! It's me! Marnie! From the plane! Remember?"

I smile and wave at Marnie. She flushes with pleasure and grabs her mother's arm.

"See?" she cries. "I told you! It really *is* her!"

Marnie waves some more. I wave back while Andrew wrestles my suitcase into the small trunk, swearing a bit. Since he's been wheeling it along the whole time, he had no idea how heavy it is until he bent to lift it.

But really, a month is a long time. I don't see how I could have packed less than ten pairs of shoes. Shari even said she was proud of me for being sensible enough not to bring my lace-up platform espadrilles. Although I did manage to squeeze them in at the last minute before I left.

"Why is that child calling you Jennifer Garner?" Mr. Marshall wants to know as he, too, waves at Marnie, whose grandparents, or whoever they are, still haven't succeeded in herding her into the car.

"Oh," I say, feeling myself begin to blush. "We sat next to each other on the plane. It's just a little game we were playing, to pass time on the flight."

"How kind of you," Mr. Marshall says, waving even more energetically now. "Not all young people realize how important it is to treat children with respect and dignity instead of condescension. It's so important to set a good example for the younger generation, especially when one considers how unstable many of today's family units really are."

"That's so true," I say in what I hope sounds like a respectful and dignified manner.

"Christ," Andrew says. He's just tried to pick up my carry-on bag from where I've set it on the ground. "What have you got in here, Liz? A dead body?"

"Oh," I say, my respectful and dignified demeanor threatening to crumble, "just a few necessities."

"I'm sorry my chariot isn't more stylish," Mr. Marshall says, opening the driver's door to his car. "It's certainly not what you're used to, I'm sure, back in America. But I hardly use it, since I walk to the school where I teach most days."

I am instantly charmed by the vision of Mr. Marshall strolling down a tree-lined country lane in a herringbone jacket with leather elbow patches—rather than the extremely uninspired windbreaker he is currently wearing—and perhaps a cocker spaniel or two nipping at his heels.

"Oh, it's fine," I say about his car. "Mine isn't much bigger."

I wonder why he's just standing there by the door, instead of getting in, until he goes, "After you, er, Liz."

He wants *me* to drive? But . . . I just got here! I don't even know my way around!

Then I realize he isn't holding open the driver's door at all . . . it's the passenger side. The steering wheel is on the right side of the car.

Of course! We're in England!

I laugh at my own mistake and sit down in the front seat.

Andrew slams down the trunk and comes around to see me sitting in the passenger seat. He looks at his dad and says, "What, I'm supposed to sit in the boot, then?"

"Mind your manners, Andy," Mr. Marshall says. It seems so strange to hear Andrew called Andy. He is such an Andrew to me. But evidently not to his family.

Although truthfully, in that jacket, he looks a bit more like an Andy than an Andrew.

"Ladies in the front seat," Mr. Marshall goes on with a smile at me. "And gentlemen in the back."

"Liz, I thought you were a feminist," Andrew says (only it comes out sounding like, *Liz, I fought you were a feminist*). "Are you going to stand for this kind of treatment?"

"Oh," I say. "Of course. Andrew should sit in front, he's got longer legs—"

"I won't hear of it," Mr. Marshall says. "You'll muss your pretty Chinese dress, climbing about." Then he shuts my car door, firmly, for me.

Next thing I know, he's come around the right side and is holding the driver's-side seat back for Andrew to crawl behind. There's a brief argument I can't really hear, and then Andrew appears. I don't really know any other word I can use to describe the expression on Andrew's face except peevish.

But I feel bad for even *thinking* Andrew might be feeling peevish about me getting to sit in the front seat. Most likely he's just embarrassed about not having his own car to pick me up in. Yes, that's probably it. Poor thing. He probably thinks I'm holding him to American standards of capitalist materialism! I'll have to find some way to assure him that I find his poverty extremely sexy, seeing as how all the sacrifices he's making, he's making for the children.

Not Andrew Jr., Henry, Stella, and Beatrice, of course. I mean the children of the world, the ones he'll be teaching someday.

Wow. Just thinking about all the little lives Andrew's going to improve with his sacrifices in the teaching profession is making me kind of horny.

Mr. Marshall climbs into the driver's seat and smiles at me. "Ready?" he asks cheerfully.

"Ready," I say, and I'm filled with a spurt of excitement despite my jet lag. England! I'm in England at last! I'm about to be driven along the English countryside, into London! Maybe I'll even see some sheep!

Before we're able to pull out, however, an SUV drives up behind us, and a back window powers down. Marnie, my little friend from the plane, leans out the window to yell, "Good-bye, Jennifer Garner!"

I roll down my own window and wave. "Bye, Marnie!"

Then the SUV pulls away, Marnie beaming happily in the back.

"Who in heaven," Mr. Marshall asks as he backs out, "is this Jennifer Garner?"

"Just some American film star," Andrew says before I can say anything.

Just some American film star? Just some American film star who happens to look exactly like your girlfriend! I want to shriek. *Enough so that little girls on airplanes want her autograph!*

But I manage to keep my mouth shut for once, because I don't want Andrew to feel inadequate, knowing he's dating a Jennifer Garner look-alike. That could be really intimidating, you know, for a guy. Even an American one.

In contrast to Egyptian costume, in which there was a distinct division in style between the sexes, the Greek costume during this same period did not vary between men and women. Large rectangles of cloth of different sizes were draped across the body and fastened only with a decorative brooch.

This garment, which is called a toga, went on to become a favorite costume of college fraternity parties, for reasons this author cannot fathom, as the toga is neither flattering nor comfortable, especially when worn with control-top underwear.

History of Fashion
SENIOR THESIS BY ELIZABETH NICHOLS

4

Men have always detested women's gossip because they suspect the truth: their measurements are being taken and compared.

—*Erica Jong (1942–), U.S. educator and author*

don't see any sheep. It turns out Heathrow airport isn't exactly that far out in the country. As if I can't tell I'm not in Michigan anymore from the way the houses look (many of them are attached, like in that movie *The Snapper* . . . which, come to think of it, was actually set in Ireland, but oh well), I definitely know it from billboards that flash by us. I can't tell, in many cases, what the product is that they're trying to sell—one of them shows a woman in her underwear with the word *Vodafone* beneath her, which could be an ad for a phone-sex service.

But it could just as easily be an ad for panties.

But when I ask, neither Andrew nor his father is able to tell me which it is, since the word *panties* causes them to dissolve into peals of laughter.

I don't mind that they find me so (unintentionally) hilarious, though, since it means Andrew's mind has been taken off being in the backseat.

When we finally turn onto the street I recognize as Andrew's from the care packages I've been sending him all summer—boxes filled with his favorite American candy, Necco wafers, and Marlboro Lights, his preferred brand of cigarettes (though I don't smoke myself, and assume Andrew will quit well before the first baby is born)—I'm feeling much better about things than I had been back in the parking garage. That's because the sun has finally put in an appearance, peeking shyly out from behind the clouds, and because Andrew's street looks so nice and Europeany, with its clean sidewalks, flowering trees, and old-fashioned town houses. It's like something out of that movie *Notting Hill*.

I have to admit, it's something of a relief: I had been wavering between picturing Andrew's "flat" as being as high tech as Hugh Grant's in *About a Boy*, or a garret, like in *A Little Princess* (which looked very cute once that old guy fixed it up for her), only in a seedier part of town, overlooking a wharf. I'd just been assuming I wouldn't be able to go walking around his neighborhood by myself after dark for fear of being set upon by heroin addicts. Or Gypsies.

I'm glad to see it's actually somewhere between the two extremes.

We are, as Mr. Marshall assures me, just a mile away from Hampstead Heath, the park where a lot of famous stuff happened, none of which I actually remember at this current time, and where people go today to have picnics and fly kites.

I'm happily surprised to see that Andrew lives in such a nice, upscale neighborhood. I didn't think teachers made enough to rent apartments in town houses. No doubt his flat is at the top of one—just like Mickey Rooney's in *Breakfast at Tiffany's*! Maybe I'll get to meet Andrew's wacky but bighearted neighbors. Maybe I can have them—and Andrew's parents, to thank Mr. Marshall for the ride from the airport—over for a small supper to show my American hospitality. I can make Mom's spaghetti due (pronounced doo-ay). It tastes complicated, but nothing could be simpler to make. It's just pasta, garlic, olive oil, hot pepper flakes, and Parmesan cheese. I'm sure even England would have all the ingredients.

"Well, here we are," Mr. Marshall says, pulling into a parking space in front of one of the brown-brick town houses and turning off the ignition. "Home sweet home."

I'm a little surprised that Mr. Marshall is getting out with us. I would have thought he'd have dropped us off and gone on to his own house somewhere—well, wherever Andrew's family lives, a family that consists, from what I remember him saying in his e-mails, of a teacher father, a social worker mother, two younger brothers, and a collie.

But maybe Mr. Marshall wants to help us with my bags, seeing as how Andrew probably lives on the top floor of the charming town house we're parked in front of.

Except that when we get to the top of the long flight of steps that leads up to the front door, it's Mr. Marshall who takes out a key and unlocks it.

And is greeted by the inquisitive gold and white muzzle of a beautiful collie.

"Hello," Mr. Marshall calls into what I can clearly see is not the foyer of an apartment house, but the entrance to a single-family home. "We're here!"

I am lugging my carry-on bag while Andrew pulls my wheelie bag up the stairs, not even bothering to lift it, but dragging it up one step at a time—*thonk, thonk, thonk*. But I swear I nearly drop the bag—hair dryer be damned—when I see that dog.

"Andrew," I whisper, whirling around, since he's coming up the steps behind me. "Do you live . . . at home? With your parents?"

Because, unless he's dog-sitting, that's the only explanation I can think of for what I'm seeing. And even that isn't a very good one.

"Of course," Andrew says, looking annoyed. "What did you think?"

Only it comes out sounding like, *What did you fink?*

"I thought you lived in an apartment," I say. I am really not try-ing to sound accusatory. I'm not. I'm just . . . surprised. "A flat, I mean. You told me, in school last May, that you were getting a flat for the summer when you got back to England."

"Oh, right," Andrew says. Since we've paused on the steps, he seems to think (fink) this is a good time for a cigarette break and pulls out a pack and lights up.

Well, it *was* a long trip from the airport. And his father *did* tell him he couldn't smoke in the car.

"Yeah, the flat didn't work out. My mate—you remember, I wrote you about him? He was going to loan me his place, since he got a gig on a pearl farm in Australia. But then he met a bird and decided not to go after all, so I moved in with the parentals. Why? Is that a problem?"

Is that a problem? IS THAT A PROBLEM? All of my fantasies about Andrew bringing me breakfast in bed—his king-size bed, with the thousand-count sheets—crumble into bits and float away. I won't be making spaghetti due for the neighbors and Andrew's parents. Well, maybe his parents, but it won't be the same if they just come down the stairs for it, as opposed to from their own place . . .

Then I have a thought that causes my blood to run cold.

"But, Andrew," I say, "I mean, how are you—how are you and I going to—if your parents are around?"

"Ah, don't worry about that," Andrew says, blowing smoke out of one side of his mouth in a manner I have to admit to finding thrillingly sexy. No one back home smokes . . . not even Grandma, since that time she lit the living-room carpet on fire. "This is London, you know, not Bible Belt America. We're cool about that kind of thing here. And my parents are the coolest."

"Right," I say. "Sorry. I was just, you know. Sort of surprised. But it really doesn't matter. As long as we can be together. Your parents really won't mind? About us sharing a bedroom, I mean?"

"Yeah," Andrew says, sort of distractedly, giving my suitcase a yank. *Thonk.* "About that. I don't actually have a bedroom in this house. See, my parents moved here with my brothers this past year, while I was in America. I'd told them I wouldn't be coming home summers, you know, but that was before I had those troubles with my student visa ... Anyway, they figured, you know, I'd basically moved out, so they only got a three-bedroom. But don't worry, I'm—how do you say it in the States? Right, bunking up—I'm bunking up with my brother Alex—"

I look at Andrew on the step below me. He's so tall that even when he's standing below me, I still have to tilt my chin up a little to look into his gray-green eyes.

"Oh, Andrew," I say, my heart melting. "Your other brother's given up his room for me? He shouldn't have!"

A strange look passes across Andrew's face.

"He didn't," Andrew says. "He wouldn't. You know kids." He gives me a crooked grin. "But don't worry, though. My mom's a whiz at do-it-yourself projects, and she's rigged up a loft bed for you—well, for me, actually. But you can use it while you're here."

I raise my eyebrows. "A loft bed?"

"Yeah, it's fantastic. She's made the whole thing out of MDF, in the laundry room. Right over the washer/dryer!" Andrew, seeing my expression, adds, "But don't worry. She's strung a curtain up between the laundry room and the kitchen. You'll have plenty of privacy. No one goes back there anyway, except the dog. That's where his food bowl is."

Dog? Food bowl? So ... instead of sleeping with my boyfriend, I'll be sleeping with the family dog. And its food bowl.

That's okay, though. That's fine. Educators like Andrew's dad—and social workers like his mom—don't make a lot of money, and real estate in England is expensive. I'm lucky they have any room at all for me! I mean, they don't even have a room for their own eldest child, and they've found a way to squeeze in a bed for me!

And why would one of Andrew's brothers give up his room for

me? Just because back home I always had to give up MY room for whatever out-of-town guest was coming to stay doesn't mean Andrew's family necessarily does things the same way . . .

Especially since I'm not even an important visitor. I'm only Andrew's future wife, after all.

Well, in my mind.

"Come on now," Andrew says. "Get a move on. I have to change for work."

I'm about to climb another step when I freeze all over again. "Work? You have to go to work? *Today?*"

"Yeah." At least he has the grace to look apologetic. "But it's no big deal, Liz, I just have to do the lunch and dinner shifts—"

"You're . . . you're a *waiter?*"

I don't mean to sound pejorative. I don't. I have nothing against people who work in restaurants, I really don't. I did my stint in food service just like everybody else, wore the polyester pants with pride.

But . . .

"What happened to your internship?" I ask. "The one at the prestigious primary school for gifted children?"

"Internship?" Andrew flicks ash off his cigarette. It falls in the rosebushes below. But ash is often used as fertilizer so this doesn't necessarily count as littering. "Oh, *that* turned out to be a disaster of epic proportions. Did you know they weren't going to pay me? Not a fucking cent."

"But—" I swallow. I can hear birds singing in the treetops along the street. At least the birds sound the same here as they do back in Michigan. "That's why it's called an internship. Your pay is all the experience you get."

"Well, experience won't pay for pints with my mates, will it?" Andrew jokes. "And of course it turned out they had two thousand applications for the position . . . a position that doesn't even pay! It's not like it is back in the States, either, where you've got an edge over everybody else if you've got a British accent, since you Yanks are convinced anyone who says 'tomahto' over 'tomato' is somehow more intelligent ... The truth is, Lizzie, I didn't even bother applying. What would have been the point?"

I just stare at him. What happened to taking on a job for the pure challenge and experience of it? What happened to teaching the children to read?

"Besides," he adds, "I want to work with *real* kids, not posh little geniuses ... kids who actually *need* positive male role models in their lives ..."

"So," I say, my heart lifting, "you applied to teach in some inner-city schools for the summer?"

"Oh, fuck no," Andrew says. "Those positions paid shit. The only way you can make ends meet in this town is in food service. And I've got the best shift, eleven to eleven. In fact, I've got to run right now if I'm going to make it there in time ..."

But I've just gotten here! I want to cry. *I've just gotten here, and you're leaving? Not just leaving, but leaving me alone with your family, whom I've never met—for TWELVE HOURS?*

But I don't say any of these things. I mean, here Andrew is, inviting me to stay, rent-free, in his family's home with him, and I'm freaking out over his having to work—and the *kind* of work he's doing. What kind of girlfriend am I, anyway?

Except I guess my expression must have given away the fact that I am less than enthusiastic about the situation, since Andrew says, reaching out to wrap an arm around my waist and bringing me up close against him, "Look, don't worry, Liz. I'll see you tonight when I get off work."

Suddenly he's grinding the cigarette beneath his heel and his lips are against my throat.

"And when I do," he murmurs, "I'm going to show you the best time you ever had. All right?"

It's very hard to think properly when a cute guy with a British accent is nuzzling your neck.

Not that there's anything to think about, really. My boyfriend obviously adores me. I'm the luckiest girl in the world.

"Well," I say, "that sounds—"

And the next thing I know, Andrew's mouth is on mine, and we're making out on the front steps of his parents' house.

I hope the Marshalls don't have any easily startled little old ladies as neighbors, and that if they do, they aren't actually looking out their windows right now.

"Fuck," Andrew breaks off our kiss to say, "I have to go to work. But look, I'll see you tonight, yeah?"

My lips are still tingling from where his razor stubble chafed them. They're probably about as swollen as Angelina Jolie's by now, from all the pressure on them.

Not that I mind. I don't have a lot of experience in the kissing department.

But I think Andrew may just be the best kisser in the world.

Plus I can't help noticing that there appears to be something going on in the vicinity of the crotch of Andrew's jeans that I also like very much.

"Do you really have to go to work?" I ask him. "Can't you blow it off?"

"Not today. But I've got tomorrow off," he says. "There's something I've got to do in the city. But after that, we'll do whatever you like. Oh God." He kisses me a few more times, then rests his forehead against mine. "I can't believe I'm doing this. You'll be all right, yeah?"

I stare at him, thinking how good-looking he is, in spite of the hideous jacket, and how sweet and unassuming he is as well. I mean, he's just so determined to follow in his father's footsteps and teach all those children to read. Only he's not going to settle for just any situation. He's waiting for the right one to come along . . .

I am so lucky that I was taking a shower at the *exact* moment that girl's potpourri caught on fire and that Andrew happened to have been the R.A. on duty at the time.

I think of the first time he kissed me, outside McCracken Hall (with me in my towel and him in those Levi's that were faded in just the right places), his breath smoky—but from cigarettes, not the fire—and hot in my mouth.

I remember all the phone calls and e-mails between us since. I remember the fact that I blew all my money on a plane ticket to England, since I'm not moving to New York with Shari and Chaz, so I can live at home and be near Andrew in the fall instead.

And I say with a big smile, "I'll be fine."

"Cheers, then," Andrew says. And gives me one last kiss.

And then he turns around and leaves.

One of the earliest known female arbiters of fashion was the Byzantine empress Theodora, the daughter of a bear trainer who beat out thousands of other girls for the hand of Emperor Justinian. Rumor had it she was helped in no small part during the talent portion of the Empress Hunt by her background in dancing and acrobatics.

Though it took a special act of legislation to allow Justinian to marry one of such lowly stature, Theodora proved herself a worthy empress, commissioning two royal spies to sneak into China and steal silkworms so that she could drape herself in the manner in which she felt she could become accustomed. If Theodora couldn't get to Chanel, well, she just had Chanel brought to her.

History of Fashion
SENIOR THESIS BY ELIZABETH NICHOLS

5

"I never repeat anything." That is the ritual phrase of society people, by which the gossip is reassured every time.
—*Marcel Proust (1871–1922), French novelist, critic, and essayist*

I'm here! I'm finally here, in England!

And okay, it's not *exactly* what I'd expected. I really did think Andrew had his own place.

But it's not like he LIED to me.

And maybe this is better than if the two of us had just holed up in his flat, making sweet love all night and day. This way, I'll be forced to interact with his family. We can sort of test each other out, the Marshalls and I, and see if we are compatible. After all, you don't want to marry into a family that hates you.

Plus, while Andrew's out working, I can start my thesis. Maybe one of the Marshalls will let me borrow a computer. And I can do some research at the British Museum. Or whatever it's called.

Yes, honestly, it's much better this way. I'll really get to know Andrew and his family, and I'll get a good solid start on my thesis. Maybe I can even get it done before I get home! That would be so great! My parents will never even know there was a slight delay in my actual graduation.

Mmm . . . I smell something coming from the kitchen. I wonder what it is. It smells good . . . sort of. It doesn't smell a bit like the scrambled eggs and bacon that are my mom's specialty. Really, it's just so kind of Mrs. Marshall to make breakfast for me. I told her she didn't have to . . . She seems so nice, with her sandy-brown bob. She told me to call her Tanya—though of course I never will. Her eyes got kind of wide when I walked in and Mr. Marshall introduced me. But whatever it was that was freaking her out about me, she didn't let on.

I certainly hope she didn't guess about my underwear. Or lack thereof. What if THAT'S why she'd stared at me like that? She's probably thinking, Of all the girls in America for my son to bring home, he had to pick a slut. I knew I should have worn something different getting off the plane. And I'm so cold in this stupid dress, I know I must have had some nipple action going on. Maybe I should change into something a little less . . . thin. Yes, that's what I'll do. I'll change into some jeans and my beaded sweater set—even though I was saving that for evenings, when I thought it might be a bit cooler . . .

Little did I know it's evening cool here all day long.

Okay. Wow, whatever Mrs. M is cooking in there sure smells—strongly. I wonder what it is? Also why it seems familiar.

You know, my MDF bed isn't so bad. It's kind of cute, really. It's like the kind of bed Ty Pennington would make for some kid who has cancer on that *Extreme Makeover: Home Edition* show.

Only his version would be shaped like a heart ventricle, or a spaceship, or something.

Okay, there, I'm ready. Just give the hair a little toss, and—hmm, too bad there's not a mirror in here. Oh well, British people clearly aren't as vain as we are in the U.S. Who cares if my mascara is smudged or whatever? I'm sure I look fine. Okay. I'll just throw the curtain back, and—

"Oh my," Mrs. Marshall says brightly. "I thought you were going to have a bit of a lie-down."

Had *that* been what she'd been saying to me a little while ago? I couldn't really understand her. Oh, *why* did Andrew have to go off to work? I clearly need a translator.

"I'm sorry," I apologize. "I'm just way too excited to sleep!"

"Is this your first time in England, then?" Mrs. M wants to know.

"It's my first time outside of the U.S. ever," I say. "Whatever you're cooking smells delicious." This is a slight lie. What she's cooking just . . . smells. Still, it will *probably* be delicious. "Is there anything I can do to help?"

"Oh no, dear, I think I've got it under control. How are you liking your bed, then? Not too hard? It's all right?"

"Oh, it's great," I say, slipping onto a stool at the end of the kitchen counter. I can't tell what's sizzling in the pans on the stove in front of her because they all have lids. But it sure smells . . . a lot. The kitchen is tiny, more of a galley than an actual kitchen. There is a window at the end of it that looks out onto a bright, sunlit garden bursting with rose blossoms. Mrs. M looks like a rose herself, all pink-cheeked and shiny in jeans and a peasant top.

Although the peasant top doesn't appear to be from this season's crop of them. In fact, it might actually be a peasant top from all the way back when peasant tops first made an appearance in serf-free society, way back in the days of Haight-Ashbury!

Now I know why Andrew thinks it's okay to go around in a break-dancing jacket. But while some vintage pieces—like Mrs. Marshall's blouse—are great, other examples—such as Andrew's jacket—aren't. Clearly the Marshall family needs to be brought into the vintage-know.

It's a good thing they have me to help. I'll have to be very sensitive to the fact that they don't have a lot of money to spend on clothes. But I'm living proof you don't have to spend a lot in order to look great. I got this sweater set on eBay for twenty dollars! And my stretch Levi's are from Sears. And okay, they came from the juniors department . . . but how thrilled was I at being able to *fit* into something from the juniors department?

Not that, in our weight-obsessed society, this is something to brag about. Why should women have to fit into child sizes in order to be considered desirable? That is both sick and depressing.

Although . . . they're nines! I fit into a nine! I never fit into a nine, even back when I was the age I was supposed to wear one.

"That's a very pretty top," Mrs. M says about my sweater set.

"Thanks," I say. "I was just admiring yours!"

She laughs when she hears this. "What, this old thing? It must be thirty years old if it's a day. Very likely older."

"That's neat," I say. "I love old clothes."

This is so cool! Andrew's mother and I are bonding. Maybe later we can go shopping, just Mrs. M and me. She probably doesn't have many opportunities for girl talk, having three sons and all. Maybe we can get manis and pedis and go to Harrods for champagne! Wait—do people in England get manis and pedis?

"I just can't tell you how great it is to meet you, after hearing about you for so long," I say. I'm not trying to suck up, either. I really mean it. "I'm so excited to be here!"

"How nice," Mrs. Marshall says, looking genuinely pleased for me.

I can see that her fingernails are square and strong-looking and completely without polish. Well, she probably doesn't have time for frivolities like manicures, being a busy social worker. "And what do you look forward to seeing most here, then?"

For some reason my mind flashes to the picture of Andrew's naked ass. I can't believe I thought of that! It must be the jet lag.

I say, "Oh, Buckingham Palace, of course. And the British Museum." I don't mention that the only parts of the museum I'm interested in touring are the rooms where they keep the historical costumes. If they even have any rooms like that. I can see boring old art back home anytime I want. I'm moving to New York City after Andrew gets his master's, anyway. He already agreed.

"Oh, and the Tower of London." Because I hear that's where they keep all the fancy jewels. "And . . . oh, Jane Austen's house."

"Oh, you're a fan, are you?" Mrs. Marshall looks a bit surprised. Clearly none of Andrew's previous girlfriends had such sophisticated taste in literature. "Which one's your favorite, then?"

"Oh, the A&E version with Colin Firth, of course," I say. "Although the costumes in the Gwyneth Paltrow one were really nice, too."

Mrs. Marshall looks at me a bit oddly—maybe she can't understand my Midwestern accent any easier than I can understand her British one. But I'm really trying to enunciate clearly. Then I realize what she means and say, "Oh, you mean of the *books*? I don't know. They're all so good." Except there aren't nearly enough descriptions of what the characters are wearing.

Mrs. Marshall laughs and asks, "Would you like to help yourself to some tea? I'm certain you must be parched after your trip."

What I'd really like, of course, is a diet Coke. But when I ask if the Marshalls have any, Mrs. Marshall gives me another odd look and says she'll have to pick some up at "the market."

"Oh no," I say, mortified. "Really, it's all right. I'll just have some tea."

Mrs. Marshall looks relieved. "Oh, good," she says. "Because I don't like the thought of your putting all those nasty, unnatural chemicals into your body. They can't be good for you."

I smile at her, even though I have no idea what she's talking about. Diet Coke does not contain nasty chemicals. It contains lovely and delicious carbonation, caffeine, and aspartame. What's unnatural about that?

But I'm in England now, so I will do as the English do. I pour myself some tea from the ceramic pot sitting by the electric kettle and, at Mrs. M's urging, put milk in it, because that is apparently how British people drink it, instead of with honey or lemon.

I'm surprised to discover that it's actually quite good that way. Which I mention out loud.

"What's good?" A sandy-haired boy, maybe fifteen or sixteen, wearing a dark-rinse jean jacket with acid-washed jeans (ouch— although beneath the jacket he's got on a Killers T-shirt, which redeems him a bit), has come into the kitchen, then freezes when he sees me.

"Who's *that*?" he wants to know.

"What do you mean, who's that?" Mrs. M demands tartly. "This is Liz, your brother Andy's girlfriend from America—"

"Oh, c'mon, Mum," Alex says, grinning. "What do I look like? That's not her. She's not—"

"Alex, this is Liz," Mrs. M interrupts even more tartly. She doesn't look as much like a rose now. Or I guess she does, just one whose thorns are showing. "Say hello to her properly, please."

Alex, looking sheepish, sticks his right hand out. I shake it.

"Sorry," he says. "Pleased to meet you. It's just that Andy said—"

"Alex, please take this out to the table," Mrs. M says, shoving a handful of knives and forks at her youngest son. "Breakfast will be ready soon."

"Breakfast? It's nearly time for lunch, isn't it?"

"Well, Liz hasn't had breakfast yet, so that's what we're having."

Alex takes the silverware from his mother and goes out into the dining room. Geronimo, which is what they named their collie— isn't that the cutest?—who had been pressing against the side of my legs the whole time I'd been sitting down, trails after him, apparently in hopes of coming across a stray piece of food.

"Do you have any brothers, Liz?" Mrs. M asks me, all prickliness gone now that her son has left the room.

"No," I say. "Just two older sisters."

"Your mother was very fortunate," Mrs. M says. "Boys are quite a handful." Then she turns off the oven and calls, "Alex, tell your dad breakfast is ready. Give a shout to Alistair as well."

Andrew, Alistair, and Alexander. I love the names Andrew's parents picked out for their three boys! How cute to give them all *A* names . . . just like Paul Anka did, only he had daughters—Alexandra, Amanda, Alicia, Anthea, and Amelia.

And how cute that they all call me Liz and not Lizzie. Nobody ever calls me Liz. Nobody except Andrew, of course. Not that I ever told him to. He just . . . does.

"Well," Mrs. Marshall says, smiling at me. "Why don't you have a seat, Liz? Then we can eat."

"Let me help you bring things to the table," I say, sliding down from my stool.

But Mrs. Marshall shoos me out of the kitchen, saying she doesn't need any help. I go into the dining room—which is really just part of an L off the living room, where the family's dining table is. Geronimo is already sitting next to the chair at the head of the table, alert for any scraps that might fall his way.

"Where should I sit?" I ask Alex, who, in typical teen fashion—I guess it's universal—shrugs.

Just then Mr. Marshall walks in and pulls out a chair for me with gallant flair. I thank him and sit in it, trying to remember when my own father ever pulled out a chair for me, and failing.

"Here we are," Mrs. Marshall says, emerging from the kitchen with several platters that are steaming. "In honor of Andy's friend Liz's first visit to this country, a genuine English country breakfast!"

I sit up a bit straighter in my seat to show how excited and flattered I am. "Thank you so much," I say. "You really didn't have to go to so much—"

Then I see what's on the platters.

"Tomato ratatouille," Mrs. Marshall says proudly. "Your favorite! And our own very English interpretation of the same dish, stewed tomatoes. Also stuffed tomatoes, and an egg and tomato omelet. Andy told me how much you love tomatoes, Liz. I hope this meal will make you feel right at home!"

Oh. My. God.

"Liz?" Mrs. Marshall, I realize, is looking down at me with concern on her rosy face. "Are you all right, dear? You look a little . . . peaked."

"I'm fine," I say. And take a big gulp of my milky tea. "It looks great, Mrs. Marshall. Thanks so much for going to all this trouble. You didn't have to."

"It was my pleasure," Mrs. Marshall says, beaming as she takes a seat in a chair across the table from mine. "And please, call me Tanya."

"Right. Tanya," I say, hoping my eyes don't look as wet as they feel. How can he have made such a mistake? Did he not even READ my e-mails? Was he not even *listening* that night of the fire?

"Who's missing?" Mrs. Marshall asks, looking at the empty chair across from Andrew.

"Alistair," Alex says, reaching for a piece of toast. Toast! I can eat toast. No, wait, I can't. Not if I want to stay a junior size nine. Oh God. I'm going to have to eat something. The egg and tomato omelet. Maybe the egg will drown out the taste of the tomato.

"ALISTAIR!" Mr. Marshall bellows.

From somewhere deep in the house, a male voice calls, "Oy! I'm coming!"

I take a bite of the omelet. It's good. You can barely taste the—

Oh no. Yes you can, actually.

The thing is, it was an honest mistake. About the tomatoes, I mean. Anyone could get something like that mixed up. Even a soul mate.

And, I mean, at least he remembered I'd *mentioned* tomatoes. He may not have remembered what I actually said about them. But he obviously knows I said *something*.

And it's not like he's not busy, teaching the children to read and all.

And waitering, apparently.

Seeing that no one is looking at me, I knock some of the omelet on my plate and down onto the napkin on my lap. Then I look over at Geronimo, who has left Mr. Marshall's side, apparently sensing he's not going to be scoring any scraps over there.

The collie meets my gaze.

Next thing I know, I have dog nose in my crotch.

"What's this now?" A boy who must be Andrew's second-youngest brother, Alistair, appears in the doorway. Unlike his mom and two brothers, Alistair's hair is bright, coppery red—probably the same color his dad's had been, before he lost it all . . . judging from his eyebrows, anyway.

"Oh, hullo, Ali," Mrs. Marshall says. "Take your seat. We're having a traditional English breakfast to welcome Andrew's friend Liz from America."

"Hi," I say, looking up at the redhead, who appears to be just a year or two younger than me. He is dressed from head to toe in Adidas apparel . . . Adidas warm-up pants, jacket, T-shirt, and shoes. Perhaps they've asked for his personal endorsement. "I'm Lizzie. Nice to meet you."

Alistair stares at me for a minute. Then he bursts out laughing.

"Right!" he says. "Come off it, Mum. What kind of joke is this supposed to be, anyway?"

"It's not a joke at all, Alistair," Mr. Marshall says in a cold voice.

"But," Alistair bleats, "she can't be Liz! Andy said Liz is a fatty!"

Little is known about costume from the period of the second century until well into the 700s, thanks to barbarian invasions by the Goths, Visigoths, Ostrogoths, Huns, and Franks. We do know, thanks to these invasions, that few people had time to think about fashion, as they were busy fleeing for their lives.

It isn't until Charlemagne came to rule in 800 that we have any sort of detailed description of wardrobe at the time, which included cross-gartered trousers that came to be known as braies, or breeches, that garment so well beloved by historical romance authors around the world.

History of Fashion
SENIOR THESIS BY ELIZABETH NICHOLS

6

But speak the truth, and all nature and all spirits help you with unexpected furtherance. Speak the truth, and all things alive or brute are vouchers, and the very roots of the grass underground there do seem to stir and move to bear you witness.

—*Ralph Waldo Emerson (1803–1882),*
U.S. essayist, poet, and philosopher

It takes five rings before Shari answers. For a minute I'm worried she won't pick up at all. What if she's asleep? I know it's only nine o'clock after all, Europe time, but what if she hasn't adjusted to the time difference as well as I have? Even though she's been over here longer. She was supposed to have gotten to Paris two days ago, stayed one night in a hotel there, then traveled down to the château the next day.

But then again, she's Shari—great at school stuff, not so good at everyday life stuff. She's dropped her cell phone in the toilet more times than I can count. Who knows if I'll even get through to her?

Then, to my relief, she finally picks up. And it's clear I haven't wakened her—because there is music blaring in the background. A song in which the refrain, *Vamos a la playa*, plays over and over, to a Latin beat.

"Liz-ZIE!" Shari yells into the phone. "Is that YOOOOOU?"

Oh yes. She's drunk.

"How are yooooouuuuu?" she wants to know. "How's London? How's hot, hot, hot Andrew? How's his aaaaaaaasssssssssss?"

"Shari," I say in a low voice. I don't want the Marshalls to hear me, so I'm running the water in the bathtub. I'm not wasting it. I really do plan to take a bath. In a minute. "Things are weird here. Really weird. I need to talk to someone normal for a minute."

"Wait, let me see if I can find Chaz," Shari says. Then she cackles. "Just kidding! Oh my God, Lizzie, you should see this place. You'd die. It's like *Under the Tuscan Sun* and *Valmont* combined. Luke's house is HUGE. HUGE. It has a name—Mirac. It has its own VINEYARD. Lizzie, they make their own champagne. THEY MAKE IT THEMSELVES."

"That's great," I say. "Shari, I think Andrew told his brothers I was fat."

Shari is silent for a moment. I am urged once again to *Vamos a la playa*. Then Shari explodes.

"He fucking said that? He fucking said you were fat? Stay where you are. Stay right where you fucking are. I'm getting on the Chunnel train thingie and I'm coming over there and I'm going to cut his balls off—"

"Shari," I say. She is yelling so loudly I'm worried the Marshalls might hear her. Through the closed door. Over the TV and the running water. "Shari, wait, that isn't what I meant. I mean, I don't *know* what he said. Things are just really weird. I got here, and the very first thing, Andrew took off for work. Which was okay. I mean it was fine. Because the truth is"—I can feel the tears coming. Oh, great—"Andrew isn't working with children. He's a waiter. He works from eleven in the morning until eleven at night. I didn't even know that was *legal*. Plus, he doesn't even have his own place. We're staying with his parents. And his little brothers. Who he told I was fat. Also, he told his mom that I like tomatoes."

"I take it back," Shari says, "I'm not going there. You're coming here. Buy a train ticket and get over here. Be sure to ask for a youth pass. You'll have to change trains in Paris. Buy a ticket there for Souillac. And then just call me. We'll pick you up at the station."

"Shari," I say, "I can't do that. I can't just *leave*."

"Like fuck you can't," Shari says. I hear another voice in the background. Then Shari is saying to someone else, "It's Lizzie. That fucker Andrew works all day and all night and is fucking making her stay at his parents' and eat tomatoes. And he said she was fat."

"Shari," I say, feeling a twinge of guilt, "I don't know that he said that. And he's not—who are you telling this to, anyway?"

"Chaz says get your far-from-fat ass on a train in the morning. He will personally pick you up at the train station tomorrow night."

"I can't go to *France*," I say, horrified. "My return ticket home is from Heathrow. It's nonreturnable and nontransferable and non—everything."

"So? You can go back to England at the end of the month and fly home from there. Come on, Lizzie. We'll have SO MUCH fun."

"Shari, I can't go to France," I say miserably. "I don't *want* to go to France. I love Andrew. You don't understand. That night outside McCracken Hall . . . it was magical, Shar. He saw into my soul, and I saw into his."

"How could you?" Shari demands. "It was dark."

"No it wasn't. We had the glow of the flames from that girl's room to see by."

"Well, then maybe you just saw what you wanted to see. Or maybe you just *felt* what you wanted to *feel*."

She's talking, I know, about Andrew's stiffy. I stare blindly down at the water splashing into the tub.

The thing is, I am generally a very happy person. I even laughed after Alistair said that thing at the table, about me being a fatty. Because what else are you supposed to do when you find out your boyfriend's been going around telling people you're fat?

Especially since the last time Andrew saw me, I *had* been fat. Or at least thirty pounds heavier than I am now.

I *had* to laugh, because I didn't want the Marshalls to think I'm some kind of oversensitive freak.

I think I succeeded, too, because all Mrs. Marshall did was shoot her son an outraged look . . . Then, since I guess I didn't appear to be offended, she seemed to forget about it. So did everyone else.

And Alistair turned out to be quite nice, offering to let me use his computer in order to start my thesis, which I then worked on for the rest of the day, until breaking for a "curry supper" from the "takeaway" shop on the corner with the two elder Marshalls, the boys having gone out. We ate while watching a British mystery show, during which I only understood approximately one word out of every seven, due to the actors' accents.

The thing is, I was *determined* not to let the fat thing get me down. Because despite what my sisters might think—and they were always more than happy to let their feelings on the matter be known to me, growing up—weight doesn't matter. It really doesn't. I mean, it does if you're a model or whatever.

But in general being a few pounds overweight hasn't ever kept me from doing what I wanted to. Sure, there were all those times I was the last one picked for volleyball in gym class.

And the occasional mortification of having to appear in front of a guy I had a crush on in a bathing suit at the lake or whatever.

And then there were the dumb frat guys who wouldn't look twice at me because I was heavier than the kind of girls they preferred.

But who wants to hang around *frat guys*? I want to be with guys who have more on their minds than where the next keg party is. I want to be with guys who care about making this world a better place—the way Andrew does. I want to be with guys who know that what's important isn't the size of a girl's waistband but the size of her heart—like Andrew. I want to be with guys who are able to see past a girl's outward appearance, and into her soul—like Andrew.

It's just that . . . well, based on Alistair's remark, it seems like maybe Andrew *didn't* see into my soul that night outside Mc-Cracken Hall.

The tomato thing, too. I TOLD Andrew—or wrote to him, actually—that I hate tomatoes. I told him it's the one single food I totally can't stand. I even went on, at great length, about how horrible it was, growing up in a household that was half Italian, hating tomatoes. Mom was always brewing up huge batches of tomato sauce to use in her pastas and lasagnas. She had a huge tomato garden in the backyard that I was in charge of weeding, since I wouldn't touch the ugly red things and so was no help in the picking or cleaning department.

I *told* Andrew all this, not just in my reply to his question about what foods I liked, but that night we spent together as well, three months ago, me in my towel and him in his Aerosmith T-shirt—it must have been laundry day—and R.A. badge, under the stars and smoke.

And he didn't listen. He hadn't paid a bit of attention to a word I'd said.

But he *had* managed to let his family know I was a—what was it again? Oh yes—"fatty."

Is it possible I've made a mistake? Is it possible—as Shari once suggested—that the reason I love Andrew is not because of who he actually is, but because I've projected onto him the personality I *want* him to have?

Could she be right that I've stubbornly refused all along to see him for what he really is, because making out with him had been so much fun (and I'd been so flattered by his full stiffy) I don't want to admit my attraction to him is merely physical?

I hadn't spoken to Shari for nearly two hours after she said this, it had made me so mad, and she'd finally apologized.

But what if she's right? Because the Andrew I knew—or felt like I knew—wouldn't have told his brother I'm fat. The Andrew I know wouldn't even have noticed I was fat.

"Lizzie?" Shari's voice crackles over the phone I'm pressing to my cheek. "Did you die?"

"No, I'm here," I say. I can still hear rock music booming in the background. Shari, it's clear, isn't a bit jet-lagged. Shari's boyfriend isn't at work. Or, rather, he is. But they're working together. "I just . . . Look, I gotta go. I'll call you later."

"Wait," Shari says. "Does this mean you'll be coming to New York with me in the fall after all?"

I hang up. It's not that I'm mad at her, exactly. I'm just . . .

So tired.

I don't even remember bathing or changing into my pajamas and dragging myself into bed. All I know is, it seems like it's about a million o'clock when Andrew gently shakes me awake. But it's really only midnight—at least according to the watchface he shows me when I groggily ask what time it is.

I never realized he wears a glow-in-the-dark digital watch. That's kind of . . . not sexy.

But maybe he needs it. For telling time when he's slaving away in that dark, candlelit restaurant . . .

"Sorry to wake you," he says. He is standing beside my loft bed, which is just high enough off the ground that he doesn't even have to stoop to whisper to me. "But I wanted to make sure you were all right. You don't need anything?"

I squint at him in the semidarkness. The only light is the moonlight that streams through the laundry room's single narrow window. Andrew, I can see, is wearing black jeans and a white shirt—a waiter's uniform.

I don't know what makes me do it. Maybe because I've been so lonely and depressed all evening. Maybe because I'm still half asleep.

Or maybe because I truly do love him. But the next thing I know, I'm sitting up and, my fingers entwined in his shirtfront, I'm whispering, "Oh, Andrew, everything's so awful! Your brother Alistair—he said something today about your having said I was a fatty. That's not true, is it?"

"What?" Andrew is laughing into my hair as he nuzzles my neck. He is quite a neck nuzzler, I'm finding out. "What are you talking about?"

"Your brother, Alistair. He acted all shocked when he met me, because he said you'd told him I was fat."

Andrew stops nuzzling my neck and peers down at me in the moonlight.

"Wait," he says. "He said that? Are you taking the mickey?"

"I don't know anything about Mickey," I say. "But, yes, he really did say he'd been expecting me to be fat. 'A fatty' were his exact words."

I realize, a little belatedly, that Andrew might possibly become a little ticked off with his brother for having said this—especially if it's not true. Which it can't be. Right? Andrew would never say something like that . . .

"Oh, Andrew, I'm sorry," I say, wrapping my arms around his neck and kissing him tenderly. "I can't believe I even brought it up. Forget I said anything. Alistair was obviously pulling my leg. And I fell for it. Let's just forget the whole thing, all right?"

But Andrew doesn't seem willing to forget it. His arms tighten around me, and he uses some very choice adjectives to describe his brother, which he whispers against my lips. Then he says, "I think you look fucking fantastic. I always have. Sure, when we first met, you were a bit plumper than you are now. When I first saw you coming out of Customs at the airport in that little Chinese dress, I didn't even recognize you. I couldn't stop staring. I kept wondering who the lucky bloke was who was meeting such a hot little number."

I can only blink at him. Somehow his words are not as encouraging as I think he means them to be.

Maybe it's because of his seeming inability to pronounce his *th*'s as anything but *f*'s, so his *thinks* come out as *finks*.

"Then, when I got the page, and I came over and saw you were—well, *you*—I realized *I* was the lucky bloke," Andrew goes on. "I'm sorry everything has been such a cock-up so far—my mate's flat falling through, and your not having a proper bed, and my arsehole of a brother, and my fucking work schedule. But you have to know"—here he snakes an arm around my waist—"I'm over the moon that you're finally here." This is where he leans down and kisses my neck some more.

I nod. Much as I am enjoying the neck kissing, there is still something weighing on my mind. So I say, "Andrew. Just one more thing."

"Yeah, what's that, Liz?" he wants to know as his lips approach my ear.

"The thing is, Andrew," I say slowly, "I really . . . I . . ."

"What is it, Liz?" Andrew asks again.

I take a deep breath. I have to do this. I *have* to say it. Otherwise it will be hanging over our heads for my entire stay.

"I really hate tomatoes," I say all in a rush, to get it over with.

Andrew raises his head to look at me blankly. Then he throws back his head and laughs.

"Oh God!" he whispers. "That's right! You wrote me that! Mum asked me what you particularly liked, so she could be sure to have it for your arrival breakfast. But I couldn't remember. I knew you'd said something about tomatoes—"

I try not to take it personally that he remembered I'd said something about tomatoes, but not WHAT I'd said about them. Like that I hated them more than anything in the world.

Andrew is guffawing now. I'm glad he finds the situation so uproarious. "Oh, you poor girl. Don't worry, I'll drop a hint. Come here, let me kiss you again—" He does so. "You really *are* a keeper, aren't you?"

I hadn't been aware there'd been any doubt on that score.

But I know what he means.

Or I think I do, anyway. It's hard to tell what I think while he's kissing me, except *Hooray! He's kissing me!*

And then there's no whispering at all for a while, as we kiss.

And I can tell that Andrew's brother is wrong—he *doesn't* think I'm a fatty . . . unless he means fatty in a *good* way. He likes me. RE-ALLY likes me. I can feel that like pressing against me through his waiter pants.

Which I feel duty-bound to help him remove. Because they seem so binding.

When he's laughingly scrambled up into my loft bed with me—thank God it holds. Or, I should say, thank you, Mrs. Marshall—and the two of us are in each other's arms again, I see why. The pants were so binding, I mean.

"Andrew," I whisper, "have you got any condoms?"

"Condoms?" Andrew whispers the word back like it's foreign. "Aren't you on the pill? I thought all American girls were on the pill."

"Well," I say uncomfortably, "I am. But—you know, the pill doesn't protect you against diseases."

"Are you suggesting I have a disease?" Andrew demands—not in a joking way, either.

Oh dear. Why can't I ever learn to keep my mouth shut?

"Um," I say, thinking fast. Which is hard to do when I'm so tired. And horny. "No. But, um, *I* might have one. You never know."

"Oh," Andrew says with a chuckle. "Right. You? Never. You're too sweet." And he goes back to nuzzling my neck.

Which is very nice. But he still hasn't answered my question.

"Well?" I ask. "Have you got one?"

"For God's sake, Liz," Andrew says, sitting up. He fumbles around and finally produces a Trojan from the pocket of his waiter pants, which are wadded up at the end of the bed. "Happy now?"

"Yes," I say. Because I am. Happy, I mean. Even though my boy-friend apparently goes to work with a condom in his pocket, which might make one ask oneself, if one were of a suspicious nature (which I am not), just what he intended to do with said condom. I mean, considering that his girlfriend is at home, and not at his place of work.

But that is not the point. The point is that he has a condom, and now we can get down to business.

Which we proceed to do without further delay.

Except.

Well, things are going the way I suppose they should, given that my experience in these matters is pretty much limited to some awk-ward fumblings in an extralong dorm bed with Jeff, my only long-term boyfriend (three months), whom I dated sophomore year and who later that semester tearfully confessed that he was in love with his roommate, Jim.

Still, I have read enough issues of *Cosmo* to know every girl is re-sponsible for her own orgasm—just like every guest is responsible for her own good time at a party . . . no hostess can control EVERY-THING! I mean, you really can't leave this kind of thing up to a guy. He's just going to mess it up or, worse, not even bother to give it a try (unless, of course, he's like Jeff, who was very interested in my orgasms . . . just as he was very interested in my circa 1950 Herbert Levine pumps with the rhinestone buckle, as I discovered when I caught him admiring himself in them).

But while I might have taken care of my own good time, An-drew is apparently having some trouble with his own. He's abruptly stopped what he was doing and has flopped back onto the bed.

"Um, Andrew," I say, filled with concern, "is everything all right?"

"I can't fucking come," is his romantic reply. "It's this fucking bed. There's not enough room."

I am, to put it mildly, astonished. I have never heard of a man who can't come. While I know that to some people—Shari, for instance—a man who is perpetually hard would be a godsend, for me it is merely inconvenient. I have already taken care of my own good time, as *Cosmo* advised. The truth is, I'm not sure how much longer I can hold out down there. I'm starting to chafe.

Still, it's wrong to think of yourself when the person next to you is in so much agony and pain. I can't imagine how Andrew must be feeling.

Feeling very bad for him, I kiss him and ask, "Well, is there anything I can do to help?"

I soon learn that there is. At least if the way Andrew starts pushing my head in a southerly direction is any indication.

The thing is, I've never given one of *those* before. I'm not even sure I know how . . . although that girl Brianna from my dorm floor did try to teach me once, using a banana.

Still. This is really not how I pictured the two of us consummating our relationship.

And yet these are the kinds of things you do for the people you love when they are in need.

I make him change the condom first, though. I don't love anybody THAT much. Not even Andrew.

The Crusades weren't all about one culture trying to inflict their religious views on another. They were also about fashion! Returning Crusaders brought back to their womenfolk not only their vanquished enemy's gold, but also beauty tips from the ladies of the Orient, including pubic shaving (not heard of in most parts of Europe since the age of the early Roman Empire).

Whether or not English ladies adopted this practice from their sisters in the Far East can be left to the imagination of the reader, but we do know from portraits of that era that many of them took matters a little too far, plucking and shaving all the hair from their heads—including eyelashes and eyebrows. As most of them could not read or write at the time, it is no small wonder they got the message wrong.

History of Fashion
SENIOR THESIS BY ELIZABETH NICHOLS

7

Keep your own secret, and get out other people's.
—*Philip Dormer Stanhope, fourth Earl of Chesterfield (1694–1773),*
British statesman

I wake up with a feeling of deep and utter contentment, even though I'm sleeping alone, Andrew having stumbled to his own bed after an attempt at sleeping together in the narrow MDF bed failed miserably, thanks to his long legs and my tendency to sleep with my knees curled up to my chest.

Still, he left grateful and happy. I saw to that. I may be a beginner, but I learn quickly.

As I stretch, I replay the night before over in my head. Andrew is lovely. Well, not lovely, because you can't really call a guy lovely. But sweet. All that worry over him thinking I was fat . . . I can't believe I wasted so much time over something so silly! Of course he never thought I was fat, or said anything about that to his family. His brother probably got me mixed up with some other girl.

No, Andrew is the perfect boyfriend. And I'll soon have him weaned off the red leather jacket. Maybe, to make it up to him, I'll even get him a new one while we're out shopping today—because this is what Andrew had promised me (during our postcoital chit-chat last night) that we'd do today—shop and see the sights (once he'd completed a quick errand he had to do in the city).

Of course, the sights I'm most interested in seeing—besides An-

drew, of course—are the Oxfams where I can find some undiscov-
ered treasure, and maybe this place I've heard about called Topshop,
which is like the British equivalent of T.J. Maxx, or maybe H&M,
which we don't actually have in Michigan, but that I've heard about,
of course, as a fashion lover's mecca.

Only I don't mention this to Andrew, because of course I want
to seem more intellectual than that. I should be interested in his
country's history, which is incredibly rich and goes back many
thousands of years . . . or at least two hundred, as far as interesting
fashion goes. Andrew is so sweet. All of his family has been so lovely,
fatty remark aside—I wish there were some way I could show my
appreciation for their kindness to me . . .

And then it comes to me, as I'm shaving my legs in the bathtub a
little while later, Andrew not being up yet, and the rest of the family
appearing to have gone off to their various jobs: I'll do it with food!
Yes! Tonight I'll show my appreciation to the Marshall family for
all their hospitality by making them my mother's famous spaghetti
due! I'm sure they probably have all the ingredients right here in the
house—it's just pasta, garlic, oil, Parmesan, and hot pepper flakes,
after all.

And if there's something they don't have—like a nice crusty baguette, which you really need, to sop up the delicious oil—Andrew
and I can stop on our way home from sightseeing to pick it up!

Imagine how surprised and happy Mr. and Mrs. Marshall will be
to come home from a long day of work to find supper already waiting for them!

Superpleased with my scheme, I put on my makeup, and am
just applying an extra layer of topcoat to my pedicure—since I'll be
traipsing around the city in open-toed shoes, and I want to protect
my French tips—when Andrew finally stumbles down the stairs,
blinking groggily. We have a very nice good-morning lovemaking
session in the MDF bed before I throw on my fun 1960s Alex Col-

man sundress with the leaf pattern (I have a cashmere sweater that matches . . . thank God I brought it along at the last minute, since I'm going to need it) and urge Andrew to get dressed so we can get started on our many activities for the day. I still have to change money, and he has his appointment downtown.

My first proper day in London—yesterday doesn't count, because I was so sleepy I hardly remember any of it—has already started out so well (a tomato-free breakfast; a leisurely bath; sex) that I can hardly hope for it to get better, but it does: the sun is shining, and it's too hot for Andrew to wear his break-dancing jacket!

We leave the Marshalls' house hand in hand—Geronimo gazing sadly after us ("That dog really likes you," Andrew observes. Yes! I've won over the family pet through the surreptitious slipping of food! Can the actual family be far behind?) through the glass door—and head for the Tube. I am traveling on the London Tube for the very first time!

And I am not at all frightened of being blown up, because if you let that kind of fear consume you, you have allowed the terrorists to win.

Still, I keep a sharp eye out for young men (and women—it's as wrong to profile by sex as it is by race) wearing bulky coats on such a gorgeous day. While I look for terrorists, I can't help noticing how much better dressed everyone in London is than they are back in Ann Arbor. It is a terrible thing to say about one's own country, but it appears that Londoners simply care about how they look more than people back home. I haven't seen a single person—except for Alistair, who is, after all, a teenager—in sweats, or even an elastic waistband.

Granted, no one appears to be as vastly overweight here as many people back in America are. What makes Londoners so slim? Could it be all the tea?

And the ads! The ads they have on the walls of the Tube station!

They're so . . . interesting. I don't really understand what it is they're advertising in many cases. But this might be because I have never seen topless women used to sell orange juice before.

I guess Shari is right. The British are much less inhibited about their bodies—although they dress them better—than we are.

When we finally reach the stop where Andrew's got his appointment—he says there's a bank close by where I can change money—we scramble back out into the sunshine—and I catch my breath . . .

I'm in London! The town center! The place where so many significant historical events have taken place, including the introduction of the punk movement (where would we be today if Madonna hadn't donned that first bustier, and Seditionaries on Kings Road hadn't introduced the world to Vivienne Westwood?) and that black evening gown Princess Diana (still only Lady Diana then) wore the night of her engagement party?

But before I can really absorb the richness of it all, Andrew drags me into a bank, where I stand in line (or in the queue, as Andrew calls it) to exchange some of my traveler's checks for British pounds. When I get to the teller, she asks to see my passport and I hand it over, and she eyes my photo suspiciously.

Well, and why not? I was thirty pounds heavier when I had that photo taken.

When she returns my passport to me, Andrew asks to see it, and he has a good chuckle over the photo.

"I can't believe you were ever that fat," he says. "Look at you now! You look like a model. Doesn't she look like a model?" he asks the teller.

The teller says, "Uh, yuh," in a noncommittal way.

It is always nice, of course, to be told you look like a model. But I can't help wondering—did I really look that bad before? I mean, when Andrew first saw me that night of the fire, I was thirty pounds heavier than I am now, but he was still attracted to me. I know. I felt his stiffy.

And okay, I was dressed in a towel since the fire department wouldn't let us back into the building. But still.

I am distracted from thinking about all this when the teller finally hands me my money—it's so pretty! So much prettier than American money, which is just so . . . green. And it comes in so many sizes—the British pound coin looks and feels like gold in my hand.

I am completely excited to go out and spend some of my new British money, so I urge Andrew to hurry up and get his appointment over with so we can get to Harrods (I've already mentioned that this is where I want to go first. I don't want to buy anything there, though . . . I just want to see the shrine the owner, Mohamed Al Fayed, has erected to his son, who was killed in the car crash with Princess Diana).

Andrew says, "Let's go then," and we head toward a very dull-looking office building with Job Centre (it's so cute how the British spell everything wrong!) written across the entrance, where Andrew gets in a long line with a lot of other people because, he says, he has to "sign on" for work, or something like that.

I am very interested in all things British, of course, because once Andrew and I are married, this could become my adopted country, the way Madonna has made it hers, so I pay attention to the signs we are passing as the line moves along. The signs all say things like: Ask Us About New Deal for Jobseekers—Part of the Department for Work and Pensions and Thought About Working in Europe? Ask Us How.

And I think how strange it is that in England they call Europe Europe like they aren't a part of it, but in the U.S. we all think of England as part of Europe. Probably incorrectly.

And that the man behind the counter is asking Andrew if he's looked for work, and Andrew says he has but he hasn't found any.

What? What is he talking about, hasn't found work? That's all he's been doing since I got here: working.

"But, Andrew," I hear myself cry, "what about your waitering job?"

Andrew goes pale. Which is an accomplishment for him since he's already so pasty. In a sexy way . . . like Hugh Grant.

"Ha," Andrew says to the man behind the counter. "She's kidding."

Kidding? What is he *talking* about?

"You were there all day yesterday," I remind him. "Eleven to eleven."

"Liz," Andrew says in a strained voice, "don't joke with the nice man. He's busy working, can't you see?"

Of course I can see that. The question is, why can't Andrew?

"Right," I say. "Like you were busy yesterday at the waitering job you had to get because the school thing didn't pay enough. Remember?"

Could Andrew be on drugs? How could he not remember the fact that the very day I arrived for my first-ever trip to England, he was working?

A glance at his face, however, reveals that he not only remembers but doesn't seem to be on drugs. Not if the look he gives me—a look that could kill—is any indication.

Well. It's clear I've done something wrong. But what? I'm only telling the truth.

So I say, to Andrew, "Wait. What's going on here?"

That's when the man behind the counter at the Job Centre picks up a phone and says, "Mr. Williams, I have a problem. Yeah, be right there."

Then he plops a Closed sign down in front of him and says, "Come with me, please, Mr. Marshall, miss," while holding up the partition in the counter so we can pass through it.

Then he escorts us into a little room—empty except for a desk, some shelves with nothing on them, and a chair—in the back of the Job Centre office.

On the way there, I can feel the gazes of everyone else—both in line and working behind the counter—burning into the back of my neck. Some people are whispering. Some of them are laughing.

It takes a good five seconds before I finally realize why.

And when I do, my cheeks go as red as Andrew's had gone pale a minute earlier.

Because that's when I know that I've done it again. Yes. Opened my big, fat, stupid mouth when I should have kept it closed.

But how was I to know that a Job Centre is where British people go to sign up for unemployment benefits?

And what is Andrew doing, anyway, signing up for unemployment benefits when he ISN'T UNEMPLOYED?

Except that Andrew doesn't seem to see it that way—you know, as illegal. He keeps opening his mouth to bleat, "But everybody does it!"

But that's not how the Job Centre people seem to feel, if the look the man gives us before he leaves to find his "superior" is any indication.

"Look, Liz," Andrew says to me the minute the Job Centre man is out of the room, "I know you didn't mean to, but you've completely cocked things up for me. It'll be all right, though, if, when the bloke comes back, you just tell him you made a mistake. That we had a little misunderstanding and I wasn't working yesterday. All right?"

I stare at him, confused.

"But Andrew—" I can't believe this is happening. There has to be some mistake. Andrew—MY Andrew, who's going to teach the children to read?—can't be a welfare cheat. That's just not possible.

"You *were* working yesterday," I say. "I mean . . . weren't you? That's where you told me you were. That's why you left me alone with your family for the whole day and most of the night. Because you were waitering. Right?"

"Right," Andrew says. He is, I notice, sweating. I've never seen Andrew sweat before. But there is a definite sheen along his hairline. Which, I notice, is receding just a little. Will he be as bald as his father someday? "Right, Liz. But you've got to tell a little lie for me."

"Lie for you," I say confusedly. It's like . . . I realize what he's saying. I understand the words.

I just can't believe Andrew—MY Andrew—is saying them.

"It's just a white lie," Andrew elaborates. "I mean, it's not as bad as you're thinking, really, Liz. Waiters make SHIT here, it's not like back in the States, where they're guaranteed a fifteen percent tip. I swear to you, every single waiter I know is on the dole as well—"

"Still," I say. I can't believe this is happening. I really can't. "That doesn't make it right. I mean, it's still . . . it's kind of dishonest, Andrew. You're taking money from people who actually NEED it."

How could he not realize this? He wants to teach underprivileged children . . . the very people that welfare money he seems to feel so entitled to is actually *for*. How could he not know this? His mother is a social worker, for crying out loud! Does she know how her son comes by his extra cash?

"*I* need it," Andrew insists. He's sweating harder now, even though it's actually quite pleasant, temperaturewise, in the little office. "*I'm* one of those people. I mean, I've got to live, Liz. And it's not easy, finding a decent-paying job when everyone knows you're going to be leaving in a few months to go back to school, anyway—"

Well . . . he's right about that. I mean, the only way I managed to work my way up to assistant manager at Vintage to Vavoom is because I live in town year-round.

Also because I'm so good at what I do.

But still . . .

"And I wasn't doing it just for me, you know. I wanted to show you a nice time while you were here," he goes on, darting a nervous glace at the open office door. "Take you nice places, have some nice meals. Maybe even take you . . . I dunno. On a cruise or something."

"Oh, Andrew!" My heart swells with love for him. How could I have thought—well, what I was thinking about him? He may have gone about it the wrong way, but his intentions were in the right place.

"But Andrew," I say, "I have tons of money saved up. You don't have to do this for me—work all these hours, and . . . um, collect the dole, or whatever it is. I have plenty of money. For the both of us."

Suddenly he doesn't look quite so sweaty.

"You do? More than what you changed today, at the bank?"

"Of course," I say. "I've been saving my earnings from the shop for ages. I'm happy to share." I really mean it, too. After all, I'm a feminist. I have no problem supporting the man I love. No problem at all.

"How much?" Andrew asks quickly.

"How much have I got?" I blink at him. "Well, a couple thousand—"

"Honestly? Brilliant! Can I borrow a bit, then?"

"Andrew, I told you," I say. "I'm more than happy to pay for us to go out—"

"No, I mean, can I borrow a bit in advance?" Andrew wants to know. He's stopped sweating, but his face has taken on a bit of a pinched look. He keeps looking at the doorway where the man behind the counter's supervisor is due to appear at any moment. "See, I haven't paid my matriculation fees for school yet—"

"Matriculation fees?" I echo.

"Right," Andrew says. Now he's grinning sort of sheepishly, in the manner of a child with his hand caught in a cookie jar. "See, I had a bit of a cock-up myself just before you got here. Did you ever go to any of the Friday poker nights, back at McCracken Hall?"

My head is spinning. Seriously. "Poker nights? McCracken Hall?" *What is he talking about?*

"Yeah, there was a whole group of residents who played Texas Hold'em every Friday night. I used to play with them, and I got to be quite good . . ."

The British guy, Chaz had said about someone . . . someone I now realize was Andrew. *The one who was running the illegal poker ring on the seventh floor.*

"That was *you*?" I'm staring at him. "But . . . but you're an R.A. Gambling in the dorms is illegal."

Andrew shoots me an incredulous look.

"Right," he says. "Well, maybe, but everybody did it . . ."

If everybody suddenly started wearing epaulets, would you do it, too? I start to ask . . . then stop myself just in time.

Because, of course, I know the answer.

"Anyway," Andrew says, "I got involved with a game here not long ago, and . . . well, the stakes were a bit higher than I'm used to, and the players a bit more experienced, and I—"

"You lost," I say flatly.

"I told you I was a bit overconfident and thought I could clean up at that game I got into . . . but instead I got my arse kicked, and lost the money for my matriculation fees for next semester. That's why I was working so much, see? I can't tell my parents what happened to their money—they're dead set against gambling, and they'd probably kick me out of the house . . . I've barely got a bed there as it is, as you well know. But if you can spare it . . . well, then I'm golden, right? I won't have to work, and then we can be together all day"—He snakes out an arm, wrapping it around my waist and pulling me to him—"and all night, too," he adds with a suggestive wag of his eyebrows. "Wouldn't that be *brilliant*?"

My head is still spinning. Even though he's explained, somehow none of this is making sense . . . or rather, it *is* . . .

But I don't think I like the sense it's making.

I blink at him. "A few hundred? To pay your matriculation fees?"

"Two hundred quid or so, yeah," Andrew says. "Which is . . . what, five hundred dollars? Not so much if you consider it's all going to my future . . . *our* future. And I'll make it up to you. If it takes me the rest of my life, I'll make it up to you." He lowers his head to my neck, to nuzzle it. "Not," he adds into my hair, "that spending the rest of my life making it up to a girl like you will be such a hardship."

"Um," I say, "I guess I can spare it . . ." Inside my head, though, a voice is screaming something entirely different. "We could . . . we could go wire it to the university after we leave here."

"Right," Andrew says. "Listen, about that . . . It might just be better if you gave me the cash and I sent it. There's a bloke I know at work, he can get it there for nothing, no fees, no nothing . . ."

"You want me to give you cash," I repeat.

"Right," Andrew says. "It'll be cheaper than if we wired the money from here in town. They kill you with fees . . ." Then, hearing footsteps in the hallways outside the little office, he says quickly, "Listen, tell that wanker, when he gets in here, that you were wrong about my having a job. That you misunderstood. All right? Can you do that for me, Liz?"

"Lizzie," I say in a sort of daze.

He looks at me blankly. "What?"

"Lizzie. Not Liz. You always call me Liz. No one calls me that. My name's Lizzie."

"Right," Andrew says. "Whatever. Look, he's coming. Just tell him, will you? Tell him you made a mistake."

"Oh," I say, "I will."

But the mistake, I realize, was not about Andy's employment status.

While the Elizabethan age is considered by many historians to be one of enlightenment, given the rise of such geniuses as Shakespeare and Sir Walter Raleigh (see: cape in the mud, etc.), there is no question that Elizabeth, toward the end of her reign, began to behave in an unpredictable and skittish fashion. Many believe this may have been due to the copious amount of white foundation she wore upon her face in order to give it what was then considered a youthful appearance. Unfortunately for Queen Elizabeth, there was lead in her face paint, which may have caused lead poisoning, affecting her brain.

Elizabeth I is not the last to suffer hardship in the pursuit of beauty (see: Jackson, Michael).

History of Fashion
SENIOR THESIS BY ELIZABETH NICHOLS

8

Women speak because they wish to speak, whereas a man speaks only when driven to speak by something outside himself—like, for instance, he can't find any clean socks.
—*Jean Kerr (1923–2003), U.S. author and playwright*

𝕴 don't know what made me do it.

One minute I was asking Mr. Williams—the supervisor of the man who'd escorted us to the little back office—if he could direct me to the ladies' room (although here in England they apparently call it a toilet, since it took some seconds before I could make anyone understand what it was that I needed), and the next I was making a run for it.

That's right. I left. I left the Job Centre—and Andrew. I pretended like I was going to the women's toilet.

But instead I exited the building, hurrying out onto the busy London streets with no idea where I was going, let alone how to get there.

I don't know why I did it. I'd said what Andrew had told me to say—that I'd been mistaken about his having been at work. I suppose that since Andrew gets paid under the table, the Job Centre people have no way to check on whether this is really true. So it wasn't as if Mr. Williams could really *do* anything to Andrew . . . like have him arrested.

In fact, all Mr. Williams was doing when I interrupted to ask where the bathroom was was giving Andrew a lecture on how wrong it is for people who don't truly need the welfare system to abuse it.

That's when I left.

And I never returned.

Which is why I'm wandering the streets of London, with no idea where I am. I don't have a guidebook or a map or anything. All I have is a purseful of British money and a sinking feeling that Andrew isn't going to be too pleased to see me when I get back to his parents' house—if I can even figure out *how* to get back there.

Maybe I should have stayed. It was wrong of me just to leave like that. Andrew's right, it really *is* hard for students to make ends meet ...

Although obviously it doesn't help if they gamble away their savings.

And what about the money? I promised him five hundred dollars for his matriculation fees and then I just ... left. How could I walk out like that? If Andrew doesn't pay his matriculation fees, he won't be able to come back to school in the fall. How could I just turn my back on him like this?

But how could I stay?

It isn't the money. It *isn't*. I'd gladly give him every cent I have. Because the truth is, I really can put up with the fact that he thought I was fat.

And I can put up with the fact that he apparently complained about my fatness to his family.

And I can put up with the gambling, and even with the fact that he pretended like he couldn't come so I would give him a blow job.

But defrauding poor people? Because that is basically what someone who takes unemployment while having a paying job is doing.

That I cannot tolerate.

And he wants to be a teacher! A TEACHER! Can you imagine a man like that molding the minds of impressionable young people?

I'm such an idiot. I can't believe I fell for his whole "I want to teach the children to read" thing. It was all so obviously just an act so he could get into my pants—and, later, my wallet. Why didn't I see the signs? I mean, what kind of man who wants to teach the children to read—really and sincerely—also e-mails photos of his naked butt to innocent American girls?

I'm so stupid. How could I have been so blind?

Shari's right, of course. It was his accent. That has to be it. I was completely swayed by his accent. It's just so . . . charming.

But now I know that just because a guy sounds like James Bond doesn't mean he's necessarily going to ACT like him. Would James Bond collect unemployment while also working? Of course not.

Oh God, and to think I wanted to MARRY him!!! I wanted to marry and support him for the rest of my life. I wanted to have children with him—Andrew Jr., Henry, Stella, and Beatrice. And a dog! What was the dog's name?

Oh, never mind.

I'm the biggest idiot this side of the Atlantic. Possibly both sides. God, I wish I'd figured that out before I gave him that blow job. I can't believe I did that.

You know what? I want that blow job back. Andrew Marshall isn't worthy of a blow job by me. That blow job was special. It was my first. And it was meant for a teacher, not a welfare fraud!

Or a dole fraud. Or whatever they call it here.

What am I going to do? It's only two days into my trip to visit my boyfriend and I've already decided I never want to see him again. And I'm staying with his *family*! It's not like I can avoid him there.

Oh God. I want to go home.

But I can't. Even if I could afford it—even if I could call home right now and have them buy me a ticket—I'd never hear the end of it. Sarah and Rose—Mrs. Rajghatta—even my mother—everyone. They'll never let me live it down. They all told me—ALL OF THEM—not to do this, not to go all the way to England to visit a guy I hardly knew, a guy who'd, yeah, okay, saved my life . . .

But chances are I wouldn't have died. I mean, eventually I'd have noticed the smoke and gotten out on my own.

They will never let me forget the fact that they were right. God! They were all right! I can't believe this. They've never been right about *anything*. They all said I'd never graduate . . . well, I have.

Well, okay, almost. I just have to write one little paper.

And they all said I'd never lose my baby fat.

Well, I did. Except for those last five pounds. But they're hardly noticeable to anyone but me.

They said I'd never get a job or an apartment in New York—well, I'm going to prove them wrong about that. I hope. Actually, I can't think about that right now or I'll throw up.

All I know is, I can't go back home. I can't let them think they were right about this.

But I can't stay, either! Not after walking out like that—Andrew will never forgive me. I mean, I just *left*. It was like my feet developed little brains all their own and just took off, trying to put as much distance between Andrew and me as they could.

It isn't his fault. Not really. I mean, gambling is an addiction! If I were a decent person, I would have stayed and tried to help him. I'd have given him the money so he could come back in the fall and make a fresh start . . . I'd have *been* there for him. Together, we could have worked to lick it . . .

But instead I just *left*. Oh, good job, Lizzie. Some girlfriend you are.

My chest feels tight. I think I might be having a panic attack. I've never had one before, but Brianna Dunleavy, back in the dorm, used to get them all the time, and end up at the student health center, where they'd give her a note to get out of her exams.

I can't have a panic attack on the street. I can't! I'm wearing a skirt. Supposing I fall down and everyone sees my underwear? It's true they're the cute polka-dot ones with the bows from Target. But still. I need to sit down. I need to—

Oh—a bookshop. Bookshops are excellent for panic attacks. At least, I hope so, never having had one before.

I plunge past the latest releases and the checkout counter, deep into the bowels of the store. Then, spying a leather chair in the self-help section, which is otherwise empty (British people evidently don't feel the need for much self-help. Which is too bad, because some of them—namely Andrew Marshall—really need it), I sink down into it and put my head between my knees.

Then I breathe. In. Out. In. Out.

This. Can't. Be. Happening. I. Can't. Be. Having. A. Panic. Attack. In. A. Foreign. Country. My. Boyfriend. Can't. Have. Lost. All. His. Grad. School. Money. Playing. Texas. Hold'em.

"Pardon me, miss?"

I lift up my head. Oh no! One of the bookstore clerks is looking down at me curiously.

"Um," I say, "hi."

"Hullo," he says. He seems nice enough. He is wearing jeans and a black T-shirt. His dreadlocks are very clean. He doesn't seem like the kind of person who would kick a woman who is having a panic attack out of his shop.

"Are you all right?" he wants to know. A tag on his shirt says his name is Jamal.

"Yes," I squeak. "Thank you. I'm just . . . I'm not feeling very well."

"You don't look well," Jamal confirms. "Would you like a glass of water?"

I realize then how incredibly thirsty I am. A diet Coke. That's what I really need. Is there no diet Coke in this benighted country?

But I say, "That would be so nice of you," to Jamal's offer of water.

He nods and goes off, looking concerned. Such a nice person. Why can't I be dating him instead of Andrew? Why did I have to fall in love with a guy who claims he WANTS to teach children to read, as opposed to one who really is helping them to do it?

Well, okay, Jamal doesn't work in the children's department.

But still. I bet there are children who have been in this shop that he's encouraged to read.

But maybe I'm just projecting. Again. Maybe I'm just believing what I *want* to believe about Jamal.

Just like I wanted to believe that Andrew is really an Andrew and not an Andy. When in reality he's the biggest Andy I've ever met.

Not that there's anything wrong with the name Andy. It's just that—

Suddenly I know what I need, and it's not water.

I don't want to. I really don't want to. But I realize I have to hear my mother's voice. I simply *have* to.

With trembling fingers, I dial my house. I won't tell her about Andrew, I decide, and how he's turned out to be an Andy. I just need to hear a familiar voice. A voice that calls me Lizzie instead of Liz. A voice—

"Mom?" I cry when a woman picks up the phone on the other end and says hello.

"What the hell are you doing calling so early in the morning?" Grandma demands. "Dontcha know what time it is here?"

"Grandma," I say. I close my eyes. My chest still feels tight. "Is Mom there?"

"Hell no," Grandma says. "She's over at the hospital. You know she helps Father Mack give out communion on Tuesdays."

I don't dispute this, even though it isn't Tuesday. "Well, is Dad there, then? Or Rose? Or Sarah?"

"What's the matter, I'm not good enough for you?"

"No," I say. "You're fine. I just—"

"You sound like you're coming down with something. You catching one of those avian flus over there?"

"No," I say. "Grandma . . ."

And that's when I start to cry.

Why? WHY??? I'm too angry to cry. I already told myself that!

"What's with the waterworks?" Grandma wants to know. "You lose your passport? Don't worry, they'll still let you come home. They let anybody in here. Even people who want to blow us all to kingdom come."

"Grandma," I say, "I think . . ." It's hard to whisper when I'm sobbing, but I try. I don't want to disturb the bookstore customers and get kicked back out onto the street. I know Jamal will be coming back with my water at any moment. "I think I made a mistake in coming here. Andrew . . . he isn't the person I thought he was."

"What did he do?" Grandma wants to know.

"He . . . he . . . told his family I was fat. And he gambles. And he's defrauding the government. And he . . . he . . . he said I liked tomatoes!"

"Come home," Grandma says. "Come home right now."

"That's just it," I say. "I c-can't come home. Sarah and Rose—everybody—they all told me this was going to happen. And now it has. If I come home, they'll all just say they told me so. Because they did. Oh, Grandma." Now the tears are coming even faster. "I'm never going to get a boyfriend! A real one, I mean, who loves me for me, and not my savings account."

"Bullshit," Grandma says.

Startled, I say, "W-what?"

"You're going to get a boyfriend," Grandma says. "Only unlike your sisters, you're choosy. You're not going to marry the first asshole who comes along who tells you he likes you, then knocks you up."

This is a very sobering assessment of my older sisters' relationships. It has the effect of drying up my tears instantly.

"Grandma," I say, "I mean, really. Isn't that a little harsh?"

"So this latest one turned out to be a dud," Grandma goes on. "Good riddance. What are you going to do, stay with him anyway until your flight leaves?"

"I don't see what choice I have," I say. "I mean, I can't just . . . leave him."

"Where is he now?"

"Well," I say, "he's back at the Job Centre, I guess." Would he have come looking for me?

Yes, of course. I have his five hundred dollars.

"Then you already left him," Grandma says. "Look. I don't get what the big deal is. You're in Europe. You're young. Young people have been going to Europe on a shoestring for a hundred years. Use your head, for God's sake. What about your friend Shari? Isn't she over there somewhere?"

Shari. I forgot all about her. Shari, who is right across the English Channel, in France. Shari, who actually invited me, just last night, to come stay with her at—what was it called again? Oh yes. Mirac.

Mirac. The word might as well mean heaven, it sounds so magical right now.

"Grandma," I say, climbing out from my chair, "do you really think . . . I mean . . . should I?"

"You said he gambles?" Grandma asks.

"Apparently," I say, "he has a fondness for Texas Hold'em."

Grandma sighs. "Just like your uncle Ted. By all means stay with him if you want to live the rest of your life trying to bail him out financially. That's what your aunt Olivia did. But if you're smart—and I think you are—you'll get the hell out now, while you still can."

"Grandma," I say, choking back tears, "I . . . I think I'll take your advice. Thank you."

"Well," Grandma says flatly, "this is an occasion. One of you girls actually listening to me for a change. Somebody needs to break out the champagne."

"I'll toast you in absentia, Grandma," I say. "And now I'd better call Shari. Thank you so much. And, um, don't tell anyone about this conversation, okay, Grandma?"

"Who would I tell?" Grandma grumbles, and hangs up.

I hang up as well and hurriedly dial Shari's number. Shari. I can't believe I didn't think of SHARI! Shari's in France. And she said I could come see her. The Chunnel. Didn't she say something about taking the Chunnel? Can I really do this? *Should* I?

Oh no. It goes to Shari's voice mail. Where *is* she? Out in the vineyard squishing grapes between her toes? Shari, where are you? I need you!

I leave a message: "Hi, Shar? It's me, Lizzie. I really need to talk to you. It's really important. I think . . . I'm pretty sure Andrew and I are breaking up." I flash back to the expression on his face as he was telling me about his friend from work who could wire my money to the States with no fees.

My heart twists.

"Um, in fact, I think we've *definitely* broken up. So could you call me? Because I'm probably going to need to take you up on your France offer. So call me back. Right away. Well. Bye."

Saying the words out loud makes it suddenly seem much more real. My boyfriend and I are breaking up. If I had just kept my mouth shut about his waitering job, none of this would have happened. It's all because of me. Because of my big mouth.

Really, I have put my foot in it before. But never this big.

On the other hand . . . if I hadn't said anything, would he ever have told me? About the gambling, I mean? Or would he have tried to keep a secret from me for the rest of our lives together—as he seemed to have done, pretty successfully, for the past three months? Would we have ended up like Uncle Ted and Aunt Olivia—bitter, divorced, financially insolvent, and living in Cleveland and Reno, respectively?

I can't let that happen. I *won't* let that happen.

I can't go back to the Marshalls' house. That's all there is to it. I mean, obviously, I have to, in order to get my things. But I can't sleep there tonight. Not in the MDF bed, the same bed Andrew and I made love in . . . the bed I gave him that blow job in.

The blow job I want back.

And, I realize, I don't *have* to sleep there tonight. Because I have somewhere to go.

I stand up so suddenly that I get a head rush. I am staggering around, clutching my head, when Jamal comes back with a glass of water for me.

"Miss?" he says worriedly.

"Oh," I say, seeing the water. I snatch it from him and down the glass's contents. I don't mean to be rude, but my head is pounding. "Thanks so much," I say when I'm done drinking. And hand the glass back to him. I'm feeling better already.

"Is there someone I can telephone for you?" Jamal wants to know. Really, he is so kind. So attentive! I almost feel like I'm back in Ann Arbor. Except for the English accent.

"No," I say. "But there is something you can help me with. I need to know how to get to the Chunnel."

Part Two

The French Revolution in the late 1700s wasn't just an uprising of common people overthrowing the monarchy in favor of democracy and republicanism. No! It was also about fashion—the haves (who favored powdered wigs, fake facial moles, and hooped skirts, sometimes as much as fifteen feet wide) versus the have-nots (who wore stout boots, narrow skirts, and plain cloth). In this particular uprising, as history shows, the peasants won.

But fashion lost.

History of Fashion
SENIOR THESIS BY ELIZABETH NICHOLS

9

Good talkers are only found in Paris.
—*François Villon (1431–1463), French poet*

I'm pulling my wheelie bag down the aisles of the Paris-Souillac train, and I'm trying not to cry.

Not because of the bag. Well, sort of because of the bag. I mean, the aisle is very narrow, and I have my carry-on bag over my shoulder, and I sort of have to walk sideways, like a crab, in order not to bang people in the head with it as I search—apparently fruitlessly—for a front-facing first-class seat in a nonsmoking car.

If I smoked and I didn't mind facing backward, I'd be all set. Except that I don't smoke, and I'm afraid if I ride facing backward, I might throw up. In fact, I am *sure* I will throw up, because I have felt like throwing up ever since I woke up in Paris—having conked out in my comfy seat on the train from London, like Grandma after too much cooking sherry—and realized what I'd done.

Which is, pretty much, set off by myself through Europe, with no idea whether I am actually going to find the place, much less the person, I'm looking for. Especially since Shari still isn't answering her cell phone, much less calling me back.

Of course, part of the reason why I feel like throwing up might be that I am so incredibly hungry I can hardly see. All I've had to eat since breakfast is an apple I bought at Waterloo Station, since that was the only nutritious food I could find for sale there that didn't have tomatoes on it. If I'd wanted a Cadbury bar or an egg and to- mato sandwich, I'd have been all right.

But since I didn't, I was out of luck.

I'm hoping there'll be a dining car on this train. But before I can go look for it, I need to find a decent seat where I can dump my stuff.

And that's proving difficult. My bag is so wide and awkward that it keeps bumping people in the knees as I go by them, and even though I'm apologizing like crazy—*"Pardonnez-moi,"* I say to them, when I'm not *"Excusez-moi"*-ing them—nobody seems to appre- ciate my apologies very much. Maybe because they're all French and I'm American and no one here seems to like Americans. At least, judging by the way the kid next to me in the backward-facing smoking seat I found—but consequently had to abandon—had gone, *"Êtes-vous américaine?"* in a disgusted voice when he over- heard me leaving yet another message for Shari on my cell.

"Um," I said, *"oui?"*

And he made a face and pulled out an iPod, inserted his ear- phones, and turned his face to the window so he wouldn't have to look at me again.

Vamos a la playa, screamed the song I could plainly hear from his earphones. *Vamos a la playa.*

I know that song is going to be stuck in my head for the rest of the day. Or night, I should say, since it's already afternoon and my train won't be arriving at the station in Souillac for six hours.

That's another reason I'm going in search of a new seat. How am I supposed to spend six hours next to a snot-nosed seventeen-year- old in an Eminem T-shirt who listens to Europop, hates Americans, and *smokes*?

Of course, now it's looking like that seat was actually the last va- cant one on this train.

Can I stand for six hours? Because if so, I'll be golden. There's plenty of space for me and my gargantuan bags in the spaces between the cars.

How can this be happening to me? It all seemed so simple when Jamal, back at the bookshop, explained what I'd have to do to get to France. He'd been so knowing and kind, it had sounded as if getting from London to where Shari is was going to be a snap.

He didn't mention, of course, the fact that the minute you open your mouth to speak to anyone in this country and they realize from your accent that you're American, they just answer you in English anyway.

And usually not very nicely, either.

But still. I was able to follow most of the signage at the Gare du Nord. Enough to get my ticket, anyway—which I'd reserved over the phone—out of the machines. Enough to find my train. Enough to stumble onto the first car I reached and plop down into the first available seat.

Too bad I didn't notice the smoke—and the fact that I was facing the wrong way—until the train actually started moving.

It's hard not to feel like this whole thing was a very bad idea. Not the moving-to-the-different-seat thing—I already know THAT was a bad idea. But the coming-to-France thing. I mean, what if I never get ahold of Shari? What if her cell phone fell into the toilet again, the way it did that time back in the dorm, and she can't afford a new one or there's no cell phone store nearby and she's just going without one for the rest of her trip? How will I ever find her?

I suppose I could ask people, when I get to Souillac, if they know where Château Mirac is. But supposing they've never heard of Château Mirac? Shari didn't say how far the château was from the train station. What if it's really, really far?

And it's not like I can call Shari's parents and ask them if they know where she is and how I can get in touch with her. Because then they'll want to know why I want to know, and if I tell them, they'll tell my mom and dad, and then they'll know things didn't work out with Andrew—I mean, Andy—and tell my sisters.

And then I will never hear the end of it.

Oh God, how did I get myself into this? Maybe I should have just stayed at Andy's. What's the worst that would have happened? I could have gone to Jane Austen's house by myself and just used Andy's house as a sort of home base. I didn't have to leave. I could have just been like, "Look, Andy, it's not working out between us, because you're not who I thought you were. I have a thesis to write, so let's just agree to ignore each other the rest of the time I'm here and I'll do my thing and you do yours."

I could have just said that to him. Of course, it's too late now. I can't go back. Not after that note I left him when I took that taxi back to his house—best fifteen pounds I ever spent—to get my stuff. Thank GOD no one had been home . . .

. . . and thank God Andy had thought to give me my own key this morning before we'd left, which I'd dropped into the Marshalls' mailbox on my way out.

Oh my God. A seat! An empty seat! Facing the right way! In a nonsmoking car! And it's next to a window!

Okay, be calm. It might be taken and the person just got up to use the bathroom or whatever—oh jeez, I bonked that lady in the head with my bag—"*Je suis désolée, madame,*" I say. That means "I'm sorry," right? Oh, who cares. A seat! A seat!

Oh my God. A seat next to a guy who looks to be about my age, with curly dark hair, big brown eyes, and a gray button-down shirt that is actually tucked into his faded-in-all-the-right-places Levi's. That he is wearing with a mesh weave leather belt.

It is possible that I have died. That I have passed out in the aisles of the train—and died of hunger, dehydration, and heartache.

And that this is heaven.

"*Pardonnez-moi*," I say to the totally hot guy. "*Mais est-ce que . . . est-ce que—*"

"Is that seat next to you taken?" is what I want to ask. Only in French, obviously. Only I can't remember the word for seat. Or taken. In fact, I don't think we ever covered this phrase in French 101 or 102. Or maybe we did but I was too busy daydreaming about Andrew—I mean, Andy—that I wasn't paying attention that day.

Or maybe it's just that this guy is so good-looking I can't think of anything else.

"Do you want to sit here?"

That's what the guy in the aisle seat asks, indicating the empty window seat beside him.

In perfect English. In perfect AMERICAN English.

"Oh my God!" I burst out. "Are you American? Is that seat really not taken? Can I sit there?"

"Yes," the guy says with a smile that reveals perfect white teeth. Perfect white AMERICAN teeth. "To all three."

And he gets up to let me into the window seat.

Not only that, but he actually leans over, grabs my gargantuan wheelie bag that has just popped a thousand French kneecaps during its long drag through several train cars, and says, "Let me help you with this."

And, seemingly without effort, he lifts the bag and shoves it up onto the rack above our heads.

Okay. *Now* I'm crying.

Because this is not a hallucination. I am not dead. This is really happening. I know because I've just slung my carry-on bag down from my shoulder and put it under the seat in front of mine, and my entire right side has gone numb from the weight not being there anymore. If I were dead, would I feel numb?

No.

I sink down into the seat—the soft, cushiony seat—and just sit there, blinking at the buildings flashing by so unbelievably quickly, completely unable to believe my good fortune. How could my luck, which has been so totally rotten lately, have taken such an incredible turn for the better? This can't be right. There has to be a catch. There just has to be.

"Water?" the guy next to me asks, holding out a plastic bottle of Evian.

I can barely see him through my tears. "You're . . . you're giving me your water?"

"Um," he says, "no. They come with the seats. This is first class. Everyone gets one."

"Oh," I say, feeling stupid (so what else is new?). I hadn't noticed the water at my last seat. Probably that French kid had bogarted mine. He looked like the type who would steal someone else's water.

I take the water from my new—and vastly improved—seatmate.

"Thank you," I say. "I'm sorry. It's just . . . it's been a long day."

"I can see that," he says. "Unless you always cry on trains."

"I don't," I say, shaking my head and sniffling. "Really."

"Well, that's good to know," he says. "I've heard of fear of flying, of course. But I've never heard of a fear of trains."

"I've had the worst day," I say, opening the water. "Really. You have no idea. It's so nice to hear an American accent. I can't believe how much everybody here hates us."

"Oh," the guy says with another flash of those perfect white teeth, "they aren't so bad. If you saw how the typical American tourist acted, you'd probably feel the same way about us that the French do."

I've chugged most of my water. I'm starting to feel a little better— not so much like death warmed over. Although I'm sure I probably look it. Which is great since now that I have an even closer view of him, I can see that my seatmate isn't just handsome. His face is filled with kindness, intelligence, and good humor as well.

Unless that's just the starvation talking.

"Well." I reach up to dab at my eyes with my wrist. I wonder if my mascara is running down my cheeks in streaks. Did I wear the waterproof kind? I can't even remember. "I'll just have to take your word for it."

"Your first time in France?" he asks sympathetically. Even his *voice* is nice. Sort of deep, and very understanding.

"My first time anywhere in Europe," I say. "Well, except for London, where I was this morning."

And then, like a dam bursting, I'm crying again.

I try not to do it loudly. You know, without sobbing or anything. I just can't think about London—I never even got to go to Topshop!—without tearing up.

My seatmate nudges my elbow with his. When I open my streaming eyes, I see that he is holding a plastic bag in front of me.

"Honey-roasted peanuts?" he asks.

I am overwhelmed by hunger. Without a word, I dive my hand into the bag, grab a handful of nuts, and stuff them into my mouth. I don't care if they're honey-roasted and jam-packed with carbs. I'm starved.

"Do . . . do they come with the seats, too?" I ask between sniffles.

"No," he says, "they're mine. Help yourself to more, if you want some."

I do. They are the best thing I have ever tasted. And not just because I haven't had sugar in so long.

"Thanks," I say. "I . . . I'm s-sorry."

"For what?" my seatmate asks.

"For s-sitting here crying like this. I'm not usually like this. I swear."

"Travel can be very stressful," he says. "Especially in this day and age."

"It's true," I say, taking some more nuts. "You can just never tell. I mean, you meet people and they seem perfectly nice. And then it turns out that all along they were just lying to you to get you to pay their matriculation fees because they lost all their money in a game of Texas Hold'em."

"I was actually referring to terrorist alerts," my seatmate says somewhat dryly. "But I guess what, er, you mentioned could be troubling as well."

"Oh, it is," I assure him through my tears. "You have no idea. I mean, he just outright lied to me—telling me that he loved me and all of that—when all along I think he was just using me. I mean, Andy—that's the guy I left, back in London—he seemed so nice, you know? He was going to be a teacher. He said he was going to devote his life to teaching little children to read. Have you ever heard of anything that noble?"

"Um," my seatmate says, "no?"

"No. Because who even does that in today's day and age? People our age—how old are you?"

"I'm twenty-five," my seatmate says, a little smile on his lips.

"Right," I say. I open my purse, fishing inside it for some tissue. "Well, haven't you noticed that people our age . . . all they seem to think about is making money? Okay, not everyone. But a lot of them. No one wants to be a teacher anymore, or even a doctor . . . not with HMOs and all of that. There's not enough money in it. Everyone wants to be an investment banker, or a corporate head- hunter, or a lawyer . . . because that's where the money is. They don't care if they're doing anything good for mankind. They just want to own a McMansion and a BMW. Seriously."

"Or pay back their student loans," says my seatmate.

"Right. But it's like, you don't *have* to go to the world's most expensive college in order to get a good education." I've managed to locate a wadded-up piece of tissue at the bottom of my purse. I use it to mop up some of my tears. "Education is what you *make* out of it."

"I never actually thought of it that way," says my seatmate. "But you could have a point."

"I think I do," I say. The buildings that had been whizzing past my window have turned to open fields. The sky is a golden red as the sun begins to slide down toward the western horizon. "I mean, I've been out there. I've seen it for myself. If you're studying something like—I don't know. History of fashion or something—people think you're a freak. No one wants to pursue anything creative anymore, because that's too risky. They may not get the kind of return on the financial investment they've made in their education that they think they should. So they all go into business or accounting or law or . . . or they look for stupid American girls to marry so they can live off them."

"You sound as if you're speaking from personal experience," my seatmate observes.

"Well, what else am I supposed to think?" I'm babbling. I know I'm babbling. But I can't seem to stop myself. Any more than I can stop the tears that continue to flow down my cheeks. "I mean, what kind of person—you know, who wants to be a teacher—works as a waiter, and ALSO collects the dole?"

My seatmate seems to consider this. "A financially needy one?"

"You would think that," I say, sniffling into the tissue. "But what if I told you that this was also a person who lost all his money playing Texas Hold'em, then asked his girlfriend to pay his matriculation fees, and then, as if that were not enough, also told his entire family that . . . she's . . . I mean, I'm . . . a fatty?"

"You?" My seatmate sounds suitably stunned. "But you're not. Fat, I mean."

"Not now," I say with a little sob. "But I was. When we met. But I lost thirty pounds since the last time I saw him. But even if I *was* fat—he shouldn't go around telling people that! Not if he really loved me. Right? If he really loved me, he wouldn't have *noticed*

I was fat. Or he would have, but it wouldn't have mattered. Not enough to tell his family."

"That's true," my seatmate says.

"But he did. He told them I was fat!" New tears erupt. "And when I got there, they were all, 'You're not fat!' Which is how I knew he'd said something about it. And then he goes and gambles away the money his parents—his hardworking parents—gave him for school! I mean, his mother—his poor mother! You should have seen her. She's a social worker, and she made me a giant breakfast and everything. Even though I don't like tomatoes, and every single thing she made had tomatoes in it. Which is another sign Andy never loved me at all—I specifically told him I don't like tomatoes, and yet he didn't pay any attention. It was like he didn't even know me at all. I mean, he e-mailed me a picture of his naked butt. What would make a guy think a girl would WANT to see a picture of his naked butt? I mean, seriously? Why would he think that was an okay thing to do?"

"I really couldn't say," my seatmate says.

I blow my nose. "But see, that's just typical cluelessness on Andy's part. The scariest part is, I felt *sorry* for him. Seriously. I didn't know about the welfare fraud or that he was going around calling me fat, or that he was using me just to pay his gambling debts. And the worst part is . . . Oh God, I can't be the only one this has ever happened to, can I? I mean, haven't you ever thought you loved someone and done things you regretted with that person? And then wished you could get them back, only you can't? I mean, haven't you?"

"What kind of things are we talking about?" my seatmate wants to know.

"Oh," I say. It's amazing, but I'm starting to feel a little bit better. Maybe it's the comfortable seat, or the golden glow flooding the train car as well as the tranquil countryside we're passing. Maybe it's the fact that I finally got some liquids into me. Maybe it's the sugar from the peanuts.

Or maybe, just maybe, it's that saying all of this out loud is restoring my faith in myself. I mean, anyone might have been tricked by as smooth an operator as Andrew—I mean, Andy. ANYONE. Maybe not my seatmate, since he's a guy. But any girl. ANY girl.

"You know the kinds of things I'm talking about," I say. I look around to make sure no one is listening. All the other passengers appear to be dozing, listening to things through headphones, or too French to understand me anyway. Still, I lower my voice. *Blow job,* I mouth meaningfully.

"Oh," my seatmate says, both of his dark eyebrows going up. "*That* kind of thing."

The thing is, he's American. And he's my age. And he's *so* nice. I feel totally comfortable talking about this with him, because I know he's not going to make any judgments about me.

Besides, I'm never going to see him again.

"Seriously," I say, "guys have no idea. Oh, wait, maybe you do. Are you gay?"

He nearly chokes on the water he is sipping. "No! Do I seem gay?"

"No," I say. "But then my gaydar isn't the best. My last relationship before Andy was with a guy who dumped me for his roommate. His MALE roommate."

"Well, I'm not gay."

"Oh. Well, the thing is, unless you've given one, you can't know. It's a major deal."

"What is?"

"*Blow job,*" I whisper again.

"Oh," he says. "Right."

"I mean, I know you guys all want them, but they're not easy. And the thing is, did he so much as attempt to give me anything in return? No! Of course not! Not that I didn't take care of, you know. Myself. But still. That's just impolite. Especially since I only did it out of pity for him."

"A . . . pity blow job?" My seatmate has the strangest expression on his face. Sort of like he's trying not to laugh. Or that he can't believe he's having this conversation. Or maybe a combination of both.

Oh well. Now he'll have a funny story to tell his family when he gets back home. If he is from the kind of family where it's okay to talk about blow jobs. Which I am definitely not. Except with Grandma, maybe.

"Right," I say. "I did it out of pity for him because he couldn't come. But now I realize that the whole couldn't-come thing was just a ruse. He was faking it! So I'd blow him! I feel so used. I'm telling you . . . I want it back."

"The . . . blow job?" he asks.

"Exactly. If only there was a way I could take it back."

"Well," my seatmate says, "it sounds like you did. You left. If that's not taking a blow job back, I don't know what is."

"It's not the same thing," I say dejectedly.

"*Billets.*" I see someone in a uniform standing in the aisle. "*Billets, s'il vous plaît.*"

"Do you have your ticket?" my seatmate asks me.

I nod, and open my purse. I manage to locate my ticket, and the guy next to me takes it. A second later the conductor moves on, and my seatmate says, "You're going to Souillac, I see. Any particular reason? Do you know someone there?"

"My best friend, Shari," I say. "She's supposed to meet me there. At the station. If she gets my message. Which I don't even know if she did, since she doesn't seem to be picking up her phone. Which she's probably dropped in the toilet again. Because she's always doing things like that."

"So . . . Shari doesn't even know you're coming?"

"No. I mean, she invited me. But I said no. Because back then I thought I could work things out with Andy. Only it turned out I couldn't."

"Well, not through any fault of your own."

I look at him then. The sun, sliding into the car, has outlined his profile in gold. I notice that he has really long eyelashes. Sort of like a girl. Also that his lips are very full and squishy-looking. In a good way.

"You're really nice," I say to him. My tears have totally dried up now. It's amazing how therapeutic telling all your problems to a total stranger can be. No wonder so many of my peers are in therapy. "Thanks for listening to me. Although I must sound completely psychotic to you. I bet you're wondering what you did to deserve having such a total wack job sit down next to you."

"I think you've just been through a rotten time," my seatmate says with a smile. "And so you have every right to sound psychotic. But I don't consider you a wack job. At least, not a total one."

"Really?" He also has, in addition to the lovely eyelashes and lips, really nice-looking hands. Strong and clean—tanned, too—with just a light spatter of dark hair on the back of them. "I just don't want you to think I go around giving blow jobs to all the guys I feel sorry for. I really don't. That was my first one. Ever."

"You don't? That's too bad. I was going to tell you about how I was raised in a Romanian orphanage."

I stare at him. "You're Romanian?"

"That was a joke," he says. "To make you feel sorry for me. So you'll—"

"I get it," I say. "Funny."

"Not really," he says with a sigh. "I suck at jokes. I always have. Hey, listen. Are you hungry? Want to go to the dining car? It's a long way to Souillac, and you've eaten all my nuts."

I look down at the empty plastic bag in my lap.

"Oh my God," I say. "I'm so sorry! I was starving—yes, let's go to the dining car. I'll buy you dinner. To make up for the nuts. And the crying. And the thing about the blow job. I'm really sorry about that."

"I'll take *you* to dinner," he says gallantly. "To make up for your recent mistreatment at the hands of one of my gender. How's that?"

"Um," I say, "okay. But . . . I don't even know your name. I'm Lizzie Nichols."

"I'm Jean-Luc de Villiers," he says, holding out his right hand. "And I think you should know, I'm an investment banker. But I don't own a McMansion or a BMW. I swear."

I automatically take his hand, but instead of shaking it, I just stare at him, momentarily flustered.

"Oh," I say, "I'm sorry. I didn't mean . . . I'm sure not *all* investment bankers are bad—"

"It's okay," Jean-Luc says, giving my hand a squeeze. "Most of us are. Just not me. Now come on. Let's go eat."

His fingers are warm and just slightly rough. I gaze up at him, wondering if the rosy glow all around him is really just caused by the setting sun, or if he is, by some chance, an angel sent down from heaven to rescue me.

Hey. You never know. Even an investment banker could be an angel. God moves in mysterious ways.

The "Empire waist"—a waistline beginning just beneath the bust—was popularized by Napoléon Bonaparte's wife, Joséphine, who, during her husband's reign as emperor beginning in 1804, favored the "classical" style of Greek art, and emulated the togalike robes worn by figures on ancient pottery from that time.

In order to better simulate the look of the pottery figures, many young women dampened their skirts so that their legs, beneath the sopping garments, were more apparent. It is from this tradition that the modern-day "wet T-shirt contest" is believed to have derived.

History of Fashion
SENIOR THESIS BY ELIZABETH NICHOLS

10

The way to get a man interested and to hold his interest was
to talk about him, and then gradually lead the conversation
around to yourself—and keep it there.
        —*Margaret Mitchell (1900–1949), U.S. author*

He isn't an angel. At least, not unless angels are born and
raised in Houston, which is where he's from.

Also, angels don't have degrees from the University of
Pennsylvania, the way Jean-Luc does.

Also, angels don't have parents who are going through an acri-
monious divorce, the way Jean-Luc's are, so that when they want to
come visit their father—the way Jean-Luc's taken a few weeks off
from his job at the investment firm of Lazard Frères to do—they
have to come all the way to France, since that's where Jean-Luc's
dad, a Frenchman, lives.

Also, angels tell better jokes. He wasn't lying about the joke thing.
He really does suck at them.

But that's okay. Because I would rather be with a bad joke-teller
who remembers I hate tomatoes than with a gambling welfare cheat
who doesn't.

Because Jean-Luc does—remember about the tomatoes, I mean.
When I come back from the ladies' room (picturesquely referred to
on French trains as the "toilet"), where I went to repair the damage
done to my face by my tears—fortunately, nothing a new application of eyeliner, undereye cover-up, lipstick, and powder couldn't

cure, along with some hair combing—I find the waiter already at our table, taking our order. Jean-Luc does all the talking because, being half French, he speaks the language fluently. And quickly. I can't catch everything he says, but I hear *"pas de tomates"* several times.

Which even I, with my summer-school French, know means "no tomatoes."

It is all I can do to keep from bursting into tears all over again. Because Jean-Luc has renewed my faith in men. There *are* nice, funny, totally good-looking guys out there. You just have to know where to look . . . and apparently, where NOT to look. Which is in the ladies' shower of your dorm.

Of course, I've found this one on a train . . . which means after I get off this train, I'll probably never see him again.

But that's okay. It's fine. I mean, what did I expect, to walk out of one relationship right into another? Right. Like that's even healthy. Like it would have had a chance of lasting, since I'm so obviously on the rebound from Andy.

Plus, you know. The whole two-ships-passing-in-the-night thing.

Oh, and the fact that I told him about the blow job. (WHY? WHY DID I DO THAT??? WHY DO I HAVE TO HAVE THE BIGGEST MOUTH IN THE ENTIRE UNIVERSE???)

Still. He's just so . . . cute. And not married—no ring. Maybe he's got a girlfriend—actually, no guy this cute could *not* have a girlfriend—but if so, he certainly isn't talking about her.

Which is good. Because why would I want to sit here and listen to this totally cute guy talk about his girlfriend? I mean, obviously, if he talked about her I *would* listen, since he listened so patiently when I was talking about Andy.

But, you know. I'm glad he's not.

He orders wine to go with dinner, and when it arrives and the waiter pours it out for us, Jean-Luc lifts his glass, clinks it with mine, and says, "To blow jobs."

I nearly choke on the bread I'm scarfing down. Because even though we're on a train, we're on a train in *France,* so the food is incredible. At least the bread is. So incredible there's no possible way I can resist it after I take a tiny nibble from a roll in the basket on the table. Perfectly crunchy crust with a warm, soft middle? How can I abstain? Sure, I'll regret it later, when my size nine jeans won't zip up.

But for right now, I'm still in heaven. Because, for such a bad joke-teller, Jean-Luc is still pretty funny.

And I've missed bread. I've really, really missed it.

"To blow jobs we want *back,*" I correct him.

"I can only pray," Jean-Luc says, "there's no woman out there wishing she could take back one she's given me."

"Oh," I say, gently laying a curl of salted butter on top of the center of my roll and watching it melt into the warm bread, "I'm sure there's not. I mean, you don't seem like a user to me."

"Yes," he says, "but then neither did—what's his name again? Blow-job boy?"

"Andy," I say, blushing. God, why did I ever open my big mouth about that? "And my instincts were off about him. Because of the accent. And his wardrobe. If he'd been American, I never would have fallen for him. Or his lies."

"His wardrobe?" Jean-Luc asks as the waiter brings over my pan-seared pork medallions and his poached salmon.

"Sure," I say. "You can tell a lot about a guy from what he's wearing. But Andy was British, so that threw everything off a little. I mean, until I got there, I just figured everyone in England wore Aerosmith T-shirts, like Andy was wearing the night we met."

Jean-Luc's dark eyebrows go up. "Aerosmith?"

"Right. Obviously, I assumed he was being ironic, or possibly that it was laundry day. But then I got to London and I saw that is how he really dresses. There was nothing ironic about it. If things had worked out between us, I might eventually have gotten him into decent clothes. But . . ." I shrug. Which is a very French thing to do, I notice. All the other ladies in the dining car are shrugging as well, and saying, "*ouais*," which is French slang for *oui*, at least according to the copy of *Let's Go: France* I bought from Jamal and skimmed before I zonked out in the Chunnel.

"So you're saying," Jean-Luc says, "that you can tell what someone is like just by the clothes they're wearing?"

"Oh, absolutely," I say, digging into my pork tenderloin. Which, I might add, is totally delicious, even by non-train-food standards. "What someone wears reveals so much about themselves. Like you, for instance."

Jean-Luc grins. "Okay. Hit me."

I squint at him. "Are you sure?"

"I can take it," Jean-Luc assures me.

"Well . . . all right, then." I study him. "I can tell by the fact that you tuck your shirt into your jeans—which are Levi's; I doubt you own any other brand—that you're confident about your body and also that you care about how you look, but you aren't vain. You probably don't think much about how you look, but you glance in the mirror in the morning to shave and maybe make sure no tags are sticking out. Your mesh leather belt is casual and understated, but I bet it cost a lot, which means you're willing to spend money on quality, but you don't want it to look show-offy. Your shirt is Hugo—not Hugo Boss—which means you care, just a little, about not looking like everybody else, and you have on Cole Haan driving shoes with no socks, which means you like to be comfortable, aren't impatient about waiting in lines, don't mind having weird girls you've never met before sit next to you on trains and cry, and that you don't suffer from any sort of glandular foot-odor problems. Oh, and you're wearing a Fossil watch, which means you're athletic—I bet you run to stay in shape—and that you like to cook."

I laid down my fork and look at him. "How am I? Close?"

He stares at me across the bread basket.

"You got all that," Jean-Luc says incredulously, "just from what I'm wearing?"

"Well," I say, taking a sip of wine, "all that and the fact that you don't suffer from feelings of sexual inadequacy, because you aren't wearing cologne."

He says, "I got my belt for two hundred dollars, Hugo Boss fits weird on me, socks make my feet feel hot, I run three miles a day, I hate cologne, and I make the best cheese and scallion omelets you've ever tasted."

"I rest my case," I say, and dive into the mesclun salad the waiter's just brought us. It is loaded with blue cheese and candied walnuts.

Mmm, candied walnuts.

"But seriously," Jean-Luc says, "how'd you do that?"

"It's a talent," I say modestly. "Something I've always been able to do. Except, obviously, it doesn't always work. In fact, it seems to always fail me when I need it most—if a guy is ambivalent about his sexual orientation, I totally can't tell by what he's wearing. Unless, you know, he's in something of mine. And like I said—Andy was a foreigner. That threw me off. I'll know better next time."

"Next British guy?" Jean-Luc asks, the eyebrows going up again.

"Oh no," I say. "There will be no more British guys. Unless they're members of the royal family, of course."

"Wise strategy," Jean-Luc says.

He pours me more wine as he asks me what I have planned for after I return to the States. I tell him about how I was going to stay in Ann Arbor and wait for Andy to get his degree. But now . . .

I don't know what I'm going to do.

Then I find myself telling him—this stranger who is buying me dinner—my concerns about how if I go ahead and go with Shari to New York, she is going to ditch me eventually to go live with her boyfriend, since Chaz is going to be heading off to NYU to get a Ph.D. in philosophy, and then I'll have to room with total strangers. And also how I don't really have my degree yet since I haven't finished (or actually started) my thesis, so I probably won't even be able to get a job in my chosen field in New York—if jobs for history of fashion majors even exist—and will probably end up having to work at the Gap, my personal idea of hell on earth. All those capped-sleeved T-shirts, each one exactly the same as the other, and people mixing their denim rinses. It might actually kill me.

"Somehow," Jean-Luc says, "I can't quite picture you working at the Gap."

I look down at my Alex Colman sundress and say, "No. You're right. Do you think I'm insane?"

"No, I like that dress. It's kind of . . . retro."

"No. I mean about how I was going to stay in Ann Arbor until Andy was done with his degree and live at home. Shari says I was compromising my feminist principles, doing that."

"I don't think it's compromising your feminist principles," Jean-Luc says, "to want to stay close to someone you really love."

"Okay," I say. "But what am I going to do now? I mean, is it insane to move to New York without a job or a place to live first?"

"Oh no. Not insane. Brave. But then you seem like a fairly brave girl."

Brave? I nearly choke on a sip of wine. No one's ever called me fairly brave before.

And outside the dining car, the sun is still setting—it stays light out so late in France during the summer!—turning the sky behind the green hills and woods we're hurtling through a luscious, sultry pink. Around us, the waiters are passing out plates of assorted cheeses and chocolate truffles and tiny glasses of digestifs, and over in the smoking section our fellow diners have lit up, enjoying a lazy after-supper cigarette, the secondhand smoke from which, in this romantic setting, doesn't smell anywhere near as foul as it might coming out of, say, my ex-boyfriend's nostrils.

And I feel as if I'm in a movie. This isn't Lizzie Nichols, youngest daughter of Professor Harry Nichols, recent college nongraduate, who spent her whole life in Ann Arbor, Michigan, and has only been out with three guys her entire life (four if you count Andy).

This is Elizabeth Nichols, fairly brave (!), cosmopolitan world traveler and sophisticate, dining in a train car with a perfect (and I do mean perfect!) stranger, enjoying a cheese course (cheese course!) and sipping something called Pernod as the sun sets over the French countryside whizzing past—

And suddenly, in the middle of Jean-Luc's description of his own senior thesis, which has to do with shipping routes (I'm trying hard not to yawn—but then the history of fashion probably wouldn't light his fire, either), my cell phone chirps.

I snatch it up, thinking it must be Shari at last.

But the caller ID says Unknown Number. Which is weird, because no one Unknown *has* my cell number.

"Excuse me," I say to Jean-Luc. Then, ducking my head, I answer. "Hello?"

"Liz?"

Static crackles. The connection is terrible.

But it's unmistakably the last person in the world I want to hear from.

I don't know what to do. Why is he calling me? This is terrible. I don't want to talk to him! I have nothing to say to him. Oh dear.

"Just a minute," I say to Jean-Luc, and I leave our table to take the call in the open area beside the sliding door to the next train car, where I won't disturb the rest of the passengers.

"Andy?" I say into the cell phone.

"There you are!" Andy says, sounding relieved. "You have no idea how glad I am to hear your voice. Didn't you get my calls? I've been ringing your mobile all day. Why didn't you pick up?"

"I'm sorry, did you call? I never heard it ring." This is true. Cell phones don't work in the Chunnel.

"You have no idea what I've been through," Andy goes on, "coming out of that horrible office and finding you gone like that. The whole way home, I kept thinking, What if she's not there? What if something happened to her? I tell you, I must really love you, eh, if I was that scared something might have happened!"

I give a weak laugh. Even though I don't feel like laughing. "Yes," I say, "I guess you must."

"Liz, Christ," Andy goes on. Now he sounds . . . tense. "Where the fuck *are* you? When are you coming home?"

I gaze up at what looks, in the slanting rays of the sun, like a castle on a hillside. But that, of course, is impossible. Castles don't sit out in the middle of nowhere. Even in France.

"What do you mean, when am I coming home?" I ask him. "Didn't you get my note?" I left a note for Mrs. Marshall and the rest of Andy's family, thanking them for their hospitality, and a separate note for Andy, explaining that I was very sorry, but that I had unexpectedly been called away and would not be seeing him again.

"Of course I got your note," Andy says. "I just don't understand it."

"Oh," I say, surprised. I have excellent penmanship. But I was crying so hard maybe my handwriting was shakier than I'd thought. "Well . . . like I said in the note, Andy, I'm really very sorry, but I just had to go. I really am—"

"Look, Liz. I know what happened this morning at the Job Centre upset you. I hated having to ask you to lie like that. But you wouldn't have had to lie if you'd just kept your mouth shut in the first place."

"I realize that," I say. Oh God, this is awful. I don't want to do this. Not now. And certainly not here. "I know it's all my fault, Andy. And I really am sorry. I hope I didn't get you into trouble with Mr. Williams."

"Well, I won't lie to you, Liz," Andy says. "It was close. Very close. But . . . Wait a sec. Why are you calling me Andy?"

"Because it's your name," I say, moving out of the way of some people who've come through the sliding door from another car and are looking for an empty table.

"But you never call me Andy. You've always called me Andrew."

"Oh," I say. "Well, I don't know. You just seem like more of an Andy to me now."

"I'm not sure I like the sound of that," Andy says in a rueful tone. "Look, Liz . . . I know I made a fuck-all of everything. But you didn't have to *leave*. I can fix this, Liz. Really. Things didn't get off on the right foot between us, but everyone feels gutted about it, especially me. I'm done with Texas Hold'em . . . I swear it. And Alex has given up his room—he says you and I can share it. Or, if you like, we can go somewhere else . . . somewhere we can be alone. Where was it you wanted to go? Charlotte Brontë's house?"

"Jane Austen," I correct him.

"Right, Jane Austen's house. We can leave right away. Just tell me where you are and I'll come fetch you. We'll patch things up. I'll make it up to you—all of it—I swear it."

"Oh, Andy," I say, feeling guilt-ridden. Jean-Luc, over at our table, is paying the bill to make room at the table for the new passengers who've come in. "That just . . . I mean, it won't be possible for you to come fetch me. Because I'm in France."

"You're WHAT?" Andy sounds a bit more surprised than is necessarily flattering. I guess he doesn't consider me fairly brave, the way Jean-Luc does. At least, not brave enough to get to France on my own. "How did you get *there*? What are you *doing* there? Where are you? I'll join you."

"Andy," I say. This is terrible. I *hate* confrontations. It's so much easier to walk away than it is to have to explain to someone that you never want to see them again. "I want . . . I *need* to be by myself for a bit. I just need some time alone to think."

"But for God's sake, Liz, you've never been in Europe before. You don't have the slightest idea what you're doing. This isn't funny, you know. I'm really worried. Just tell me where you are and I'll—"

"No, Andy," I say softly. Jean-Luc is coming toward me, looking concerned. "Listen, I can't talk right now. I really have to go. I'm so sorry, Andy, but . . . like you said, I made a mistake."

"I forgive you!" Andy says. "Lizzie! I forgive you! Just—listen. What about the money?"

"The . . . what?" I am so stunned I nearly drop the phone.

"The money," Andy says urgently. "Can you still wire me the money?"

"I can't talk about that right now," I say. Jean-Luc has reached my side. He is, I note, really very tall—taller, even, than Andy. "I'm so sorry. Good-bye."

I hang up, and for a second or two my vision swims. I would not have thought it possible to have any tears left, but apparently I do.

"Are you all right?" I hear—since I cannot see—Jean-Luc ask gently.

"I will be," I assure him, more heartily than I actually feel.

"Was that him?" he wants to know.

I nod. It's feeling a little hard to breathe. I can't tell if it's because of my barely repressed tears or Jean-Luc's proximity . . . which, given how often the swaying of the train occasionally causes his arm to brush mine, is considerable.

"Did you tell him you were here with your attorney," Jean-Luc wants to know, "and that he was busy drawing up your demand for your blow job back?"

I am so shocked by this I forget about not being able to breathe. Instead I find myself grinning . . . and the tears mysteriously drying up in my eyes.

"Did you let him know that if he can't see fit to return your blow job immediately, you will have no choice but to sue?"

Now the tears in my eyes are from laughter.

"You said you can't tell jokes," I say accusingly when I've stopped laughing long enough to catch my breath.

"I can't." Jean-Luc looks grave. "That was a horrible one. I can't believe you laughed."

I'm still giggling as I collapse back into my seat beside him, feeling pleasantly full and more than a little sleepy. I struggle to stay awake, however, keeping my gaze on the window on the far side of the car, just behind Jean-Luc's head, where the sun—still not quite sunk—seems to be silhouetting another castle. I point at it and say, "You know, it's so weird. But that looks like a castle over there."

Jean-Luc turns his head. "That's because it *is* a castle."

"It is not," I say drowsily.

"Of course it is," Jean-Luc says with a laugh. "You're in France, Lizzie. What did you expect?"

Not castles, just sitting there for anyone to see by train. Not this breathtaking sunset, filling our car with this rosy light. Not this perfectly kind, perfectly lovely man sitting next to me.

"Not this," I murmur. "Not this."

And then I close my eyes.

The so-called Empire dresses worn by women at the dawn of the nineteenth century were often as sheer as today's nightgowns. To keep warm, women wore flesh-toned pantaloons, made of stockinette (a closely woven cotton) and reaching all the way to the ankles or to just below the knee. This is why, when seen in paintings of the era, women in Empire gowns often appear to be wearing no underwear at all, though the idea of "going commando" would not actually occur to anyone for at least two more centuries.

History of Fashion
SENIOR THESIS BY ELIZABETH NICHOLS

We feel safer with a madman who talks than with one who cannot open his mouth.

—*E. M. Cioran (1911–1995), Romania-born French philosopher*

I wake up to someone saying my name and gently shaking me.

"Lizzie. Lizzie, wake up. We're at your station."

I open my eyes with a start. I'd been dreaming about New York— of Shari and me moving there, and finding no better place to live than a cardboard refrigerator box on some kind of highway meridian, and my having to get a job folding T-shirts—miles and miles of capped-sleeved T-shirts—at the Gap.

I am startled to find I am not in New York but on a train. In France. That is stopped at my station. At least if the sign outside the window, silhouetted against the night sky (when did it get so dark out?), which says Souillac, is any indication.

"Oh no," I cry, hurtling out of my seat. "Oh. No."

"It's all right," Jean-Luc says soothingly. "I've got your bags here."

He does. My wheelie bag is down from the overhead rack, and he passes me the handle, along with my carry-on bag and purse.

"You're fine," he says with a chuckle at my panic. "They won't leave with you still on board."

"Oh," I say. My mouth tastes awful, from the wine. I can't believe I fell asleep. Had I been breathing on him? Had he smelled my disgusting wine breath? "I'm so sorry. Oh. It was so nice to meet you. Thank you so much for everything. You're so nice. I hope to see you again someday. Thanks again—"

Then I barrel from the train, saying, "*Pardon, pardon,*" the French way to everyone I bang into on my way out.

And then I'm standing on the platform. Which appears to be in the middle of nowhere. In the middle of the night.

All I can hear is crickets. There is a faint scent of woodsmoke in the air.

Around me, the other passengers who got out at the same time I did are being greeted by excited family members and escorted to waiting cars. There is a bus purring nearby that other passengers are climbing onto. The sign in the bus's windshield says Sarlat.

I have no idea what Sarlat is. All I know is the town of Souillac isn't much of a town. It appears, in fact, to be merely a train station.

Which is currently closed, if the locked door and dark windows are any indication.

This is not good. Because, despite the numerous messages I left informing her of my arrival time, Shari is not here to pick me up. I am stranded on a train platform in the middle of the French countryside.

All alone. All alone except for—

Someone beside me clears his throat. I spin around and smack—almost literally—into Jean-Luc. Who is standing behind me. With a big grin on his face.

"Hello again," he says.

"What—" I stare at him. Is he a figment of my imagination? Can blood clots form in your legs on trains and then travel to your brain? I'm almost sure not. They are from the air pressure in planes, right?

So he really is here. Standing in front of me. With a long, ex-

tremely bulky gray garment bag in his hands. As the train pulls
away.

"What are you *doing* here?" I shriek. "This isn't your stop!"

"How do you know? You never even asked where I was going."

This is totally true, I realize belatedly.

"But—but," I stammer, "you saw my ticket. You knew I was getting off at Souillac. You didn't say you were, too."

"No," Jean-Luc says, "I didn't."

"But . . . *why*?" I'm suddenly seized with a horrible thought. What
if charming, handsome Jean-Luc is some kind of serial killer? Who
woos vulnerable American girls on foreign trains, lulls them into a
false sense of trust, then kills them when they get to their destina-
tions? What if he's got some kind of scythe or garrote in that garment bag? He totally could. It looks awfully bulky. Way too bulky to
be a suit jacket or hemmed trousers.

I look around and see that the last car in the parking lot is pulling away—along with the Sarlat bus—leaving us alone on the platform. Totally alone.

"I wanted to tell you I was getting off at Souillac," Jean-Luc is
saying when I am able to focus on him, and not my complete and
utter lack of recourse if he starts trying to kill me, "but I was afraid
you'd feel embarrassed."

"About what?" I ask.

"Well," Jean-Luc says. He's starting to look a little sheepish in the
bright glare of the streetlamp, around which moths are throwing
themselves about as noisily as the crickets are chirping. Why does
he look sheepish? Because he realizes he has to kill me now and I'm
probably not going to like it? "I haven't exactly been honest with
you . . . I mean, you thought I was just some random stranger on a
train you could pour out all your problems to . . ."

"I'm really sorry about that," I say. My God, what kind of person
would kill another person just because she told her life story to him

on a train? This is totally unreasonable. All he had to do was pull out a book and pretend to read or something, and I'd have shut up. Probably. "I was very upset—"

"But it was so entertaining," Jean-Luc says with a shrug. "I have to tell you. I've never had a girl sit down next to me and start talking about—well, what you did. Ever."

This can't be happening. Why did I tell a total stranger so much about my personal life? Even a totally cute one in a Hugo shirt?

"I think you've got the wrong idea about me," I say, backing slowly toward the train platform's stairs. "I'm not that type of girl. I'm really not."

"Lizzie," Jean-Luc says. He takes a step toward me. He is not letting me back away toward the steps. "The reason I didn't tell you I was getting off at Souillac—besides the fact that you didn't ask—is because I'm *not* some random stranger you met on a train."

Oh, great. This is the part where he starts telling me something psychotic about how we knew each other in a past life. It's like T.J. from my freshman year all over again. Why am I such a weirdo magnet? WHY?

And he seemed so great back on the train! Really! He said I was fairly brave! He totally restored my faith in men! Why does he have to turn out to be a murdering psycho? WHY?

"Really," I say. This is all Shari's fault, of course. If she would just answer her freaking cell phone once in a while, none of this would be happening. "What do you mean?"

"I mean, I'm actually your host. Jean-Luc de Villiers? Your friend Shari's staying at my father's place, Mirac."

I stop backing up. I stop staring at the garment bag. I stop thinking about my imminent death.

Mirac. He said Mirac.

"I never told you the place I was going was called Mirac," I say. Because, while it's true I'd babbled almost nonstop to him, I don't remember ever saying the word *Mirac*. Which I'd actually forgotten until that very moment.

"No, you didn't," Jean-Luc says. "But that's where your friend Shari is staying, isn't it? With her boyfriend, Charles Pendergast?"

Charles Pendergast? He knows Chaz's real name! I *know* I never told him that. No one ever uses Chaz's real name, because he tells hardly anyone what it is.

Who would know Chaz's real name? Only someone who knew him. Well.

"Wait," I say, my mind lurching for some—*any*—reasonable explanation for what's happening. "You're . . . *Luke*? *Chaz's* friend Luke? But . . . you said your name was Jean-Luc."

"Well," Luke—or Luc—or Jean-Luc—or whatever his name is—says, still looking sheepish, "that's my full name. Jean-Luc de Villiers. But Chaz has always just called me Luke."

"But . . . but aren't you supposed to be at Mirac with Chaz and Shari?"

He swings the garment bag off his shoulder. "I had to go into Paris for the day to pick up my cousin's wedding gown. She didn't trust the shop's courier to get it here in one piece. See?"

He unzips the bag a little and a froth of white lace—unmistakably bridal—spills out. He tucks it back in and rezips.

"I never thought in a million years, when you sat down next to me, that you were the Lizzie I've heard so much about from Shari and Chaz. But then when you said Shari's name, I knew it. But by that time you'd already mentioned . . . you know." Now he looks more embarrassed than sheepish. "And I knew you'd only done that because you thought you were never going to see me again . . ."

"Oh," I say, feeling suddenly sick to my stomach. Since that's exactly what I HAD thought to myself. "My. God."

"Yeah," Luke says with a very French shrug. For an American.

Which makes sense. Since he's half French. "Sorry about that. Although you have to admit . . . it's kind of funny."

"No," I say, "it's really not."

"Yeah." He sighs, not smiling anymore. "I sort of guessed you'd see it that way. That's why I didn't tell you."

"So you knew," I say, feeling my cheeks heating up. "You knew all along we'd be seeing each other again. A lot. And you didn't try to stop me. You just let me go on and on like that. Like a moron."

"No, not like a moron," he says, *really* not smiling anymore. In fact, he looks a little worried. "Nothing like that. I thought you were really charming. And funny. That's why I didn't try to stop you. I mean, in the first place, I didn't know, until you were almost through with your—um, venting—who you were. I just knew you needed to vent, and so I let you, because I actually enjoyed it. I thought you were sweet."

"Oh God!" I want to throw his garment bag over my head and hide in it. "*Sweet?* Talking about how I gave my boyfriend a blow job?"

"You talked about it in a very sweet manner," Luke assures me.

"I'm going to kill myself," I say from between my fingers, since I've buried my burning face in my hands.

"Hey."

I hear footsteps, then feel hands go around my wrists. I look up, startled, and find that Luke has laid the garment bag across my suitcase and is standing very, very close to me, looking down into my face while gently pulling my hands from my eyes.

"Hey," he says again, his voice as gentle as his touch. "Seriously. I'm sorry. I wasn't thinking. I didn't . . . I didn't know what to do. I wanted to tell you, but then I thought . . . well, I thought it would be a funny joke. But. Like I said. Jokes aren't really my thing."

I am intensely aware of how dark his eyes are—as dark as the tree branches behind the train station, silhouetted against the navy-blue sky—and how kissable his lips look. Especially since they're only just a few inches away from mine.

"If you tell anyone," I hear myself say in a voice that has gone strangely throaty, "about what I told you on the train—especially Chaz—I will kill you. About my not finishing my thesis yet AND the other thing. The you-know-what. You can't tell *anyone*. Do you understand? I will *kill* you if you do."

"I totally understand," Luke says, his grip on my wrists even firmer now that I've dropped my hands from my face. He's essentially holding them in his big warm hands. And it feels nice. Really nice. "You have my complete and total word. I won't say a thing. Your blow job is totally safe with me."

"Ack!" I cry. "I mean it! Don't mention those words again!"

"What words?" he asks. Now his dark eyes are as lit up as the smattering of stars I see winking down at us, like sequins on a blue cashmere sweater set. "Blow job?"

"Stop it," I say, and let myself sway toward him.

Just in case, you know, he wants to kiss me.

Because I'm starting to realize that the fact that Luke is Jean-Luc is hardly what anyone can call bad news. Considering that now I don't have to worry about getting hold of Shari. And about where I'm going to stay tonight.

Not to mention the fact that he's the nicest, hottest guy I've met in a really long time. Who doesn't have an addiction to Texas Hold'em . . . that I know of, anyway.

And that he seems to like me.

And that I'm going to be spending the rest of the summer with him.

And that he's holding my hands.

Suddenly things are looking up. Way up.

"So," Luke says, "am I forgiven?"

"You're forgiven," I say. I can't help smiling up at him like the moron he claims I'm not. He's just so . . . cute.

And not just cute, either. He's nice, too. I mean, he bought me dinner.

And he was totally sympathetic when I was crying like a maniac.

Plus he's an investment banker. He's working hard to . . . protect rich people's money. Or something.

And he made me laugh instead of cry after I got off the phone with Andy.

And I'm going to be with him. All summer. All—

"Good," Luke says. "Because I'd hate for you to think you were wrong. You know, about my character assessment. The one you made based on my clothes."

"I don't think," I say, lowering my gaze to the opening of his shirt, where I see a few promising-looking chest hairs poking out, "that I'm wrong."

"Good," he says again. "I think you're really going to like Mirac."

I *know* I'm going to like it, I think—but for once restrain myself from saying out loud—if *you're* there, Luke.

"Thanks," I say. And wonder if he's going to kiss me now.

And then we both hear a car coming and Luke says, "Oh, great. Here's our ride." And abruptly drops my wrists.

And an ancient butter-yellow convertible Mercedes pulls into the parking lot, driven by a honey-colored blonde who calls out in a French accent, "Sorry I'm late, *chéri!*"

And I know, even before he hurries down to kiss her, who she is.

His girlfriend.

It so figures.

Women were not the only ones who were interested in showing off their figures in the early 1800s. This period saw the introduction of the "dandy," followers of the fashion icon George "Beau" Brummell, a gentleman who insisted his trousers fit tightly as a second skin and could not abide a wrinkle in his waistcoat. A dandy's neckwear consisted of a collar so high he could not turn his head from side to side.

It is not known how many gentlemen met their deaths from stepping out in front of oncoming carriages they failed to see.

History of Fashion
SENIOR THESIS BY ELIZABETH NICHOLS

12

Gossip is the opiate of the oppressed.
—*Erica Jong (1942–), U.S. educator and author*

Because of course he has a girlfriend. He's way too fabulous not to—that little keeping-his-true-identity-a-secret-from-me thing aside.

The thing is, she seems really nice. She's definitely gorgeous, with all that hair and her slim tanned shoulders and long, equally tanned legs. She's wearing a very simple black tank top and a longish peasant skirt (new, not vintage, and expensive-looking, too) with jeweled flip-flops. She's definitely in vacation mode.

Although my fashion radar may be off, because Dominique Desautels—that's her name—like Andy, is foreign. She's Canadian. *French* Canadian. She works at the same investment banking company in Houston that Luke does.

And they've been going out for six months.

At least that's what I'm able to gather from my careful questioning of them both from the backseat of the Mercedes before my voice dies.

Because it's very hard to concentrate on gathering information about the two of them when we're whizzing past such beautiful scenery. The sun has set, but the moon's rising, so I can still make out enormous oaks, their branches twisting across the road to make a sort of canopy of leaves above us. We're careening down a twisting two-lane country road that winds alongside a wide, burbling river. It's hard to tell, judging by the scenery, where, exactly, we are.

Or even *when* we are. Judging by the lack of telephone poles and streetlights, this could be *any* century, not just the twenty-first. We even pass an old-fashioned mill—a mill! With one of those big paddle wheels on the side of it!—with a thatched roof and beautiful garden.

There are electric lights on in the windows of the mill, though, indicating that this isn't the 1800s.

Still, I see a family in there, sitting down to dinner.

In a millhouse!

It's very hard to remember that I am depressed about my boyfriend turning out to have a gambling problem when the scenery whizzing past me is so picturesque.

Then we pass out from beneath the canopy of trees and I see towering cliffs above us, with castles on top of them, and Luke explains that this area of France (known as the Dordogne, after the river) is famous for its castles, having over a thousand of them, as well as for its caves, on the walls of some of which are paintings dating back to 15,000 BCE.

Then Dominique adds that Périgord, which is the part of the Dordogne we are in, is also known for its black truffles and foie gras. I am barely listening, though. It's hard not to be distracted by the sight of a set of high-fortified walls—Luke says they belong to the ancient medieval village of Sarlat, and that we can go there to shop if I want to.

Shop! They couldn't possibly have a vintage store there. But maybe a thrift shop . . . God, could you imagine the finds just waiting for someone like me? Givenchy, Dior, Chanel . . . who KNOWS?

Then we turn off the road onto what appears to be a very steep gravel-covered mountain track, barely wide enough for the car to pass. Branches, in fact, are whipping the side of it—and nearly me, as well, until I move into the middle of the backseat.

Dominique notices when I move and says, "You've got to get the men to trim that back before your mother gets here, Jean-Luc. You know how she is."

Luke says, "I know, I know," and then, to me, says, "You all right back there?"

"I'm good," I say, clutching the back of the seats in front of me. I am being bounced around quite a bit. The driveway—if that's what it is—needs some maintenance.

And then, just when I think the shuddering car can't take it anymore—and am starting to wonder if we'll ever reach the top of this hill, or if tree limbs are going to whip our heads off first—we burst through the last of the trees onto a wide, grassy plateau overlooking the valley below. Bright torches line the driveway, leading up to what appears to be—if my eyes are not deceiving me—the same house Mr. Darcy lived in in the A&E version of *Pride and Prejudice*.

Only this mansion is bigger. And more elegant-looking. With more outbuildings.

And it has electric light, which is making what looks like hundreds of windows blaze brightly against the blue satin sky. Arcing out from the circular driveway is a wide lawn dotted with huge, elegant oak trees, a massive swimming pool—lit up and gleaming like a sapphire in the night—and a scattering of white wrought-iron lawn furniture.

It is the most perfect place for a wedding that I have ever seen. The entire well-manicured lawn is fenced in with a low stone wall. All I can see beyond the wall, which appears to drop off into thin air, is a vast expanse of moonlit trees, far below, and then, off in the distance, another cliff like the one we're on, topped by a château that could be a sister to this one, its own lights blazing in the night sky.

It is breathtaking. Literally. I find I've stopped breathing, gazing at it all.

Luke pulls the car into the circular driveway and switches the motor off. All I can hear is crickets.

"Well?" he says, turning around in his seat. "What do you think?"

I am, for the first time in my life, speechless. It is an historic occasion, but Luke doesn't even know it.

The crickets sound very loud in the silence that follows Luke's question. I still can't breathe.

"Yes," Dominique says, getting out of the car and heading toward the château's massive oak doors, the garment bag with the wedding gown in it in both her hands. "It tends to have that effect on people. It's pretty, isn't it?"

Pretty? *Pretty?* That's like calling the Grand Canyon big.

"It's," I say, not finally finding my voice until Dominique has gone inside and Luke is helping me pull my suitcases from the trunk, "the most beautiful place I've ever seen."

"Really?" Luke looks down at me, his dark eyes hooded in the moonlight. "Do you think so?"

He keeps saying he's bad at telling jokes. But he has to be kidding me. There can't be any more beautiful place on the entire planet.

"Completely," I say, though even that seems like a total understatement.

And then I hear familiar voices from the grassy terrace overlooking the valley.

"Is that Monsieur de Villiers, returned from Paris?" Chaz, striding out from the shadows of one of the massive trees, demands. "Why, yes, it is. And who is that with him?"

Then, midway across the circular drive, Chaz stops, recognizing me. It's hard to tell, with the moon at his back—and the bill of his University of Michigan baseball cap pulled low over his eyes, as always—but I think he's smiling.

"Well, well, well," he says in a pleased way. "Look what the cat drug in."

"What?" And Shari appears behind him. "Oh, hi, Luke. Did you get the—"

Then her voice trails off. And a second later she shrieks, "LIZZIE? IS THAT YOU?"

Then she's leaping across the driveway and all over me, and shouting, "You came! You came! I can't believe you came! How did you get here? Luke, where did you find her?"

"On the train," Luke says, smiling at the panicky look I throw him over Shari's shoulder as she's hugging me.

But he doesn't elaborate. Just like I'd asked him not to.

"But that's amazing," Shari cries. "I mean, that you two, of all people, would run into each other—"

"Not really," Chaz says mildly. "I mean, considering they were probably the only two Americans heading for Souillac—"

"Oh, not another one of your philosophical speeches on the nature of randomness," Shari says to Chaz. "PLEASE." To me, she cries, "But why didn't you call? We'd have met you at the station."

"I *did* call," I say. "About a hundred times. But I kept getting your voice mail."

"That's impossible," Shari says, pulling her cell phone out of the pocket of her shorts. "I have my . . . Oh." She squints at the screen in the moonlight. "I forgot to turn it on this morning."

"I figured you'd dropped it in the toilet," I said.

"Not this time," Chaz says, wrapping an arm around my shoulders to give me a quick welcoming hug. As he does so, he whispers, "Is there anybody back in England that I have to beat up? Because, with God as my witness, I'll go over there and kick his scrawny naked ass for you. Just say the word."

"No," I assure him, laughing a little painfully. "It's okay. Really. It's as much my fault as it is his. I should have listened to you. You were right. You're always right."

"Not always," Chaz says, dropping his arm. "It's just that the times I'm wrong don't register in your memory with as much clarity as the times I'm right. Still, go right ahead thinking I'm always right if you want to."

"Cut it out, Chaz," Shari says. "Who cares about what happened in England, anyway? She's here now. It's okay if she stays, right, Luke?"

"I don't know," Luke says teasingly. "Can she pull her weight? We don't need any more slackers around here. We've already got this one." He slaps Chaz on the shoulder.

"Hey," Chaz says, "I'm helping out. I'm testing all the alcohol for purity and freshness before Luke's mom gets here."

Shari shakes her head at her boyfriend and says, "You're insufferable." To Luke, she says, "Lizzie's superhandy. Well, with a needle. If you've got any seamstressy stuff to do . . ."

Luke seems surprised to learn that I can actually sew. Most people are. It's not something many people know how to do anymore.

"I just might," he says. "I'll check with, ahem, Mom when she gets here tomorrow. But right now I think we have more pressing concerns—helping Chaz with the alcohol testing."

"This way, ladies," Chaz says, indicating, with a courtly bow, the path to the outdoor bar he's apparently set up, "and gentleman."

Shari and I follow the guys into the cool, slightly damp grass. As we get closer to the low stone wall, I glance over it and see the valley stretched below, the river—just as Chaz promised—winking in the moonlight like a long, silver snake. It is so beautiful my throat catches. I feel as if I am in a daze. Or a dream.

And I am not the only one.

"I can't believe this," Shari whispers, still hanging on to my arm. "What happened? I know I was pretty drunk last time I talked to you, but I thought you said you were going to try to work things out with Andy."

"Yeah," I whisper back. "Well, I did try. But then I found out—well, it's a long story. I'll tell you sometime when"—I nod my head in Luke and Chaz's direction—"*they're* not around."

Although of course Luke already knows most of it.

Well, okay. All of it.

And I do mean *all*.

"Was it bad?" Shari asks, concern creasing her pretty face. "Are you okay?"

"I'm fine," I assure her. "Really. I wasn't before, but . . ." I glance in Luke's direction again. "Well, I had a very sympathetic shoulder to cry on."

Shari's dark-eyed gaze follows mine. I see her eyebrows go up beneath her curly bangs. I wonder what she's thinking. Not, I hope, *Oh, poor little Lizzie, in love with a guy so out of her league.*

Because I'm not. In love with him, I mean.

But all she says is, "Well, I'm glad about that. So your heart's not broken?"

"You know," I say thoughtfully, "I don't think it is. A little bruised, is all. Is it really all right that I'm here? What's Chaz talking about, Luke's mom coming tomorrow?"

Shari grimaces. "Luke's mom and dad are getting divorced, but apparently she—Mrs. de Villiers—promised her niece a long time ago that she could get married at Mirac. So she—Mrs. de Villiers, I mean—is arriving tomorrow, with her sister, the niece, the groom—the whole family. It should be a helluva party. Especially considering Luke's parents are barely speaking, and he's caught up in the middle of the whole thing. According to Chaz, Luke's mom is some kind of battle-ax."

I wince, remembering Dominique's warning about Luke needing to get the brush along the driveway cleared before his mom's arrival.

"So they won't want me here," I whisper, to make sure Luke doesn't overhear us. I say *they,* but I mean Luke, of course. "I mean, I don't want to crash—"

"Lizzie, it's *totally* okay," Shari says. "This place is huge, and there's plenty of room. Even with Luke's entire extended family here, there are rooms to spare. And there'll be plenty to do. It's actually good you're here. We could use the help. Apparently this niece—Luke's cousin, Vicky—is some kind of Texas socialite. She already browbeat Luke into making the trip to Paris and back just to pick up her dress from the fancy Parisian seamstress who made it, and she's not even here yet. Plus, she's apparently invited half of Houston for this wedding, including her brother's garage band, who just got some kind of recording contract and are supposed to be the Next Hot Thing. So it's not exactly going to be intimate."

"Oh," I say. "Well, good. Because I really couldn't think what else to do other than come here. I couldn't go home—"

"Of course you couldn't," Shari says, sounding horrified. "Your sisters would have had a field day!"

"I know," I say. "So I just figured . . . well, you'd said it was okay to come here—"

"I'm so glad you did. I mean, look at the two of them." She nods toward her boyfriend and Luke, who've drifted over to one of the wrought-iron tables and are mixing up some kind of concoction in fluted champagne glasses. "They're like long-lost twins. All they do is yak, yak, yak about everything under the sun—Nietzsche, Tiger Woods, beer, the probability of coincident birth dates, the good old days at prep school. I've been feeling like a total third wheel." She puts her arm around me. "But now I've got my own friend to yak with."

"Well," I say with a grin, "you know I'm always good for a bit of yaking. But what about Luke's girlfriend, Dominique? You can't yak with her?"

Shari makes a face. "Sure. If you want to yak about Dominique."

"Oh," I say. "I sort of got the idea, what with the flip-flops."

"Really?" Shari looks interested. She's always valued my fashion analyses. "They give you a bad vibe?"

"No," I say hastily. "Nothing like that. Just sort of like she's trying too hard. But then she's Canadian. I think my radar is off when it comes to foreigners."

Shari winces. "You mean Andy? Yeah, well, I always did wonder what you saw in him. But you're not wrong about Dominique. Those flip-flops? They're Manolo Blahniks."

"No!" Manolo Blahnik flip-flops, I know from my *Vogue* perusing, can cost upward of six hundred dollars. "Gosh. I always wondered who bought them—"

"Hey, you two." Chaz strolls across the moonlit grass toward us. "No shirking your duties. There's alcohol to inspect."

"Hang on." Luke is one step behind him. "I've got their first test subjects here." He hands each of us a champagne flute filled with sparkling liquid. "Kir royales," he says, "with champagne made right here at Mirac."

I don't know what a kir royale is, but I'm game to try one. Dominique reappears and lays claim to a glass as well.

"What shall we drink to?" she asks, raising her glass.

"How about," Luke says, "to strangers meeting on a train."

I smile at him across the few feet of grass separating us.

"Sounds good to me," I say, and clink glasses with everyone. Then I take a sip.

It is like drinking liquid gold. The mingled flavors of berry, sunlight, and champagne dance on my tongue. Kir royale turns out to be champagne with a sort of liqueur in it—cassis, Shari explains, which is a type of berry.

"Now *you* explain something to me," Shari says when she's through with her cassis commentary.

"Hmm?" I am pretty fairly convinced by now that this is all just a dream from which I'm going to wake up eventually. But until that moment, I plan on enjoying myself. "What's that?"

"What did Luke mean with that toast? Strangers on a train and all that?"

"Oh." I glance over at him, where he's laughing with Chaz. "I don't know. Nothing."

Shari narrows her eyes at me. "Don't you nothing me, Lizzie. Spill. What happened on that train?"

"Nothing!" I cry, laughing a little myself. "Well, I mean, I was upset—you know, about Andy. And I cried a bit. But like I said . . . he was very sympathetic."

Shari just shakes her head. "There's more to this story. Something you aren't telling me. I know it."

"There's not," I assure her.

"Well," Shari says, "if there is, I know I'll find out eventually. You've never kept a secret in your life."

I just smile at her. There are a couple of secrets I've managed to keep from her so far. And I don't plan on spilling them anytime soon.

But all I say is, "Really, Shari. Nothing happened."

Which is, basically, the truth.

A little while later, I stroll toward the low stone wall and stand there, trying to take it all in—the valley; the moon rising over the roof of the château across from ours; the starry night sky; the crickets; the sweet smell of some kind of night-blooming flower.

It's too much. It's all too much. To go from that horrible little office in the Job Centre to this, all in one day . . .

Beside me, Luke, who has somehow managed to break away from Chaz and Dominique for a minute, asks softly, "Better now?"

"Getting there," I reply, smiling up at him. "I can't thank you enough for letting me stay here. And thanks for . . . you know. Not telling them. Anything."

He looks genuinely surprised. "Of course," he says. "What else are friends for?"

Friends. So that's what we are.

And somehow, there in the moonlight? That's more than enough.

The Romantic movement of the 1820s brought back a yearning for narrow-waisted heroines like the ones in the novels of Sir Walter Scott (the Dan Brown of his day—though Sir Walter would not have dared dress a French heroine in a big sweater and black leggings, as Mr. Brown did poor Sophie Neveu in *The Da Vinci Code*), and corsets gained popularity while skirts became wider. So beloved was Sir Walter that a brief craze for tartan overtook a few of the less sensible ladies of the time, though thankfully they soon realized the error of their ways.

History of Fashion
SENIOR THESIS BY ELIZABETH NICHOLS

13

I should not talk so much about myself if there were anybody else whom I knew as well.
—*Henry David Thoreau (1817–1862),*
U.S. philosopher, author, and naturalist

When I wake up the following morning, I look around the tiny, low-ceilinged room I'm in, with its bright white walls and dark wood rafters, in confusion. The curtains—cream-colored, with large pink roses splotched on them—are drawn across the room's single window, so I can't see outside. For a second I can't remember where I am—whose bedroom, or even what *country.*

Then I see the old-fashioned door, with its latch you press down on instead of turn—like the latch to a garden gate—and I realize I'm at Château Mirac. In one of the dozen attic bedrooms—which, in the château's glory days, housed the serving staff—and which now house Shari, Chaz, and myself—not to mention Jean-Luc and his girlfriend, Dominique.

That's because the château's formal bedrooms, below us, are reserved for the wedding party—and guests—that are due to arrive this afternoon. While renting out the main house, Luke's father—whom Shari refers to as Monsieur de Villiers—stays in a small thatched-roofed cottage near the outbuildings, where he keeps the oak casks of his wine before it's ready for bottling. Shari told me last night, as we climbed the seemingly hundreds of stairs to our rooms after four—or was it five?—more kir royales, that birds regularly nest in the thatch and have to be chased away lest their waste eat through the roof.

Somehow a thatched roof will never seem picturesque to me again.

After blinking groggily at the cracks in the ceiling above, I realize what's wakened me. Someone is knocking on the door.

"Lizzie," I hear Shari say, "are you up yet? It's noon. What are you going to do, sleep all day?"

I throw back the duvet and rush to the door to hurl it open. Shari is standing there in a bikini and a sarong holding two enormous, steaming mugs. Her hair, which is normally dark and curly, is look-ing enormous, a sure sign that it's hot outside.

"Is it really noon?" I ask, freaking out that I slept so long and wondering if people—okay, Luke—are going to think I'm a rude slacker.

"Five after," Shari says. "I hope you brought a swimsuit. We've got to try to catch as many rays as we can before Luke's mom and her guests arrive and we have to start setting things up for the meals and wine tastings. That only gives us about four hours. But first"—she thrusts one of the steaming mugs at me—"cappuccino. Lots of aspartame, just the way you like it."

"Oh," I say appreciatively as the milky steam bathes my face. "You are a lifesaver."

"I know," Shari says, and comes into the room to make herself comfortable on the end of my rumpled bed. "Now. I want to know everything that happened with Andy. And with Luke, on the train. So spill."

I do, settling in beside her. Well, I don't tell her *everything*, of course. I've still never told her the truth about my thesis, and I'm definitely never telling her about the blow job. Of course, I told a total stranger on a train about both. But somehow that was much

easier than telling my best friend, who would, I know, only disap-
prove of both—especially the latter. I mean, a blow job, without re-
ciprocation, is the height of antifeminism.

"So," Shari says when I'm through, "you and Andy are really
over."

"Definitely," I say, sipping the last of my delicious cappuccino.

"You told him that. You told him it's over."

"Totally," I say. Didn't I? I think I did.

"Lizzie." Shari gives me a hard look. "I know how much you hate
confrontation. Did you *really* tell him it's over?"

"I told him I need to be alone," I say . . . realizing, a little belatedly, that that's not the same thing as telling someone it's over.

Still, Andy got the message. I *know* he did.

But just in case, maybe I won't pick up if he calls again.

"And you're really okay with that?" Shari wants to know.

"Mostly," I say. "I mean, I guess I feel pretty guilty about the
money—"

"What money?"

"The money he wanted to borrow," I say. "For his matriculation
fees. I probably should have given it to him. Because now he's not
going to be able to go to school in the fall—"

"Lizzie," Shari says in tones of disbelief, "he *had* the money . . .
he gambled it away! If you'd given him more, he just would have
gambled that away, too. You'd have been enabling him to continue
his destructive behavior. Is that what you want? To be an enabler?"

"No," I say mournfully, "but, you know. I did really love him. You
can't turn love on and off, like a faucet."

"You can if the guy's trying to take advantage of your generous
nature."

"I guess." I sigh. "I really shouldn't feel bad. He *was* getting unemployment money while being employed."

One corner of Shari's mouth turns up. "I love how, to you, that's obviously the worst thing he did. What about the gambling? What about the fat thing?"

"But cheating the government is way worse than either of those."

"Okay. If you say so. Anyway, good riddance to him. Now will you stop being such a pain in my ass and just move to New York with me and Chaz?"

"Shari," I say. "Really. I just—" How can I tell her the truth? That I can't possibly go job-hunting in New York City without a college degree, and I don't know if I'll be done with my thesis by the time she and Chaz are ready to leave. Also the whole even-if-I-have-a-degree-I'm-not-so-sure-I-can-make-it-in-the-big-city thing.

"Fine," Shari says, clearly misinterpreting my reluctance. "I get it. It's a big step. You need time to adjust to the idea. I know. Well, what about the other thing?"

"What other thing?"

"About you and Luke. On that train."

"Shari, I already told you. Nothing happened. I mean, come on. I just got out of a disastrous relationship with a guy I hardly knew. You think I'm going to rush into another one right away? Give me some credit. Besides, have you had a good look at his girlfriend? Why would a guy who has that go for a girl like me?"

"I can think of a few reasons," Shari says darkly.

But before I have a chance to ask what she means, she says, "All right, listen. I know you've been through a lot the past couple days, so I won't bug you about the New York thing for a while. How about you take some time off from worrying about the future? God knows you deserve it. Consider the next few days a well-earned vacation. We'll revisit the subject later, when you've had a chance to recover from finding out that the man of your dreams was actually more of a nightmare. Now"—she smacks me on the leg—"throw on your suit and meet me at the pool. We have tanning to do."

I don't argue. I hurry to grab my beauty supplies so I can have a quick wash before hitting the pool.

"And hurry up," she says before stomping away. "Prime tanning hours are a-wasting."

I rush to comply, since Shari doesn't like having her orders disobeyed. I dart across the hall into an ancient bathroom that comes complete with a massive claw-foot tub and a toilet with a wooden seat and one of those chain-pull flushers. After a quick bath and makeup application, I pull on my bikini—the first time I've ever worn one in my life. My sisters used to mock me mercilessly every time I tried to put a two-piece on, back in my pre-weight-loss days.

Of course, that might have been because all my bathing suits were vintage one-pieces, many of which had built-in little skirts and had a distinct Annette Funicello flare to them.

Still, while I may have been the chubbiest girl at the pool, I was always the most originally dressed . . . or, as Rose used to put it, the biggest "fashion freak."

My new suit doesn't make me look like a freak at all. At least, I don't think so. It's a two-piece, but it's vintage, too . . . vintage Lilly Pulitzer, from the sixties. Sarah used to say it was gross to wear someone else's old swimsuit, but it's actually perfectly hygienic if you wash it a few times before you wear it.

Now, checking out my reflection in the somewhat dim but otherwise fairly reliable mirror on the back of the bathroom door, I think I look . . . all right. I'm no Dominique, of course. But then, who among us can be?

Except, of course, for Dominique.

I hurry back to my room, tug a matching Lilly Pulitzer sundress over my suit, and hurriedly make my bed, pausing to throw back the rose curtains, then open the small diamond-shaped window so I can let in some fresh air . . .

And catch my breath, struck by what I see out my window . . .

Which is nothing less than the daylight view of the valley stretching out below the château. Green velvet treetops and rolling hills, pale brown cliffsides and, high above it all, the bluest, most cloudless sky I have ever seen.

And it's all so beautiful. I can see, seemingly, for miles, nothing but trees, and the silver river winding through them, dotted by tiny village hamlets, with the occasional château or castle perched on a cliffside above. It's like something out of a book of fairy tales.

How can Luke, I wonder, go back to Houston after having spent any amount of time here? How can anyone go *anywhere* else?

But I don't have time to mull over this. I have to meet Shari at the pool or face her wrath.

It's no joke, trying to find my way back downstairs through the myriad hallways and staircases that seem to make up Château Mirac, but I manage somehow to end up in the marble foyer, and slip outside into the soft, sweetly scented summer air. Somewhere in the distance I hear the whine of a motor—possibly a lawn mower, judging by the smell of freshly cut grass—and the tinkle of . . . cowbells? It can't be.

Or can it?

I don't pause to investigate. I put on my rhinestone-studded sunglasses, then hurry across the driveway, and finally across the lawn to the pool, where I see Shari, Dominique, and another girl all stretched out across chaise longues with blue-and-white striped cushions. The chaise longues face the valley, and the sun. Dominique and the other girl are already brown—this is undoubtedly not the first day they've spent lying out. Shari, I can see, is determined to gain on them before the summer is over.

"Good morning," I say to Dominique and the other girl, who is on the chubby side and looks like a teenager. She's in a blue one-piece Speedo while Dominique, beside her, is in a black Calvin Klein string bikini.

And the strings don't seem to be tied very tightly.

"*Bonjour*," the teenager says to me cheerfully.

"Lizzie, this is Agnès," Shari says. Only she pronounces it the French way, which is *Ahn-yes*. "She's staying here for the summer as the resident au pair. Her family lives in the millhouse down the road."

"Oh!" I cry. "I saw the millhouse! It's so beautiful!"

Agnès continues to smile at me pleasantly. It's Dominique who says, "Don't bother. She doesn't understand a word of English. She claimed she did when she applied to work here, but she doesn't, beyond hello, good-bye, and thank you."

"Oh," I say. And smile back at Agnès. "*Bonjour! Je m'appelle Lizzie*," which pretty much exhausts what French phrases I know, with the exception of *Excusez-moi* and *J'aime pas des tomates*.

Agnès says a lot of stuff back to me, none of which I understand. Shari says, "Just smile and nod and you two'll get along fine."

And so I do. Agnès beams at me, then hands me a white towel and a bottle of cold water from a cooler she's brought with her. I wonder if there's any diet Coke in the cooler, but a glimpse before she closes the lid tells me there's not. Do they even HAVE diet Coke in France? They must. It's not the Third World, for crying out loud.

I thank Agnès for the water and spread the towel out on the chaise longue between hers and Dominique's. I peel off my dress, then kick off my sandals. Then I lie back against the comfy cushion and find myself gazing at a cloudless blue sky.

This, I realize, is something I could get used to. Fast. England, and its cool, moist air, seems a long time ago.

So, for that matter, does Andy.

"That's an . . . unusual swimsuit," Dominique says.

"Thank you," I say, even though I have a sneaking suspicion she didn't mean it as a compliment. But I'm probably just projecting again, on account of the six-hundred-dollar flip-flops. "So where are Luke and Chaz?"

"Trimming the branches along the driveway," Shari says.

"Ouch," I say. "Don't they have—I don't know. A tree-trimming company who does that?"

Dominique shoots me a very sarcastic look from behind her Gucci sunglasses.

"Certainly—if someone had thought to call them in time. But as usual, Jean-Luc's father waited until the last minute and couldn't get anyone. So now Jean-Luc has to do it, if he doesn't want Bibi to have a fit when she arrives."

"Bibi?"

"Jean-Luc's mother," Dominique explains.

"Mrs. de Villiers is kind of . . . particular, from what I understand," Shari says tonelessly from her chaise longue.

Dominique lets out a delicate snort. "You could say that," she says. "You could also say, of course, that she's merely frustrated by her husband's complete and total absentmindedness. All he thinks about are his stupid grapes."

"Grapes?"

Dominique waves a hand behind us, toward some of the château's outbuildings behind which I'd seen some kind of orchard stretching.

"The vineyard," she says.

So it was a vineyard, not an orchard! Of course!

"Oh," I say. "Well, shouldn't Monsieur de Villiers think about his grapes? This place is primarily a vineyard, isn't it? Isn't the wedding thing just sort of a side business?"

"Of course," Dominique says, "but Mirac hasn't had a decent harvest in years. First there were the droughts, then a blight . . . anyone else would take this as a hint to move on, but not Jean-Luc's father. He says the de Villiers family has been in the wine business since the 1600s, when Mirac was first built, and he's not going to be the one to give up on it."

"Well," I say admiringly, "that's kind of . . . noble. I mean, isn't it?"

Dominique makes a disgusted noise. "Noble? It is a total waste. Mirac has got such tremendous potential, if only Jean-Luc and his father would see it."

"Potential?" What is she talking about? It's gorgeous the way it is. The perfect grounds, the beautiful house, the frothy cappuccino . . . what needs changing?

Dominique has a few suggestions, it turns out.

"Well, it's obviously in terrible need of updating. The place needs a total renovation—particularly the bathrooms. We need to replace those tacky claw-foot tubs with Jacuzzis . . . and pull-chain toilets! My God. They have to go as well."

"I kind of like the pull-chain toilets," I say. "I think they're sort of . . . charming."

"Well, yes, of course *you* would think that," Dominique says, and raises an eyebrow meaningfully in the direction of my swimsuit. "But most people do not. The kitchen, too, needs a total overhaul. Do you know they still have a—what do you call it? Oh yes. A larder. Ridiculous. No chef in his right mind could be hired who would work under the current conditions."

"Chef?" I say. And even as I think of cooking food, my stomach rumbles. I'm starving. I know I've missed breakfast, but when's lunch? Is there really a chef? Did he make the cappuccino?

"But of course. In order to turn Mirac into a true world-class hotel, it will need a five-star Michelin chef."

Oh. So . . .

"Turn it into a . . ." I sit up and stare down at Dominique. "Wait. They're thinking of turning this place into a *hotel*?"

"Not yet," Dominique says, reaching for a bottle of water she has sitting by her chaise longue. "But as I keep telling Jean-Luc, they ought to. Just think of the fortune that could be made in cor-porate retreat and convention business alone! And then, of course, there's the spa route—they could easily get rid of the vineyards—turn them into jogging paths or horseback-riding trails—and convert the outbuildings into massage, acupuncture, and hydro-therapy rooms. The plastic surgery recovery industry is booming right now—"

"The what?" I interrupt. I'm sorry to say I yelled it, too. But I was just so shocked at the idea of anyone wanting to turn this fabulous place into a *spa.*

"The plastic surgery recovery industry," Dominique repeats, looking annoyed. "People who've recently undergone liposuction or a face-lift need a place to recover, and I've always thought Mirac would be outstanding in that capacity—"

I can't help it. I have to look over to see what Shari thinks about all this.

But she merely holds the book she is pretending to read even closer to her face, in order to hide her expression.

Still, I can see her shoulders shaking. She can't stop laughing.

"Really," Dominique goes on, taking another sip of her water. "The de Villiers family has failed to see the entrepreneurial poten-tial of this property. By hiring trained professional servers—instead of the local riffraff—and offering services such as broadband and satellite television—installing air-conditioning, and perhaps even a home movie theater—they will attract a much wealthier clientele. And turn over a much bigger profit than Jean-Luc's father's puny wine business ever has."

Before I can make any sort of reply to this horrifying speech, my stomach chooses to do my talking for me, letting out an extremely loud gurgle of hunger. Dominique ignores it, but Agnès sits up and babbles something that sounds like a question. I do hear the word *goûter,* which I know means "to taste."

"She wants to know if you want her to get you something to eat," Dominique translates in a bored voice.

I say, "Oh. Uh . . ."

Agnès babbles some more, and Dominique says in the same bored voice, "It's no trouble. She's getting herself a snack anyway."

"Oh," I say. "Then, yes, thank you, I'd love one." I beam at Agnès and say, *"Oui, merci."* Then I add, *"Est-ce que vous . . . Est-ce que vous . . ."*

"What are you trying to ask her?" Dominique asks—a little waspishly, I think. But maybe I'm projecting, because of the liposuction thing. I'm still having a hard time believing that she really wants to turn this beautiful place into one of those hotels where they send contestants on *The Swan* after they get their new noses.

"I wanted to know if they've got any diet Coke," I say.

Dominique makes a face. "Of course not. Why would you want to put those kinds of terrible chemicals in your body?"

Because they're delicious, I want to say. But instead I say, "Oh. Okay. Then . . . nothing."

Dominique snaps something at Agnès, who nods, leaps up from her towel, stuffs her feet into a pair of rubber clogs—which seem like the appropriate footwear for walking through gravel and grass. WAY more appropriate than suede Manolos—grabs her sarong, and takes off for the house.

"Wow," I say. "She's so nice."

"She's *supposed* to do what you say. She's the *help*," Dominique says.

I look over at Shari. "Um . . . but aren't we, too? The help, I mean?"

"But you aren't expected to fetch and carry for people," Dominique says. "And you mustn't *vous* her."

"I'm sorry." I shake my head. "I mustn't *what*?"

"You *vous*'d her," Dominique says. "When you tried to speak

French to her just now. That isn't proper. She's younger than you, and she's a servant. You should *tu* her—the informal version of *you*—*tu* as opposed to *vous*. You'll give her airs above her station. Not that she doesn't already suffer from them—I don't actually think it's appropriate for her to be using the pool during her time off. But Jean-Luc said it was all right, so now there's no getting rid of her."

I sit there gaping at her some more, completely unable to believe the words that have just come out of Dominique's mouth. Shari, for her part, is actually covering her face with her book, she's trying so hard not to let it show how much she's laughing.

As if Dominique would even notice. Not when she's busy doing what she does next, which is say, "It's *so* hot . . ."

Which, actually, it is. It's broiling out. In fact, before Dominique started in on that *vous*-versus-*tu* thing, I'd been thinking about taking a plunge into that clear blue water shimmering so tantalizingly in front of us . . .

But then Dominique does me one better by suddenly sitting up, undoing her bikini top, flipping it over the back of her chaise longue, then stretching and saying, "Ah. That's better."

The year 1848 (aptly nicknamed the Year of Revolutions) saw many peasant uprisings throughout Europe and the fall of the monarchy in France, as well as the potato famine in Ireland, and fashion responded to the unrest by requiring women to look as covered up as possible, with "poke" bonnets and skirts that trailed filthily to the floor declared the season's "must-haves."

This was the age of Jane Eyre, whom we all remember refused to accept Mr. Rochester's generous offer to make over her wardrobe, preferring merino wool to the silk organzas he ordered for her. If only she'd had Melania Trump to set her straight on this wrongheaded attitude toward fashion.

History of Fashion
SENIOR THESIS BY ELIZABETH NICHOLS

14

Never to talk about ourselves is a very noble piece of hypocrisy.
—*Friedrich Nietzsche (1844–1900),*
German philosopher, classical scholar, and critic

*a*nd okay. I *know* this is Europe and people here are much more laid-back about their bodies and nudity than we are (except that Dominique isn't European. She's Canadian. Which I guess is sort of like European. But still).

It's just very hard to sit and talk to someone whose bare nipples are sort of . . . *pointing* at you.

And Shari's no help at all. She's keeping her gaze resolutely on the pages of the book she's reading. Though I notice she's not actually *turning* any of those pages.

I realize there's nothing I can do except try to act normal. I mean, it's not like I'm not used to seeing bare-chested women, considering the gang showers back in McCracken Hall.

Still. I *knew* all those girls.

Plus, Dominique's knockers are—how can I put this?—a bit more suspiciously perky than even Brianna Dunleavy's.

And Brianna worked part-time at Bare Assets Cocktail Lounge.

"So," I say, casually, "have you mentioned all these ideas you have for, um, improving Mirac to Luke?"

Because I can't help wondering what *he* thinks of Dominique's plans.

"Of course," Dominique says, lifting a hand to slick back her long blond hair. "And to his father as well. But the old man is only interested in one thing. His wine. So until he dies . . ." Dominique gives a metaphoric shrug.

"Luke's waiting for his father to die before turning this place into a Hyatt Regency?" I ask, my voice cracking a little in my astonishment. Because I simply can't believe the Luke I met yesterday would ever do such a thing.

"A Hyatt?" Dominique looks scandalized. "I told you, it will be five-star luxury accommodation, not part of a cheap American hotel chain. And no, Jean-Luc is not entirely enthusiastic about my plans. Yet. For one thing because he would have to move to France full-time to see them implemented, and he isn't interested in giving up his job at Lazard Frères. Although I've told him it would be a simple thing to transfer to their Paris offices. Then we could—"

"We?" I'm on the word like Grandma on a can of Bud. "You two are getting married?"

"Well, certainly," Dominique says. "Someday."

It's ridiculous that this statement sends a shaft of pain through my heart. I barely know him. I only met him yesterday.

But then I'm the same girl who traveled all the way to England to see a guy I had only spent twenty-four hours with three months earlier.

And look how *that* turned out.

"Oh," Shari finally pipes up, "you and Luke are engaged? That's funny, Chaz never mentioned that to me. I'd have thought Luke would have told him."

"Well, nothing so formal as an engagement," Dominique says with obvious reluctance. "Who even gets engaged anymore? It's so old-fashioned. Today's couples, they form partnerships, not marriages. It's all about combining incomes and investing in a shared future. And I knew, from the first moment I saw Mirac, that this is a future I wanted to invest in."

I blink at her. Today's couples form partnerships, not marriages? They combine incomes and invest in a shared future?

And what's this about *from the first moment I saw Mirac*? Doesn't she mean *from the first moment I saw Jean-Luc*?

"It *is* a beautiful place," Shari says, turning a page of her book that I know she hasn't read. "Why do you think it is that Luke doesn't want to move to Paris?"

"Because Jean-Luc doesn't know what he wants," Dominique says with a frustrated sigh.

"Does any man?" Shari asks mildly. And I can tell, from her tone, that she is highly amused by the conversation.

"Maybe he doesn't want to be that far away from you," I offer— very generously, in my opinion, considering my little crush on her boyfriend. Since that's all it is. Just a crush. Really.

Dominique turns her head to look at me. "I have offered to transfer to Paris with him," she says tonelessly.

"Oh," I say. "Well. His mom lives in Houston, right? Maybe he doesn't want to leave her."

"That's not it," Dominique says. "It's that if he puts in a request to transfer to Paris and it goes through, he'll have to go. And then he'll be stuck there. And there'll be no chance for him ever to pursue the career he really wants."

"What's the career he really wants?" I ask.

"He wants," Dominique says, picking up the bottle of water she has by her chaise longue and raising it to her lips, then swallowing, "to be a doctor."

"A doctor?" I'm thrilled. I can't believe Luke didn't mention this on the train when I said all those bad things about investment bankers. "Really? But that's so great. I mean, doctors ... they heal people."

Dominique looks at me as if I've just said the most obvious thing in the world. Which, of course, I have.

But she obviously hasn't figured out that I routinely say the first thing that pops into my head. Seriously. It's like a disease.

"What I mean is," I hasten to add, "doctors are so important. You know. To society. Because without them, we'd all . . . be a lot sicker."

I look over at her to see what she thinks of this stroke of deductive brilliance on my part. Dominique has leaned up on her elbows—though the movement, mysteriously enough, did not cause her breasts to move at all—to look past me, over at Shari.

"Your friend," she says to Shari, "talks very much."

"Yes," Shari says. "Lizzie does have a tendency to do that."

"I'm sorry," I say, feeling myself blush. But it's not like I'm going to shut up. Because I physically *can't*. "But why doesn't Luke go to medical school? I mean, if that's what he wants to do? Because it can't be that doctors don't make enough money." The Luke I know—the one who let me, a total stranger, cry on his shoulder on that train yesterday—and shared his nuts with me—would never choose a career based on what kind of salary he might earn in said career.

I mean, would he?

No. No way. Hugo instead of Hugo Boss! Come on! That is the choice of a man who prefers personal comfort over style . . .

"Is it the cost of medical school?" I ask. "Because surely Luke's parents would support him while he was in school. Have you thought of talking about it to Luke's mom and dad?"

Dominique's expression changes from one of mild disgust—with me, apparently—to one of horror.

"Why would I do that?" Dominique looks completely perplexed. "I want Luke to transfer to Paris with me and work at Lazard Frères so that he and I can turn this place into a five-star hotel, turn over a considerable profit, and come here on weekends. I don't want to be a doctor's wife and continue to live in *Texas*. Is that so hard to understand?"

I blink at her. "Um," I say, "no."

But inwardly, I'm thinking, *Wow. This is one lady who knows what she wants. I bet SHE wouldn't have any reservations about moving to New York City with no degree, no job, and no place to stay already lined up.*

In fact, I bet she'd EAT New York City.

It's at this point Agnès returns from the kitchen, holding a plate of snacks.

"*Voilà*," she says to me, looking extremely pleased with herself as she hands me the creation she's prepared for me.

Which appears to be half a French baguette, sliced down the middle and stuffed with—

"Hershey bar!" Agnès cries, excited to be using the only English words she apparently knows.

I have just been handed a Hershey bar sandwich.

Agnès holds out the plate to Shari, who takes one look and says, "No thank you."

Shrugging, Agnès then offers the plate to Dominique. The teenager doesn't appear the least shocked that her boss's girlfriend is half naked, proving that French people of all ages are way cooler about nudity than I am.

Dominique takes one look at the sandwich on the platter in front of her, shudders, and says, "*Mon Dieu. Non.*"

Well, okay. Maybe she wouldn't eat New York City after all. Too fattening.

Agnès shrugs again, takes her own chocolate sandwich off the plate, sinks back down onto her chaise longue, and digs in. Crispy bits of crust fall all over the front of her bathing suit as she takes her first bite. Chewing, she gives me a chocolaty smile.

"*C'est bon, ça,*" she says, indicating the sandwich.

That much is obvious. The real question, of course, is how could it not be good?

Also, how can I say no to such a thoughtful and lovingly prepared snack? I don't want to hurt the girl's feelings.

There's really only one thing I can do, of course. And so I do it.

And it is, without a doubt, the best sandwich I have ever eaten.

But it's the kind of sandwich I can tell that Dominique—if she were to sink her business-oriented claws into this place—would outlaw immediately! Women recovering from lipo don't want to be offered Hershey bar and baguette sandwiches! People on a corporate retreat can't be served candy bars! I can practically see Dominique thinking this, even as she lifts a bottle of sunscreen and resolutely sprays her chest with it.

Agnès, and her Hershey bar sandwiches, will soon be a thing of the past if Dominique has her way with the running of Mirac.

Unless, of course, someone stops her.

"Ladies."

I nearly choke on the huge bite of chocolate bar sandwich I've just taken. That's because Luke and Chaz have just shown up at the far end of the pool, looking sweaty and dirt-smeared from their morning spent hacking at the underbrush along the driveway.

"*Salut,*" Dominique says, lifting a darkly tanned arm to wave at them. Her breasts, I notice, don't move at all as she does this. It is a miracle of gravity.

"Hello, boys," Shari says.

I don't say anything for once, because I'm still too busy trying to swallow.

"Are you girls having a nice time?" Chaz wants to know. He is grinning, and I know why: half-naked Dominique. It's hard to miss the amused glance he throws Shari, who only says, mildly, "Oh, we're having a *dandy* time. You?"

"Dandy," Chaz replied. "Thought we'd go for a swim to cool off a little." Even as he says it, he's peeling off his shirt.

One thing I'll say about Chaz. He may have a master's in philosophy, but he's got the body of a physical trainer.

But Luke—I'm able to note all too clearly when he, too, pulls off his shirt a second later—is an even more spectacular example of athletic masculinity than Chaz. There's not an ounce of body fat on his tanned, well-muscled body, and his dark chest hair, while not copious, still forms a very distinct arrow that seems to point directly down to his . . .

SPLASH! Both guys leap into the sparkling water, not bothering to drop their shorts first, robbing me of the pleasure of seeing just what that trail of hair from Luke's chest down into his waistband leads to.

"Christ, that feels good," Chaz says when he surfaces. "Shar, get in here."

"Your wish is my command, master," Shari says. She lays down her book, stands up, and jumps. Some of the spray from the splash she makes gets on Dominique, who flicks it off.

"Dominique," Luke calls from where he surfaces at the deep end. "Come on in. The water's great."

Dominique prattles something in French that I don't completely catch, although the word *cheveux* is mentioned several times. I try to remember if *cheveux* means hair or horses. Somehow I don't think Dominique is saying that she doesn't want to get her horses wet.

Shari swims to the side of the pool and, folding her arms on the edge, leans out to say to me, "Lizzie, you have to get in here. The water is fabulous."

"Let me finish my sandwich first," I say, since I'm still working on the messy—but sinfully delicious—concoction Agnès handed me.

"Better wait half an hour after eating," Luke says, teasingly, from the deep end. "You don't want to get a cramp."

Fortunately, I'm busy chewing, so my mouth is too full for me to ask, *If I get one, will you rescue me, Luke?* Flirting would be totally inappropriate, considering the fact that his girlfriend is sitting right next to me. Topless.

And looking way better that way than I could ever hope to.

"Ah, the new girl!"

I practically spit out the wad of bread and chocolate in my mouth, I'm so startled by the heavily French-accented male voice behind me. When I whip around on my chaise longue, I find myself staring at an older gentleman in a white shirt and khaki pants held up by a pair of stylishly embroidered suspenders.

"Um," I say after I've swallowed, "hello."

"This is the new girl?" the old man asks Dominique as he points at me.

Dominique turns around, looks at the old guy, and says, in a much pleasanter tone than I've ever heard her use before, "Why, yes, monsieur. This is Shari's friend Lizzie."

"*Enchanté*," the old man says, lifting my hand—the one that isn't clutching the remains of my Hershey bar sandwich—and bringing it to the vicinity of—but not touching it with—his lips. "I am Guillaume de Villiers. Would you like to see my vineyard?"

"Dad," Luke says from the side of the pool he's hastily climbing out of, "Lizzie doesn't want to see your vineyard right now, okay? She's relaxing by the pool."

So this charming old man is Luke's father! I can't say I can really see a resemblance—Monsieur de Villiers's hair is wispy, not curly, like Luke's, and snow white, not dark.

But he does have Luke's same twinkling brown eyes.

"Oh, that's all right," I say, reaching for my sundress. "I want to see your vineyard, Monsieur de Villiers. I've heard so much about it. And last night I had some of your delicious champagne . . ."

"Ah." Monsieur de Villiers looks delighted. "But technically it is not correct to call it champagne, unless it was made in the region of Champagne. What I make can only be called sparkling wine."

"Well," I said, having polished off the remains of my sandwich so that I have both hands free to struggle into my dress, "whatever it was, it was lovely."

"*Merci, merci!*" Monsieur de Villiers exclaims. To Luke, who has come up to my chaise longue and is dripping on Dominique's legs—causing her to give him an annoyed look—he says, "I like this girl!"

"You don't have to go with him," Luke says to me. "Really. Don't let him bully you. He's notorious for it."

"I *want* to go," I assure Luke, laughing. "I've never been to a vineyard before. I'd love to see it, if Monsieur de Villiers has time to show it to me."

"I have all the time in the world!" Luke's father cries.

"You don't, actually," Dominique says, with a glance at her slim gold watch. "Bibi will be here in less than two hours. Don't you need to—"

"No, no, no," Monsieur de Villiers says. He takes hold of my elbow to help me balance while I slip on my sandals. Or maybe to keep me from running away. Because that's sort of what I feel like doing, considering that Luke's dad is having this conversation with Luke's girlfriend while the latter is completely TOPLESS!!!

I try to imagine a scenario in which I would ever have felt comfortable being topless in front of one of my ex-boyfriends' fathers, and fail.

"We will make it short," Monsieur de Villiers assures Dominique.

"I'll just go along to make sure you stick to that, Dad," Luke says, accepting a towel Agnès is handing him. "We don't want to bore Lizzie to death her first day here."

But now that I know Luke is coming along, I know that's one thing I definitely won't be: bored, I mean.

Especially since, as we move away from the pool and toward the vineyard behind the main house, I realize Luke has left his shirt behind.

Really, there's something to be said for this topless thing after all.

The Industrial Revolution did not just introduce the concepts of the steam engine and the rotation of nitrogen-fixing and cereal crops. No! The mid 1850s saw the invention of something much more crucial and useful to humankind: the crinoline, or hooped petticoat. By being able to step into a cage of steel hoops rather than having to don pounds and pounds of petticoats in order to give her skirts the mandatory width a fashionable woman of the day demanded, women everywhere were now at liberty to actually move their legs.

What seemed a brilliant stroke of genius, however, soon revealed itself to be the fatal undoing of many an unsuspecting country lass, for the crinoline not only attracted improper suitors, but was also responsible for hundreds upon hundreds of young picnicking ladies being torched by lightning.

History of Fashion
SENIOR THESIS BY ELIZABETH NICHOLS

15

Man, truly the animal that talks, is the only one that needs conversations to propagate its species ... In love, conversations play an almost greater role than anything else. Love is the most talkative of all feelings and consists to a great extent completely of talkativeness.

—*Robert Musil (1880–1942), Austrian author*

Okay, so it's the middle of the afternoon and I'm drunk.

But it's not my fault! All I've had to eat today is a cappuccino, a Hershey bar sandwich, and a few dusty, not-very-ripe grapes Monsieur de Villiers picked for me when we were touring his vineyard.

Then, after we headed into the cask room, Luke's dad kept pouring me cups of wine from all the different oak barrels, making me taste each individual one. After a while, I tried saying no. But he looked so hurt!

And he's been so kind to me, taking me all around the vineyard—the farm behind it, too, waiting tolerantly while I patted the velvet nose of the enormous horse that stuck his head over the stone wall to greet us, and while I squealed over the source of those cowbells I knew I'd heard (actual cows, three of them, that supply the milk for the château).

Then there were the dogs that showed up, eager to greet their master, a basset hound named Patapouf and a dachshund called Minouche. They needed sticks thrown to them—even though the basset hound tripped over his own ears going after them—and their entire life histories told to me.

And there was the farmer to greet, and his gnarled hand to shake, and his incomprehensible French—after which Monsieur de Villiers asked how much I understood, and when I said none, caused him to laugh uproariously—to listen to.

And there was the tractor to ride on the back of, and the history of the area to learn—it's no wonder I'm tipsy. All that, and ten different kinds of wine, too? I mean, they were all totally delicious.

But I'm starting to feel a little light-headed.

Or maybe that's just because of Luke's proximity. Sadly, he went back to the house and changed into a clean shirt and pair of jeans before rejoining us.

But his hair was still wet and clung damply to the back of his tanned neck in a way that made me, out on the back of that tractor, long to throw my arms around him. Even now, in the relative cool of the cask room, I can't help glancing at the sun-kissed skin of his forearms and wondering what it would feel like beneath my fingertips . . .

Oh my God, what's WRONG with me? I really *must* be drunk. I mean, he's TAKEN. And by someone way prettier and more accomplished than I am.

Plus, there's the whole rebound factor. I mean, I'm barely over Andy.

But still. I can't help thinking Dominique isn't right for Luke. And I'm not talking about her shoes, either. Lots of totally otherwise nice people own totally overpriced shoes.

And I'm not talking about her whole turning-Mirac-into-a-hotel scheme, either. Or even her disdain for Luke's secret dream of being a doctor (not, of course, that he's shared this secret dream with me. I'll just have to take Dominique's word for it that Luke even *has* a secret dream).

No, it's the fact that Luke is *so* good with his father, showing endless patience with the old man's fixation on his winery and its history and the telling of it. How he made sure the old man didn't trip over any of the machinery he was climbing on top of in order to show me how it worked. The way he ordered Patapouf and Minouche to sit when he felt they'd jumped all over his father for long enough. The way he gently pried his father's shirtsleeve from the mouth of that enormous horse.

You just don't see that sort of kindness from a son toward his father every day. I mean, Chaz doesn't even *speak* to his dad. And okay, Charles Pendergast Sr. is, by all reports, sort of an ass.

But still.

A guy like that—so patient and tolerant and sweet—deserves better than a girl who doesn't support his secret dreams. . . .

"You are very old-fashioned," Monsieur de Villiers is saying, breaking in on my unkind thoughts about Luke's girlfriend. The three of us are leaning in companionable silence against a cask, sipping a cabernet sauvignon Luke's dad has told me is very young . . . too young to bottle yet. As if I'd even know the difference.

"Excuse me?" I know I'm drunk. But what on earth is he talking about? I'm not old-fashioned. I totally gave my last boyfriend a blow job.

"This dress." Monsieur de Villiers points at my sundress. "It is very old, no? You are very old-fashioned for a young American girl."

"Oh," I say, realizing at last what he means. "You mean I like vintage. Yes. Well, this dress *is* old. Older than me, probably."

"I have seen a dress like this before," Monsieur de Villiers says. It's clear from the way he waves a fly away from his face—none too steadily—that he, too, has had a few too many sips of his own wine. Well, it's a hot day. All that running—and riding—around makes a person thirsty. And the cask room isn't air-conditioned.

Still, it's a comfortably cool temperature inside. It has to be, Monsieur de Villiers told me, in order for the wine to ferment properly.

"Upstairs," he goes on. "In the . . ." He looks questioningly at Luke. "*Grenier?*"

"The attic," Luke says, and nods. "Right. There are a bunch of old clothes up there."

"In the attic?" I instantly forget how drunk I feel—and how hot Luke looks. I straighten up and stare at the two of them with my eyes narrowed. "*There are vintage Lilly Pulitzer dresses in your attic?*"

Monsieur de Villiers looks confused.

"I do not know that name," he says. "But I have seen dresses like this up there. My mother's, I think. I have been meaning to donate them to the poor—"

"Can I see them?" I ask. I don't mean to sound overeager.

But I guess I do, anyway, since Luke's dad chuckles and says, "Ah! You love the old clothes the same way I love my wine!"

I start to blush—how embarrassing! I didn't mean to sound so greedy.

But Monsieur de Villiers lays a comforting hand on my shoulder and says, "No, no. I do not mean to laugh at you. I am just very pleased. I like to see people show passion for something, because, you know, I have my own passion." He holds his glass of wine aloft to illustrate just what that passion is—in case I hadn't guessed.

"But it is especially nice to see a young person with a passion for something," he goes on. "Too many young people today—they care for nothing but making money!"

I glance nervously at Luke. Because of course if what Dominique said is true about Luke choosing a business degree over medicine, he is one of the "young people" his dad is talking about.

But Luke is showing no guilt that I can see.

"I'll take you up into the attic if you really want to see it," Luke volunteers. "But don't get your hopes up that any of it's in decent condition. We had a pretty bad leak last year and a lot of the stuff stored up there got ruined."

"It's not *ruined*," Monsieur de Villiers says. "Just a little moldy, perhaps."

But I'll take moldy Lilly Pulitzer over no Lilly Pulitzer any day.

Luke must sense my eagerness since he says, with a laugh, "Okay. Let's go." To his father, he adds, "Don't you think you'd better go inside and have some coffee? You might want to sober up before Mom gets here."

"Your mother." Monsieur de Villiers rolls his eyes. "Yes, I suppose you are right."

Which is how a few minutes later, after thanking the elder Monsieur de Villiers profusely for the lovely tour and dropping him off in the château's enormous—but, as Dominique mentioned, hardly high tech—kitchen, I find myself in the cobweb-filled attic with the younger Monsieur de Villiers, riffling through old trunks of clothes and trying unsuccessfully to contain my excitement.

"Oh my God!" I exclaim as I open the first trunk and find, beneath a bone china tea set, an Emilio Pucci slip skirt. "Whose stuff did your dad say this is? His mother's?"

"There's no telling, really," Luke says. He's examining the rafters above our heads, ostensibly for more leaks. "Some of these trunks have been here since well before I was born. The de Villiers, I'm sorry to say, are definite pack rats. Help yourself to whatever you like."

"I couldn't," I say—even as I'm holding the skirt to my hips to see if it might fit. "I mean, this skirt right here? You could get two hundred bucks for it on eBay, easy." Then I gasp and dive incredulously back into the trunk.

But it's true. I've found the rarest of rare—Lilly Pulitzer's elusive tiger-print housedress . . . *with matching kerchief.*

"Well, I'm not going to go to the trouble of selling it," Luke is saying. "So it might as well go to someone who can appreciate it. Which, from the way things look, is you."

"Seriously," I say, bending down and finding what appears to be a wadded-up—but genuine—John Frederics blue velvet hat, "you have some great stuff in here, Luke. All it needs is a little TLC."

"That's a pretty good description"—Luke spins a wooden chair around and straddles it, backward, leaning his elbows on its back while he watches me—"for Mirac in general."

"No," I say, "this place is gorgeous. You guys have done a fantastic job of keeping it up all these years."

"Well, it hasn't been easy," Luke says. "When the Crash came—in 1929—my grandfather lost nearly everything—including that year's crop, to a blight. We had to sell off a lot of the land just to afford to pay the taxes on the place that year."

"Really?" Suddenly the unopened trunks all around me aren't nearly as interesting anymore. At least, not as interesting as what Luke is saying. "That's amazing."

"Then came the Nazi occupation—my grandfather avoided having SS officers housed in the place by claiming my father had contagious yellow fever . . . which he didn't, but it tricked the Germans into going elsewhere. Still, the war years weren't the best for wine-making."

I sink down onto the top of a trunk next to the one I've just plundered. There's something lumpy beneath me, but I hardly notice.

"It must be so weird," I say, "to own something that has such a *history*. Especially if . . ."

"If?"

"Well," I say hesitantly, "if owning a château isn't exactly your dream job. Dominique was saying something about how you actually wanted to be a, um, doctor."

"*What?*" His back straightens and his gaze, in the golden light that flows in from the diamond-shaped panes on either end of the long, sloped ceiling, is impenetrably dark. "When did she say *that*?"

"Today," I say innocently. Because I *am* innocent. Dominique didn't say it was a secret. Not that, given my history, it would have made a difference if she had. "By the pool. Why? Is it not true?"

"No, it's not true," Luke says. "Well, I mean, sure, at one time—Jesus, what else did she say?"

That you're an attentive and thoughtful lover in bed, I want to say. *That a girl doesn't have to worry about taking care of her own needs when she's with you because you are totally willing to take care of them for her.*

"Nothing," is what I say instead. Because of course Dominique didn't say any of those things. That's just my totally dirty, filthy imagination talking. "Oh, except some stuff about how she wants to turn Mirac into a hotel or a spa for people to go to while they're recovering from plastic surgery."

Luke looks even more startled. *"Plastic surgery?"*

Oops.

"Nothing," I say, turning crimson. Oh. No. I. Did. Not. Just. Do. It. Again. I turn back to the trunks to hide my blush. "Gosh, Luke. This stuff is *amazing.*"

"Wait. *What* did Dominique say?"

I fling him a guilt-stricken look.

"Nothing," I say. "Really. I shouldn't have—I mean, it's between you and her. I . . . I know it's none of my business—"

But it all comes spilling out anyway.

"—but I don't think you ought to turn this place into a hotel," I say all in a rush. "Mirac just seems so special. Commercializing it like that would just ruin it, I think."

"Plastic surgery?" Luke repeats, still looking incredulous.

"I guess I can understand the appeal," I say. "Since you wanted to be a doctor and all, but—"

"I didn't—" Luke springs up from the chair and takes a few quick steps toward the far end of the attic, raking one hand through his thick, curly hair. "I told her I wanted to be a doctor when I was a *kid.* Then I grew up and realized I'd have to be in school for another *four* years after college . . . plus three more years as a resident. And I don't like school that much."

"Oh," I say, sinking back down onto the lumpy trunk-top. "Then it's not just because doctors don't make as much money as investment bankers these days?"

"Did she—" He spins around to face me. "Is that what she told you I said?"

I can see I am treading on rocky terrain here. I hop up and, eager to change the subject, say, "What is this lumpy thing I've been sitting on?"

"Because it's not true," Luke says, striding toward me as I bend to lift up the long white object. "It had nothing to do with the money. I mean, it's true that for the years I'd be in school, there'd be no money coming in. And, yeah, okay, that's a concern. I'm not going to lie. I like having my own money so I don't have to depend on my parents for support. A guy wants to be able to pay his own bills, you know?"

"Oh," I say, unwinding what appears to be a length of white satin from the long, hard object it's been wrapped around. "Totally."

"And, okay, I looked into the postbaccalaureate premedical programs at a few schools—because, you know, not having been premed in college, even if I wanted to try to get into med school now, I'd have to take some postgrad science classes."

"Sure," I say, still working at unraveling whatever's been wrapped inside what appears to be some kind of tablecloth.

"And, yeah, okay, maybe I applied to a few of them. And maybe I got into the ones at Columbia and New York University. But I mean even if I go full-time, with summers included, that's another year in school that doesn't even count toward whatever medical degree I eventually go for. Is that really what I want? To be in school for another *five* years? When I don't have to be?"

"Oh my God," I say. Because I have finally unraveled the long, hard thing. And gotten a good look at what was being used to wrap it.

"That," Luke says, looking alarmed, "is my dad's hunting rifle. Don't—Lizzie, don't hold it like that. Jesus Christ." He hastily takes the long thing from my hands, then opens it and looks down the barrel.

"It's still loaded," he says in a small voice.

Now that Luke's taken the gun from me, I have both hands free and can give the thing the gun was wrapped in a good shaking.

"Lizzie." Luke sounds kind of stressed. "In the future, when you're holding a hunting rifle—even an unloaded one—don't fling it around like that. And definitely don't point it at your own head. You nearly gave me a heart attack."

His voice seems far away. All my concentration is on the dress I'm holding. Even in its wrinkled, rust-stained state, I can see that it's a cream-colored full-length satin gown with slender spaghetti straps (complete with tiny snapped loops on the underside, for hiding the wearer's bra straps), fine gathers over the double-lined molded breast cups, and a row of buttons down the back that can only be real pearls.

"Luke, whose dress is this?" I ask, searching inside for a label.

"Did you hear me?" Luke says. "This thing is loaded. You could have taken the top of your head off."

Then I find them. The words that nearly cause my heart to stop, though they are discreetly stitched in black on a small white label: *Givenchy Couture.*

I feel as if someone has kicked me.

"Givenchy—" I stagger backward, to sink back down onto the top of the trunk, because my knees no longer appear to be working. "Givenchy Couture!"

"Jesus Christ," Luke says again. He's unloaded the rifle, and now he sets it down on the chair he'd abandoned and hurries across the room to bend over me solicitously. "Are you all right?"

"No, I'm not all right," I say, reaching up and grabbing a handful of his shirt, pulling him down until he's kneeling by my chair, his face just inches from mine.

He doesn't understand. He just doesn't understand. I have to *make* him understand.

"This is a Hubert de Givenchy evening gown. A priceless, one-of-a-kind couture evening gown from one of the most innovative and classic fashion designers in the world. And someone used it to wrap up an old gun that . . . that . . ."

Luke gazes down at me, concern in his dark eyes. "Yes?"

"That RUSTED on it!"

Something causes Luke's lips to twist upward a little. He's smiling. How can he be *smiling*? I can tell he still doesn't get it.

"RUST, Luke," I say desperately. "RUST. Do you have any idea how hard it is to get rust out of fine fabrics like silk? And look, look here . . . one of the straps is broken. And the hem—there's a tear here. And here. Luke, how could someone have done something like this? How could someone have . . . MURDERED a beautiful vintage gown like this?"

"I don't know," Luke says. He's still smiling, which means he still isn't getting it.

But he's also laid a hand over mine, where I'm still clutching his shirt. His fingers are warm and reassuring.

"But I have a feeling if there's anyone in the world who can resuscitate the victim," he goes on in his deep, quiet voice—which sounds even deeper and quieter in the stillness of the long attic—"it's you."

His eyes, as I gaze into them, look very dark, and very friendly . . . just as his lips, as always, look eminently kissable.

HOW CAN HE HAVE A GIRLFRIEND? It's not fair. It's just not.

I do the only thing I can, under the circumstances. I gently release his shirt and drop my hand—and my gaze—away from his.

"I guess . . ." I say, looking down at the yards of stained fabric in my lap, hoping he doesn't notice my blush—or the sudden speeding up of my heartbeat, which I can feel slamming against my ribs. "I guess I could try. I mean . . . if it's okay with you, I'd *like* to try."

"Lizzie," Luke says, "that dress has been up in this attic for God knows how long, and, as you mentioned, wasn't exactly treated very nicely. I think it deserves to belong to someone who will give it the care and attention it needs."

Just like you, Luke! I want to cry. *You deserve to belong to someone who will give YOU the care and attention YOU need . . . someone who will support your dream of being a doctor, and not nag you to move to Paris, who will stick by you for those five more years of school, and who will promise never to turn your ancestral home into a spa for people recovering from plastic surgery, even if it would bring in more money than weddings.*

But of course I can't say this.

Instead I say, "You know, Chaz is going to New York University in the fall. Maybe if you do decide to go to that postbacca-whatever-it-is thingie, you two could find a place to live together."

That is, I add silently, *if Dominique doesn't insist on coming with you . . .*

"Yeah," Luke says, still smiling. "It'd be just like old times."

"Because," I go on, keeping my hands strictly away from him, and on the silky smoothness of the dress in my lap, "I think, if there's something you really want to do—like being a doctor—you should go for it. I mean, because otherwise you'll never know. And you might regret it your whole life."

Luke, I can't help noticing, is still kneeling beside my chair, his face still way too close to mine for comfort. I'm trying not to think about how my advice—about how he should go for it—could also apply to my kissing him. Because, you know, I might never get another chance to see what it would be like.

But kissing a guy who has a girlfriend is just wrong. Even a girlfriend who doesn't necessarily have his best interests in mind, like I do. It's the kind of thing Brianna Dunleavy, back at McCracken Hall, would do.

And no one liked Brianna.

"I don't know," Luke says. Is it my imagination, or is his gaze on my mouth? Do I have something stuck to my lip gloss? Or—oh God—are my teeth purple from all that red wine? "It's a really big step. A life-changing one. A risky one."

"Sometimes," I say, my gaze on his own lips—his teeth, I note, are not purple at all, "we need to take big risks if we want to find out who we are, and what we were put on this planet for. Like me, jumping on that train and coming to France, instead of staying in England."

Okay, he is definitely leaning in. He's *leaning in toward me*. What does this mean? Does he want to kiss me? How can he want to kiss *me* when he has the world's most gorgeous girlfriend lying half naked out there by the pool?

I can't let him kiss me. Even if he wants to. Because that would be wrong. He is taken.

And besides, I'm sure I still have stinky wine breath.

"Was the risk worth it?" he wants to know.

I can't seem to tear my gaze from his lips, which are coming closer and closer toward mine.

"Totally," I say. And close my eyes.

He's going to kiss me. He's going to kiss me! Oh no!

Oh. Yes.

It was an American woman named Amelia Bloomer who first spoke out against the dangers of the crinoline (and also the unhygienic practice of wearing skirts that swept the earth and floor). She encouraged women to adopt the "bloomer," a baggy-legged pant worn beneath a knee-length skirt that would not in any way be considered immodest today. The Victorians, however, objected strongly to women wearing the pants in the family, and "bloomers" went the way of Members Only jackets and Hall & Oates.

History of Fashion
SENIOR THESIS BY ELIZABETH NICHOLS

16

A lover without indiscretion is no lover at all. Circumspection and devotion are a contradiction in terms.
—*Thomas Hardy (1840–1928), British author and poet*

*J*ean-Luc?"

Wait. Who said that?

"Jean-Luc?"

My eyes fly open. Luke is already on his feet and rushing for the attic door.

"I'm up here," he calls down the narrow staircase to the third floor. "In the attic!"

Okay. What just happened? One minute he was about to kiss me—I'm almost sure of it—and the next—

"Well, you had better come down now." Dominique's voice sounds prim. "Your mother's just arrived."

"Shit," Luke says. But not to Dominique. To Dominique, he calls, "Right. I'll be down in a second."

He turns around to look at me. I'm sitting there, the Givenchy evening gown still spilling off my lap, feeling as if something was just ripped from me. My heart, maybe?

But that's ridiculous. I didn't want him to kiss me. I *didn't*. Even if he was going to.

Which he wasn't.

"We should go," Luke says. "Unless you want to stay up here. You're welcome to anything you want to take—"

Except the one thing I'm starting to realize I want most.

"Oh," I say, standing up. I'm mildly surprised to find that my knees can still support me. "No. I couldn't."

But I haven't let go of the evening dress, a fact Luke notices, and which causes one corner of his mouth to go up in a knowing way.

"I mean," I say, looking down guiltily at the armful of silk I'm holding, "if I could just take this and maybe try to restore it—"

"By all means," Luke says, still trying to hide his smile.

He's laughing at me. But I don't care, because now we have another secret together. Soon I'll have more secrets with Luke de Villiers than I do with anyone else.

Although, thanks to the Lizzie Broadcasting System, I don't have secrets with *anyone* else. This is definitely something I need to work on.

I follow Luke down the stairs. Dominique is waiting at the bottom. She's changed from her bathing suit into a cream-colored, very contemporary linen dress that leaves her shoulders bare and makes her waist look tiny. On her feet, I'm quick to note, are a pair of slides with wickedly pointy toes.

"Well," she says when she sees me trailing behind Luke, "you certainly got the full tour, didn't you, Lizzie?"

"Luke and his father were very thorough," I say, trying to hide my guilt. Why should I feel guilty, though? Nothing happened. And nothing was *going* to happen.

Probably.

"I'm sure they were," Dominique says in a bored voice. Then she casts a critical eye over Luke. "Look at you. You're all dusty. You cannot greet your mother like this. Go and change."

If Luke doesn't like being bossed around like this, he doesn't show it. Instead he heads off down the hall, calling, "Tell Mom I'll be there in a minute," over his shoulder.

I start for my own room, where I intend to stash the evening gown until I can find some lemons or, even better, cream of tartar to soak it in. I've had luck in the past getting rust stains out of silk with both.

But Dominique stops me before I can take a single step.

"What is it that you have there?" Dominique asks.

"Oh," I say. I unfold the dress and hold it up for her to see. "It's just an old dress I found up there. It's such a shame, it's covered in rust stains now. I'm going to see if I can get them out."

Dominique casts a critical eye up and down the garment. If she recognizes its significance as a piece of fashion history, she doesn't let on.

"It is very old, I think," she says.

"Not that old," I say. "Sixties. Maybe early seventies."

She wrinkles her nose. "It smells."

"Well," I say, "it's been sitting in a moldy attic. I'm going to soak it for a while to see if I can get the stains out. That will help with the smell as well."

Dominique reaches out to finger the smooth silk. A second later she's reaching for the label.

Uh-oh. She's seen it.

She doesn't squeal, though, the way I did. That's because Dominique can actually control herself.

"You are good at sewing?" she asks very calmly. "I thought I heard your friend Shari say so . . ."

"Oh, I'm just okay," I say modestly.

"If you cut off the skirt here," Dominique says, indicating a place where, if I were to cut off the skirt, the hem would hit her just above the knee, "it would be a cute cocktail dress. I would have to dye it black, of course. Otherwise it looks too much like an evening gown, I think."

Whoa. Wait a minute.

"Because it *is* an evening gown," I say. "And I'm sure it belongs to someone. I'm just going to try to restore it. I'm sure whoever it belongs to would love to have it back."

"But that could be anyone," Dominique says. "And if whoever it belongs to really cared for it, she would not have left it here. If it is a matter of cost, I will gladly pay you—"

I snatch the dress from her fingers. I can't help it. It's like she's turned into Cruella De Vil, and the gown is a dalmatian puppy. I can't believe anyone would be so vicious as to suggest cutting—not to mention dyeing—a Givenchy original.

"Why don't we see if I can get the stains out first," I say as calmly as I'm able to, seeing as how I am practically hyperventilating in shock.

Dominique shrugs in her French Canadian way. At least, I suppose it's French Canadian, since I've never met one before.

"Fine," she says. "I suppose we can just let Jean-Luc decide what to do with it since it's his house . . ."

She doesn't add, . . . *and I'm his girlfriend, and therefore all couture spoils in his house should rightfully go to me.*

Because she doesn't have to.

"I'll just go put it away," I say, "and then come down to meet Mrs. de Villiers."

Mention of the name seems to remind Dominique that she's wanted elsewhere.

"Yes, of course," she says, and hurries to the stairs.

Hideously relieved, I dart into my room and close the door behind me, then lean against it as if I have to catch my breath. Cut a Givenchy! Dye a Givenchy! What kind of sick, twisted . . .

But I don't have time to worry about that now. I want to go see what Luke's mother is like. I gently hang the evening gown from a peg in the wall (my room not having a closet), then strip off the swimsuit and dress I've been wearing all day. Then I throw on my robe and zip into the bathroom for a quick wash, makeup reapplication, and hair combing before coming back into my room to throw on my Suzy Perette party dress (I finally got the paint out).

Then, following the sounds of conversation drifting up from downstairs, I hurry to meet Bibi de Villiers.

Who turns out to be nothing like what I expected. Having met Luke's father, I had built up a picture in my head of the kind of woman he would marry—diminutive, dark, and soft-spoken, to go with his dreamy absentmindedness.

But none of the women I see from the second-floor landing when I reach it fit this description. There are three women standing in the foyer—not including Shari, Dominique, and Agnès—and none of them is dark or diminutive.

And they're DEFINITELY not soft-spoken.

"But then where are Lauren and Nicole going to stay?" a girl about my own age, only considerably blonder, is demanding in a heavy Southern accent.

"Vicky darlin', I told you." Another blonde, who has to be the girl's mother, since the resemblance between the two is uncanny (except that Mom has about twenty pounds on her daughter), is speaking in long-suffering, but still distinctly Texan, tones. "They're just going to have to stay in Sarlat. Aunt Bibi told you she could only fit so many people here in Mirac—"

"But why do Blaine's friends get to stay here," Vicky is whining, "and my friends have to go to a hotel? And what about Craig? Where are *his* friends going to stay?"

A sullen-looking young man lurking in the corner by a marble pillar says, "I didn't know Craig *had* any friends."

"Shut up, you retard," Vicky hurls at him.

"Well," declares the other blond middle-aged woman, "I know I could sure use a drink. Anybody with me on that one?"

"Here, Bibi." Monsieur de Villiers is quick to move in with a tray of champagne flutes he's had standing by, apparently in case of an emergency just like this one.

"Oh, thank the Lord," says Luke's mother, quickly taking hold of a glass. Nearly a head taller than her French soon-to-be-ex-husband (although maybe that's just because her hair is so big), she is a striking woman in a brightly patterned Diane von Furstenberg wrap dress that shows off her still-trim figure to advantage.

"Here, Ginny," she says, taking another glass of champagne and handing it to her sister. "You need one of these even more than I do, I'll bet."

Vicky's mother doesn't even wait until everyone else is served before downing the contents of her glass. She looks like a woman on the verge of . . . well, something not very good.

Dominique, I see, has already made her way back downstairs and is standing at Mrs. de Villiers's elbow, supervising the handing out of the champagne. When Monsieur de Villiers gets to Agnès, Dominique says something rather sharp in French and Luke's dad looks startled.

"Oh, surely just a taste," he says. "It's my new demi-sec . . ."

Dominique looks disapproving.

But this apparently doesn't bother Luke, who steps forward, plucks a champagne glass off the tray his father is holding, and hands it to Agnès, who looks surprised and thrilled.

"It's a special occasion," Luke says, seemingly to everyone in general. But I can't help thinking his remark is directed at Dominique. "My cousin is here for her wedding. Everyone needs to be in on the celebration."

I see Shari—changed out of her swimsuit into a neat white blouse and olive capris—exchange glances with Chaz, who's also changed—into khakis and a clean polo shirt—since I last saw him. Her look seems to say, *See? I told you so.*

Told you so about what, though? What's going on?

"Well," Mrs. de Villiers says, holding up her glass, "let's toast, then. To the bride and groom. Who isn't here yet. The lucky bastard." She throws back her head and laughs. "Just kidding."

Then, having spied me when she threw her head back, Mrs. de Villiers adds, "Oops, Guillaume, one more. There's one more comin.'" And Monsieur de Villiers turns, spots me coming down the stairs, and breaks into a wide grin.

"Ah, there she is," he says, holding the last glass of champagne out to me. "Better late than never. And definitely worth waiting for."

Blushing, I take the glass and say, speaking to the room in general, the way Luke had, "Hello. I'm Lizzie Nichols. Thank you so much for having me here," as if I'd actually been an invited guest and not the complete party crasher that I am.

Then I stand there wishing something heavy would fall on my head and knock me unconscious.

"Lizzie, how do you do?" Mrs. de Villiers steps forward to shake my hand. "You must be the friend of Chaz's I've been hearing about. So nice to meet you. Any friend of Chaz's is a friend of ours. He was just so sweet to our Luke when he was at school. Always helping him get into trouble."

I glance at Chaz, who is grinning. "I'm sure," I say, "knowing Chaz."

"Not true," Chaz is saying. "Not true. Luke got into plenty of trouble on his own with no help from me."

"This is my sister, Ginny Thibodaux, and her daughter Vicky," Bibi de Villiers is saying as she steers me around the foyer to meet her family. Mrs. Thibodaux's handshake, compared to her sister's hearty one, is like holding a wet sponge, and Vicky's is only a little better. "And this is Blaine, Vicky's not-so-little-anymore brother—" Blaine's handshake is a little better than his sister's, but his face seems to be molded into a permanent sneer and he has a letter of the alphabet tattooed on each of his fingers. I can't tell what they spell when seen in a row, though.

"Well," Bibi says when she's done introducing me, "here's to the lovely couple."

Then she polishes off her champagne. Fortunately, her husband is standing nearby with a new bottle, ready to freshen everybody's glass.

"It's good, no?" he's asking eagerly of anyone who will reply. "The demi-sec? They don't make many demi-secs anymore. Everyone is always clamoring for the bruts. But I think to myself, why not?"

"Way to think outside the box, Guillaume," Chaz says amiably. I sidle over toward him and Shari and lean over to ask, "Do you have any idea what a demi-sec is?"

"Oh, hell, no," Chaz says, just as amiably, and drains his glass. "Hey, I'll take some more," he says, hurrying after Luke's father.

Shari looks up at me—she's never gotten over being only five four, whereas I've never gotten over having a butt that's twice as big as hers (until recently)—and says, "Where did you disappear to all afternoon? And how come you're so dressed up?"

"Luke and his dad gave me a tour of the vineyard," I say. "And I'm not dressed up. This dress got downgraded to everyday wear after Maggie got paint on it. Remember?"

"There's no paint on it now," Shari observes.

"Well, it was water-soluble. Nobody gives a four-year-old non-water-soluble paint. Not even my sister."

"Whatever," Shari says. She's never understood my complicated wardrobe rules, though I've offered to explain them multiple times. "We're invited to dinner tonight. It'll just be the bride's family, which is why. Groom's family and the rest of the guests get here tomorrow. You up for helping out in the kitchen?"

"Totally," I say, picturing me with a cute apron on, preparing spaghetti due for everyone.

"Great," Shari says. "Agnès's mother is making it. She's supposed to be a fantastic cook. We'll be on dish patrol. Let's get nice and toasted to make it go faster."

"Sounds like a plan to me," I say, and follow her over to where Luke is standing, having taken over champagne-pouring duties from his dad, for refills.

"Ah," Luke says when he notices me. "There she is. Nice dress."

"Thanks," I say. "You don't clean up so badly yourself. Do you know if you have any cream of tartar in your kitchen?"

Shari chokes on the sip of champagne she's just taken. Luke, however, calmly replies, "I have no idea. Tell me what cream of tartar would be called in French and I'll ask."

"I don't know," I say. "You're the Frenchman."

"Half," Luke says, casting a glance at his mother, who is throwing her head back and laughing at something else Chaz has said.

"*Crème de tartre?*" Shari suggests.

"I'll ask," Luke says, and goes to refill his aunt's glass.

"What was that all about?" Shari wants to know when he's out of earshot.

"Oh, nothing," I say innocently. It's kind of fun, I'm discovering, keeping secrets from her. It's something I've never done before in my life.

But there are quite a few things I've never done before in my life that I've been trying lately. Some without success, but some . . . well, time would tell.

"Lizzie." Shari narrows her eyes at me. "Is there something going on between you and Luke?"

"No! God, no."

But I can't help blushing, thinking about that near-kiss in the attic. And what about last night at the train station? Had Luke been about to kiss me then? Somehow I had sort of thought he might . . . if Dominique hadn't showed up. Both times.

"He has a girlfriend," I remind Shari, hoping saying it out loud will also help me remind myself. "Like I would ever make a move on a guy who has a girlfriend. Who do you think I am, anyway? Brianna Dunleavy?"

"No need to get huffy," Shari says. "I was just asking."

"I'm not huffy," I say, trying to sound very unhuffy. "Did I seem huffy? Because I didn't mean to."

"Whatever you say, psycho." Shari shoots me an amused glance. "I'm gonna get another refill. Care to join me?"

I look in the direction she's nodding toward. Luke is just opening a new bottle of his dad's champagne. He happens to lift his head and see us looking at him from across the room. He smiles.

"Um," I say. "Well, okay. Maybe one more."

The mid-1870s saw something of a fashion revolution, thanks to the invention of the sewing machine and the introduction of synthetic dyes. While mass manufacturing meant inexpensive, stylish clothes were available to everyone, it also meant that, for the first time in recorded history, you could be walking down the street and actually see someone wearing your exact same outfit. The hoop skirt disappeared, transformed into the "bustle," the last time it was stylish to look as if one had a big butt until the birth of J.Lo.

History of Fashion
SENIOR THESIS BY ELIZABETH NICHOLS

17

Talk is a pure art. Its only limits are the patience of listeners
who, when they get tired, can always pay for their coffee or
change it with a friendly waiter and walk out.
—*John Dos Passos (1896–1970),*
U.S. novelist, poet, playwright, and painter

Dinner isn't so much a meal as it is a war council.

That's because Vicky and her mother want to make sure
everything is ready for when the guests—and Vicky's future husband and in-laws—start arriving tomorrow.

I guess I can understand their concern. I mean, you only have
one wedding (hopefully). So you want to make sure you do it right.

Still, it would be nice if we could concentrate more on the food
Agnès's mother, Madame Laurent, has prepared for us than on Mrs.
Thibodaux's complaints about the bumpiness of the driveway.

Because this is possibly one of the most delicious meals I've
ever had, starting with a creamy fish *cassoulet* (which means stew)
with slices of apple in it as a starter; then duck caramelized in some
kind of delicious sweet sauce; a salad of baby lettuce in a garlicky
dressing; and an enormous cheese platter, all of it accompanied by
huge chunks of perfectly baked bread—crunchy and golden on the
outside, soft and warm in the middle—and a wine to go with each
course, poured by Monsieur de Villiers, who tries to tell us about
each glass we're sampling but who keeps getting interrupted by
Luke's aunt Ginny, who says things like "Speaking of bouquet, has
anyone talked to that florist over in Sarlat? She knows we changed

to the white roses from the white lilies, right? What's the French word for rose again?"

To which Luke replies dryly, *"Rose,"* causing some of the water I've just sipped to go up my nose, I start laughing so hard.

Fortunately he doesn't notice—Luke, I mean—because he's sitting all the way down at the opposite end of the enormous dining table—which Dominique informed me (on our way into the impressively high-ceilinged and dramatically decorated dining room) seats twenty-six—with his mother on one side and Dominique at the other. I'm at the other end, by Luke's father, with the surly Blaine on my other side.

Not that I mind. Especially since I don't even like Luke that way. Or so I am telling myself, now that Shari is on to me.

At least I got the opportunity to observe up close what the letters tattooed on Blaine's fingers spell: F-U-C-K Y-O-U!

I think the exclamation mark is a nice touch. I imagine his mother must be very proud of him.

If she thinks anything about him at all, which seems unlikely given the amount of gushing she is doing over her daughter, who isn't, to put it mildly, a very happy bride. Nothing, apparently, has been done right so far, and Vicky doesn't seem to have much faith that anything is going to be done right in the future, despite protestations to the contrary from her mother, Luke, and even Monsieur de Villiers.

"Darlin', I already called the hotel and the concierge assures me there's plenty of space there for your sorority sisters. Or there will be tomorrow after some German tourists check out. At least"—Mrs. Thibodaux shoots her sister a look—"I think that's what he said. It was hard to tell with that accent . . ."

"But why can't Blaine's friends stay in the hotel?" Vicky wants to know. "Why do mine have to? I'm the bride!"

"Blaine's friends are in the wedding party," her mother reminds her. "You're the one who wanted them to play at the reception."

"Huh," Blaine, beside me, grunts as he stabs a piece of Camembert over and over with his butter knife. "Yeah, only *after* we landed that recording contract."

"You guys aren't celebrity recording artists yet," Vicky hurls at him from the far end of the table. "I don't see where you get off acting like one. Your stupid friends could stay in their VAN and not know the difference."

"My stupid friends," Blaine hurls back, "are the only remotely cool thing about your wedding, and you know it."

"Um, excuse me. I think getting married at a *French château* is plenty cool enough," Vicky snaps.

"Oh, right," Blaine says, rolling his eyes. "Like having the hottest band on the Houston music scene right now play at your wedding isn't something you've been bragging about to every publicist in town."

"Would you two kindly *shut the hell up*?" their aunt Bibi asks in a voice I suspect is even more slurry than usual, thanks to all the champagne she put back earlier, while stonily ignoring her estranged husband, who continues to make every effort possible to sit or stand near her and include her in the conversation. It is kind of sad, actually, to watch how excited Monsieur de Villiers is to have his wife back—even if only temporarily and even if only for her niece's wedding—and how totally unexcited she is to *be* back.

"Really, you two," Mrs. Thibodaux says, looking close to tears, "now is not a time for bickering. It's a time for pulling together, to try to weather this crisis as best we can."

"Crisis?" Monsieur de Villiers looks confused. "What crisis? Victoria is getting married! How is this a crisis? It is a joyous occasion, no?"

Both Bibi and her sister look at him and say at the same time, "No."

Vicky, after looking from one woman to the other, suddenly pushes her chair back, leaps to her feet, and runs from the dining room, a hand flung dramatically over her face.

Which is when Shari stands up and says, "On that note . . . thank you so much. We've had a lovely evening. And I'm pretty sure we're all clear on what we'll be needed to do tomorrow when the rest of your guests start arriving. But right now I think Lizzie and I will just get a head start on the dishes."

"I'll help you," Chaz says, springing to his feet, obviously eager to get away from the fighting and talk of floral arrangements.

"Me, too," Luke says.

But the minute he starts to get up, his mother lays a restraining hand upon his wrist and says, not slurring the word at all now, "Sit."

Luke sinks slowly back into his chair, a pained expression on his face.

I start clearing the empty plates around my end of the table. I don't think I can get out of that tense silence fast enough.

As I come into the high-ceilinged—but still old-fashioned—kitchen, I smile at Agnès and her mother when they look up from the supper they're sharing at the massive butcher-block table.

"*Ne pas se lever,*" I say to them, not sure if this is the right way of saying "Don't get up." But I guess it is, since it has the desired effect—they both sit back down to finish their meal.

"Oh my God," Shari says to me after smiling at the Laurents. "Oh my God. Oh my God. What *was* that out there?"

Chaz looks visibly shaken. "I feel violated," he says.

"Oh, whatever," I say, grabbing a trash can and beginning to scrape the remains on the plates off into it. "My own family is way more embarrassing."

"Well," Shari says, "I hadn't thought of it quite like that. But that is a good point."

"Weddings are just stressful, you guys," I say, reaching for the plates Chaz has carried in and scraping them as well. "I mean, the expectations are so high, and then if things don't go perfectly, people melt down."

"Sure," Shari says. "Melt down. But not spontaneously combust. You know what her problem is, don't you? Vicky's, I mean?"

"She's a Bridezilla?" Chaz asks.

"No," Shari says. "She's marrying beneath her."

"Shut up," I say, laughing.

"I'm serious," Shari says. "Dominique was telling us all about it at the pool today after you left for your little vineyard tour, Lizzie. Vicky's marrying some computer software programmer whose family all comes from Minnesota or something, instead of the rich Texas oil baron her mom had all picked out for her. Mrs. Thibodaux is fit to be tied about it, but there's nothing she can do to change Vicky's mind. It's *lurve*."

"Where's *Mr.* Thibodaux in all this?" Chaz wants to know. "Vicky's dad?"

"Oh, he has some big important meeting to go to in New York for his investment company or something. He'll be here just in time to walk her down the aisle, and not a minute before, if he's smart." Shari hands Chaz a dish towel. "Here. I'll rinse. You dry."

"Oh, I love it when you talk dirty dishes to me," Chaz says.

I gaze at the two of them as they bicker at each other over the sink, thinking how lucky they are to have found each other. It hasn't all been funny one-liners and trips to France for them, of course. There was the time Shari had to kill and dissect Mr. Jingles, her university-assigned lab rat, in order to pass advanced behavioral neuroscience, and Chaz urged her to spare Mr. Jingles by surreptitiously replacing him with a look-alike rat he found at PetSmart in the mall.

But Shari wouldn't swap rats because she said as a scientist she needed to learn how to distance herself from her subjects . . . after which Chaz wouldn't speak to her for two weeks.

Still. Overall, they are the cutest couple I know. Besides my mom and dad.

And I would give anything to have a relationship like that of my own.

Except, of course, I wouldn't resort to busting up someone else's to get it. Even if I could. Which I can't.

So I don't even know why I'm standing here thinking about a certain person I met on a train just the day before.

Agnès and her mother, once they finish their meal, refuse to leave without helping us with the rest of the dishes, and the job is done sooner than I would have thought, given the number of courses we had and the number of utensils we'd ended up using to eat them.

But even better than being done with our chores sooner than I thought we would be is the fact that Madame Laurent actually understands me when I ask her if she knows whether there's any *crème de tartre* in the kitchen. Even better yet—she manages to produce a container of it for me. She looks a little confused at my joy over securing a common acidic compound but seems pleased to have been able to help. She and her daughter both wish us a *bonne nuit*—which we enthusiastically return—before returning to the millhouse for the night.

Chaz announces he's going to see if he can't rescue Luke from the clutches of his mother and Mrs. Thibodaux and cajole him into having a nightcap. He and Shari invite me along, but I tell them I'm tired and am going to bed.

Which is a lie, but I'm embarrassed to admit that I have other plans . . . and that they involve needing to find a basin big enough to soak the Givenchy dress in—with the cream of tartar—overnight.

I'm on my hands and knees with my head in the cabinet under

the kitchen sink examining something I think might work—a plastic bucket that must have been placed there during some ancient leak—when I hear a door open behind me. Worried it might be Luke, and that if so he'll be seeing me from my least flattering angle, I start to get up, misjudge the distance between the sink and my scalp, and bang my head on the inside of the cabinet.

"Ouch," says a male voice from behind me. "That had to hurt."

Clutching my head with one hand, I look over my shoulder and see Blaine, in his baggy black jeans, dyed-black hair, and Marilyn Manson T-shirt, which I believe he is wearing to be ironic.

"You okay?" he asks, eyebrows raised.

"Yeah," I say. Letting go of my head, I reach for the bucket and climb to my feet.

"Whatcha doing down there, anyway?" Blaine wants to know.

"Just getting something," I say, trying to hide the bucket behind my voluminous skirt. Don't even ask me why. I just don't feel like getting into an explanation of why I have it.

"Oh," Blaine says. That's when I notice the unlit, apparently hand-rolled cigarette dangling from his lips. "Okay. Well, listen. You got a light, by any chance?"

"Sorry," I say. "No."

He sags in the doorway. Really. He looks genuinely crushed. "Shit."

I don't approve of smoking, of course, but considering what this guy has had to sit through all night, I don't blame him for needing a little stimulant.

"You could use one of the burners," I suggest, pointing at the massive—and ancient—stove in the corner.

"Oh," Blaine says. "Sweet."

He slouches toward the stove, switches on the flame, bends down, and inhales.

"Ahhhh," he says after he's straightened again and exhaled. "Now that's what I'm talkin' about."

And I recognize a sweet, pungent scent that immediately reminds me of McCracken Hall. That's when I realize what's rolled into his cigarette is not tobacco.

"How," I ask, truly stunned, "did you get that onto a transatlantic flight?"

"They're called tighty-whities, baby," Blaine says, dropping down into the kitchen chair Madame Laurent only recently vacated and swinging his combat-booted feet up onto the butcher-block table.

"You smuggled marijuana into France in your *underwear*?" I am stunned.

He looks at me and chuckles. "Marijuana," he echoes. "You're cute, you know that?"

"They have those sniffy dogs at airports now," I remind him.

"Sure they do," he says. "They're trained to sniff for bombs, though, not ganja. Here." He takes a deep toke on the joint, then holds it out to me. "Have some."

"Oh," I say, wrapping both arms around my bucket, then realizing, belatedly, that I must look very prim. "No thank you."

He eyes me incredulously. "What? You don't smoke weed?"

"Oh no," I say, "I can't afford to lose any more brain cells. I didn't have that many to start with."

He chuckles some more. "Good one," he says. "So what's a nice girl like you doing in a dump like this?"

I assume he's joking, since Château Mirac is hardly a dump.

"Oh," I say, "I'm just visiting with my friends."

"That tall dude," Blaine says, "and the dyke?"

I take umbrage at this. "Shari isn't a lesbian! Not that there's anything wrong with being a lesbian. But Shari isn't one."

He looks surprised. "She isn't? Whoa. Coulda fooled me. Sorry."

"She and Chaz have been dating for two years!" I'm still shocked.

"Okay, okay. Jeez, no need to jump all over me. I said I was sorry. She just seems kinda dykey to me."

"She hardly said two words to you!"

"Right."

"What, any woman who doesn't fall all over you is a lesbian?"

"Relax," Blaine says, "would you? God, you're worse than my sister, for Christ's sake."

"Well, I can see why your sister might be upset with you," I say, "if you go around accusing her friends of being lesbians when they're not. Again, not that there's anything wrong with that."

"Jesus," Blaine says, "chill out. What, are you a lesbian or something?"

"No," I say, feeling my cheeks start to heat up, "I'm not a lesbian. Not that—"

"—there's anything wrong with it. I know, I know. Sorry. It's just, you know, you're here by yourself, and you got so upset when I asked about your friend . . ."

"For your information," I say, "I'm here by myself because I just got out of a very bad relationship with a British guy. Yesterday. That's why I'm here, as a matter of fact."

"Yeah? What'd he do? Cheat on you?"

"Worse. He cheated on the British government. Welfare fraud."

"Oh." Blaine looks impressed. "Hey, that's bad. My last girlfriend turned out to be a disappointment as well. Only *she* dumped *me*."

"Really? What for? Did you accuse her of being a lesbian, too?"

He smiles. "Funny. No. *She* accused *me* of being a sellout when my band signed with Atlantic Records. Dating a musician with a trust fund is one thing. Dating a musician with an actual recording contract turns out to be something else completely."

"Oh," I say. And he looks so sad that for a moment I really do feel sorry for him. "Well, I'm sure you'll meet someone else. There must

be lots of girls out there who'd enjoy dating someone with a recording contract *and* a trust fund."

"I don't know," Blaine says, looking depressed. "If so, I haven't
met any."

"Well," I say, "give it time. You don't want to rush into anything
right away. You need to give yourself a chance to heal emotionally."
This sounds like such good advice. I should give serious consider-
ation to taking it myself.

"Yeah," Blaine says, sucking on his joint, "I hear ya. That's what I
told my sister about Craig. But did she listen? No."

"Oh? Craig is your sister's fiancé? Is he a rebound?"

"Oh, hell, yeah. I mean, he's better than the last guy she almost
married—least this one's not part of Houston 'society'"—he makes
quotes around the word with the fingers that aren't holding the
joint—"but talk about boring. I mean, the guy practically makes
Bill Gates look like freaking Jam Master Jay, if you get my drift."

"Right," I say.

"Still," Blaine says with a shrug. "He makes her happy. Or as
happy as any guy can. Still, Mom'd much rather have her marrying
some guy like ol' Jean-Luc."

I am disgusted with myself for the way my heart turns over even
at the mention of Luke's name.

"Oh really?" I say in an attempt to appear only casually interested
in the topic.

"Shit," Blaine says, "are you serious? If Mom could get Vicks to
hook up with some guy who went to one of those fruity boarding schools, like Luke did, and has a castle in France, she'd frigging cream herself. Instead," he says with a sigh, "she got stuck
with Craig." He holds out a hand and examines the fingers that say
F-U-C-K. "And me."

"Oh yes," I say, "I noticed your tattoos at dinner. That must
have . . . hurt."

"Truthfully," Blaine says, "I don't remember if it did or not, I was so wasted. Soon as I get back home, I'm having 'em lasered off. I mean, it was funny for a while, but I'm makin' serious business deals now and shit. It's embarrassing to walk into those corporate meetings with 'Fuck You!' tattooed on your hands, you know? We just sold one of our songs to Lexus, for a commercial. Six figures, dawg. It's unbelievable."

"Wow," I say. "I'll be sure to look out for it. What's the name of your band, anyway?"

He blows a blue plume of marijuana smoke toward the ceiling.

"Satan's Shadow," he says reverently.

I cough. And not because of the smoke.

"Well," I say, "that's an . . . unusual name."

"Vicky thinks it's dumb," Blaine says. "But I notice she still wants us to play her gig."

"Well," I say, "weddings are a big deal to girls. You should probably go apologize to your sister, don't you think? I mean, she's really stressed. I'm sure she didn't mean to take it out on you."

"Yeah," Blaine says, lumbering, with an effort, from his chair, "you're probably right. Hey, you wouldn't be interested, would you?"

I blink, confused. "Interested? In what?"

"You know," Blaine says. "*Me*. I'd never cheat the government. I've got a CPA for that."

"Oh." I smile at him, startled but flattered. "Thank you very much for the offer. Ordinarily, of course, I'd jump at the chance. But like I said, I'm just coming out of a relationship and I probably shouldn't rush into anything new too soon."

"Yeah," Blaine says with a sigh, "it's all about the timing. Well, g'night."

"Night," I say. "And, um, good luck. With Satan's Shadow and all."

He waves and shuffles from the kitchen. And I hurry out as well, clutching my bucket.

The late 1800s saw the prominence of the "puffed sleeve" on women's gowns for which Anne Shirley so longed in the classic children's book series *Anne of Green Gables*. Dresses were longer than ever, requiring skirts to be lifted while crossing the street, thus revealing lace-trimmed petticoats available now not only to the rich, thanks to mass production.

Amelia Bloomer's trousers, meanwhile, finally found eager supporters in young female enthusiasts of the newly invented bicycle, and no amount of chastising from their parents, priests, or the press could induce girls to give up their "bloomers," or their bicycles.

History of Fashion
SENIOR THESIS BY ELIZABETH NICHOLS

18

His talk was like a spring, which runs
With rapid change from rocks to roses
—*Winthrop Mackworth Praed (1802–1839), British poet*

I got the rust stains out.

I know. I can barely believe it myself. I'm standing in the kitchen of Château Mirac early the next morning, having soaked the gown overnight in my room, then hurried downstairs—seemingly at the crack of dawn, but a glance at my cell phone tells me it's only eight—to rinse it in the kitchen sink, which is much wider than the one in the bathroom across the hall from my room.

I swear that's the only reason. It has nothing to do with my fearing Dominique might find me there and demand I hand the dress over to her now that it's saved.

Really. Nothing to do with that.

Saved, but still not perfect. I have to mend the torn strap and the jaggedy parts along the hem, plus give the thing a supergood ironing when it finally dries.

But I did it. I got the rust stains out.

It's a French miracle.

I'm gazing at the dress with rapturous self-satisfaction when I hear someone behind me say, "You did it!"

And I nearly have a heart attack, I'm so startled.

"GOD!" I cry, spinning around to find a smiling Luke in the doorway, looking excited. "What are you trying to do, kill me?"

"Sorry," Luke says, "I didn't mean to scare you. But . . . you did it! The stains are gone!"

My heart is hammering a mile a minute—but I have to admit it's not just because he startled me. It's also because he looks so gorgeous in the morning light. His freshly shaved face is still glowing a little pinkly from whatever he uses as aftershave (I suspect plain alcohol, since he doesn't smell like anything in particular, except clean), and the ends of his dark hair are curling damply against the collar of his blue polo shirt. He's got on those jeans again—the ones he was wearing the first time I met him, the Levi's that fit his butt so perfectly, not too snug, but not too loose, either. He looks like something dropped from a helicopter—you know, the perfect guy, for a needy girl trapped on a desert island.

That girl being me, and the desert island being my life.

Except, of course, he isn't mine.

A fact about which he is undoubtedly vastly relieved, I realize, when I see his gaze going from the gown I'm holding to the clothes I'm wearing—which happen to be my Sears jeans and Run Katie Run T-shirt.

Well, Mrs. Thibodaux had been pretty explicit about what we'd be doing all day—setting up tables and chairs in preparation for tomorrow's wedding. I don't want to get one of my nice dresses dirty.

Plus I couldn't be bothered with my hair this morning, so it's piled into a ponytail coming out of the top of my head. At least I have makeup on. Some, anyway. Enough to keep my eyes from looking piglike.

"Cream of tartar works, huh?" is all Luke says, though, as his gaze goes from me back to the dress. Which is something of a relief. I get positively jumpy when those dark brown eyes turn in my direction.

"It sure does," I say, giving the gown a satisfied flick. "Of course, it doesn't always work this fast. Sometimes you have to go through multiple soakings. I don't think that gun could have been there that long. The grease and rust didn't really set in that deeply. Now I just need to mend and iron it, and it'll be as good as new. Whoever it belongs to is going to be stoked to get it back good as new."

Luke grins. "I think tracing its ownership is going to be a tad difficult. We've had a lot of guests here over the past few centuries."

"Well, this one probably stayed here sometime in the past few decades," I say. "I'm thinking late sixties, early seventies. Though, I grant you, with Givenchy it's hard to tell. His lines are so classic . . . he really isn't influenced by the vagaries of popular trends."

Luke's grin broadens. "The vagaries of popular trends?"

I blush. "I thought that sounded good."

"Oh, it did. You've got me convinced. So. Want to come with me to get the croissants?"

I stare at him. "Croissants?"

"Yeah. For breakfast. I'm going into town to the bakery now, to get them before everybody wakes up and comes downstairs, whining for breakfast. I know you haven't seen Sarlat and I think you'll like it. Want to come with me?"

If he'd asked me if I wanted to go to Family Day at the local Gap, where all Gap employees give their friends and relatives thirty-five percent off all Gap products—which is basically my idea of hell on earth—I would have wanted to come with him. That's how far gone I am about him.

Except, of course, for that one trifling detail.

"Um," I say, "where's Dominique?"

I feel like that's a nice, neutral way to ask if his girlfriend is going along, too. Without coming right out and asking it that way. Because "Is your girlfriend coming?" might sound as if I don't like her, or that I only want to go if I can get him alone, or something like that. Which isn't true. At all.

Although if she is coming along, I might find something else I have to do instead. Just because having to sit and watch the two of them together isn't really high on my list of fun things to do while on vacation in the south of France.

"She's still sleeping," Luke says. "Little too much champagne with Mom last night."

"Oh," I say, keeping my expression carefully neutral. "Well, just let me hang this to dry. And I'll be right back."

"I'll be out in the car," Luke says, indicating the back door to the kitchen, in front of which the butter-colored convertible is parked.

I run like the wind. I hang the dress from the peg (what servants used for their uniforms in the olden days?) on my wall, with the bucket underneath to catch the drips.

Then I grab my purse and tear back downstairs.

Luke is sitting behind the wheel. There is no one else in the car. Around us, the morning air smells as fresh as newly folded laundry, and the sun, already getting hot, feels delicious on my skin. It's completely quiet except for birdsong and the huffing of Patapouf, the basset hound, who has come sniffing around the back kitchen door in hopes of getting some handouts.

"Ready?" Luke asks me with a smile.

And, despite all my best efforts, my heart bursts right out of my chest and flies around my head on little cherub wings. Just like in a cartoon.

"Yes," I say to him in what I think sounds like a perfectly normal voice—considering the fact that my heart is twittering around and around my head—and hurry to slide into the front passenger seat.

I am so, so dead.

But so what? I'm on vacation! It's okay to have a little crush. In fact, it's better to have a crush on Luke, who is safely taken, than it would be to have one on, say, Blaine. Because I might actually end up hooking up with Blaine, who is available, and that would be very emotionally risky, considering my fragile state of rebound.

No, it's fine that I have a crush on Luke. He's safe. Because nothing will come of it. Nothing at all.

The ride down the same driveway it took us so long to climb up the night before last is hilariously bouncy. I have to hang on to keep from being thrown around the massive front seat. But Luke and Chaz really did do a good job cutting the tree branches back—none of them whip at us.

And then suddenly we're bursting out of the trees onto the same road along the river that we'd traveled from the train station the other night . . . but that had been in the dark. Seeing the river up close for the first time in daylight, I can't help gasping.

"It's so beautiful!" I cry. Because it is. A sun-dappled, gently flowing river, with wide, grassy banks, over which tall oak trees tower, their leafy branches providing bathers and rafters with welcome shade.

"The Dordogne," Luke explains. "I used to go rafting on it when I was a kid. Although that makes it sounds like there are rapids, which there aren't, really. We'd go down it on inflatable tires. It's a nice, lazy ride."

Impressed by so much natural beauty, I shake my head. "Luke, I don't get how you can go back to Houston when you have all this."

Luke laughs and says, "Well, much as I love my dad, I don't exactly want to live with him."

"No," I say mournfully. "Neither does your mom, I guess."

"He drives her crazy," Luke agrees. "She thinks all he cares about is his wine. When he's here, all he does is fuss over his vines, and when he's back in Texas, with her, all he ever did was worry about them."

"But he loves her so much," I say. "I mean, can't she tell that? He can barely take his eyes off her."

"I guess she needs more than that," Luke says. "Some kind of proof that when she's not around, he thinks about her, too. And not just his grapes."

I'm mulling this over when we turn a corner and I see the Laurents' millhouse—with Madame Laurent outside, watering the explosion of blossoms in her arbored garden.

"Oh!" I cry. "It's Agnès's mom!" I wave. *"Bonjour! Bonjour, madame!"*

Madame Laurent looks up from her flowers and waves back, smiling, as we whiz past.

"Well," Luke says, glancing at me with a grin, "you're certainly in a good mood this morning."

"Oh," I say, sinking back into my seat in embarrassment over my excitement at seeing the Château Mirac cook in her own habitat. "This place is so beautiful. And I'm just. So happy. To be here."

With you, I almost add. But for once, I manage to shut my mouth before it runs away with me.

"I suspect," Luke says, making a turn toward the high-walled city I'd seen perched up on a cliff the night I'd arrived, "that you're the kind of person who's in a good mood wherever you are. Except when you've just discovered your boyfriend is a welfare cheat," he adds with a wink.

I smile a little queasily back at him, still feeling mortified. Of all the people I had to open my big mouth to about my romantic problems, why did it have to be *him*?

But a second later, as we enter the city of Sarlat, I forget my chagrin at the sight of all the red geraniums spilling down from window boxes above my head; the narrow cobblestoned streets; the villagers, hurrying along to the open-air market with their baskets filled with baguettes and vegetables. It's like a movie-set version of a French medieval village—only it isn't a movie set. It's a real medieval village!

And I'm right in the middle of it!

Luke pulls up in front of a quaint old shop with the word *boulangerie* written in gold on the large front window and from which the smell of freshly baked bread wafts, causing my stomach to growl hungrily.

"Do you mind waiting in the car?" Luke asks. "That way I don't have to find a parking space. It'll just take a second, I already phoned in the order. I just have to pick it up."

"Pas un problème," I say, which I think means "Not a problem." I guess I'm right since Luke smiles and hurries inside.

Still, my grasp of French is put to the test a second later when a carefully dressed old woman approaches the car and begins babbling to me a mile a minute. The name "Jean-Luc" is the only word I recognize.

"Je suis désolée, madame," I begin to say, which means "I'm sorry." I think. *"Mais je ne parle pas français—"*

Before the words are all the way out of my mouth, the old woman is saying, in French-accented English, looking scandalized, "But I understood Jean-Luc's *petite amie* was French!"

At least I know what the words *petite amie* mean.

"Oh, I'm not Jean-Luc's girlfriend," I say hastily. "I'm just a friend. I'm staying at Mirac for a little while. He's inside picking up some croissants—"

The old woman looks infinitely relieved. "Oh!" she says, laughing. "I recognized the car, you see, and I just assumed . . . you must forgive me. That was quite a shock. For Jean-Luc not to marry a Frenchwoman . . . it would be quite a scandal!"

I take in the woman's carefully knotted scarf—obviously Hermès—and light wool suit (she must be broiling in this heat) and say, "You must be a friend of Monsieur de Villiers, then?"

"Oh, I have known Guillaume for years. It was very shocking to all of us when *he* married that woman from Texas. Tell me"—the old woman narrows her perfectly made-up eyes—"is she there now? Madame de Villiers? At Château Mirac? I heard a rumor she was . . ."

"Um," I say. "Well, yes. Her niece is getting married there tomorrow, and—"

"Madame Castille," Luke says as he comes out of the bakery with two large paper bags in his arms. "What a pleasure." His smile, though, doesn't reach his eyes.

"Oh, Jean-Luc," the old woman says, beaming with pleasure at the sight of him (well, who wouldn't?).

And then she launches into a torrent of French against which Luke, I can tell, feels defenseless. Which is why I say, when Madame Castille pauses for breath, "Uh, Luke? Hadn't we better get back? People are going to be waking up and wanting their breakfast."

"Right," Luke says quickly. "We have to go, madame. It was lovely seeing you. I'll give my father your best, don't worry."

It isn't until we've pulled away that Luke gives a mighty exhalation and says, "Thanks for that. I thought she was going to talk all day."

"She's a big fan of yours," I say with cautious nonchalance. "She thought I was your girlfriend and she about had a heart attack that I wasn't French. She said it will be a big scandal if you don't marry a French girl. It was a big scandal when your dad married your mom, apparently."

Luke throws the car into gear with more force than is strictly necessary. "The only person who was scandalized was her. She's been after my dad since they were kids. Now that he and my mom are on the rocks, she can't wait for the chance to sink her claws into him."

"But it won't work," I say, "because your dad still loves your mom. Right?"

"Right," Luke says. "Although I could see the old guy marrying that witch just to get her off his back. Oh, here. I got you something." He pokes the bag of heavenly scented croissants that sits between us.

"A croissant?" I ask, opening up the bag. A wave of yeasty steam hits me. They're still warm from the oven. "Thanks!" I decide not to mention anything about my carb-free diet. I've pretty much given up on that since those rolls on the train down here, anyway.

"Not that bag," Luke says, looking at me like I'm crazy. "The other one."

I notice a smaller bag behind the one containing the croissants and open it.

And my eyes nearly pop out of my head.

"Wha—" I gasp. I am, for only the second time in my life, speechless. "How—how did you know?"

"Chaz said something about it," Luke says.

I pull the six-pack—glistening with moisture—from the bag and stare at it.

"They're . . . they're still cold," I say wonderingly.

"Well," Luke says a little dryly, "yes. I know Sarlat looks old, but they do have refrigeration."

I know it's ridiculous. But my eyes have actually filled with tears. I do my best to blink them away. I don't want him to know that I'm crying with joy over the fact that he's given me a six-pack of diet Coke. Because I'm not. It's the gesture, not the beverage.

"Th-thank you," I say. I know I need to keep the conversation short, or he'll hear the tremor in my voice. "D-do you want one?"

"You're welcome," Luke says. "And no, thank you. I prefer to get my caffeine the old-fashioned way, with a Colombian drip. So. What have you decided?"

I've taken one of the cans from the plastic holder and am about to crack it open. "Decided?"

"About what you're going to do," Luke says. "When you get back to the States. Are you going to stay in Ann Arbor? Or move to New York?"

"Oh." I crack open the can. The sharp hiss of carbonation is every bit as musical to my ears as the burble of the river to my left.

"I don't know. I want to move to New York. You know, with Shari. But what would I do there?"

"In New York?"

"Right. I mean, let's face it. It turns out there's not a whole lot you can do with an individualized major in history of fashion. I don't know what I was thinking."

"Oh," Luke says with a mysterious smile, "I'm pretty sure you'll figure something out."

"Right," I say—very sarcastically. I mean, for me, anyway. "And then there's the small fact that I haven't exactly graduated yet. How can I find a job if I don't even have my B.A. yet?"

"Well," Luke says, "I think that depends on the job."

"I don't know," I say. And take a sip of my diet Coke. The bubbles from the carbonation tickle my tongue. God, I've missed this. "It might just be simpler to stay in Ann Arbor for one last semester."

"Right," Luke says. "And see if you can patch things up with what's-his-name."

I am so shocked by this I nearly spit out the diet Coke I've just swallowed. Yes! Nearly one of sixteenth of one my six precious cans!

"WHAT?" I cry after I swallow. "Patch things up with—what are you TALKING about?"

"Just checking," Luke says. "I mean, you say you want to stay in Ann Arbor . . . and he'll be in Ann Arbor. Right?"

"Well, yeah," I say. "But that's not why. I mean, at least in Ann Arbor I still have my job at the shop. I could live at home and save up my money, then join Shari in January." If she hasn't already found another roommate.

"That," Luke says as he turns the car up the driveway to Mirac, "doesn't sound much like the girl I met on the train the other day, the one who took off for France without even knowing if she'd have a place to stay when she got there."

"I knew I'd have a place to stay," I say. "I mean, I knew Shari was here *somewhere*. I knew I wouldn't be alone."

"Just like you wouldn't be alone in New York," Luke says.

I laugh. "Oh, you're one to talk," I say. "Why aren't *you* moving to New York? You told me you got into NYU."

"Yeah," Luke says as we bounce along the steep driveway. "But I don't know if that's really what I want to do. I mean, give up my six-figure salary for five more years of school?"

"Oh, you'd rather help rich people figure out how to make more money than save lives?"

"Ouch," Luke says with a grin.

I shrug. Or as best I can when I'm being jounced around so much and am also trying to protect the precious elixir in the can I'm holding. "I'm just saying. I mean, managing stock portfolios is important. But if it turns out what you're actually good at is healing sick people, isn't it kind of a waste not to do that instead?"

"But that's just it," Luke says. "I don't know if I am. Good at healing sick people, I mean."

"Just like I don't know if there's anything I'm good at that someone in New York will actually pay me to do."

"But," he says, "as a certain person keeps telling me, you'll never know if you don't even give it a try."

Then we're bursting out of the trees again and onto the circular drive that leads to the house. It's even more impressive, it turns out, in daylight than it is at nighttime.

Not that Luke seems to notice. I guess because he's seen it so many times already.

"That's different," I say. "I mean, you already know there's something you can do. Someone's paying you a six-figure salary to do it. You know how much I get paid? I get eight bucks an hour at Vintage to Vavoom. You know how far eight bucks an hour goes in New York City? Well, I don't, either. But I'm guessing not very far."

Luke, I notice when I glance nervously his way to see what he thinks of my admission, is grinning more broadly than ever.

"Is this how you are with everybody?" he wants to know. "Or am I just lucky because, in a moment of weakness, you revealed all your deepest secrets to me?"

"You promised not to tell anyone about those," I remind him. "Especially Shari, about the thesis—"

"Hey," Luke says, pulling up in front of the château. His gaze is steady on mine. He's not smiling anymore. "I said I wouldn't tell. Remember? And I'm not going to. You can trust me."

And for a second—while we sit there looking at each other across the bag of croissants—I can swear that something . . . *happens* . . . between us.

I don't know what. But it's different from all the times I thought he was going to kiss me. There's nothing sexual about what happens there in the car. It's more like some sort of . . . mutual understanding. Some sort of acknowledgment that we are spiritual kin. Some sort of magnetic pull—

Or maybe it's just the smell of the croissants. It's been a really long time since I've had any kind of pastry.

Whatever it is that's going on between Luke and me—if anything—it's over a second later when the door to the château is thrown open and Vicky, standing there in a pale blue kimono, says, "God, what took you so long? We're all *starving*. You know I get hypoglycemic if I don't eat first thing in the morning."

And the moment between Luke and me—whatever it was—is gone.

"Got your cure for hypoglycemia right here," Luke says cheerfully, grabbing the bag of croissants.

Then, when Vicky stomps back into the house, Luke turns to me and winks.

"Look at that," he says. "I'm healing people already."

The dawn of the twentieth century is often referred to as "la Belle Époque," or "the beautiful age." Certainly the fashions of the age were beautiful, featuring, as they did, big hair, low décolletage, and tons and tons of lace (see: Winslet, Kate, *Titanic,* and Kidman, Nicole, *Moulin Rouge*). Achieving the look of a Gibson girl (created by a popular artist of the same name) became the rage, with even President Roosevelt's vivacious daughter, "Princess" Alice, wearing her hair in the Gibson girl's pompadour style—a look very hard to maintain while "motoring," Alice's favorite hobby.

History of Fashion
SENIOR THESIS BY ELIZABETH NICHOLS

19

Keep silence for the most part,
and speak only when you must,
and then briefly.
—*Epictetus (c. ACE 55–135), Greek Stoic philosopher*

The rest of the morning is a blur of deliveries. The first truck to arrive is the one carrying the dance-floor, stage, and sound equipment for the wedding's band—in this case, not the string quartet Luke tells me plays most weddings at Mirac, but Blaine's band, Satan's Shadow. As workers from the company in charge of setting this up begin their work, another truck—this one filled with folding tables and chairs for the rehearsal dinner and wedding reception (both of which are to be held on the lawn)—rumbles up the driveway (knocking down everything Luke and Chaz couldn't reach, and forcing the two of them to have to scramble back down the driveway to clear it of all the newly fallen branches) and needs help unloading.

Just as Shari, Chaz, Blaine—who, his band not having arrived yet, declares, "I'm bored," and begins pitching in—and I get the last of the folding chairs off the truck, another one arrives, this one carrying all the food the chef and staff from a local restaurant will be preparing for the festivities. This food needs to be unloaded and carried to the kitchen, where Madame Laurent supervises its storage, and the restaurant chef begins preparing canapés for the cocktail hour, which begins in the late afternoon . . .

Which is when the out-of-town guests begin showing up, either in their own rented vehicles or ferried from the train station by Dominique, who has managed to avoid having to do any hard labor by volunteering to do this instead. The groom arrives first, with his dazed-looking parents. I am very curious to see this computer programmer Vicky is marrying instead of the rich Texas oil baron her mother wanted for her, and I have to say, when I finally see Craig, I can understand the attraction. Not that he's good-looking—because he's not.

But when Vicky comes flying at him from inside the house, blathering about everything that's going wrong, from her friends still not having hotel rooms to Blaine having told her that she looks fat in her rehearsal-dinner dress, Craig's reply is as phlegmatic as his parents' reaction to Mirac.

"Vic. It's all right," he says.

And Vicky actually stops crying.

At least until half a dozen of Vicky's friends—as pretty and blond as she is—pile out of minivans and stumble across the gravel driveway in their wobbly high heels to hug her. Then she starts bawling all over again, and Craig, not looking in the least bothered by this, gently leads his parents to the vineyard, where Monsieur de Villiers happily shows them around the cavernous cask room.

Soon it seems the entire château is under attack by what appears to be the upper crust of Houston society, stylishly clad matrons with their navy-blue-blazer-wearing husbands in tow, with whom Dominique mingles and laughs.

These Houstonians, in turn, raise their eyebrows at the arrival of the remaining members of Satan's Shadow, who show up in an extremely disreputable-looking van and are greeted by Blaine with their signature Satanic cry, which involves tipping back the head and ululating (which causes Vicky to run inside, screaming, "Mo-o-o-om!" and Shari, as she helps me spread a tablecloth over the last of the twenty-five or so tables on the lawn, to shake her head and go, "God, am I glad I'm an only child").

I'm happy when the staff from the restaurant takes over and begins setting the tables. This leaves us free to run inside to change before the cocktails are served—a necessity since we're going to be manning the bar for the event, opening the bottles of wine and champagne Monsieur de Villiers will be supplying, and I personally don't want to gross anyone out with my sweat stains. I don't exactly have the most experience opening wine bottles, either, so I'm suspecting the evening should be pretty interesting, on the whole.

I'm just coming back down the stairs, feeling refreshed and semi-presentable in a black sleeveless Anne Fogarty linen dress, when I nearly collide with a group of people coming *up* the stairs, led by Luke, who is hauling a couple of really heavy-looking suitcases.

"I'm telling you, son," a portly bald gentleman in khaki pants and a black polo shirt is saying to Luke. "It's an opportunity you can't afford to miss. You were the first person I thought of when I heard."

Behind the balding man hovers Ginny Thibodaux, looking flustered.

"Gerald," she says, "did you hear me? I said I think Blaine's smoking again. I could swear I smelled cigarettes on him just now. That funny foreign kind he and all his friends like so much . . ."

Behind Mrs. Thibodaux, Vicky is saying, "Mom, you have got to talk to him. Now he's saying his stupid band won't play covers. Mom, he swore they'd play covers. Now he's saying they're only doing their songs. How am I supposed to have my father-daughter dance to some song called 'Cheetah Whip'?"

"I don't know, dear," Mrs. Thibodaux says. "Your brother just hasn't been the same since that Nancy left him. I wish he'd meet a nice girl. Wouldn't any of your friends—"

"Jesus, Mom. Would you worry about something that actually

matters for a change? What are we going to do about the fact that he won't play any covers? Craig and I are not having our first dance as a married couple to a song called 'I Wanna Bang Your Box' . . ."

"Well, hello," Luke says with a grin as I make room for him and the Thibodauxes to pass me. "Don't you look nice."

"Thanks," I say, looking carefully at the bald man. This, I assume, is Vicky's long-awaited dad.

"Think about it, son," Mr. Thibodaux is saying eagerly to Luke. "It's a tremendous opportunity."

Luke says, "Thanks, Uncle Gerald," with a wink at me, and continues up the stairs, with the Thibodauxes trailing along after him, still talking a mile a minute, and none of them listening to the other. Hurrying the rest of the way down the stairs, I find Mrs. de Villiers and Dominique in the foyer having a little tête-à-tête of their own . . .

But not in voices low enough for me not to overhear what they're saying.

"—opening a branch in Paris," Dominique is going on excitedly. "Gerald says he thought of Jean-Luc immediately. It's an incredible offer. Far more responsibility—and money—than Jean-Luc is getting at Lazard Frères. Thibodaux, Davies, and Stern is one of the most exclusive private-client investment companies in the world!"

"I'm familiar with my brother-in-law's company," Mrs. de Villiers says with a hint of irony in her voice. "What I'm not so sure of is just when Luke decided he wanted to move to Paris."

"Are you joking?" Dominique asks. "It's always been our dream!"

I am rooted to the spot by the words. *Our dream.*

And then Dominique is racing excitedly up the stairs after Luke, barely acknowledging me as she hurries past, except to give me a tight little smile.

So Luke's uncle has offered him a job. An investment banking job. In Paris. For a lot more money than he's making now.

It's ridiculous that I should feel so physically affected by the news. I mean, I only met Luke two days ago. All I have is a tiny crush on him. Just a crush. That thing in the car this morning—that thing I thought I felt pass between us . . . that was probably just my undying gratitude to him for buying me that six-pack of diet Coke. That's all.

But there's no denying that a lump has formed in my throat. Paris! He can't move to Paris! It's bad enough that he lives in Houston! But a whole *ocean* away from me? No.

What am I thinking? What's wrong with me? It's none of my business. *None* of my business.

I tell myself that firmly as I come the rest of the way down the stairs . . .

. . . and find that Mrs. de Villiers has sunk onto one of the velvet couches in the foyer and is looking perturbed. She smiles briefly when she sees me, then continues to look troubled, lost in her own thoughts.

I start to walk by. I know I'm probably wanted outside. I can hear the murmur of all the guests gathering on the lawn for aperitifs. I'm sure there are champagne bottles that need uncorking. And I did, after all, promise to help.

But suddenly I'm wondering if there's someone else I need to help first. Maybe this *is* my business. I mean, why else was it that Luke and I ended up sitting next to each other on that train? Granted, there were no other seats available. But *why* were there no other seats available?

Maybe because I was *supposed* to sit by him. So that I can do what I'm doing now.

Which is save him.

And so, before I can change my mind, I turn around and come back to where Mrs. de Villiers is sitting.

Seeing me standing in front of her, Luke's mother looks up.

"Yes, dear?" she says with a hesitant smile. "I'm sorry, I've forgotten your name . . ."

"Lizzie," I say. My heart has begun beating very hard within my chest. I can't believe I'm doing what I'm about to do. But on the other hand, I feel it's my duty, as lead anchor of the Lizzie Broadcasting System. "Lizzie Nichols. I couldn't help overhearing what Dominique told you just now"—I nod my head toward the stairs Dominique has just taken—"and I just wanted to say, strictly between you and me, that I'm not sure it's *entirely* true."

Mrs. de Villiers blinks. She really is a very attractive woman. I can totally see why Monsieur de Villiers fell so much in love with her and is so depressed about her not feeling the same way about him.

"What's not entirely true, honey?" she asks me.

"About Luke, wanting to move to Paris," I say in a rush, to get it all out before someone interrupts us. Or I come to my senses. "I know Dominique wants to move there, but I'm not so sure Luke does. In fact, he's playing with the idea of going to medical school. He's already applied to a program at NYU and gotten in. He hasn't told anyone, I guess—anyone but me—because he's not sure it's what he wants to do. But I personally think if he doesn't go, he'll always regret it. He told me he used to dream of being a doctor, but that he couldn't imagine going to school for four more years—well, five, counting the program he'd have to take to get all the science credits he'd need before he can even start . . ."

My voice trails off as I realize, from her stunned expression, how stupid what I'm saying must sound to her.

"Medical school?" Mrs. de Villiers's eyes are lined in pale blue. It brings out the green in her hazel eyes. The green is even more noticeable when she widens her eyes at me, which she does now.

"Luke always did want to be a doctor when he was a little boy," she says in a breathy, excited way. "He was forever bringing home sick and injured animals to try to cure, both here and back in Houston . . ."

"I think medicine is really what he would have preferred to go into," I say, nodding eagerly. "But I don't think converting Mirac into a place for plastic surgery patients to recover from their liposuction is necessarily a substitute for—"

"*What?*" A look of horror crosses Luke's mother's face.

Oh. No. Please don't tell me I've done it again.

But it's clear from the look on Mrs. de Villiers's face that I have. She looks as shocked as if I'd just told her that Jimmy Choo doesn't design the shoes with his name on them anymore. Which he doesn't.

Okay. So the lipo thing isn't something Dominique has run by Luke's parents yet.

"Um," I say. This is definitely *not* what I'd intended when I approached Luke's mom. I had never meant to rat out Dominique. All I'd wanted to do was let Mrs. de Villiers know that her son had a secret dream . . . a dream that, now that I think about it, he'd probably meant to *stay* secret. But, of course, I'd blown that.

"I'm just . . . I mean—if the vineyard really isn't doing all that well," I stammer, trying to change the subject, "I was thinking that a better alternative might be to rent Mirac out to people—rich people, obviously—who want a nice château to vacation in for a month, or maybe for a family or college reunion or something . . ."

"*Plastic surgery?*" Mrs. de Villiers repeats, in a stunned tone not unlike the one Luke had employed when I'd mentioned Dominique's idea to him. I can see that my attempt to change the subject hadn't gone over too well. "Who on earth ever suggested—"

"No one," I assure her quickly. "It was just an idea I heard being kicked around—"

"By *whom?*" Mrs. de Villiers wants to know, still looking horrified.

"You know what," I say, wanting to die. "I think I hear my friend Shari calling. I have to go—"

And then I do just that, jumping up and darting out of the house just as quickly as I can.

I'm dead. I'm so dead. I can't believe I did that. *Why* did I do that? Why did I open my big mouth? Especially about something that has nothing whatsoever to do with me. NOTHING. God, I'm such an *idiot*.

My cheeks flaming scarlet, I hurry across the lawn to where Chaz is already manning the bar (a long folding table covered with a white cloth). There is a long line of thirsty Houstonians, eager for their first cocktail of the day, in front of him.

"There you are," Chaz says when he sees me. He seems to notice neither my flaming cheeks nor my advanced state of nervous paranoia. "Thank God. Start cracking open some of those champagne bottles. Where's Shari?"

"I thought she was out here with you," I say, reaching for a bottle with trembling fingers.

"What, she's still inside changing?" Chaz shakes his head, then looks at the frat-boy type standing in front of him. "What can I get for you?"

"Stoli on the rocks," Frat Boy says.

"Sorry," Chaz says. "Beer and wine only, man."

"What the fuck?" cries Frat Boy.

Chaz levels him with a look. "You're on a vineyard, pal. What did you expect?"

"Fine." Frat Boy is sulking. "Beer, then."

Chaz all but throws a bottle at him, then looks at me. I've gotten the little metal cage off the champagne bottle, but the cork is eluding me. I don't want it to pop off and hit anyone.

Why did I tell Mrs. de Villiers that Luke wants to be a doctor? Why did I let slip that thing about the lipo? Why am I physically incapable of keeping my mouth *shut*?

"Use a napkin," Chaz says, throwing me one.

I give him a blank look. I have no idea what he's talking about. Am I drooling now, on top of everything else?

"To pull the cork," Chaz says impatiently.

Oh! Looking down, I wrap the napkin around the cork and pull—and it comes out easily, with a gentle pop, and no bodily harm to anyone.

Sweet. Okay. So there's one thing I can do right, anyway.

I am totally getting the hang of this. Chaz and I have a nice little rhythm going . . . that is, until Shari suddenly appears.

"Where have you been?" Chaz wants to know.

Shari ignores him. It's only then that I notice her eyes are blazing. And that she's staring straight at me.

"So just when," Shari demands, "were you going to tell me you didn't actually graduate yet, huh, Lizzie?"

The dawning of World War I found women's fashion going through a change almost as hot as the political climate. Corsets were abandoned as waistlines dropped and hemlines rose, sometimes to ankle length. For the first time in modern history, it became stylish not to have a bustline. Small-breasted women everywhere rejoiced as their more endowed sisters were forced to purchase chest "flatteners" in order to fit into the most popular fashions.

History of Fashion
SENIOR THESIS BY ELIZABETH NICHOLS

If you can't say something good about someone,
sit right here by me.
—*Alice Roosevelt Longworth (1884–1980), U.S. author and wit*

can't believe he told. I trusted him and he completely betrayed me!

"I . . . I was going to tell you," I say to Shari.

"Kir royale, please," says a woman who looks as if she might be regretting her decision to wear long sleeves in such warm weather.

"When?" Shari demands.

"You know," I say, pouring a glass of champagne for the woman, then adding a splash of cassis. "Soon. I mean, I only just found out myself! How was I supposed to know I had to write a thesis?"

"If you paid a little more attention," Shari says, "to your studies, and a little less to clothes and a certain Englishman, you might have realized it."

"That's not fair," I say, passing the woman her kir royale and only splashing a little of it down on her hand. "My field of study *is* clothes."

"You're impossible," Shari spits. "How are you going to move to New York City with Chaz and me if you don't even have a degree?"

"I never said I was going to move to New York with you and Chaz!"

"Well, you're definitely not *now*," Shari declares.

"Hey," Chaz says, looking annoyed, "would you two cool it? We have a lot of Texans here who want their liquor and you're holding up the line."

Shari steps in front of me and says, "May I help you?" to the large woman I'd just been about to wait on.

"Hey," I say, hurt. "That's where I was standing."

"Why don't you go do something useful," Shari says, "and go finish your thesis."

"Shari, that's not fair. I *am* finishing it. I've been working on it all—"

It's right then that a shriek rends the stillness of the evening. It seems to be coming from the second floor of the house. It is followed by the words "No, no, no," uttered at the unmistakably high decibel achieved by one person, and only one person, staying at Mirac:

Vicky Thibodaux.

Craig, who is standing in front of the table where we're serving, glances at the house. Blaine, behind him in line, says, "Don't do it, man. Don't go. Whatever it is, you do not want to know."

But Craig looks resigned.

"I'll be right back," he says, and starts toward the house.

"You'll regret it," Blaine calls after him. Then, to me, he says, "There's a sucker born every minute."

"Did it ever occur to you that there might be something seriously wrong?" Shari, who is clearly in no joking mood, asks him. It's clear she's not sharing Blaine's unconcern—though she's one of the few. Everyone else on the lawn, seemingly used to Vicky's outbursts, is steadfastly ignoring what they've just heard.

"With my sister?" Blaine nods. "There's been something seriously wrong with her since the day she was born. It's called being a spoiled brat."

It's right then that Agnès comes running up to me, out of breath and panting, and says, "Mademoiselle. Mademoiselle. They want you to come. You must come now."

"Who wants me to come?" I ask in wonder.

"Madame Thibodaux," Agnès replies. "And her daughter. In the house. They say it is an emergency . . ."

"All right," I say, putting down my napkin. "I'll come. But—" Then, stunned, I gasp. "Wait. Agnès, you spoke English!"

Agnès blanches, then realizes she's been caught.

"Don't tell Mademoiselle Desautels," Agnès begs.

Chaz, amused, grins at her. "But if you speak English, why did you pretend you didn't?"

Now Agnès, instead of being pale, is blushing.

"Because I do not like her," she says with a shrug. "And my not understanding English annoys her very much. And I like to annoy her."

Whoa.

"Um," I say, "okay." To Chaz and Shari, I say, "I'll be back in a minute. Is that okay?"

Shari, her lips pressed into a thin line, refuses to comment. But Chaz, rapidly filling glasses, looks at me and says, "Go on. Agnès can take over for you. Can't you, Agnès?"

"Oh yes," Agnès says, and begins opening champagne bottles with the ease of someone who happens to be an old hand at it.

I don't hesitate a moment longer. I race around the table and head for the house, relieved to be out from under Shari's glare . . . but also furious that Luke told her. Why? Why did he say anything when only just this morning he promised he wouldn't?

And okay, I may not exactly have kept *his* secret . . .

But his secret isn't guaranteed to make anyone mad at him, the way mine was.

I should have known, of course. Men can't be trusted to keep a secret. Well, okay, I can't be trusted to keep one, either. But I thought

Luke was different from other guys. I thought I could tell him anything . . .

Oh my God! What *else* did he tell Shari? Did he tell her about the
you-know-what? No, surely not. If he had, she'd have said something. She wouldn't have cared about shocking all those Daughters
of the American Revolution. She'd have been like, "YOU GAVE
ANDY A PITY BLOW JOB? ARE YOU INSANE?"

At least, I think she would have . . .

This is what I'm thinking to myself as I race into the house and
up the stairs. I don't see anyone on my way to the second floor,
where I find Craig, tapping on the door to Vicky's room and saying,
"Vic. Let me in. Now."

"NO!" Vicky cries in an anguished voice from behind the door.
"You can't see me! Go away!"

I approach, a little out of breath.

"What's wrong?" I ask Craig.

"I don't know," the groom-to-be says with a shrug. "Something
to do with her dress. I'm not allowed to see it, or it's bad luck. She
won't let me in."

Something to do with her dress?

I tap on the door.

"Vicky?" I say. "It's Lizzie. Can I come in?"

"No!" Vicky cries.

But the next thing I know, the door has been flung open.

Only not by Vicky. By her mother. Who snakes out an arm, grabs
me by the shoulder, and pulls me into the room with a terse "Please
go away, Craig" to her future son-in-law before slamming the door
shut behind us.

As I stand in the large corner room, with its pink-papered walls
and enormous canopy bed, my gaze is instantly drawn to the girl
sobbing on a pink stuffed chair in the corner. Mrs. de Villiers is
stroking her niece's hair in an attempt to calm her down. Domi-

nique, looking darkly malevolent for some reason, glares daggers at me.

"Dominique says you know how to sew," Mrs. Thibodaux says, still not having let go of my shoulders. "Is that true?"

"Um," I say, completely confused, "yes. I mean, I *can* sew—"

"Can you do anything about this?" Mrs. Thibodaux demands, and spins me around so that I can get a look at her daughter, who has climbed to her feet and is now standing . . .

. . . in the most hideous wedding dress I have ever seen in my life.

It looks as if a lace factory threw up on her. There is lace every-where . . . the poufed sleeves . . . the insert above the neckline . . . dripping from the bodice and skirt, then looped up in bunches all around the hem. It's the kind of wedding dress some girls dream of . . .

When they're nine.

"What *happened*?" I ask.

This just makes Vicky cry harder.

"You see?" she wails to her mother. "I knew it!"

Mrs. Thibodaux is chewing her lower lip. "I told her it wasn't that bad. She's so upset . . ."

I walk around the stricken bride to get a look at the back of the dress. Just as I suspected. There is an enormous lace butt bow in the back.

A butt bow.

Things could not be worse.

I exchange glances with Luke's mother. She looks, very briefly, to the ceiling.

I have no choice but to admit the truth.

"It's bad," I say.

Vicky lets out a hiccupy sob. "How c-could you let this happen, Mother?"

"What?" Mrs. Thibodaux looks indignant. "I'm the one who warned you! I'm the one who kept saying not to overdo it! She designed it herself," Mrs. Thibodaux explains to me, "and had a Parisian dressmaker hand-sew it, based on Vicky's sketch."

Oh. Well, that explains everything. Amateurs should never design their own dresses. And certainly not their own *wedding dress.*

"But I didn't mean it to look like *this,*" Vicky wails. "It didn't even look like this at the last fitting!"

"I told you," Mrs. Thibodaux says to her daughter. "I told you not to wait until twelve hours before your wedding to try your dress on! And I told you not to add all that lace! But you wouldn't listen. You kept saying it would be fine. You kept saying you wanted more."

"I wanted something *original,*" Vicky cries.

"Well, it's original all right," Mrs. de Villiers says wryly.

"The question is," Dominique says, speaking for the first time since I've entered the room, "can you fix it?"

"Me?" I fling a panicky glance at the gown. "Fix it? How?"

"Get rid of all this," Vicky says with a sniffle, lifting up a limp layer of lace that hangs, inexplicably, from the gown's bodice.

I stoop to examine the gown. It is, just as she asserted, hand-sewn. The stitching is superb.

And is going to be nearly impossible to rip out without damaging the material underneath.

"I don't know," I say. "I mean, it's sewn on there really well. Removing it might leave holes. It could end up looking really weird."

"Weirder than this?" Vicky demands, lifting her arms and revealing what appear to be wings of lace coming down from the sleeves.

"Good God in heaven!" Luke's mother exclaims, seeing the wings.

The wings seem to have clinched the matter for Mrs. Thibodaux.

"Can't you sew up the holes?" she asks me.

"In time for her to wear it tomorrow afternoon?" Luke's mother's tone is still wry. "Ginny, be reasonable. Even a professional seamstress—if we could find someone this late in the day—couldn't do it."

"Oh, Lizzie is quite accomplished," Dominique chimes in. "Jean-Luc can't stop raving about her many talents."

Luke can't stop raving about me? Many talents? What talents? What is Dominique talking about?

"Really?" Mrs. de Villiers is looking at me with pointed interest. I can't tell if it's because of what Dominique just said, or if it's residual curiosity concerning what I told her earlier in the evening, about her son's medical aspirations.

"Jean-Luc says she makes all her own clothes," Dominique says. "She even made that dress she's got on right now."

"What?" I'm so startled I jump. "No I didn't. This is by Anne Fogarty from, like, the 1960s. I didn't *make* it."

"Oh, don't be modest, Lizzie," Dominique says with a laugh. "Jean-Luc told me everything."

What is she *talking* about? What is going on? What did Luke say to her about me? What did Luke say to *Shari* about me? What is Luke doing, going around talking about me all over the place?

"It won't take Lizzie any time at all," Dominique is saying, "to whip Victoria's dress into shape."

"Oh!" Mrs. Thibodaux claps her hands together, tears—actual tears—glistening at the corners of her eyes. "Is that really true, Lizzie? Can you really do it?"

I look from Mrs. Thibodaux to Mrs. de Villiers to Dominique, then back again. Something is going on here. Something that, I'm starting to suspect, has more to do with Dominique than it does anything else.

"Do you think you can salvage it, Lizzie?" Mrs. de Villiers asks me, looking worried.

Did Luke really say I have many talents? That I'm accomplished?

I can't let him down. Even if he did rat me out to Shari.

"I'll see what I can do," I say hesitantly. "I mean, I can't promise anything—"

"I don't care," Vicky says. "I just don't want to look like Stevie Nicks on my wedding day."

I can see her point. Still—

"Take off your dress and give it to Lizzie," Mrs. Thibodaux tells her daughter. "And change into your rehearsal-dinner dress. There are a lot of people waiting to see us down there. God knows what they think is happening up here."

I didn't point out that it seemed as if most people hadn't been too alarmed by Vicky's screams, since she seems to let them out so often.

A minute later I find myself standing there clutching an armful of satin and lace.

"Do what you can," Mrs. Thibodaux says to me as Vicky, having changed into a demure pink sundress and repaired her tear-stained makeup, opens the door and goes out to greet Craig, who has been calmly waiting for her all this time.

"You can't possibly make it look any worse," is what Luke's mother says as she sails past me.

It's Dominique who adds, as she follows the sisters, "Good luck," with such malicious glee in her eye that I realize—belatedly—that I've just dug myself a grave I'll never be able to climb out of.

And that Dominique is the one who handed me the shovel.

Part Three

World War I was responsible for millions of deaths, but perhaps none more noticeable than the death of prewar conventions. A generation of women who had been doing "war work" in the absence of men, who were away fighting, realized that with the world about to end, they might as well start smoking, drinking, and in general doing everything else they had been forbidden from doing for so many years.

Girls who engaged in these activities soon earned themselves a special name—flappers—so-called because they were like baby birds, "flapping" the wings of their independence for the first time. In defiance of their parents and, in some cases, lawmakers, these girls bobbed their hair, hiked their skirts to knee length, and began paving the way for the fashion trendsetters of today's youth (see: Stefani, Gwen, L.A.M.B designs, and Spears, Britney, banana snake halter top).

History of Fashion
SENIOR THESIS BY ELIZABETH NICHOLS

21

It is vain to keep a secret from one who has a right to know it.
It will tell itself.
—*Ralph Waldo Emerson (1803–1882),*
U.S. essayist, poet, and philosopher

Okay. It's all right. I can do this. I can totally do this.

I'll just rip out the stitches. I have my sewing kit with me, with its seam ripper and stitch scissors. It'll be a snap. I'll just rip off all the lace and see what I've got to work with when I'm done. It'll be fine. Just fine. It has to be fine, because if it isn't, I'll have ruined a bride's big day. Not only that, but I'll have let down all these people who've been so kind to me.

Okay. I have to do a good job. I have to.

Rip.

Oh. Oh, okay, that looks really bad. Maybe I'll start with the butt bow. Rip. Yes, that looks better already. Good. Rip.

The thing is, one person, I know, wants me to fail. It's so obvious that's why Dominique said the things she did. Luke probably didn't say any of those things—rip—about me having many talents, or being so accomplished. I can't believe I fell for that. She only said those things because she knew if I heard them, it would be harder for me to say no.

And she wanted me to say yes so I could screw up.

It's just—rip—why would she want me to screw up? What did I ever do to her? I mean, I have been nothing but nice to her.

Well, okay, there was that thing about telling Luke's mom that he wants to be a doctor. She might be a *little* peeved about that, seeing as how she wants to move to Paris.

And then there's the fact that I let her little plan about converting Mirac to a lipo-recovery hotel slip.

But I never told Mrs. de Villiers that Dominique was the one who came up with it.

So why would she do something so incredibly bitchy? She knows as well as I do this dress is a lost cause. *Vera Wang* couldn't salvage this thing. Nobody could. What was Vicky thinking? How could she possibly ever have thought—

"Lizzie?"

Chaz. Chaz is at my bedroom door.

"Come in," I call.

He opens the door and pokes his head inside.

"Hey, what are you doing in here? We need you out—"

His voice trails off as he takes in the mess my room has become. Snowy fields of lace lay . . . well, everywhere.

"Sweet mother of God," Chaz says. "Did the Sugar Plum Fairy explode in here?"

"Bridal gown emergency," I say, holding up Vicky's gown.

"Who's getting married?" Chaz wants to know. "Björk?"

"Very funny," I say. "Anyway, don't expect me back at the bar anytime soon. I've got my hands full up here."

"That's kinda obvious. But not for nothing, Lizzie . . . do you even know anything about fixing wedding dresses?"

I am trying hard not to let him see me cry.

"I guess we'll find out, won't we?" I say brightly.

"Yeah. I guess we will. Well, don't worry, you're not missing much down there. Just a lot of windbags going on about their yachts. Oh, hey, listen, what's going on between you and Shar?"

I sniffle, and rub my nose with a shoulder as if it just tickles and isn't running.

"She found out I didn't actually graduate," I say.

Chaz looks relieved. "Is that all? Jesus, the way she's carrying on, I thought you said something about Mr. Jingles. You know she still feels guilty about that—"

"No," I say. "I just neglected to inform her that I haven't finished my thesis. And she found out. Somehow."

You know, it serves me right. Luke telling Shari about me not graduating, I mean. Since I told his mom about the doctor thing.

It's just that I physically *can't* keep a secret. What's his excuse?

"Didn't finish your thesis? Jesus, that's nothing," Chaz says dismissively. "You can crank that puppy out in no time. I'll tell Shar to cool it."

"Right," I say, sniffling. When he throws me a questioning look, I say, "Allergies. Really. And thanks, Chaz."

"Okay. Well. Good luck." Chaz looks around the room speculatively. "Looks like you're going to need it."

Then he leaves.

I let out a little sob but quickly pull myself together. I can do this. I can do this. I've done this hundreds of times to dresses at Vintage to Vavoom, dresses no one wanted to buy because they were too ugly. A few swipes of my scissors and a velvet rose here and there, and ... *voilà! Parfait!*

And we were generally able to sell them at a fifty percent markup.

I've just managed to get the wings dripping from the sleeves off when there's another knock at the door. I have no idea how long I've been working, or what time it is, but I can see outside the tiny diamond-shaped window at the end of my bed that the sun is setting, turning the sky a brilliant ruby color. I can hear laughter drifting up from the lawn and the clink of silverware. The guests are eating.

And, having helped to carry in the food from the delivery truck it arrived in, I'm pretty sure, based on what I've seen, that what they're eating is delicious. I'm pretty sure, in fact, that truffles and foie gras are involved.

"Come in," I say in response to the knock, thinking maybe it's Chaz again.

I am totally shocked to see that it's not Chaz at all, but Luke.

"Hey," he says, letting himself into the tiny room, then looking around, clearly concerned.

And why shouldn't he be concerned? The place looks like a confetti factory.

"Chaz just told me what's up," he says. "I had no idea they'd roped you into this. This is completely insane."

"Yeah," I say stiffly. I am determined not to cry. At least, not in front of him. "It's insane all right."

Hold it together, Lizzie. You can do it.

"How did they talk you into this?" he wants to know. "I mean, Lizzie, no one can possibly make a wedding dress in one night. Why didn't you say no?"

"Why didn't I say no?" Oh no. Here come the tears. I can feel them, hot and wet, behind my eyelids. "Gosh, Luke, I don't know. Maybe because your girlfriend was standing there telling them how talented you said I was."

Luke looks taken aback. "What? I didn't—"

"I realize that," I cut him off. "*Now*. But at the time, I don't know, a part of me was hoping it was true or something. You know, that you had said something nice about me. I should have realized, of course, that it was all just a trick."

"What are you talking about?" Luke asks. "Lizzie—are you crying?"

"No," I insist, lifting a wrist to wipe my streaming eyes. "I'm not crying. I'm just really tired. It's been a really long day. And I really don't appreciate your doing what you did."

"What *I* did?" Luke looks totally confused.

He also, in the light from the little lamp by my bed, looks totally hot. He's changed into his party clothes, a collared white linen shirt and black trousers with a razor-sharp crease down the front of each leg. The white shirt brings out the deep tan of his neck and arms.

But I will not be swayed by masculine hotness. Not this time.

"Oh, right," I say. "Like you don't know."

"I *don't* know," Luke says. "I don't know what Dominique said that I said, Lizzie, but I swear—"

"I'm not talking about what you said to Dominique," I interrupt. "I already know that was a lie. But why . . ." My voice catches. So much for refusing to cry in front of him. Oh well. It's not like he's never seen my tears before. ". . . why did you tell Shari about my thesis?"

"*What?*" His expression, in the lamplight, is a mixture of incredulity and confusion. "Lizzie. I swear. I never said a word."

Wow. I really hadn't expected that. You know, denial. I'd fully expected him simply to come clean . . . to admit he'd done it and ask for an apology.

Which I'd been willing to accept, of course, on account of my own guilt for having spilled the beans about him to his mom. It's true things would never be the same between us, of course. But maybe, with time, we might have been able to build up some modicum of mutual trust . . .

But to stand there and deny it? To my *face*?

"Luke," I say, my disappointment causing my voice to throb a little, "it had to be you. No one else knew."

"It *wasn't*," Luke says. A glance at his face shows he's no longer feeling incredulous or confused. Now he's mad. At least if his frown is any indication. "Look, I don't know how Shari found out about your not graduating. But I didn't tell her. Unlike *some* people in this room, I can keep a secret. Or are you not the one who told my mother that I want to go to medical school?"

Oops. In the silence before I reply, I can hear more rattling of silverware from below, along with the chirp of crickets, and Vicky's voice, crying out very distinctly, "Lauren! Nicole! You made it!"

I swallow.

I. Am. So. Dead.

"Well," I say, "yes. Yes, I did. But I can explain—"

"Do you really think," Luke interrupts, "that it's okay for you to go around accusing people of failing to keep a secret when you obviously can't keep one yourself?"

"But—" I say, feeling all the blood drain from my face. Because he's right. Of course. I'm the biggest hypocrite in the world.

"But," I say again, "you don't understand. Your girlfriend—your uncle—everyone was going around saying you were going to take that job, and I just thought—"

"You just thought you'd get involved in something that was none of your business?" Luke demands.

I. Am. So. Stupid.

"I was trying to help," I say in a small voice.

"I never asked for your help, Lizzie," Luke says. "Help was never what I wanted from you. What I wanted from you was . . . what I thought we might have—"

Wait. Luke wanted something from me? Luke thought we might have—*what*?

Suddenly my heart starts pounding a mile a minute. Oh my God. Oh my God.

"You know what?" Luke says suddenly. "Never mind."

And he turns around and stalks from the room, closing the door very firmly behind him.

Some argue that the rise of Hitler—and Fascism—can be blamed for the return, in the 1930s, to longer skirt lengths and the restrictively tight waistline, sending women into corsets once again. The onset of the Depression made it nearly impossible for ordinary women actually to own the expensive Parisian fashions they saw sultry stars wearing in the movies—but talented seamstresses who could imitate the designs with less costly fabrics found plenty of business, and the "knockoff" was born at last . . . long may it live (see: Vuitton, Louis).

History of Fashion
SENIOR THESIS BY ELIZABETH NICHOLS

Gossip is charming! History is merely gossip.
But scandal is gossip made tedious by morality.
—*Oscar Wilde (1854–1900), Anglo-Irish playwright, novelist, and poet*

Can I just say it's really hard to snip straight when you're crying so hard you can't see?

Well, whatever. Who needs him, anyway? I mean, okay, sure, he seems really nice. And he's definitely good-looking. And smart and funny, too.

But he's a liar. I mean, obviously he told Shari about my thesis. How else could she have found out? I don't know why he couldn't have just admitted it, the way I did, about having told his mom about his secret dream of being a doctor.

At least I did that for a good cause. Because I suspect Bibi de Villiers is the kind of woman who, upon learning her child has a secret dream, will do everything in her power to see that that dream is achieved. Should a mother like that really be kept in the dark about her son's most heartfelt ambition?

I was actually doing Luke a *service* in telling his mother. How can he fail to see that?

Oh, all right. I'm a busybody and a loudmouth and a big stupid jerk.

And because of it, I've lost him . . . though the truth is, I never really had him. Oh, sure, there was that moment this morning, when he bought me the diet Coke—

But no. That was clearly all in my head. There's no doubt about it now. I am destined to live and die alone. Romance and Lizzie Nichols simply do not mix.

And that's just fine. I mean, there have been plenty of people who have had perfectly happy, fulfilled lives without a significant other. I can't think of any right now. But I'm sure there have been. I'll just be like one of them. I'll just be Lizzie . . . alone.

I'm trying to angle my scissors beneath a particularly tight row of stitches when there's yet another knock on my door.

Seriously. I don't know how much more of this I can take.

The door opens before I even have a chance to say "Come in."

And, much to my surprise, Dominique is standing there, looking tall and cool in high-heeled Manolo slides and a low-cut slinky green dress.

I shake my head.

"Look," I say, "I know it looks bad, but it's always worse before the storm. I'll get the dress done if people would just leave me alone so I can work."

Dominique steps into the room, looking around carefully, as if afraid there might be trip wires across the floor, instead of just mounds and mounds of lace.

"I didn't come here about the dress," Dominique says. She stops by my open suitcase and looks down at the jumble of vintage dresses and Sears jeans that are lying there. Then she smirks.

"Look," I say. I have really taken about all I can mentally stand. "If you want me to finish this thing by morning, you're going to have to leave me alone, okay? Tell Vicky I'm doing the best I can."

"I told you," Dominique says. "I'm not here about Victoria or her dress. I'm here about Luke."

Luke? That causes me to lay down my scissors. What could Dominique have to say to me about *Luke*?

"I know you're in love with him," she says, lifting my family-size pack of Tums from the top of the dresser and examining it closely.

I stare at her openmouthed. "Wh-what?"

"It's quite obvious," Dominique says, putting the Tums back where she found them. "At first I was not alarmed because . . . well, look at you."

Like the total jerk that I am, I actually do look down at myself. There are now approximately eighty-five thousand bits of white lace stuck to my black dress. I've pulled my hair into a haphazard ponytail and lost my shoes somewhere under all the folds of material lining my floor.

"But I know he's . . . *fond* of you," Dominique says, lifting her pointed chin.

Yeah. Well. Maybe at one time. Now? Not so much, I suspect.

"He thinks of you, I think, like a big brother thinks of a funny little sister," Dominique goes on.

Great. The way Blaine thinks of Vicky. Just great.

Although it's better than hating me, I guess.

"He tells you things, I think." She's found one of my many book lights and lifts it up to examine it. "I'm wondering if he has said anything to you about his uncle's offer."

I feign ignorance. What else can I do? I can't let on that I was eavesdropping. Even though of course I was.

"Offer?"

"Surely you heard? A job in Paris with Monsieur Thibodaux's very exclusive firm. Making a great deal more than he is making even now. Hasn't he mentioned it to you?"

"No," I say. And for once, I'm not even lying.

"How odd," Dominique says. "He's acting so strangely."

"Well," I say conversationally, "that can happen. You know, when a lot of money suddenly gets thrown your way. People freak. Look at what happened to Blaine."

"Blaine?" Dominique looks blank.

"Right. Blaine Thibodaux." When Dominique continues to look blank, I explain, "His band got signed by a record company, and Blaine's girlfriend left him. Because she says he's too rich now. Like I said. When it comes to large amounts of money, some people just . . . freak."

Dominique looks startled. My book light sits forgotten in her hand.

"Record companies pay that much?"

"Well, sure," I say. "Plus, you know, Blaine just sold the rights to one of his songs to Lexus. For a commercial."

Dominique's eyes narrow. "Really." She puts down the book light. "How interesting." Her tone suggests she finds it anything but. "Then you don't know why Luke is acting so strangely?"

"I have no idea," I say. Because I really don't. At least, not why he'd be acting strangely toward *Dominique*. Unless she, like me, accused him of being a liar. Then, of course, I'd understand.

"Well," she says. And starts for the door. "Thank you. Good luck with the dress." Her mouth twists at one end into something like a smile. "It looks as if you'll need it."

Then she's gone, before I can even say "Thanks."

Oh well. If that's the kind of woman Luke prefers—tall, naturally skinny, artificially inflated in the chest area (I'd stake Grandma's life on it), and obsessed with money, more power to him.

Although, you know. I can sort of understand why he might prefer that kind of woman to one who accuses him of being a liar. Even if he is one.

And that doesn't seem like something Dominique would do. She's way too crafty.

Crafty enough to have gotten me to commit to a project there's no way I'll ever complete on time. At least, not to anyone's satisfaction. By the time the toasts start downstairs—I can hear the clink of spoons on crystal, then a lull, then appreciative laughter—I've denuded Vicky's gown of lace.

And found that what the lace was covering is actually worse-looking than the lace.

I'm standing there asking myself if I should just put the lace back on and admit defeat, or possibly pack up all my things and just make a run for it, when the door to my room opens and Shari comes in, without knocking. In her hands is a plate of food.

"Before you open your mouth and make things even worse than they actually are," she says angrily as she sets the plate on top of my dresser, by the book lights, "I want you to know that I got my period today, and like a fool, I forgot to bring any tampons. So I came in here to look for some, because I know you always pack like you're going to Mount Everest and won't see civilization for weeks, even for an overnighter. And that's how I found the notebook you're writing your thesis in. I mean, you left it open, right on your bed. There's no way I could avoid looking at it. I thought it was your diary. And I had PMS. I *had* to read it, obviously."

I stare at her openmouthed.

"I know it was wrong," she goes on. "But I read it anyway. And that's how I knew you hadn't actually graduated. Luke didn't tell me. Although may I just take this moment to say I can't believe you told Luke, a man you only met a few days ago, and not me, who has been your best friend since kindergarten?"

I feel something rumble beneath me. At first I think it's the floor. Then I realize it's my entrails, clenching.

"Luke didn't tell you?" I ask in a weak voice.

"No," Shari says. She flops down onto my bed, heedless of the piles of lace there. "So it was really nice of you to accuse him of it. He seems to really appreciate it. And you."

"Oh God." Clutching my stomach, I sink down on the bed beside her. "What have I done?"

"Fucked up," Shari says. "Big time. I mean, considering you're in love with him and all."

I glance at her miserably. "Does it show that much?"

"To those of us who have known you for eighteen years? Yes. To him? Probably not."

I collapse back against the bed and stare with tear-filled eyes at the raftered ceiling.

"I'm such an idiot," I say.

"Yes," Shari replies. "You are. Why didn't you just tell me about your thesis in the first place?"

"Because," I say, "I knew you'd be mad at me."

"I *am* mad at you."

"See? I knew it."

"Well, come on, Lizzie," Shari says. "Just because your education was free doesn't mean it's all right for you to squander it. *History of fashion?* As a major?"

"Well, at least I didn't have to kill any rats!"

The minute the words are out of my mouth, I regret them. Because now Shari's eyes have filled with tears.

"I told you," she says. "I had to kill Mr. Jingles. A scientist has to be able to distance herself."

"I know," I say, sitting up and wrapping my arms around her. "I know, and I'm sorry I said that. I don't know what's wrong with me. I'm just . . . I'm just a mess."

Shari doesn't hug me back. Instead she looks across my room and says, "You *are* a mess, and you've gotten yourself *into* a mess. Lizzie, what are you going to do about that girl's dress?"

"I don't know," I say sadly, surveying the damage. "It actually looks worse than before."

"Well," Shari says, "I didn't see it before. But I don't see how it could look worse than it does now."

I take a deep breath.

"I'm going to fix it," I say. And I'm not just talking about Vicky's dress, either. "I don't know how. But I'm going to fix it. If I have to stay up all night."

"Well," Shari says. And she gets up off the bed and goes to retrieve the plate from the dresser. "Here. Peace offering."

She puts the plate in my lap. On it is an assortment of some of the food from the rehearsal dinner—what appears to be Cornish game hen, some kind of vegetable gratin, a salad in a vinaigrette, assorted chunks of cheese, and . . .

"That's foie gras," Shari says, pointing at a blob of brown on the edge of the plate. "I know you wanted to try some. I didn't get you any bread, because I trust you're still doing the low-carb thing—croissants and Hershey bar sandwiches aside. Here's a fork. Oh, and here—"

She goes to the door to my room, opens it, stoops down, and retrieves something from the floor outside.

It's an ice bucket. She lifts the lid to reveal—

"My diet Cokes," I say, fighting back a new wave of tears.

"Yeah," Shari says. "I found them wedged way back in the fridge, behind the Nutella. I figured you could use some if you were going to pull an all-nighter up here. Which"—she glances at the remains of Vicky's wedding dress—"is what it looks like you'll be doing."

"Thanks, Shar," I say, starting to sniffle. "And . . . I'm sorry. I don't know why I didn't stay more on top of things with school. I was just too wrapped up in Andy toward the end there, I guess, to really pay attention to what was going on."

"That's not it," Shari says. "I mean, that's probably part of it, but let's face it, Lizzie. School was never your thing." She nods at my sewing basket. "*This* is. And if anybody can fix that ugly dress, well, I guess it's you."

My eyes well up again. "Thanks. Only . . . I mean, what am I going to do about Luke? Does he . . . does he really hate me?"

"Hate might be a strong word for it," Shari says. "I'd say he's more . . . bitter."

"Bitter?" I wipe my eyes with my hands. "Bitter's better. I can deal with bitter. Not," I add quickly, seeing the curious look Shari darts at me, "that it matters. Since he's already got a girlfriend, and he lives in Houston, and I'm just coming out of a dead-end relationship, and I'm not interested in starting something new and all."

"Right," Shari says with one eyebrow raised. "Okay, then. Well, get to it, Coco. We'll all be eagerly awaiting your creation in the morning."

I try to laugh, but all that comes out is a hiccupy sob.

"And Lizzie?" she asks as she pauses on her way out the door.

Uh-oh. "Yeah?"

"Is there anything else I need to know?" Shari asks. "Any other secrets you might be harboring from me?"

I swallow. "Absolutely not," I say.

"Good," Shari says. "Let's keep it that way."

And then she stomps out of my room.

The thing is, I don't feel at all bad about not telling her about the blow job. There are some things even your best friend doesn't need to know.

When the Germans invaded Paris in 1940, fashion as the world knew it came to a standstill. The war put an end to the export of couture, and rationing to save resources for the war effort meant that items like silk, which was needed to make parachutes, were impossible to come by. Die-hard lovers of fashion, however, would not give up their stockings, and so stained their legs and drew seams down them to imitate the look of their favorite hosiery. Women who were not so artistically inclined opted instead to wear trousers, a look finally acceptable to a society becoming used to things like air raids and bebop.

History of Fashion
SENIOR THESIS BY ELIZABETH NICHOLS

23

Gossip is news running ahead of itself in a red satin dress.
—*Liz Smith (1923–), U.S. journalist and author*

awake to find a strip of lace stuck to my face. Also to an urgent knocking on my door.

I look around blearily. A wan gray light fills my room. I realize I forgot to close my drapes the night before. I realize I forgot to do a lot of things the night before. Such as change into pajamas. Wash my makeup off. Or brush my teeth.

The banging on my door continues.

"Coming," I say, rolling out of bed—then staggering a little as a wicked head rush seizes my temples in a vise. This is what comes, I know, of pulling a diet-Coke-fueled all-nighter.

I make my way to the door and pull it open a few cautious inches.

Vicky Thibodaux, in a pale blue peignoir, stands in the hallway.

"Well?" she demands anxiously. "Are you finished? Did you do it? Could you save it?"

"What time is it?" I ask, rubbing my gritty eyes.

"Eight," she says. "I'm getting married in four hours. FOUR HOURS. *Did you finish?*"

"Vicky," I say, slowly forming the words that I have been going over and over in my head since around two in the morning. "Here's the thing—"

"Oh, fuck it," Vicky says, and throws her full body weight against the door, shoving it open, and me aside.

Three steps into the room, she freezes when she sees what's hanging from the hook on my wall.

"Th-that . . ." she stammers, her eyes wide. "Th-that's—"

"Vicky," I say. "Let me explain. The gown that your dressmaker used to sew all that lace onto didn't have enough structural integrity in and of itself to exist on its own without—"

"I love it," Vicky breathes.

"—all the lace that covered it. In essence, your bridal gown *was* lace . . . and that's it. So I—wait. You what?"

"I love it," Vicky says. She reaches excitedly for my hand and squeezes it. She hasn't once taken her eyes off the gown on the wall. "It's the most beautiful gown I've ever seen."

"Um," I say, relief coursing through me. "Thanks. I think so, too. I found it in the attic upstairs the other day. It was kind of stained, but I got those out, and fixed a few tears along the hem, and reattached one strap. Last night I adjusted the fit according to the measurements on your old dress. It should fit, so long as you haven't shrunk—or grown—in the night. Then I spent about an hour pressing it . . . thank God I found an iron down in the kitchen . . ."

Vicky, I realize, is barely listening to me. She still hasn't unglued her gaze from the glistening Givenchy.

"Um," I say, "do you want to try it on?"

Vicky nods, apparently unable to speak, and begins stripping off her peignoir without another word.

I gently pluck the gown from its hanger. Vicky's original dress—the lace disaster—hangs on another hook nearby. I'd put the two side by side in order to let her choose. Her original gown doesn't look *that* bad—if I do say so myself. I managed to tone down the lace, though there was no way I could remove it all and still have a dress left. Instead of looking like something Stevie Nicks might wear, it now resembled something Oksana Baiul might sport at *Barbie on Ice*.

But next to the Givenchy, it hadn't stood a chance.

Which was just what I was hoping.

I find myself holding my own breath as I drop the yards and yards of creamy white silk over Vicky's head. Then, as she slips her arms through the straps, I step behind her to begin fastening the pearl buttons. One by one, they easily close. And she isn't, I know, holding her breath, because I can hear her excited panting as she looks down at herself.

"It fits," she cries excitedly as I get to the top buttons. "It fits *perfectly*."

"Well," I say, "it should. I moved the darts—"

Vicky whirls away from me. "I want to see," she cries. "Where's a mirror?"

"Um," I say. "There's one in the bathroom across the hall—"

She runs from my room, noisily banging the door, then just as noisily barges into the bathroom.

From which I hear, "Oh my God! It's *perfect*!"

I find myself sagging against my bedroom wall in relief. She likes it.

I finally did *something* right, anyway.

Vicky barges back into my room.

"I love it," she says. For the first time since I've met her, she's all smiles.

And, smiling, Vicky transforms into an entirely different girl. She's no longer the spoiled socialite who hates her brother and just about everyone else in the world.

Instead I get a glimpse of the sweet, engaging girl who chose to marry a phlegmatic computer programmer from Minnesota instead of the rich heir to a Texas oil fortune her mom had picked out for her.

It's true, I guess, what they say about brides on their wedding day. They're all beautiful. Even this early in the morning, with no makeup on, Vicky looks stunning.

"I love it, and I love *you*," she gushes. "I'm going to go show my mom." She leans over to plant a kiss on my cheek and pulls me into a surprisingly hard bear hug. "Thank you. Thank you so much. I will never forget this. You're a genius. An absolute genius."

Then, in a whirl of white silk, she's gone.

And, completely exhausted, I fall back into bed, desperate for a few more minutes of sleep.

I'm able to snatch one, maybe two, more hours before I'm rudely awakened again, this time by someone hurling herself bodily against me. Someone who sounds very much like Shari as she says, "Oh my God, oh my God, Lizzie, wake up! You'll never believe this—WAKE UP!"

I wedge a pillow over my head, keeping my eyes tightly closed.

"Whatever it is," I say, "I don't want to know. Seriously. I'm exhausted. Go away."

"You'll want to know this," Shari assures me, prying the pillow out of my hands.

When she's successfully lifted my only protection from the bright sunlight spilling into my bedroom, I peer at her through my puffy eyelids and say, in tones of great hostility, "This better be good, Shar. I was up till five in the morning working on that stupid dress."

"Oh, this is good," Shari says. "Luke dumped her."

I just stare at her. "Who?"

"What do you mean who?" Shari hits me in the head with the pillow she's taken from me. "Dominique, you idiot. He just told Chaz, who told me. And I rushed up here to tell you."

"Wait." I raise up to my elbows. "Luke broke up with Dominique?"

"Last night, apparently, after we all went to bed. I thought I heard them fighting, but the walls in this place are so thick—"

"Wait." This is seriously too much for me to handle on a diet-Coke-buzz hangover. "They broke up last night?"

"They didn't break up," Shari says gleefully. "He *dumped* her. He told Chaz he finally realized they wanted totally different things in life. Also that her tits were fake."

"*What?*"

"Well, that's not one of the reasons why he broke up with her, of course. It's just something he said in passing."

"Oh my God." I lay there, trying to figure out how I feel. Mostly I feel bad. But maybe that's because I've only had, like, three hours of sleep, total.

"It's my fault," I say finally.

Shari looks at me as if I'm insane. "Your fault? How is it your fault?"

"I told Luke's mom what Dominique told us . . . about him wanting to be a doctor. And I also let slip that stuff about turning this place into a lipo-recovery hotel. I bet she said something about it to Luke. His mom, I mean."

Shari gives me a very sarcastic look.

"Lizzie," she says, "guys don't break up with their girlfriends because their mom doesn't like them."

"Still," I say. I feel terrible. "If I had kept my mouth shut—"

"Lizzie," Shari says, "Luke and his girlfriend were having problems way before you ever came along."

"But—"

"I know, because Chaz told me. I mean, the woman has six-hundred-dollar flip-flops. Come on. Get over yourself. It had nothing to do with you or anything you may or may not have said to Luke's mom."

I digest this. Shari's right, of course. It would be way conceited of me to think that what had happened between Luke and his girlfriend had anything to do with me.

"I knew they were fake," I say at last.

"I know," Shari says. "I mean, they never moved. Like when she was waving."

"I know!" I cry. "Whose boobs don't jiggle when they move? When they're that big, I mean."

"So you know what this means," Shari says. "You've totally got a chance with him after all."

"Shari," I say, feeling alarmed. Because I know I'm only going to get my hopes up for nothing. "He hates me. Remember?"

Shari frowns. "He doesn't hate you."

"You said he was bitter."

"Well. Yeah. He did sound kind of bitter about you last night."

"See," I say.

"But that was before he dumped his girlfriend!"

I flop back against the pillows. "Nothing's changed between him and me since last night, though," I say to the ceiling. "I still accused him of telling you about my thesis. When he totally didn't."

"Well, here's a brilliant idea. Why don't you try apologizing to him?"

"It won't change anything," I say, still speaking to the ceiling. "Not if he's still bitter. And he probably is. I know I would be, if it were me."

"Actually, you wouldn't. But that's another issue. Look, there's no doubt in my mind you're going to have to do some groveling," Shari says. "But come on. Don't you think he might be worth it?"

"Yes," I say. "Of course." I think about that day on the train, how kind and patient and funny he was. How long his eyelashes had looked against the setting sun. How sweet he was to me that day in the attic. The diet Coke he bought me.

The way he'd insisted I'm brave, in spite of all the evidence to the contrary.

And my heart lurches with longing.

"But, Shari," I say, "there's no point. I mean, look at—"

The door to my room thumps open and Chaz sticks his head in, looking annoyed.

"Excuse me, ladies," he said. "I know it's fun sitting around gossiping about my friend Luke. But has it occurred to either of you that we have a WEDDING WE PROMISED TO HELP SET UP?"

Which is how, an hour later, I find myself carrying around a tray of mimosas, offering welcome libations to the thirsty—and cranky—hordes gathered on the lawn for the wedding of Victoria Rose Thibodaux and Craig Peter Parkinson. It's much hotter than anyone anticipated it would be, and the men are all sweating in their suit jackets and ties while the women are using the wedding programs to fan themselves. The wedding is supposed to start at noon, and by all indications it actually will. The minister—imported all the way from the bride's own church in Houston—has arrived, as has the florist, the wedding cake, and even the string quartet that will march in the bride (Satan's Shadow still refusing to play covers, including *Lohengrin*).

Even the bride, to everyone's surprise, is actually ready, and is rumored to be waiting coolly in the house for the strike of twelve.

I wish I could be doing anything coolly, but I'm basically a mess. That's because I still haven't seen Luke yet. Well, I mean, I've *seen* him—he's running around all over the place, greeting guests, fielding problems, looking stunning in a dark suit, and, unlike so many of the men at Mirac, not at all uncomfortable in it in this heat.

But never once has he come anywhere close to me, much less even glanced my way.

I can totally understand why he's angry—I mean, bitter—with me.

But the least he could do is give me a chance to explain.

"Is there alcohol in that?" Baz, Satan's Shadow's drummer, asks me as he points at the glasses I'm carrying.

"Yes," I say. "Champagne."

"Thank God," Baz says, and grabs two glasses, downs both of them, and puts them back on my tray empty. "It's frigging hot out here, huh?"

"Well," I observe politely, "at least you're dressed for it." Vicky's brother's band has, as far as I can tell, opted to eschew the dress code by wearing shorts, flip-flops, and, in the case of Kurt, the keyboardist, no shirt.

"Man," Baz says, "have you seen Blaine?"

"I have not," I say, my attention wandering. That's because I see Luke nearby, helping an elderly woman in one of the folding chairs Chaz and he were apparently up at seven in the morning setting in rows to form an aisle down which they're about to unroll a white carpet.

Baz follows my gaze and, spying Luke, raises an arm. "Luke!" he yells. "Yo, over here."

No! Oh God, no! I want to have a word with Luke, of course, but not like this . . . a *private* word. I do not want our first meeting since that unpleasant scene the night before to be in front of anyone—particularly not a drummer named Baz.

"Yes?" Luke asks politely as he comes over.

As usual, the sight of him causes my pulse to flutter like a tween at a sale at Claire's. He just looks so gorgeous standing there in the sunlight with his broad shoulders and freshly shaved face and, oh God, wingtips. Shiny, newly polished WINGTIPS!

It's all I can do to keep from dropping my tray.

Why did I have to do something as stupid as accuse him of telling Shari about my thesis? Why, just because *I* can't keep a secret, do I go around assuming no one else can, either?

"Dude, have you seen your cousin Blaine?" Baz asks Luke. "Nobody can find him anywhere."

"I haven't seen him," Luke says. His gaze, I can't help noting, is on mine. Though I can't for the life of me read what's going on behind those dark eyes. Does he hate me? Does he like me? Or does he ever even think about me at all? "Has anyone tried his room? Blaine's a late sleeper, if I remember correctly."

"Oh yeah," Baz says. "Good idea."

And he shuffles off, leaving Luke and me standing awkwardly alone together—an opportunity I seize before Luke has a chance to slip away.

"Luke," I say, my voice sounding very soft compared to the drum of my heartbeat in my ears, "I just wanted to say . . . about last night . . . Shari told me—"

"Let's forget about it, okay?" Luke says tersely.

Tears spring to my eyes.

Shari had said he was bitter. And he has a right to be.

But won't he even let me *apologize*?

But before I have a chance to say another word, Monsieur de Villiers, looking spry in a cream-colored suit and tie, comes up to me, holding a bottle of champagne.

"Lizzie, Lizzie," he chastises me merrily, "I see empty glasses on this tray. I think you need to go back to Madame Laurent for a refill."

"Here." Luke tries to take the tray from me. "I'll do it."

"*I'll* do it," I say, snatching the tray back. Only the fact that there are three glasses sitting on it, including Baz's two empty ones, keeps disaster from ensuing.

"I said," Luke says, reaching out again, "*I'll* do it."

"And I said, *I will*—"

"Lizzie!"

Luke, his father, and I all turn at the sound of Bibi de Villiers's excited voice. Looking stunning in butter yellow, with a picture hat framing her face, she exclaims, "Lizzie, where did you find that dress?"

I look down at myself. I have on the mandarin dress I last wore at Heathrow, when I'd been hoping to impress Andy . . . a million years ago. It's the only thing I brought with me that seems remotely appropriate for a wedding. Well, the fact that I can't wear panties with it aside. Besides, no one has to know about that but me.

"Um," I say, "at this shop where I work back in Michigan called Vin—"

"Not *that* dress," Luke's mother says. Her expression is a strange combination of excited and anxious. Not that that seems to matter to Luke's dad, who's staring at her as if she were something Santa had just dropped down the chimney.

"I mean the dress Vicky is wearing," Mrs. de Villiers says. "The one she says you fitted for her overnight."

Beside me, Luke grows very still. His father, on the other hand, is still staring at his wife in a thoroughly besotted manner.

Alerted by Luke's stiffness that something is up, I answer his mother's question very carefully.

"I found it here at Mirac," I say. "In the attic."

"The attic?" Mrs. de Villiers looks stunned. "*Where* in the attic?"

I don't have the slightest idea what's going on. But I do know that Mrs. de Villiers's interest in the Givenchy isn't casual. Was the dress hers? The size is right . . . it fit Vicky, and Vicky is Bibi's niece, so . . .

I'm not taking any chances. No way am I telling her the horrifying condition in which I found her dress. That's one secret I'll take with me to the grave.

Unlike all the rest I know.

"I found it in a special box," I say, fabricating rapidly. "It was wrapped in tissue. I would almost say *lovingly* wrapped—"

I know I've said the right thing when Mrs. de Villiers turns toward her husband and cries, "You saved it! After all these years!"

And suddenly she's thrown her arms around the neck of Luke's father, who is glowing with pleasure.

"Why, yes," Monsieur de Villiers is saying, "of course I saved it! What do you think, Bibi?"

Though it's clear—to me, anyway—he has no idea what his wife is talking about. He's just happy to be holding her in his arms again.

Beside me, I hear Luke swear beneath his breath.

But when I look up at him, alarmed that I've done the wrong thing—again—I see that he's smiling.

"What's this all about?" I ask him out of the corner of my mouth.

"I knew that dress looked familiar," Luke says in a low voice so his parents—who are nuzzling each other—won't overhear. "But I've only seen it in black-and-white pictures, so I never . . . That dress you found? The one you took to get the rust out of? That was her wedding gown."

I gasp. I can't help it. "But—"

"I know," Luke says, taking me by the arm and steering me away from his parents, "I know."

"But . . . a gun! It was wrapped around—"

"I know," Luke says again as he guides me across the lawn, toward the table where Madame Laurent has the orange juice pitcher. "That dress has been a bone of contention between them for years. She thought he threw it out along with everything else after the attic leaked—"

"But he didn't. He—"

"I know," Luke says again. He stops walking and—much to my disappointment—drops his hand from my elbow. "Look, he really loves her. But he's not exactly the sentimental type. Mom means a lot to him. But so does his hunting rifle. I doubt he even realized what that dress was. He just saw that it was the perfect size to wrap his gun in and . . . well, there you go."

"Oh my God," I say, horror clutching my heart, "and I moved the darts to make it fit Vicky!"

"Somehow," Luke says, turning around to gaze at his parents, who are still practically making out in front of everybody across the lawn, "I don't think my mom minds."

We stand there watching his parents for almost a full thirty seconds before I remember I'm supposed to be apologizing to him. Even though last time I tried, I didn't exactly have the best results.

I open my mouth, wondering how I'm going to say this—will a simple sorry suffice? Shari had said something about groveling. Do I need to drop to my knees?

But before I can say anything, he asks, in a voice that's very different from the terse one in which, a few minutes earlier, he suggested we just forget about it, "How did you know? Not to mention the way you *really* found it? That dress, I mean?"

"Oh," I say, suddenly unable to meet his eye. I keep my gaze on my retro kitten heels, which are slowly sinking deeper and deeper into the grass the longer I stand still. "Well, you know. I could tell that dress meant something to your mom, so I just tried to imagine how I'd want a Givenchy of mine to be treated . . ."

It's then that Luke takes the tray of glasses from my hands, puts it down at the table Madame Laurent and Agnès have commandeered, and grabs my fingers in his own.

"Lizzie," he says in a deep voice.

And I have to look up from my French pedicure. I *have* to.

This is it, I realize. This is when he forgives me.

Or not.

"Luke," I say, "I'm so—"

But then, before I can say another word, the string quartet, seated in the shade of a nearby oak tree, suddenly breaks into those four familiar notes:

Dum dum da-dum.

The end of World War II brought about a new beginning in fashion. The hourglass silhouette was back, and suddenly even top designers were producing ready-to-wear styles—particularly for teenagers, who, in the economic boom following the war, had enough disposable allowance finally to afford to buy their own clothes. How else to explain the rise of the "poodle skirt"? Like today's "low-rise jeans," the appeal seemed known only to the wearers themselves.

History of Fashion
SENIOR THESIS BY ELIZABETH NICHOLS

24

Love is only chatter,
Friends are all that matter.
—*Gelett Burgess (1866–1951), U.S. artist, critic, and poet*

Vicky's wedding to Craig is lovely.

And I'm not just saying that because I'm one of the people who helped make it that way, by ensuring that the bride wore a gown of such stunning beauty. It would have been lovely even if Vicky had worn her original dress.

Just, you know. More lacy.

Shari and Chaz and Madame Laurent and Agnès and I sit in the back, watching the exchange of vows, while Madame Laurent and I dab at our eyes and Chaz smirks (what is it with guys and weddings?).

And the whole time, I keep a surreptitious eye on Luke, sitting near the front row of chairs, on the bride's side (they're actually both the bride's side, given that, with the exception of his parents, his sister, and three former college buddies, the groom's side was pretty much empty until the bride's guests were urged to fill in the seats). Luke, I can see, glances often in the direction of his parents, who are still giggling with each other and smooching like high school sweethearts.

There is no sign, that I can see, of Dominique. Either she's refusing to come down from her room or she's left the château altogether.

Then, suddenly, the minister is saying, "Craig, you may kiss the bride," and Mrs. Thibodaux lets out a huge happy sob, and it's over.

"Come on," Shari says, plucking my arm. "We're in charge of the bar again."

I look longingly after Luke. Am I *ever* going to get to tell him I'm sorry? Even if I can get him alone—will he actually listen?

We hurry to beat the rush of hot, thirsty wedding guests and immediately start popping (or, in my case, carefully pulling off) champagne corks. Everyone seems to be in a much better mood now that the ceremony is over. Men are loosening their ties and removing their jackets, and women, fearful of getting grass stains on their fabric shoes, are going barefoot. Patapouf and Minouche, the farm dogs, are hanging around, directly in the path of the caterers with their trays of canapés. Everything seems to be going exactly as planned . . .

. . . until Luke comes by and asks us, in a low voice, "Have any of you seen Blaine?"

I look across the yard and see the stage that had been set up yesterday for the band. Baz and Kurt are at the drums and keyboard, respectively. The bass player is there (I've forgotten his name), tuning up. Even a group of Vicky's friends are standing on the wooden dance floor, eagerly awaiting the concert.

But there's no one standing in front of the microphone in the middle of the stage.

"Satan's Shadow seems to have lost its lead singer," Shari observes.

It's right then that Agnès comes running up, looking angelic in what has to be her best party dress, a pink organza number better suited to the prom than a wedding.

But that's what makes it so cute.

She says something in breathless, rapid French to Luke, whose eyebrows go up.

"Oh no," he says. And hurries off in the direction of his aunt and uncle.

"Agnès," I say, hurrying to fill the glasses that are being handed to me, "what is it? What'd you just say to Luke?"

"Oh," Agnès says, brushing some of her hair from her face, "only that the room of Blaine is empty. His suitcase, everything, is gone. And so is the room of Dominique. The van of the Satan's Shadow is gone as well."

I feel something cold and wet on my hand, and look down to see that I've poured champagne all over my arm.

"Shit," Chaz is saying, having overheard. He can't seem to stop laughing. "Oh, shit!"

"What?" Shari looks annoyed. She's never coped well in food service situations. "What's so funny?"

"Blaine and Dominique," I say, through lips that have gone suddenly numb. Because I'm remembering the conversation I had in the kitchen that night with Blaine—assuring him that somewhere out there, there was a girl who wouldn't mind his newfound wealth.

And my conversation with Dominique last night, about Blaine and his new recording contract . . . not to mention his Lexus commercial.

It looks as if Blaine's found his new girlfriend, and Dominique a man who might actually listen to her get-even-richer schemes.

"Yes," Shari says impatiently. "Blaine and Dominique, what?"

"It looks like they've run off together," I say.

And it's all my fault.

Again.

It's Shari's turn to spill champagne. She's so startled she jerks the bottle she's holding, pouring sparkling wine all over Chaz's hightops.

"Hey, watch it!" he cries.

"Blaine and Dominique?" Shari echoes. "Are you sure?"

"He's not here, and neither is she," I say. I glance in the direction of the stage. "Things are not looking good for Satan's Shadow."

Vicky's friends have been joined by Vicky, who, resplendent in her bridal gown and veil, seems to be noticing for the first time that her brother has skipped out on her nuptials.

"Hope Blaine wasn't the only one who knows how to sing," Chaz says.

"Can we get the string quartet back?" Shari wonders.

"You can't have a father-daughter dance to Tchaikovsky," I say.

I can't believe this is happening. I can't believe Blaine would do this to his own sister!

Well, actually, considering the fact that Dominique is involved, I sort of can.

But that doesn't make it any less my fault. *Why* did I tell her about Blaine? He was clearly in a vulnerable state, romantically. Of course he'd have no resistance to her wiles!

And after Luke dumped her, she must have been smarting . . . of course she'd need the kind of therapeutic balm only a guy with a trust fund can provide a girl like Dominique.

And no matter what Shari might think, it's my fault Luke and Dominique broke up. Not because he secretly loves me or anything. But because of my encouraging Luke to pursue his medical school dream, instead of Dominique's living-in-Paris dream . . .

It really is all my fault.

There's only one thing, I realize, that I can do. If I want to make things right again for everyone, that is.

The only question is, am I brave enough to do it?

I guess I have to be.

"I'll be right back," I say, throwing down my cork-unscrewing napkin.

And I begin marching toward the stage.

"Hey," Shari calls after me, "where ya going?"

I keep moving. I don't *want* to do this. But it's not like I have a choice. Vicky, I see, is crying now. Craig is attempting to comfort her, as are her parents. The wedding guests are milling around, more concerned about the fact that Vicky seems so upset than about the fact that there's no music.

"How could he do this to me?" Vicky is wailing. *"How?"*

"Darling," Mrs. Thibodaux says comfortingly, "it's all right. The boys will find something to play. Won't you, boys?"

Baz, Kurt, and the bass player exchange glances. Baz is the only one with the guts to go, "Um. None of us can sing."

"But you can still *play,*" Mrs. Thibodaux snaps. "Your fingers aren't broken, are they?"

Baz actually looks down at his fingers. "No. But, like . . . what should we play? Blaine took the playlist."

"Play something appropriate for the couple's first dance," Mrs. Thibodaux hisses.

Baz and Kurt look at each other. "'Cheetah Whip'?" Baz asks.

"I don't know, man," Kurt says, looking alarmed. Or as alarmed as a twenty-year-old who is aggressively stoned *can* look. "We say 'fuck' a lot in that one."

"Yeah," Baz says, "but if no one is singing—"

I glance at Luke. He is gazing with concern at his sobbing cousin.

That's it. I know what I have to do.

Before I can talk myself out of it, I step up onto the stage. Baz and Kurt look at me. The bass player—what's his name again?—says, "Hey," and grins at my bare legs.

"Is this on?" I ask, and grab the microphone from its stand.

Is this on Is this on Is this on? My voice seems to reverberate across the valley.

"Oh," I say. "I guess it is."

is is is is is.

Everyone on the lawn before me turns to stare up at me . . . including, I see, an openmouthed Vicky.

And Luke.

Who looks like someone just kicked him.

Great.

"Hi," I say into the microphone. What am I doing? And why am I doing it again?

Oh yeah. It's all my fault.

I wonder if they can see that my knees are shaking.

"I'm Lizzie Nichols. Blaine Thibodaux was supposed to be up here—not me—but he had, ahem, an emergency—" I glance behind me for support. Baz nods energetically. "Right. An emergency crisis and he had to leave. But we still have the rest of Satan's Shadow," I say, flinging out an arm to introduce the band. "Guys?"

The band members shuffle their feet. The crowd, confused but polite, applauds a little.

I seriously cannot believe these guys just signed a multimillion-dollar recording deal.

"So, uh," I say as I notice Shari, a look of abject shock on her face, weaving her way through the guests toward me, "I just want to say congratulations to Vicky and Craig. You two make a really beautiful couple."

More applause, this time heartfelt. Vicky hasn't stopped crying, but she isn't crying as much. She looks more stunned than anything else.

Sort of like her cousin Luke.

"And, uh," I say into the microphone. *And uh And uh And uh And uh.* "Since we're missing a singer, I thought, in honor of your special day—"

I see Shari, out on the dance floor, shake her head at me, her eyes wide with alarm. *No,* she mouths. *No, don't do it.*

"—my friend Miss Shari Dennis and I will sing a song traditionally played during the newly wedded couple's first dance where we come from—".

Shari's shaking her head so fast her bushy hair is whacking her in the face. "No," she says. "Lizzie. *No*."

"—the great state of Michigan," I go on. "It's a song I'm sure you all know. Feel free to sing along if you want to. Guys." I turn around to face Satan's Shadow. "I know you know it, too. Don't act like you don't."

Baz and Kurt raise their eyebrows at each other. The bass player still hasn't torn his gaze from my legs.

"Vicky and Craig," I say, "this one is for you."

you you you you.

Then I clear my throat.

"'Now, I,'" I sing, just as I have a hundred times before, at family gatherings, grade-school talent shows, dorm competitions, karaoke nights, and anytime I've had one too many beers.

Only this time my voice is so magnified I can hear it carrying all across the lawn . . . across the vineyard . . . down the cliff and into the valley below. The German tourists floating on rubber inner tubes along the Dordogne can hear me. The tourists arriving by the busload to look at the cave paintings at Lascaux can hear me. Even Dominique and Blaine, wherever they are, can probably hear me.

But no one joins in.

Well, maybe they need more of a lead-in.

"'—had—'"

Hmm. Still no one joining in. Not even the band. I turn around to look at them. They're staring at me blankly. What is wrong with them?

"'—the time of my life—'"

It can't be that they don't know this song. Okay, sure, they're guys. But what, they didn't have sisters?

"'And I never—'"

What is going on? I *can't* be the only person here who knows this song. *Shari* knows it.

But she's still standing down there on the dance floor, shaking her head, mouthing *No, no, no.*

"Come on, guys," I say encouragingly to the band. "I know you know this one. '—felt this way before.'"

At least Vicky is smiling. And swaying a little. *She* knows this song. Although Craig looks a little confused.

Oh my God. What am I doing? *What am I doing?* I'm standing up here in front of all these people, singing my favorite song of all time—the perfect wedding song—and they're all just standing there, staring up at me.

Even Luke is staring up at me like I was just beamed down from the starship *Enterprise.*

And now Shari's disappeared. Where did she go? She was there a second ago. How can she let me down this way? We've been doing this song together since kindergarten. She always plays the girl part. *Always.*

How could she leave me hanging like this? I know I screwed up with the thesis thing, but how long can you stay mad at someone you've been friends with your whole life? Plus, I apologized for that.

Then I hear it. The snap of a snare drum.

Baz. Baz is joining in.

I *knew* he knew this song. *Everyone* knows this song.

"'Oh, I—'" I sing, turning around to grin at him gratefully. Now Kurt's playing an experimental chord. Yes, Kurt. You got it, Kurt.

"'—had the time of my life—'"

Oh, thank you, guys. Thank you for not leaving me hanging.

Then a voice not my own booms out, "'—It's the truth—'"

And Shari climbs up onstage and comes to stand beside me, singing into the microphone.

And the bass player, whatever his name is, begins plucking out the familiar notes, while below us Craig gives Vicky a twirl . . .

And everyone applauds. And starts singing along.

"'And,'" Shari and I sing, "'I owe it all to you—'"

Oh my God. It's working. It's working! People are having a good time! They're forgetting about the heat, and the fact that the brother of the bride has run off with the girlfriend of their host's son. They're starting to dance. They're singing along!

"'You're the one thing,'" Shari and I sing—along with Satan's Shadow, the Thibodauxes, and the rest of the wedding guests, "'that I can't get enough of, baby—'"

I look down and see Luke's parents dancing along with everyone else.

"'So I'll tell you something—'" I sing, not quite believing what I'm seeing below me. "'This must be love!'"

People are having a good time. People are clapping their hands and dancing. Satan's Shadow has given the song a kind of Latin beat. Which it's not supposed to have, but whatever. Now it sounds kind of like *Vamos a la playa*.

But oddly, this isn't turning out to be a bad thing.

And then, just as we're getting to our big crescendo, Shari elbows me, hard—which is not actually part of our choreography. I glance at her and see that her face has gone as white as Vicky's dress. She points.

And I see Andy Marshall making his way toward the stage.

The Swinging Sixties brought about more than just a sexual revolution. Fashion underwent a revolution as well. Suddenly the feeling was "anything goes," from miniskirts to tie-dye. A return to natural fabrics—made from the same materials with which our ancient ancestors wove their loincloths—in the seventies brought fashion full circle, when hippies revealed other uses for hemp than those popularized by the beatniks of the decade before . . . although the most popular use for it is still very much in style on college campuses.

History of Fashion
SENIOR THESIS BY ELIZABETH NICHOLS

25

While gossip among women is universally ridiculed as low and trivial, gossip among men, especially if it is about women, is called theory, or idea, or fact.

—*Andrea Dworkin (1946–2005), U.S. feminist critic*

ortunately we've just warbled our last "And I owe it all to you." Because if he'd shown up at any other part, I'd have choked on my own saliva.

The crowd bursts into enthusiastic applause, and Shari and I take our bow. While our heads are down by our knees (and I see the bass player duck to see if he can catch a glimpse of what's going on under our skirts—which, in my case, is going to be quite a lot, if he can actually see up there), Shari says, "Jesus Christ, Lizzie. What's *he* doing here?"

"I don't know," I say back, wanting to cry. "What do I do?"

"What do you mean, what do you do? You have to go talk to him."

"I don't want to talk to him! I've already said everything I have to say to him."

"Well, you obviously didn't say it forcefully enough," Shari says. "So go say it again."

We both straighten just as one of Vicky's friends, to hoots of "Go, Lauren!" and "You can do it, girl!" runs up onto the stage and grabs the microphone from us.

"Hi," she says to us. "You guys were great." Then she spins around to the band and cries, "D'you guys know 'Lady Marmalade'?"

Baz glances at Kurt. Kurt shrugs.

"We can probably figure it out," the bass player says.

And Kurt starts tapping out the beat.

"Lizzie," Andy says, standing at the bottom of the stage. He's got his leather jacket with him, strung over one arm.

What is he *doing* here? How did he find me? Why did he come? He doesn't love me. I know he doesn't love me.

So then why go to all this trouble?

My God. It must have been the blow job. Seriously!

I had no idea a blow job was such a powerful thing. If I had, I'd never have given him one, I swear.

I start climbing from the stage, Shari behind me, whispering, "Tell him to leave. Tell him you don't want anything to do with him. Tell him you're going to take out a restraining order. I'm sure they have those in France. Don't they?"

Andy is waiting for me at the bottom of the steps. His face is white and filled with anxiety.

"Liz," he says when I reach him, "there you are. I've been looking all over this place—"

"Andy," I say, "what are you doing here?"

"I'm sorry, Lizzie," he says, reaching for my hand. "But you just ran off! I couldn't leave things that way—"

"Excuse me," a woman with a heavy Texas accent interrupts us, "but are you the girl who designed the bride's gown?"

"Um," I say, "I didn't design it. It's vintage. I just rehabbed it."

"Well, I just wanted to tell you," the woman says, "you did a fantastic job. That dress is lovely. Just lovely. You'd never know it was vintage. Never in a million years."

"Well," I say, "thank you."

The woman goes away.

And I turn back to the man in front of me.

"Andy," I say. I can't believe this. I've never had a guy follow me across Europe before. Well, across a channel, anyway. "We broke up."

"No we didn't," Andy says. "I mean, you broke up with me. But you never even gave me a chance to explain—"

"Pardon me, miss." Another woman has come up to us. "But did you really make that wedding dress li'l Vicky's got on?"

"No, I didn't make it," I say. "I rehabbed it. It's a vintage gown. I just cleaned and fitted it for her."

"Well, it's beautiful," the woman says. "Just beautiful. And I liked your little song up there."

"Oh," I say, beginning to blush, "thanks." When she goes away, I say, to Andy, "Look, things just didn't work out between us. I'm really sorry about it. But you're just not the person I thought you were. And you know what? It turns out I'm not the person I thought I was, either."

It sort of surprises me to hear myself say that. But it's really true. I am not the same girl who got off that plane at Heathrow, even if I do happen to be wearing the same dress. I'm someone totally different now. I don't know who, exactly, but—

Someone else.

"Really," I say to Andy, giving his hand a squeeze. "I don't have any hard feelings toward you. We just made a mistake."

"I don't think we were a mistake," Andy says, his grip on my hand tightening. Not in a friendly squeeze like mine was, either. His is more like he isn't going to let go of me. "I think I *made* a mistake—plenty of mistakes. But, Lizzie, you never even gave me a chance to really apologize. That's why I'm here. I want to apologize properly, and then maybe take you out for a nice meal, and then take you home—"

"Andy," I say gently. Our conversation, already bizarre enough, has taken on an even weirder note, thanks to the musical accompaniment. Behind me, Lauren is shrieking, "'Gitchy gitchy ya ya da da!'" and doing some choreography that is making the bass player, at least, smile happily.

"How—how did you even know where to find me, anyway?" I ask wonderingly.

"You told me a million times in your e-mails that your friend Shari was staying the month in a château in the Dordogne called Mirac. It wasn't that hard to find. Now say you'll come home with me, Liz. We can start over. I promise it will be different this time . . . *I'll* be different."

"I'm not going back to England with you, Andy," I explain as kindly as I can. "I just don't feel that way about you anymore. It was very nice knowing you, but really. I think this is where we have to say good-bye."

Andy's jaw is slack.

"Excuse me," a woman says. I turn and find a middle-aged woman looking apologetic. "I'm sorry, I really don't mean to interrupt, but I heard you rehabbed the bride's gown. Which I assume means you took an old gown and fixed it up?"

"Yes," I say. What is going on here? "I did."

"Well—I really am sorry to interrupt—but my daughter would like to wear my grandmother's wedding dress for her wedding next June, but we just haven't been able to find anyone willing to, um, rehab it. Everyone we've seen about it says the fabric is too old and fragile, and they don't want to risk ruining it."

"Well," I say, "that is a concern with old fabric. I mean, it's much better quality than the materials used in bridal gowns today. But I've found if you use all-natural cleansers—no chemicals—you can get quite good results."

"All-natural cleansers," the woman repeats. "I see. Honey, do you have a business card? Because I would love to be in touch with you about this again"—she glances up at Andy's face—"but I can see that you're busy right now."

"Um." I pat myself, then remember my mandarin dress has no pockets. And that even if it did, I have no business cards, anyway. "No. But I'll find you and give you my contact information in a little while. Would that be all right?"

"That'd be just fine," the woman says with another nervous glance at Andy. "I'll just . . . I'll see you in a bit."

She slinks off and Andy, as if he can hold it in no longer, bursts out with, "Lizzie, you can't mean that. I understand that maybe you feel we need some time apart. Maybe after a bit of time has passed you'll realize that what we've got, you and I, is really special. I'll show you. I'll treat you the way you want to be treated. I'll make it up to you, Lizzie, I swear. When you get back to Ann Arbor in the fall, I'll call you—"

The strangest feeling comes over me when he says that. I can't really explain it, except that it's as if suddenly he's given me a glimpse into the future . . .

A future I can now see quite clearly, as if it were in high definition.

"I'm not going back to Ann Arbor in the fall, Andy," I say. "Well, I mean, except to get my stuff. I'm moving to New York City."

Behind me, I hear Shari go, "Ye-esss."

But when I turn to look at her, she's stonily watching Lauren implore the wedding guests to *coucher avec* her tonight.

"New York City?" Andy looks confused. "*You?*"

I stick out my chin. "Yes, me," I say in a voice that sounds completely unlike my own. "Why? You don't think I can do it?"

Andy's shaking his head. "Lizzie, I love you. I think you can do anything. Anything you set your mind to. I think you're amazing."

It comes out more like, *I fink you're amazing.*

But that's okay. Because right then I forgive him. I forgive him for all of it.

"Thank you, Andy," I say to him, a big grin bursting out across my face. Maybe I was wrong about him. Oh, not about the two of us not being right for each other. But, you know. Maybe he's not so bad after all. Maybe, even though we can't be lovers, we can still be friends . . .

"Excuse me," someone says.

Only this time it's not a Houston society matron who's come up to ask me how to get stains out of fifty-year-old lace.

It's Luke.

And he doesn't seem too happy.

"Luke," I say. "Hi. I—"

"Is it true?" Luke asks me. "Is this him?"

He's jerked a thumb in Andy's direction.

I can't imagine what's come over him—Luke, so unfailingly polite to everyone.

Everyone but me, I mean. But then I guess I deserve it.

"Um," I say, shifting uncomfortably, "yes. Luke, this is Andy Marshall. Andy, this is—"

But I never get to finish my sentence. Because before I can, Luke pulls back his arm and sends his fist crashing straight into Andy's face.

Anarchy! That was the cry of members of the punk movement in the 1980s. But there was nothing anarchic about their postapocalyptic style. Punk, coupled with a fitness phase that began in the eighties and has been going steady ever since, went on to influence both high fashion and street style for many years to come, giving us such wardrobe staples as motorcycle boots and yoga pants.

History of Fashion
SENIOR THESIS BY ELIZABETH NICHOLS

26

Silence is the most intolerable of answers.
—*Mason Cooley (1927–2002), U.S. aphorist*

He tried to kill me," Andy keeps saying. Although his words are somewhat indistinct behind the ice-filled dish towel Madame Laurent is pressing to his lip.

"He didn't try to kill you," Chaz says in a tired voice. "Stop being such a fucking baby."

"Hey," Andy says from his perch on the butcher-block kitchen table, "fuck you! I'd like to see how you'd react if someone sucker-punched you in the mouth!"

Only with his swollen lip and accent, the words come out sounding more like, *Oi'd loik to see how you'd weact if someone sucker-punched you in the mouf.*

"Chaz," I ask worriedly, ignoring their squabbling, "where's Luke?"

"I don't know," Chaz says. He was the one who'd jumped in and broken up the fight. Well, not that there'd been much of one. It had been more like a one-man assassination attempt. Luke had landed his punch, then backed off, waving his hand, apparently having injured it on Andy's teeth.

Which Andy is now complaining feel loose.

Chaz, who'd come over to congratulate Shari for so thoroughly embarrassing herself onstage, was able to keep Andy from returning Luke's punch merely by placing a hand on his shoulder. Andy is much more of a lover than a fighter, it turns out.

Though he doesn't seem to know it.

"It was a completely unprovoked attack!" Andy insists. "I wasn't doing *anything* to Liz! I was just talking to her!"

"Lizzie," Shari corrects him, in a bored voice, from where she's leaning against the kitchen sink, trying to keep out of the way of the caterers, who are streaming in and out of the kitchen with the first course—salmon—and glaring angrily at us as the chef tries to make progress at the stove with the second course—foie gras. "Her name's Lizzie. Not Liz."

"Whatever," Andy says into the dish towel. "When I find that bastard, I'm going to show him a thing or two."

"You're not going to be showing anybody anything," Chaz says to Andy in a firm voice. "Because you're leaving. There's a three o'clock train back to Paris, and I'm going to make sure you're on it. You, my friend, have caused quite enough trouble for one day."

"I didn't do anything!" Andy cries. "It was that French git!"

"He's not French," Shari says, still bored, as she examines her cuticles.

"Lizzie," Andy says from behind the dish towel, "listen. I'm sorry to bring it up. And now may not be the greatest time, but I was wondering about the money."

I blink at him.

"Money?"

"Right. The money you said you'd loan me for my matriculation fees? Because I really do need it, Liz."

"Oh no!" Shari bursts out. "Oh no, he did not just—"

"Shari," I say to her sharply, "I can handle this."

Because I can.

And, okay, it's not like I ever really thought he came all this way to patch things up with me because he loves me.

But it honestly never occurred to me that he did it because of the money.

"Andy," I say, "you came all this way to ask if I'd still lend you five hundred dollars?"

"Actually," Andy points out, his words muffled by the dish towel, "you said you'd give it to me. But a loan's all right, too. I feel terrible about asking, but in a way, you do sort of owe me the money. I mean, I did open up my home to you, and there was the gas money, you know, Dad spent picking you up from the airport, and—"

"Can I hit him now?" Chaz wants to know. "*Please*, Lizzie?"

"No, you can't," I say to Chaz.

Although it must be obvious from my stunned expression that I'm not about to pony up the money, since Andy's hangdog expression has completely disappeared. In fact, his eyes have squeezed shut above the dish towel.

Shari gasps.

"Oh my God," she says. "Andy, are you *crying*?"

It's clear when he speaks that he is.

"Are you telling me," he says, weeping, "that I hitched all the way here and you're not going to give me the money after all?"

I'm shocked. Crying? He's crying?

Luke must have hit him harder than any of us thought.

"You said on the phone that you couldn't talk about it!" Andy sobs. "That's all! You never said—"

"Andy." I shake my head. Can this really be happening? "I mean, Andy, we broke up. What did you think was going to happen?"

"You don't understand," Andy cries. "If I don't pay these blokes the money I owe them, they're . . . they're going to break my legs."

I exchange confused looks with Shari and Chaz. "The bursar's office is going to break your legs if you don't pay your matriculation fees?"

"No." Andy takes a shuddering breath from behind the dish

towel. "I . . . I wasn't quite truthful about that bit. It's the blokes that run the poker ring that I owe the money to, actually. They're . . . well, they're quite serious about getting it back. I can't go to Mum and Dad for it—they'll throw me out. And my mates are all tapped out as well. Really, Lizzie . . . you were my last hope."

I stare at him as his words sink in. Then I glance at Chaz and Shari, to see that both of them are looking at me, Chaz with a little grin on his face, Shari with a glower that clearly says, *Don't you back down. Don't you do it, Nichols. Not this time.*

I turn back to Andy and say, "Oh, Andy. I'm so sorry!" I reach up and give him a sympathetic pat on the shoulder. I can't believe I once loved that shoulder.

And I can't believe he really thinks I'm such a sap I'll actually give him a dime. Who does he think I am, anyway? Some kind of pushover?

"At least," I say, "have some wedding cake before you go. Good-bye."

Then I slip out the back door, where Patapouf and Minouche are waiting, eager for scraps dropped by the caterers. Behind me, I hear Chaz saying in a hearty voice, "Andy, my boy. I'm open-minded, man. And I happen to be loaded. So let's talk business. What've you got in the way of collateral? Is that jacket you've got there worth anything, by any chance?"

Agnès is outside, leaning against the butter-yellow Mercedes. She perks up when she sees me, eager for more gossip. I realize Luke's fight with Andy is the most exciting thing that's happened at Mirac in a long time. She's going to have a lot to tell her girlfriends when school starts again in the fall.

"Does the Englishman need to go to hospital?" she asks me brightly. "Because I can call my father, and he can come to take your friend to hospital."

"He's not my friend," I say. "And he doesn't need to go to hospital. I mean, to the hospital. Chaz is going to take him to the train station, and that will be the last we'll see of him."

Agnès looks disappointed. "Oh," she says, "I was hoping for more of the fighting."

"I think there's been enough fighting for one day," I say. "Speaking of which, did you see where Luke went after the fight?"

Agnès brightens again. "Oh yes! I see him go to the vineyard. I think he is in the cask room."

"Thanks, Agnès," I say, and start around the side of the house, to the lawn.

The wedding reception is in full swing and going well now that Satan's Shadow has gotten the hang of playing covers. One of Vicky's sorority sisters is onstage, shrieking lines from Alanis Morissette's "You Oughta Know." Not exactly wedding fare, but everyone appears far too drunk to notice. Most of them, thanks to the mimosas, had been too drunk even to realize there'd been a fight. Only a few people who happened to be standing nearby noticed, and Chaz's quick intervention had put a damper on any hopes for a continuation of the dramatic scene, and so they had all turned their attention back to what was happening onstage.

Still, even though no one seems aware of the fight, they all seem to know who I am. Well, I guess that's what happens when you make a complete and utter ass of yourself onstage in front of two hundred total strangers. They all feel like you're their best friend.

Or maybe it's just that word of my prowess with cream of tartar has spread. Because every woman there seems to have some question for me about an antique wedding dress—how they can get out a stain or insert a gusset; how they can update it without damaging the fine material; even how they can find a vintage wedding gown of their own.

I wrestle with these as best I can and finally manage to cross the lawn and reach the cask room—a thick-walled, cavernous struc-

ture, as centuries-old as the house itself—and pull open the heavy
oak and iron door.

Inside, it's still as a mausoleum—although unlike in a mausoleum, golden light filters in through mullion-paned windows high
up along the walls. You can't hear the sound of the band outside—
which you can probably hear clear across the valley—or the chatter
of the wedding guests. The walls are lined with waist-high oak wine
casks, the contents of many of which Luke's father had insisted I
try during my tour two days before. The glasses we—and then all
the wedding guests Monsieur de Villiers had brought through for
subsequent tours—used are piled up beside a stone sink at the far
end of the room.

The stone sink at which Luke is running water over his hand.

He doesn't hear me come in. Or, at least, if he did, he doesn't
react. He is standing with his back to me, his dark head ducked, letting the water run over his hand. He must, I realize, have really hurt
himself on Andy's teeth.

Which is when I forget that my heart is in my throat at the pros-
pect of talking to him after all the nasty things I accused him of last
night, and hurry forward.

"Let me see," I say when I reach his side.

He jumps.

"Jesus," he says, looking down at me in surprise. "Sneak up on a
guy, why don't you?"

I pull his hand from the stream of water gurgling out of the
old-fashioned faucet. His knuckle, I see, is red and swollen. But the
skin's not broken.

"You're lucky," I say, looking down at his hand. "He says his teeth
are loose. You could have cut yourself on them."

"I know," Luke says, reaching out with his left hand to turn off
the water. "I should have known better than to aim for the mouth. I
should have gone for his nose."

"You shouldn't have 'gone for' anything," I say. I let go of his hand. "I had the situation totally under control, you know."

Luke doesn't even try to argue. He dries his hand on a nearby dish towel.

"I know," he says sheepishly. "I don't know what came over me. I just couldn't believe he'd have the nerve to show up here. Unless . . ."

I stare at him. I can't help noticing how thick and dark his hair looks in the bright shafts of sunlight coming down from the windows so close to the ceiling.

"Unless what?"

"Unless you *asked* him to come here," Luke says, not meeting my gaze.

"*What?*" I have to start laughing at that one. "Are you serious? Do you honestly think—"

"Well," Luke says. He lays the dish towel aside. "I didn't know."

"I thought I made myself pretty clear on the train," I say. "Andy and I broke up. He only came after me because he thought I could bail him out of a financial situation he got himself into."

"And . . . did you?" Luke asks. His dark-eyed gaze is steady on my face.

"No," I say. "Although Chaz seems to be working on it."

"That sounds like Chaz," Luke says with a grin.

I have to look away, flustered by how handsome the grin makes him.

Then I remember that there's something I'm supposed to be saying to him, so, feeling incredibly shy, I say it, fast. To my French pedicure.

"Luke. I'm sorry about what I said last night. I should have known you didn't tell her," I say. "Shari, I mean. About my thesis. I don't know what I was thinking."

Luke doesn't say anything. I look up, just once, to see if he's heard me.

He is looking down at me with the most inscrutable expression I have ever seen—halfway between a smile and a frown. Does he hate me? Or can he possibly, in spite of my big, fat, stupid mouth—in spite of everything—like me?

With my heart hammering so hard I'm sure he must be able to see it through the silk of my dress, I look down again and say, keeping my gaze on his feet now, instead of my own—then regretting it when I notice the wingtips again—WINGTIPS! So hot! "And the thing with telling your mom about you getting into NYU. And about Dominique's plans for the château. I mean, I was really only trying to suggest alternatives to turning this place into a spa. Like maybe renting it out to wealthy families who just want a nice château to vacation in for a month, or maybe for a reunion, or whatever. Honestly, I was only trying to help—"

"Well, actually, I've managed to get along without your help pretty well for the past twenty-five years," Luke says.

Ouch!

Stung, I can't help looking up and saying, "And that's why you're so happy with your career and your life and your girlfriend? And why Vicky looked so great in her dress and your parents seem to be getting back together and everyone out there is having . . . such a . . . fun time . . ."

My voice trails off as I realize he's smiling down at me.

"Joke," he says. "That was a joke. I told you I'm no good at them."

That's when he reaches out, pulls me toward him, and starts kissing me.

I'm in complete and utter shock. I can't understand what's happening. I mean, I *can* . . . but it makes no sense. Luke de Villiers is kissing me. Luke de Villiers's arms are going around me, holding me so tightly to him I can feel his heart slamming as hard against his ribs as mine is slamming against mine. Luke de Villiers's lips are raining thousands of tiny featherlight kisses on my lips.

And now my lips are falling open, surrendering to the onslaught of his. And he's kissing me hard and long and sweet, and I'm clinging to him because my knees have given out entirely and his arms are the only thing holding me up. And his tongue is in my mouth, like he can't taste me enough, and I can feel something hard pressing against me through the fabric of his trousers. And his hand, the hand he hit Andy with, is cupping my breast through the silk of my mandarin dress, and I want him to cup more of me, and I make a sound . . .

"Christ, Lizzie," he says in a voice that doesn't sound anything like the way it usually does.

And the next thing I know, he's lifting me up and putting me down again on top of the closest wine cask, and somehow my legs have fallen open and he's standing between them. The front of my dress is open, too. I don't even know how he did that because those snaps are supposed to be hidden. And I can feel his fingers—and the hot sunlight streaming in through the high windows—on my bare breasts.

And I can't stop kissing him, or running my fingers through his thick dark hair when his mouth starts traveling down my throat, then dips below to scorch the skin on my breasts. All the places where the sun is touching me, his lips are touching me, too.

Until suddenly he mutters, "Christ, Lizzie, you haven't got on any underwear," and I say, "I know, I didn't want visible panty lines," and he puts his lips there, too.

And on top of the cask I feel as if the sunlight is piercing me all over—but piercing me in a good way—and I look down through half-lidded eyes and think how bizarre it is that Luke de Villiers's dark head is between my legs—but bizarre in a *very* good way—and then I don't think about anything at all for a while except the sun, which seems to have turned into a supernova, right there inside Monsieur de Villiers's cask room.

And then Luke straightens and wraps an arm around my waist and pulls me close against him and my legs wrap around him and I feel his naked chest beneath my fingers and wonder how. And then he's inside me, thick and hard, and it feels even better than when his mouth was there, and we're moving against each other in just the right rhythm, with him burying himself more and more deeply in me, and me trying to get closer and closer to him, and he's kissing my neck and shoulders where the sun is hitting me, and suddenly there's sun all *over* me, like I'm being showered in golden sun drops, and I cry out at how good it feels, and Luke does, too.

And then as he stands there, holding me slickly to him and panting in my hair, I realize that we just had sex on a wine cask.

And that it was fantastic. I didn't even have to worry about taking care of my own good time! Luke totally made sure I had one. Or two, actually.

"Have I mentioned," Luke wants to know when he's caught his breath, "that I think I'm in love with you?"

I laugh. I can't help it.

"Have I mentioned," I ask, "that the feeling is mutual?"

"Well," he says, "that's a relief." He doesn't move, and neither do I. It feels good to stand like that. Or, in my case, sit.

"I should also probably tell you," Luke says, "that I decided to go ahead and enter that program I got into at NYU."

I wonder if he can see my heart leap inside my chest. Although I try to sound casual.

"Really?" I say. "That's funny. I'm moving to New York, too."

"Well," Luke says, leaning his forehead against mine and smiling, "isn't that a coincidence."

"Isn't it, though?" I say, smiling back.

A little while later, we slip hand in hand from the cask room just in time to see the bride and groom cutting the multitiered cake. Agnès, spotting us first, rushes over with a tray of champagne glasses, and we each take one and stand, side by side, as Vicky and Craig feed each other the first piece.

"I hope they don't cram it into each other's faces," I say. "I hate when they do that."

"Plus," Luke says, "then you'll have chocolate stains to get out."

"Don't even say that," I say, shuddering, and hug his arm.

"Why, hello," Shari says, appearing, with Chaz in tow, a minute later. "Where did you two disappear to?"

"Nowhere," I say quickly, blushing to my hairline.

"Oh, right," Shari says with a knowing smile. "I've been there."

"What are you talking about?" Chaz, clueless, wants to know. "You've been here the whole time. *I'm* the one who had to take that freak to the train station. I've decided that from now on, Lizzie, I'll be screening all your boyfriends. You can't be trusted to choose your own."

"Is that so?" I say, exchanging an amused glance with Luke, who puts his arm around me.

"I'll give you a hand with that, Chaz," Luke volunteers. "I think Lizzie is more than you can handle on your own."

Chaz, spying Luke's arm around my shoulders, narrows his eyes at us.

"Hey," he says, "what's going on?"

"I'll explain it to you someday, baby," Shari says, patting him on the arm.

"Nobody ever tells me anything." Chaz pouts.

"That's because you've got to go straight to the source," Shari says.

"Which is?"

"The LBS. Who else?" Shari says, tipping her head in my direction.

Which is right when an extremely tipsy Ginny Thibodaux spies me and hurries over to plant a kiss on my cheek.

"Lizzie!" she exclaims. "I've been looking everywhere for you. I wanted to thank you for what you did for my Vicky. That dress—it's beautiful! You know you're a lifesaver, don't you? I've never seen anything like it. Why, you ought to open your own business!"

"Maybe," I say with a smile, "I will."

In conclusion, we have seen the important role fashion has played in the development of world culture and history. Starting from strips of fur worn for warmth and protection by cavemen gathered round a fire, to Prada shoes worn for their beauty and cachet by the modern working woman at a cocktail party, fashion has, over the centuries, come to be one of man's—and woman's—greatest and most interesting accomplishments.

This author in particular looks forward to seeing what surprises and innovations await her in the world of fashion—and beyond—in the coming years.

History of Fashion
SENIOR THESIS BY ELIZABETH NICHOLS

A+

AUTHOR
INSIGHTS,
EXTRAS, &
MORE...

FROM

**MEG
CABOT**

AND

AVON A

Big mouth. Big heart.
Big city.
Big problems.

Lizzie Nichols is back, pounding the New York City pavement, looking for a job, a place to live, and her proper place in the universe (not necessarily in that order).

When summer fling Luke uses the L word (Living Together), Lizzie is only too happy to give up her plan of being post-grad roomies with best friend, Shari, in a one-room walk-up, in exchange for co-habitation with the love of her life in his mother's Fifth Avenue pied-à-terre, complete with doorman and resident Renoir.

But Lizzie's not so lucky in her employment search. As Shari finds the perfect job, Lizzie struggles through one humiliating interview after another, being judged overqualified for the jobs in her chosen field—vintage gown rehab—and underqualified for everything else. It's Shari's boyfriend, Chaz, to the rescue when he recommends Lizzie for a receptionist position at his father's posh law firm. The non-paying gig at a local wedding gown shop Lizzie manages to land all on her own.

But Lizzie's notoriously big mouth begins to get her in trouble at work and at home almost at once—first at the law firm, where she becomes too chummy with Jill Higgins, a New York society bride with a troublesome future mother-in-law, and then back on Fifth Avenue, when she makes the mistake of bringing up the M word (Marriage) with commitment-shy Luke.

Soon Lizzie finds herself jobless as well as homeless all over again. Can Lizzie save herself—and the hapless Jill—and find career security (not to mention a mutually satisfying, committed relationship) at last?

Lizzie Nichols Wedding Gown Guide

Finding the right wedding gown for your special day isn't easy, but it shouldn't drive you to tears, either!

Even if you are planning a formal ceremony with a traditional long dress, there are many different styles of gowns to choose from.

The trick is to match the right gown to the right bride before she becomes a Bridezilla . . . and that's where a wedding gown specialist like myself comes in!

Lizzie Nichols Designs™

It is still not enough for language to have clarity and content . . . it must also have a goal and an imperative. Otherwise from language we descend to chatter, from chatter to babble, and from babble to confusion.

RENÉ DAUMAL (1908–1944), French poet, critic

I open my eyes to see the morning sunlight slanting across the Renoir hanging above my bed, and for a few seconds, I don't know where I am.

Then I remember.

And my heart swells with giddy excitement. No, really. *Giddy.* Like, first-day-of-school-and-I've-got-a-brand-new-designer-outfit-from-TJ-Maxx giddy.

And not just because that Renoir that's hanging over my head? It's real. Although it *is*, and not a print, like I had in my dorm room. An actual original work, by the impressionist master himself.

Which I couldn't actually believe, at first. I mean, how often do you walk into someone's bedroom and see an original Renoir hanging over the bed? Um, never. At least, if you're me.

When Luke left the room, I stayed behind, pretending I had to use the bathroom. But really, I slipped off my espadrilles, climbed onto the bed, and gave that canvas a closer look.

And I was right. I could see the globs of paint Renoir used to build up the lace he so carefully detailed on the cuff of the little girl's sleeve. And the stripes on the fur of the cat the little girl is holding? Raised blobby bits. It's a *real* Renoir, all right.

And it's hanging over the bed I'm waking up in . . . the same bed that's currently bathed in sunlight from the tall windows to my left . . . sunlight that's bouncing off the building across the street . . . that building being the *Metropolitan Museum of Art*. The one in front of Central Park. On Fifth Avenue. *In New York City.*

Yes! I am waking up in New York City!!!! The Big Apple! The city that never sleeps (although I try to get at least eight hours a night, or my eyelids will get puffy, and Shari says I get cranky)!

But none of that is what's making me so giddy. The sunlight, the Renoir, the Met, Fifth Avenue, New York. *None* of that can compare to what's really got me excited . . . something better than all of those things and a new back-to-school-outfit-from-TJ-Maxx put together.

And it's in the bed right next to me.

Just look how cute he is when he's sleeping! Manly cute, not kitten cute. Luke doesn't lay there with his mouth wide open with spit leaking out the side, like I do (I know I do this because my sisters told me. Also because I always wake up to a wet spot on my pillow). He manages to keep his lips together very nicely.

And his eyelashes look so long and curly. Why can't I get my eyelashes to look like that? It's not fair. I'm the girl, after all. *I'm* the one who is supposed to have long, curly eyelashes, not the stubby, short ones I have to use an eyelash curler I've heated with a hair dryer and about seven layers of mascara on if I want to look like I have any eyelashes at all.

Okay, I've got to stop. Stop obsessing over my boyfriend's eyelashes. I need to get up. I can't lounge around in bed all day. I'm in *New York City!*

And, okay, I don't have a job. Or a place to live.

Because that Renoir? Yeah, it belongs to Luke's mother. As does the bed. Oh, and the apartment.

But she only bought it when she thought she and Luke's dad were splitting up. Which they're not now. Thanks to me. So she said Luke could use it as long as he needs to.

Lucky Luke. I wish *my* mom had been planning on divorcing *my* dad and bought a totally gorgeous apartment in New York City, right across the street from the Metropolitan Museum of Art, that she now only planned on using a few times a year for shopping trips in the city, or to attend the occasional ballet.

Okay, seriously. I have to get up now. How can I stay in bed—a king-sized bed, by the way, totally comfortable, with a big, white, fluffy, goose down-stuffed duvet over it—when I have all of *New York City* right outside the door (well, down the elevator and outside the ornate marble lobby), just waiting to be explored by me?

And my boyfriend, of course.

It seems so weird to say that . . . to even think it. Me and my boyfriend. My *boyfriend.*

Because for the first time in my life, it's real! I have an honest-to-God boyfriend. One who actually considers me his girlfriend. He isn't gay and is just using me as a cover so his Christian parents don't find out he's really going out with a guy named Antonio. He isn't just trying to get me to fall so deeply in love with him that when he springs the idea of doing a threesome with his ex, I'll say yes, because I'm so afraid he'll break up with me otherwise. He isn't a compulsive gambler who knows I have a lot of money saved up and can bail him out if he gets too deeply in debt.

Not that any of those things have happened to me. More than once.

And I'm not just imagining it, either. Luke and I are *together.* I can't say I wasn't a little scared—you know, when I left France to go back to Ann Arbor—that I might never hear from him again. If he hadn't really been that into me and wanted to get rid of me, he had the perfect opportunity.

But he kept calling. First from France, and then from Houston, where he went to pack up all his stuff and get rid of his apartment and his car, and then from New York, when he got here. He kept saying he couldn't wait to see me again. He kept telling me all the stuff he was planning on doing to me when he *did* see me again.

And then when I finally got here last week, he *did* them—all those things he'd said he'd been going to do.

I can barely believe it. I mean, that a guy I like as much as I like Luke actually likes me *back*, for a change. That what we have isn't just a summer fling. Because summer's over, and it's fall now (well, okay, almost), and we're still together. Together in New York City, where he'll be going to medical school, and I'm going to get a job in the fashion industry, doing something—well, fashion-related—and together, we're going to make a go of it in the city that never sleeps!

Just as soon as I find a job. Oh, and an apartment.

But I'm sure Shari and I will find a charming pied-à-terre to call home soon. And until we do, I have Luke's place to crash in, and Shari can stay in the walk-up her boyfriend, Chaz, found last week in the East Village (he rightfully refused his parents' invitation to move back into the house in which he grew up—when he wasn't being shipped off to boarding school—in Westchester, from which his father continues to commute to the city to work every morning).

And even though it's not on the best block, exactly, it's not the worst place in the world, having the advantage of being close to NYU, where Chaz is getting his PhD, and cheap (a rent-controlled, two bedroom for only two grand a month. And okay, one of the bedrooms is an alcove. But still).

And, yeah, Shari's already witnessed a triple stabbing through the living room window. But whatever. It was a domestic dispute. The guy in the building across the courtyard stabbed his pregnant wife and mother-in-law. It's not like people in Manhattan go around getting stabbed by strangers every day.

And everyone turned out to be fine. Even the baby, who was delivered by the cops on the building's front stoop when the wife went into early labor. Eight pounds, six ounces! And okay, his dad is locked up in a prison cell on Rikers Island. But still. Welcome to New York, little Julio!

In fact, if you ask me, Chaz is sort of secretly hoping we won't find a place, and Shari will *have* to move in with him. Because Chaz is romantic that way.

And seriously, how fun would that be? Then Luke and I could come over, and the four of us could hang out just like we did back at Luke's place in France, with Chaz mixing Kir Royales and Shari bossing everyone around and me making baguette-and-Hershey-bar sandwiches for everyone, and Luke in charge of the music, or something?

And it could really happen, because Shari and I have had no luck on the apartment front so far. I mean, we've answered about a thousand ads, and so far the places are either snapped up before one of us can get there to look at them (if they're at all decent), or they're so hideous no one in their right mind would want to live there (I saw a toilet that was balanced on wooden blocks over an *open hole* in the floor. And that was in a studio apartment in Hell's Kitchen for *twenty-two hundred dollars a month*).

But it will be all right. We'll find a place eventually. Just like I'll find a job eventually. I'm not going to freak out.

Yet.

Oh! It's eight o'clock! I'd better wake up Luke. Today is his first day of orientation at New York University. He'll be attending the post-baccalaureate premedical program there, so he can study to be a doctor. He wouldn't want to be late.

But he looks so sweet lying there. With no shirt on. And his tan so dark against his mother's cream-colored, thousand-count Egyptian cotton sheets (I read the tag). How can I—

Ack! Oh, my goodness!

Um, I guess he's already awake. Considering that he's now laying on top of me.

"Good morning," he says. He hasn't even opened his eyes. His lips are nuzzling my neck. And other parts of him are nuzzling other parts of me.

"It's eight o'clock," I cry. Even though, of course, I don't want to. What could be more heavenly than just lying here all morning making sweet, sweet love to my man? Especially in a bed under a real Renoir, in an apartment across from the Metropolitan Museum of Art in *New York City!*

But he's going to be a doctor. He's going to cure children of cancer someday! I can't let him be late for his first day of orientation. Think of the children!

"Luke," I say, as his mouth moves toward mine. Oh, he doesn't even have morning breath! How does he *do* that? And why didn't I jump up first thing and hurry into the bathroom to brush my teeth?

"What?" he asks, lazily touching his tongue to my lips. Which I'm not opening, because I don't want him to smell what's going on inside my mouth. Which appears to be a small party given by the aftertaste of the chicken tikka masala and shrimp curry from Balducci's that we had delivered last night, which was apparently impervious to both the Listerine and Crest with which I attempted to combat them eight hours ago.

"You have orientation this morning," I say. Which isn't an easy thing to say when you don't want to open your lips. Also when there are a hundred and eighty pounds of delicious naked man lying on top of you. "You're going to be late!"

"I don't care," he says, and presses his lips to mine.

But it's no good. I'm not opening my mouth.

Except to say, "Well, what about me? I have to get up and go look for a job and a place to live. I have fifteen boxes of stuff sitting in my parents' garage that they're waiting to send me as soon as I can give them an address. If I don't get it all out of there soon, I just know Mom's going to have a garage sale, and I'll never see any of it again."

"It would be more expedient," Luke says, as he plucks at the straps to my vintage teddy, "if you would just sleep naked, like I do."

Only I couldn't even get mad at him for not listening to a

word I've said, because he manages to get the teddy off with an alacrity that really is breathtaking, and the next thing I know, his being late for orientation—my job and apartment search—and even those boxes sitting in my parents' garage are the last things on my mind.

A little while later he lifts his head to look at the clock and says, in some surprise, "Oh, I'm going to be late."

I am lying in a damp puddle of sweat in the middle of the bed. I feel like I've been flattened by a steamroller.

And I love it.

"I told you so," I say, mostly to the girl in the Renoir above my head.

"Hey," Luke says, getting up to head to the bathroom. "I have an idea."

"You're going to hire a helicopter to pick you up here and take you downtown?" I ask. "Because that's the only way you're going to make it to your orientation on time."

"No," Luke says. Now he's in the bathroom. I hear the shower turn on. "Why don't you just move in here with me? Then all you'll have to do today is look for a job."

He pops his head—his thick, dark hair adorably mussed from our recent activities—around the bathroom door and looks at me inquisitively. "What do you think about that?"

Only I can't reply, because I'm pretty sure my heart has just exploded with happiness.

MEG CABOT was born in Bloomington, Indiana. In addition to her adult contemporary fiction, she is the author of the bestselling young adult fiction series *The Princess Diaries*. She lives in Key West, Florida, with her husband.

www.megcabot.com

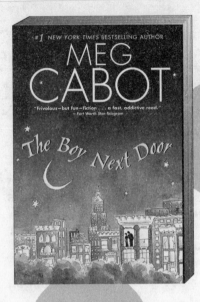

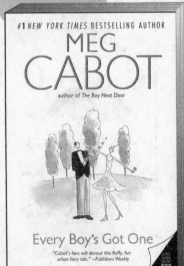